BLEST BE THE TIE

Book 1

of

THE GOINS BRICOLAGE

A Saga

of

Tecumseh & Stonewall Counties
in the State of Indiana
1925-1941

Alexander Lawrence

iUniverse, Inc.
New York Bloomington

iUniverse books may be ordered through booksellers or by contacting:

iUniverse
1663 Liberty Drive
Bloomington, IN 47403
www.iuniverse.com
1-800-Authors (1-800-288-4677)

ISBN: 978-1-4401-8695-0 (sc)
ISBN: 978-1-4401-8697-4 (ebook)
ISBN: 978-1-4401-8696-7 (hc)

Printed in the United States of America

iUniverse rev. date: 11/03/2009

Also by this author:

Author of NOTES (2009)
Anthologized in VOICES OF BROOKLYN (1973)

For Donna

CHAPTER 1
A GREAT MAN, A BLESSED PLACE,
A SUBLIME VISION

*Wherein we learn something of the history of the Goins and
of the town of Aschburgh; also of the Divine call upon young
Marva Ainsley and of her own plans for herself; reading further
in the chapter we hear of the sin of hair glory, meet the Reverend
Mister Hoheimer and discover preparations for the rebaptism of
Wilton Fox Goins, concluding with news of local import.*

1
Crossed Street Signs

The Lord God spoke to Wilton Fox Goins during the early
months of 1925. After due consideration, the middle-aged Goins
found himself in essential agreement with most of God's ideas for
his life, and so he decided to move forward. That was Wilton's
way. All advice, Divine or human, was carefully considered,
and if it seemed right, he would seize the opportunity after due
deliberation. It was a prudent yet decisive management style
that had made him a millionaire and the most powerful man in
Tecumseh County, Indiana.

1

Still rankled by the magnate Clarence Geist's comment that "You college boys are all saps," Goins grinned as he thought about the scramble going on right now to buy up his worthless land for the new reservoir planned down in Hamilton County. Geist and his *Indianapolis Water Company* were paying top dollar, even for sand pits. With thirty thousand acres of Hancock and Hamilton Counties in Wilton's pocket, Clarence and his boys were going to have to deal with him. And they were going to pay for that *sap* remark.

Wilton had learned from the abrupt destruction of Natural Gas fortunes all over central Indiana before the Great War... when the wells suddenly went dry and wealth quickly made was even more quickly lost. As he liked to say, he was "well pleased to be a Hoosier – devout, shrewd, tight and cautious". He pursued a *Hoosier Strategy* with passion. Cheap but well situated land, bonds and gold...that was the way to go if you wanted to build up something for the future. He was holding onto ten thousand acres along the projected Hamilton County reservoir just in case the area developed the way Geist thought it would. Clarence Geist might be an immoral braggart but he was no fool.

Holding to his *Hoosier Strategy,* Goins, a vigorous forty-five, tall and thin with bright blue eyes, his neatly trimmed black mustache and carefully parted black hair matching his black three piece *Brooks Brothers* suit, was now the leading banker north of Indianapolis and south of Fort Wayne. As he parked his new *Ford Tudor* in front of the *Aschburgh Savings & Trust* on the corner of *Main and Apple* he was confident that the Lord's idea to rename this intersection *Goins and Ainsley*... with all that entailed and implied...would be quickly realized.

Though his father, Louis Fox Goins, had been radical enough at fifteen to run away from home and join up with the Confederate Army near Vicksburg... Mississippi not Indiana... get himself wounded and captured by Grant's soldiers... all of that, like Louis' limp, was now in the distant past. It was not typical Goins' behavior, and the family had not been well pleased. Once his father returned from his Southern adventure, with the exception of one or two years in the gas fields up by *Power City,* he settled down to a hard but respectable life on the rich boggy soil of Tecumseh County, draining the land with constant ditching, killing off most of the remaining Massasauga rattlesnakes, and slowly and methodically increasing his corn and wheat acreage.

Like most Hoosiers of his time Wilton took little interest in family history or genealogy. The present, with all its struggles and joys, was sufficient. He knew the Goins had come from Europe... England or Germany in all likelihood...sometime around the Revolution, had settled somewhere in the East, and then come to Indiana early on. But none of that mattered when a man had opportunities to amass wealth and power and create a fresh respectability. The past was a dark place, the present bright, the future, under the anointing of a living and vibrant God... limitless.

He stepped from the automobile and stood in the bright sunshine of early Spring before the simple brick building housing the *Aschburgh Savings & Trust*. God had spoken clearly, surprisingly clearly. Not only of the street signs, but also of his marriage to Miss Marva Ainsley. There was none of the ambiguity Wilton often found in the Scriptures. Bible study rarely settled anything, but when God spoke, and you decided He was right, powerful things happened. By a step of faith, the new street names and signs would be a celebration of their union, which of course still remained a matter to be discussed with the Ainsleys and with Marva herself.

Main Street was to be renamed *Goins Boulevard*, *Apple* to become *Ainsley Street*, and Wilton was, at his own expense, to erect new street signs on the four corners by the *Bank*, with the *GOINS* and *AINSLEY* names over-lapping one another, like a railroad crossing marker. A step of faith, a celebration of the uniting of two of the three great families of Aschburgh, a testimony of praise to the Lord whose will was to be done through the merging of the Goins and Ainsley families and fortunes. Wilton waved to two merchants sweeping the sidewalk across the soon to be *Goins Boulevard*, turned and walked into his *Bank*.

In the Spring of 1925 the small town of Aschburgh, Indiana, though neither Wilton Fox Goins nor anyone else in Tecumseh

County realized it, was already five years into a steady decline which would devil it for the next seventy-five years. At the moment, though with a certain Hoosier reserve, Wilton and the Chamber of Commerce were confident that the current slump would quickly turn around. Wilton perhaps a bit less certain than the Chamber.

There was no contesting the fact that the Natural Gas Boom, having transformed Tecumseh County over the previous thirty years, was finished. But Aschburgh remained a town which not that long ago had seen the railroad stop twice a day, a place that had even possessed a small station...so surely it was merely a matter of cultivating the right opportunities. The local economy would turn around. It had to.

This was a blessed community where only decades earlier... before the nation allowed itself to be dragged by the Democrats into the European War...the fires from the gas wells lit the night skies, free gas illuminated newly erected mansions, and with businesses going up all over Giantown and Power City, scruffy strangers from the East arrived daily looking for good paying jobs in the fields, while the Ball Brothers, attracted by cheap fuel, moved their canning jar business to nearby Muncie. With that kind of recent history it seemed likely Aschburgh and the surrounding villages were going to bounce back, and with any kind of a break would soon be rivaling Fort Wayne and Indianapolis once again.

Wilton, born four and a half decades earlier near Power City where his father had moved briefly to seek a chimerical fortune, grew up surrounded by the Gas Boom. As a young man with a gift for buying and selling, and an ear always open to the voice of God, he built a modest fortune, sought out the benefits of University social contacts and education, and then moving his interests from gas to real estate ten years ago, was now well on his way to becoming one of the wealthiest men in the entire State... and a force to be reckoned with in the region.

Along with the Chamber of Commerce he continued to believe in Aschburgh as well as in the future of Tecumseh and Stonewall Counties. But unlike many enthusiasts and boosters who were hoping for a return of the Natural Gas fields, Wilton Goins was a man to hedge his bets a bit, to employ numerous baskets for his eggs, to rely on numbers rather than hopes, and in the final analysis to place ultimate trust only in the Lord, the One who from time to time spoke to him of personal and business matters.

Despite his deep confidence, despite what he said publicly at Chamber of Commerce meetings, Hoosier reserve cautioned that facts were a stubborn reality. Aschburgh had known only ten big years. That was when the three and four storey buildings went up on *Main Street*...soon to be *Goins Boulevard*. That was when the glass and brick factories were constructed just south of town, that was when the Government put up the new Post Office. But now the glass factory was closed. And the brick plant would shut down soon enough. And although the Post Office would remain, it turned out the gas fields were not limitless after all...as everyone ought to have known...so most things were stubbornly going bust, and nothing higher than one storey had been built since 1917...which was the year chiseled on the cornerstone of the *Aschburgh Savings & Trust*.

Wilton's recent spiritual and personal break-through had come three weeks earlier, in this very building, in his office, after a night spent on his knees holding conversation with the Lord. It was then he received the command to seek out union with the Ainsleys, Aschburgh farmers of prominence, whose fortune, amassed in eastern Tennessee during the now distant and murky days before the Civil War, had been cleansed and even sanctified by several generations of sober and devout lives in Aschburgh, lives focused upon crops, family and the small but intense *First Bible Baptist Holiness Church*.

Having received a clear sign that Marva, the only child of Olin and Belva Ainsley, was called to be his wife and the mother of his many children, Wilton made discreet inquiries, and learning she would soon complete her education at the *Westbury Baptist*

Holiness Women's Seminary, he prepared for her homecoming and their marriage.

Later on in the early morning of that very day…the day of his revelation, before dawn, while praying through his Bible, letting the Spirit lead him in leapfrog fashion from seemingly unrelated verse to verse, book to book, he briefly focused his attention upon the intersecting street signs on the corner post outside his office window.

MAIN STREET & APPLE DRIVE

Reflecting on the prophesy God shared in the early hours of the night, his spirit resonated, and he knew these battered street signs were *not* God's will. They had never been His will even though the signs formed a Cross…a fact he had previously noted with satisfaction. But as the sun rose that morning he saw much greater significance in these simple street markers. Once more God had touched his spirit.

Wilton smiled and carefully closed his Bible. The Lord was indeed good. The Lord God had first given to him a sign that Miss Marva Ainsley was called to be his wife and the mother of his many children, and now this same gracious One supplied the manner in which he must proceed. Truly he was ordained to *Worship the Lord in the beauty of holiness* all the days of his life, and this was as well a call upon Miss Ainsley and upon their children and their children's children.

That morning, three weeks ago now, as Wilton considered the validity of these words of prophesy, as well as his next step, recognizing the need to proceed in harmony with the plan of the Father, he noted with satisfaction the early arrival of young Harley Barnes, the assistant teller. An up and comer. "Good morning, Mr. Barnes," he called from his office in the rear of the bank. "We live in a blessed community. Do you agree?" "Yes, sir we surely do. I thought to get things prepared for the start of the week. Before Mr. Stitt arrives." "Very good. Good thought." Wilton Goins prepared to shut the door to his office. "Barring an emergency, of course, I am not to be disturbed."

His relations with Olin Ainsley were cordial and long-standing, going back to their youth. Though he lacked polish and education, Olin had always been known as a fellow with a good head for business, as well as the good sense to listen to his wife Belva, a woman born to lead. The Ainsleys' large farming operation prospered year after year, though farming was not the sort of business of which Wilton Goins thought very highly.

His father had been a farmer, of course, and though Wilton still lived on the large family farm, *The Old Goins Place*, all of the land was long since put out on rent to local men. In the long-run, he supposed, a sensible man could make a fair living from agriculture, but it was too small a return for the risks. It was hard to believe that God would ever lead a man of faith that way. The truth was, the whole proposition, while seemingly conservative, was in fact remarkably risky. No control over the weather and no way to predict the markets. Not a business to be trusted.

He recognized he had been fortunate with Natural Gas. Getting in and getting out at the right times, building up enormous capital almost overnight, that was a thing God had directed. No man had such wisdom and foresight. But it was real estate, land, which had been good to him in the long haul. Over time, land bought cheaply was always dependable.

But Olin Ainsley had done well in agriculture, and raised up a small family of which he could be well pleased. A man like Olin, a serious holiness man after his fashion, was worthy of cultivation, with an eye to family union and future investment. And so it had come to pass, as he thought and considered and prayed early that Monday morning, some three weeks earlier, isolated in his office from the commerce of the Bank, continuing to marvel at the Divine message spoken through the false signs of *MAIN and APPLE,* soon to be transformed to *GOINS and AINSLEY,* Wilton Fox Goins resolved that his first step toward uniting with Miss Marva Ainsley and in keeping with the Lord's plan, would be to join the *First Bible Baptist Holiness Church.*

The cultivation of Olin and Belva Ainsley, union with their daughter Marva, the renaming of the intersection outside his window, the birth of his many children …all these things would follow in rapid course, for it was clearly the will of the almighty God. But first there was the business of telling the Reverend Harmon Hoheimer that he was now a *Bible Baptist Holiness Man.*

2
Preparing To Slice Off The Bun Of Holiness

Westbury Bible Baptist Women's Seminary, situated just ten miles north of Indianapolis' Monument Circle on a poorly landscaped ten acre campus of single storey frame buildings, had recently experienced a touch of fame in holiness circles with the publication by the *Seminary* president, Doctor Marcus Aurelius Bound, of *Getting The Backslider Back On Track.* The pamphlet, widely circulated in *Baptist Holiness* Sunday School classes throughout the small denomination, transformed Doctor Bound into the most coveted guest speaker in the entire *Illini-Indy & Ohio Bible Baptist Holiness Convention.*

On this Spring morning, however, Doctor Bound's attention was focused not on matters of fame, but on the rumor circulating among the young ladies of the senior class that a member of their group, Marva Winslow Ainsley, planned to cut her hair short following the upcoming graduation. The girl was not well known to him, but her family was. *Families* actually since she descended from both the Winslows and the Ainsleys, each prominent in the church as steady workers and major contributors. So the whole business was disturbing...but of course if the girl waited until after graduation...well, it wouldn't be his problem. Still, considering she had been raised up in the *Bible Baptist Holiness Way* it remained troubling.

For her part, seventeen year old Marva Winslow Ainsley wasn't troubled at all. As she saw it her only problem was to struggle through these final few weeks of boredom and repression. A tall, broad-shouldered, energetic young woman, Marva had been an anomaly in the *Bible Baptist Holiness Church* at least since the age of eleven. An inch or so over six feet, with large hands and big feet, she projected a disturbing presence in a Church which preferred its women small and demure. Though everyone agreed she was reasonably graceful and attractive, given her size, and undoubtedly one of the most intelligent and artistically gifted girls at the *Women's Seminary*, she remained strong-willed and given to being out-spoken... traits which did not amuse the pious faculty and clergy.

In accord with the rules of the Church and *Seminary*, her waist-long black hair was meticulously put up in a tight bun. *But if a woman have long hair, it is a glory to her: for her hair is given to her as a covering.* And again, *For this cause ought the woman to have power on her head because of the angels.* Even so, despite both *power* and *angels*, right after graduation at the end of May, and prior to actually stepping off the dreary *Seminary* campus, Marva was determined to make a statement by slicing off this *stupid bun of holiness* and cutting her hair short. Later she'd have it styled properly. The idiotic long dresses and bonnets she'd been forced to wear would be tossed in the trash or burned, and she would exit the building in a brightly colored and stylish dress. Short. Without a nineteenth century bonnet.

Once Doctor Bound and this horrible place were literally out of her hair, she was going to Paris to study painting at the *Sorbonne*. Or London. Maybe even New York City. With her own studio on Fifth Avenue or Herald Square. She realized she knew nothing of Paris or London or New York, and precious little of painting, but she also sensed all that was out there, and she was determined to experience it. And she definitely was not setting up house for some clodhopper in Westbury or Aschburgh or Power City! Several of her watercolors had been admired at the school, and while that might not mean much, one way or another she was going to make a break and create a career, a life and a world for herself.

Marva was certain her father Olin would support her plans. The problem would be her mother, Belva Winslow Ainsley, a woman as strong willed as her daughter, and totally committed to Aschburgh and its *Bible Baptist Holiness Church*. Committed to the *better sort of people* in Aschburgh and Tecumseh County, her mother never seemed to realize there were no *better sort of people* anywhere in the area. Except for people like Daddy…and the Birdsalls…and Mister Goins, of course.

And the Birdsalls were undertakers and were odd so that hardly qualified. Indiana was a wasteland, and with the possible exception of Indianapolis, what anyone in the whole State said or did made no difference to the rest of the world. Yet here she was, despite all her dreams and all her talent, stuck in this ridiculous church, *Bible Baptist Holiness*, with the preposterous Reverend Hoheimer firm in his Aschburgh pulpit. Well, the less said the better. The bun of holiness was coming off!

Seated at a long table in the chilly dining hall, Marva had long since finished her sandwich and soup and was reading *David Copperfield*, carefully ignoring the girls around her, when her cousin Regina Winslow walked into the room.

"What've you been up to? You're too late to get anything to eat now," said Marva.

"I'm trying to skip lunch anyway." Regina lived in the center of Aschburgh with her widowed uncle Town Marshall Sevier Winslow. She was a *town girl* unlike Marva whose parents lived several miles out in the country on a large farm known throughout Tecumseh and Stonewall counties as *The Old Ainsley Place,* though in fact her family were the first Ainsleys to have ever lived there. Regina's mother, Laura Winslow, was rumored to be living in the South, maybe New Orleans, and no one ever spoke of her father. On the other hand, her uncle Sevier Winslow had been the well respected Town Marshal as long as anyone could remember, and Regina was generally considered a full Winslow despite her background and the fact that she was raised in town.

As bright as her cousin Marva, Regina was less given to dreams, and looked forward to graduation and returning to Aschburgh where she hoped to find a husband in the church. Though slender and of medium height, she was quite vigorous and strong. Her light colored hair, thick eyebrows, and black, deep-set eyes gave her, in the prosaic world of the *Westbury Bible Baptist Holiness Women's Seminary*, an exotic look. Behind her back she was called *The Blonde Jewess*, though none of the *Seminary* ladies had ever, as far as they knew, set eyes upon a child of Abraham. Or ever wanted to for that matter.

Regina favored a delicate, heavily starched white cap tied loosely under her chin rather than the black bonnet preferred by the *Seminary*. She felt the white cap accentuated her hair and made her look cute. If you had to live with holiness you could at least make it work for you.

"He walked me back to the dining hall. So I took my time," she whispered to Marva.

"Well, I hope that was the extent of it."

"Of course that was the *extent of it*."

"He's only a handyman. If Doctor Bound ever finds out he'll be fired in a second," said Marva. "Anyway, he's only a boy. I'll bet he's not even eighteen."

"Mine may still be a boy, but yours is an old man."

Marva tried her best to ignore the blush she felt rising in her cheeks and tried to continue smiling. Even if tightly. "You know I've never even spoken to him. It's all just rumors. Aschburgh is a gossip mill, a total gossip mill. And even if the rumors were true, and I'm sure they're not, it's only that he's asked a few people about me. What does that mean? You know it means nothing. There's all kinds of reasons he might've done that. I mean he's a businessman after all. Like Daddy. And he's hardly an old man. Thirty's not very old for a successful man."

"Forty-five."

"Then that. Forty or forty-five. What's so old about that? He's never been married. Not that I intend to marry either for that matter. Once I leave here, that's it. I'm going to have a career of my own, I'm going to leave this stupid place behind and go somewhere where people are alive. But in fairness to Mister Goins, I'm not saying anything against him. I think he's rather distinguished. Don't you?"

"Handsome. He has the most piercing blue eyes. But black is his color. Dark and mysterious. Have you ever noticed his nails? I think he's the only man in town with clean nails. I also think he puts some kind of clear polish on them. And rich. Very rich. And he's been every place. Uncle Sevier says he's been to France. And he has a new car. And rich. Very, very rich. Not that that matters to you, of course."

"You've noticed his finger nails?"

"I notice lots of things."

"Just keep in mind we're graduating." Marva grinned at her cousin. "So don't get yourself expelled over your little handyman. For immorality!"

"He walked me to the dining hall!"

"*Immorality* is what Doctor Bound would say."

"Backsliding!"

"We'll have to get you *back on track*. Let's just make sure we get out of this place, Regina. We've got things to do."

"Amen to that."

Later that afternoon, seated on the edge of her bed, Marva Winslow Ainsley considered reports that Wilton Fox Goins had been making what he probably thought were discreet inquiries about her. Of course Aschburgh didn't know the meaning of *discreet*. It was all rumors...but well-founded rumors near as she could tell. She'd never actually spoken to him, but last summer, standing in front of his Bank, he had spoken with her Daddy...and said hello to her naturally. Though that was as far as it went.

He spoke with Daddy as an equal. They called one another by their first names and they joked. No one else in Aschburgh would dare to joke that way with Daddy. Except maybe Mister Birdsall. And herself naturally. And Mister Wilton Fox Goins. He was supposed to be very religious. But in a peculiar way. Marva wasn't sure how she felt about that. She had hoped to put the church on the back burner...but so far as she knew he never attended any church.

He was very tall, taller than her by several inches, maybe six foot four or so. Which would be nice. And though he was thin, he wasn't skinny, he looked strong even though he was a banker. Regina was right about his hands, which were long and beautiful, with clean, clipped nails, and he had a neatly trimmed black mustache, and those bright blue eyes. It was surprising how much she remembered about him. Truth be told Mister Goins was, with the exception of Daddy, the most distinguished man she had ever met. *Seen* really. She hadn't really *met* him.

But in the end it all added up to a big nothing. What was certain was Paris or New York. Places no one around here had ever been. Except for Mister Goins. Places where she could actually meet people who were doing something with their lives. Places that were more than this little emptiness, this hollowness, this shallowness, this *Westbury Bible Baptist Holiness Women's Seminary*. Marva grinned at her wit.

Nothing to do right now but hope. Hopes and dreams were unlikely to become more than that unless she could convince Momma. And how likely was that? She carefully opened her *Bible* for her private devotions. Perhaps the Lord would answer her prayers this afternoon, revealing His will for her life through His precious Word.

3
Bible Baptist Holiness Men Stand Clear Of Hair-Glory

Reverend Harmon Hoheimer led a steady, predictable and quiet life. He and Sister Hoheimer, pleased to be humble people, were very content with their ministry in Aschburgh. For many years they had lived peacefully on *Apple Drive*, next to the sturdy, frame building which was *First Bible Baptist Holiness*. The simple parsonage, drafty in winter, but more than adequate for their basic needs...the church undisturbed, non-contentious and stable...while the living, mostly gifts of produce with small amounts of beef and pork on occasion, not to mention a tidy but dependable cash stipend...all amounted to quite a nice situation. Cozy. Brother and Sister Hoheimer bore a sorrow in that the

Lord had not seen fit to bless them with children, but that Cross, difficult to bear though it was, meant life remained peaceful, a state they both cherished. The God who owned the cattle on a thousand hills had provided for them, as a reward for faithful service, a serene and a respectable ministry in Aschburgh...one to be highly prized and cultivated.

Now all this was threatened with word that Wilton Fox Goins, a non-church going man, an unsaved man of unstable Quaker roots, a man of hair-glory, would be paying a visit to the parsonage in the late morning, something he certainly had never done before. In truth he rarely bothered to acknowledge the greeting of Reverend Hoheimer, so what could this visit be about? There were some good *non-Bible Baptist Holiness* people, thought Reverend Hoheimer...though most were odd ...but if the talk around town was to be believed Mister Goins was the oddest of the lot. And rude to boot. All the gossip about Goins hearing from God...apparently holding conversations...all the while cloaked in haughty banker's dress and behavior, made Harmon Hoheimer suspicious, not to say nervous. The vanity of hair-glory provided the window to his true condition. A powerful and apparently erratic person like Wilton Goins was an empty pasture in which the devil might graze. Someone once said satan was a better *Bible* scholar than most preachers.

One week after attending the graduation of Marva Ainsley and her cousin, Regina Winslow as a guest of Olin and Belva Ainsley, Wilton Goins approached the run-down *Bible Baptist Holiness* parsonage. The patched wooden door was opened by Pastor Harmon Hoheimer, a short man who was sweating heavily under the burden of two hundred pounds covered by a heavy wool suit.

"Reverend Hoheimer."

"Mister Goins. How good to see you again. Please come in."

"I appreciate your taking the time to see me, sir."

"Not at all. Perhaps some tea? Sister Hoheimer can have it ready in a jiffy."

"No, no thank you. May I sit down?"

"Please. Please."

Opposite one another, in simple wooden chairs, each man evaluated the other and the situation. Quickly sizing up the sparsely furnished and shabbily decorated parsonage office Wilton fixed his eyes on Reverend Hoheimer. The man was a disgrace. Fat. Grossly fat. The stereotype of the country parson who eats too much free fried chicken every Sunday afternoon. It spoke poorly of his character. The clergy ought to display discipline, not their passion for gluttony. Balding, sweating, poorly groomed. Hopefully the man's mind was still intact. *Sharp* was clearly too much to ask. Hoheimer would never be hired as a teller at the Bank.

"How may I help you, Mister Goins?" While not an *Article of Faith*, being free from facial hair, free from *hair-glory*, was a holiness standard Reverend Hoheimer insisted upon in his church. Goins' mustache was an affront, forcing the Pastor to avert his eyes from the banker's upper lip. The funds wasted on the fellow's fancy suit would easily support three humble parsonage families for a year. His eyes were hard, piercing, unpleasant. With that appalling mustache he signaled the lack of the Lord in his life. Clearly an unsaved man with a contempt for God's Word. People said the family had been Quakers some time back. An obscure group, not precisely a cult, but definitely not what he considered a Church...despite their presence in town as the *Friends Church*...no, these were not holiness people.

Wilton glanced at the torn curtains and worn rug, noted the lack of books, the absence of a radio, the clutter of Gospel tracts on the messy desk. He realized his presence was disturbing to this ignorant man, and he smiled broadly, displaying his strong white teeth.

"Reverend, I realize we have not been close, that we move in somewhat different circles, and that my presence here today must seem a bit odd."

"Not at all, Mister Goins."

"Well...there are times when we need to open ourselves to people who seem somewhat different. There are times when God requires that of us. Are you at all familiar with *Hebrews 13:2*?"

Harmon Hoheimer shut his eyes and pictured the page in his old Bible. *At all familiar!* He took pride in his perfect recall of Scripture...at least significant Scripture. *Be not forgetful to entertain strangers: for thereby some have entertained angels unawares.* "Is that the one you meant?"

"Precisely. But I've always wondered why. Do you follow me, Reverend? Why? God has a purpose there, and it's surely not that on some rare occasion we might encounter an angel. So what exactly lies behind it? An openness to new experience, new people? Do you think?"

"May I remind you that I am an ordained minister? A student of Scripture."

"And I respect that, Reverend. I respect that. But at the same time I have to say in this one way you and I are equals. Both anointed of the Lord in our grasp of the Scriptures. And while you have also been anointed to preach the Word, I have been given a special anointing to amass wealth for the purpose of seeing God's will achieved in this community. We each have special gifts of which the Church is needful. *Be not forgetful to entertain strangers: for thereby some have entertained angels unawares.* Do you see what I'm getting at here?"

"I'm afraid not. Surely you don't imagine angels are walking around Aschburgh?"

"I don't think that's funny, Pastor. God is presenting you and the Church with a remarkable opportunity." This fat man was not only dense, he was a pompous arrogant ass as well. A living, breathing example of all that was wrong with the Church of Jesus Christ. His father, Louis Fox Goins, had been right to separate himself and the family from the Quakers and all other churches. But times change, and it had to be endured. It simply had to be endured. God's plan, about to be achieved in the fulness of Divine time, was to see he and Marva Ainsley united, parents of a vigorous and fruitful family, leaders of this Church and community into future generations. And Reverend Harmon

Hoheimer, such as he was, stupid and lazy and fat, was the first link in the Lord's chain of causation. *Thy will be done.*

"Opportunities, gifts from the Lord, abound, Mister Goins. Sister Hoheimer and I have often commented during our devotions on the goodness and the grace bestowed so freely and amply by our heavenly Father. His compassion knoweth no bounds. Sister Hoheimer and I praise His name continuously and in all things."

The man was intolerable. "Let me get to the point, Pastor. I am the *opportunity* God has given to you. It is my intention to join *First Bible Baptist Holiness.* God has led me to this decision and has given me ample confirmation. If anything I have sought too much confirmation, and have delayed more than I ought. The Father has recently shown me He is not well pleased with my delays. It is His will, and I intend to be faithful."

"You are a Quaker, I believe. That's not the same as *holiness.*"

"As a young man my father was a Friend or a Quaker if you prefer. He left it early on, and I have followed my own course. God speaks and I obey."

"I'm not very familiar with the Quakers."

"Quakers have nothing to do with it. God has shown me I am to join your Church, and I intend to be obedient."

Harmon Hoheimer studied Wilton Fox Goins, knowing he needed to be careful. The man had connections. But allowing Goins to join his Church was out of the question. With his carefully parted black hair, his arrogant mustache...facial glory...carrying himself like some high fallutin' military officer...superior, arrogant ...with a Fancy-Dan necktie...the man's suit and necktie might be black, but they were definitely not *holiness.* Wilton Fox Goins would never be *holiness.*

"We do not allow facial hair in our Church, Mister Goins. I'm sorry."

Wilton leaned forward, his strong face now no more than a foot from the Pastor's. "Let us be clear that God has spoken. Surely you understand that. I am a serious person, Reverend, and I don't have time to waste. God has spoken, and I will obey.

In the light of a command from the almighty Jehovah God my mustache is irrelevant. I will join your Church."

"There's also the matter of salvation."

"I was saved by the blood of the Lord Jesus Christ when I was sixteen years old. Thursday, May the 17th, 1896 at approximately 9 p.m. That evening I went to the altar at the old *Apostolic Holiness Methodist Church* just outside Power City, prayed through, and accepted Jesus as my savior and my Lord. The evangelist was the Reverend Doctor Everett P. Thomason of Memphis, Tennessee, and he was kind enough to record my salvation in my Bible, along with his signature. A most precious document of which I am very well pleased. I have it to this day, along with Evangelist Thomason's certification of my water baptism."

"Methodist?"

"*Holiness* Methodist. Baptized by immersion. God spoke to me back then, Reverend. God had spoken of salvation and baptism and *Holiness Methodist*, and when Jehovah God speaks, I obey."

The last thing he needed was this arrogant man as a member of his Church. For years everything had been quiet, but Goins was outspoken, rich and powerful. It would never do. "*Holiness Methodist* is not *Bible Baptist Holiness*, Mister Goins. I'm sure you're aware of that. I will need time to pray and to consider all you have said. May I suggest you pray as well?"

Wilton leaned back in his chair and smiled. "I came here to tell you what God has said. In harmony with *Hebrews 13:2*. Now I have done that."

"These things cannot be rushed, Mister Goins."

"I understand. I'm a businessman, Pastor. I understand *these things*." He smiled and stood to leave, towering over Reverend Hoheimer who remained seated. "I appreciate your time, Reverend. I will be at *Bible Baptist Holiness* this Sunday, along with my good friends Olin and Belva Ainsley and their daughter Marva. Perhaps you've heard the young lady is back in our community after her graduation from *Westbury Women's Seminary*. Quite an occasion. I was delighted to be invited by the family, and to be able to be there to see her honored by the school. I failed to see you at the ceremony."

"Mister Goins--"

"I've already discussed my intention to join the Church with Olin...Mister Ainsley. One of your Board members. And he, of course, is delighted. The Lord willing and consenting, this Sunday morning I will give testimony of my salvation and baptism, and will ask to be received into membership."

"Sir!"

"The Ainsleys, who feel I ought to be rebaptized according to the *Bible Baptist Holiness Way,* have graciously offered their pond as a suitable site. With your approval, of course, Belva...Mrs. Ainsley...is planning a little picnic for the entire congregation. Following my baptism." Wilton was halfway out the door of the study when he turned back toward the Pastor. "Mister Ainsley...Olin...tells me he is certain my mustache will not be a problem."

4

Miss Fayola Fessenden treated all present at Wednesday afternoon's gathering of the Home Economy Club to as sweet a rendition of "When We Gather At The River" as this reporter believes can be imagined. Indeed the memories of many familiar with Aschburgh lore were heartily challenged to recall when ever so pleasant a rendition has been heard in these environs. Gathered for the gavel of Chairwoman Abbadean Nafe were Verona Kimes, LaDawn Hyde, Mrs. Sebert (Junita) Elzroth, Twinkle Parsons, Normalee Winslow and of course special guest Miss Fayola Fessenden. Refreshments were served, and a wonderful afternoon was experienced by all present for the festivities.

CHAPTER 2
A GOOD HEAD FOR BUSINESS
IS A CLEAR SIGN OF GOD'S
BLESSING

God's plan continues to unfold as Reverend Hoheimer is confronted with a "How's Come" question for which he has no answer; the Reverend's fate is pretty well sealed; Belva Ainsley maneuvers and believes she has her way; Wilton and Marva continue to walk in the light, having casually confronted and then quickly set behind them the boggy matter of predestination.

1
Implementing God's Will

They anticipated no difficulties and there were none. Belva Ainsley had several days to contact everyone who ought to have been contacted so the small *Bible Baptist Holiness* sanctuary was filled with the appropriate people and at the appropriate moment, with Reverend Hoheimer floundering behind the pulpit, Wilton Fox Goins rose and gave his testimony.

"Dear friends...and I feel most comfortable calling all of you friends...I've known more than a few of you all my life. One way or another I've probably had the privilege of doing business with every one of you or with your families. So I'm not standing up here this morning in the midst of strangers. I feel like I'm with family. And that's a comfort, for what I have to say is very personal, very near to my heart. Many years ago, really before some of you were even born, when I was only a boy myself, I received the Lord Jesus Christ as my savior and my lord, and I've been following Him ever since.

"For a host of reasons, of which I'd rather not speak this morning, I have not joined with any particular church doctrine, but rather I've tried my best to follow the Lord I love in a walk of holiness. Now I've been over all this with Reverend Hoheimer, and he understands it is my heart's desire to be baptized this afternoon and to be received into membership here at *First Bible Baptist Holiness of Aschburgh*. Now I'm just hoping you good people will see fit to accept me. For this is truly where I belong. This is my family."

As Reverend Hoheimer cleared his throat to add some qualifying and cautionary remarks of his own, Olin Ainsley rose to make it clear to everyone that no matter what the Reverend had to say the matter was settled. "Brother Wilton, speaking for Sister Ainsley and myself, and I believe for the rest of the congregation, we thank God for you, and we're delighted to have you as a member of this church. You are family. I'm pretty sure I speak for every single one of us when I say that. You are truly family."

Olin, his thick neck threatening to pop the top button of his tieless starched dress shirt, paused to glance around the small sanctuary daring anyone to dissent. "I'm sure most of you have already heard from Sister Ainsley about the baptism and covered dish this afternoon out at our place, but if you haven't, Belva and I want to invite you right now. Bring a plate or two or three to pass if you can, but if this notice is too short, we understand and well, don't you just worry about it. You just come. We got plenty of food. Now it's two o'clock for Wilton's baptism, and then we'll have the rest of the afternoon to eat and to chat and visit. Is that about it, Belva? O yeah. Please show up a few minutes early for the baptism. Ten or fifteen. 'Cause it'll take us a couple of minutes to get from the house up to the pond."

Belva Ainsley pursed her lips tightly and whispered to her husband who then stepped out of the pew and moved toward the pulpit. "If you don't mind, Reverend, there's a few other things I need to say, and Sister Belva feels they'd be best said from the pulpit. It won't take too much time. It's just that Sister Belva feels it should be said more officially. From the pulpit."

Harmon Hoheimer grabbed hold of the sides of the pulpit and firmly set his two hundred plus pounds as if to resist, but sensing a determined Olin Ainsley... about as heavy as the Reverend at a solid and muscular 5 '6", two hundred and five...would bull his way into the pulpit one way or the other, the preacher reluctantly retreated to his comfortable chair.

"Folks, I want to thank Reverend Hoheimer for his full support in all this. We couldn't do it without him. Now I'm going to try not to repeat myself. But Belva's right. This is all too important to say from the floor. You see having Brother Goins as a baptized member of our church is going to make all the difference for us. Now I know some preachers don't agree, but for a practical, down-to-earth fellow like me, and like you folks as well, a good head for business is a clear sign of God's blessing on a man."

"That's the truth there, Brother Olin."

"Thank you for that vote of confidence, Brother Tommy," said Olin. "I've never been in one of these here pulpits before. Frankly I'd be more comfortable behind my horses, but some things just got to be said. I'm a simple guy who's proud to have dirt under my finger-nails. You see, folks, Brother Wilton Goins is not only a good friend to all of us, not only a serious holiness man... and believe me he is that...but he's also a fellow who can bring good business sense to this church and help us start growing and reaching this community for Jesus. We've been asleep around here for too long...no offense to you Reverend...and this is a call for us to wake up. There was a time not too long ago when this church was packed with children and young families. And Brother Wilton, he's the man who can get us going again. He understands stewardship, he understands how a budget works, he knows how to get things done. This is a fellow who runs a major business. He doesn't just know the big-shots over at Giantown and Indianville...he knows the high and mighty muckity-mucks down in Indianapolis. And if you don't know those people and if they're not on your side you're not going to get nothing done. That's just the way it is in this world. Anyway, I guess that's about it. Reverend Hoheimer will baptize Brother Wilton at 2:00 out at our place, and well...*ya'll come* as my folks used to say down in Tennessee. I know Sister Belva will be expecting to see every last one of you, so you just come and we're going to have a good time. It'll be a time to chat and visit. And remember to come early for the baptism. Reverend."

Following the service the men of the congregation took care to congratulate Wilton, and to assure Olin that they would be present this afternoon, even if a bit late for the actual baptism, while the ladies all checked in with Belva to find out what extras she might want them to bring, and then hustled their husbands home so they wouldn't be late for the baptism. Marva and her cousin Regina, though shy and demure as befitted young holiness women, stopped to tell Wilton how touched they were by his testimony and how happy they would be at his baptism. Only Reverend Hoheimer, still dubious about Wilton's salvation and mustache, and stunned that Olin Ainsley had forced him from his own pulpit, refrained from offering congratulations. But that of course was of little consequence.

2
Reflecting On Marriage & Holiness

Sunday afternoon, May the 3rd was warm and sunny...a perfect day for dear Wilton's baptism, and ideal to give her Marva and the banker a chance to get to know one another a little better, thought Belva Ainsley. She saw the hand of the Lord in all of this. Had it not been for the presence of Reverend Hoheimer and the rest of the congregation tromping all over her property she would have been fully content and at peace.

Tall and slender, her auburn hair worn up, stylish but scriptural, Belva Winslow Ainsley was an attractive woman with delicate features. Except for her hands and feet, which were quite large, a trait she regretted passing along to her only child.

Attractive as she knew herself to be she might well have been cursed with vanity had it not been for the sound teaching of the *Holiness Methodist Church* of her childhood. *Holiness* was the only acceptable church. She hesitated to think or say *true* church since that smacked of the fanaticism of some of these new cults, but your faith had to be clearly reflected in your life and only *Holiness* achieved that. Early in their marriage she and Mister Ainsley who, despite his family having roots in Tennessee, had been raised in the Northern Baptist tradition, the old anti-slavery part of the Baptist Church, arrived at an acceptable compromise...*Bible Baptist Holiness*.

Olin had graciously compromised on the denomination though for many years he resisted stubbornly on some of the dress issues, insisting on rolling up his sleeves and unbuttoning his collar when working in the fields for instance. As near as Belva could tell *Bible Baptist Holiness* was virtually identical to *Holiness Methodist*, neither of which was onerous to a person of commitment...but she tried not to be a harpy about it with Olin. Ten years older than her, and well established in the Aschburgh community at the time of their wedding, Mister Ainsley could be a difficult man...excited about things one minute, dark and tense the next, always demanding she adjust herself to his changing moods.

And it wasn't just in matters of religion that they differed either. It had always pained Belva to have Olin's huge dirty barns and silos placed right at the edge of her lovely lawn, but Olin insisted they were farmers and farmers kept the barns and silos nearby the house. There was no budging him on that point. Smells, flies and general filth, none of it seemed to touch him. Olin might earn his living from agriculture, he might even have it in his blood as he insisted, but Belva was not a farmer. And the barns with their piles of manure were filthy no matter what he claimed. Still...a Christian wife had to be submissive.

She stood on the porch, which stretched all the way around the old farmhouse, looking out toward the field beside the horse barn. Olin mowed it yesterday so their guests could leave their wagons and automobiles at a distance from the house. Tables and chairs, borrowed from the church, were set up neatly on the lawn before they left for services this morning, with several nice shady areas for the ladies. Belva was pleased to see a good number of families arriving early, the women carrying baskets into the kitchen, the men gathering to chat.

Olin had taken Wilton into the house where he could change into his baptismal gown, and Reverend Hoheimer and the deacons were already up at the pond, prepared to receive him at 2:00. So things were moving along nicely. She and Olin had been married on a beautiful Spring day like this. With the reception on this very same lawn, though she hadn't noticed the barns, cattle, manure and flies as much in those days. She'd only been a girl...younger than Marva. Plus compromise and submission were the essence of a good marriage. Olin Ainsley was, on the whole, a good man, faithful to family, community and church. He didn't drink, smoke, chew or cuss around the house, and for the most part...unless planting or harvest were really pressed... he refrained from working on Sundays.

Wilton and Olin stepped out of the house and joined her on the porch as the Birdsalls...Joey at the wheel of his new Buick... drove into the parking field. Wilton, with his neat black hair and mustache, looked distinguished...like an angel...in the long white baptismal gown, she thought. She wished Olin had kept his jacket on, but that was probably asking too much on a sunny day like this. Hopefully he had remembered to sand the bottom of the pond where Wilton and the Reverend Hoheimer would be standing.

Not even born back in those days she didn't really know what the town and country around Aschburgh had been like when Olin and Wilton were boys together, swimming, hunting and doing the things boys did around here back then. They were both in their early teens when she was an infant. Amazing that her only daughter would soon be marrying Wilton Goins. Not that anything was certain…or had actually been said…but Belva could see the signs, and if it was God's will…and she was certain it was…it would be a wonderful match, and Marva would be well provided for.

3
Walking By Faith & Answering The Call

As Wilton expected the baptism had been anti-climactic. A few words, a dunk in the cool pond, a hymn followed by congratulatory slaps on the back, and that was it. Other than clearing the water from his sinuses. His first baptism wasn't that way…not at all. This afternoon was little more than going through the motions to please Belva, but in 1896, as a young fellow at the *Holiness Campgrounds* near *Power City*…well, that had been the real McCoy with the living hand of Jehovah God plunging him under the waters unto death, and then abruptly raising him out of the creek to new life in Jesus Christ. Overwhelmed that day by the power and the goodness of the Lord, the teenaged Wilton Fox Goins had been raised up out of the water of life a man anointed and empowered.

It had never changed after that, and neither had he. As he broke through the water that day in 1896 he knew God was calling him to greatness, and he embraced that call, never wavering. The Lord had blessed him with wealth and power in this world, but the defining event of his life had been the anointing, the empowerment bestowed freely upon him at the old *Holiness Campgrounds* by Jehovah God through the ministry of the Holy Ghost.

As he rose from the waters of the creek, thirty years earlier, he had been oblivious of Evangelist Thomason, that dear man, knowing only the presence of the Father, the Son and the Holy Comforter. Just as in the Gospels, as he stepped from his Jordan, the teen-age Wilton Goins had lifted his hands to the heavens and blessed the people with the power of Jehovah's anointing. Their glory cries of praise and delight were still vivid in his memory, along with Evangelist Thomason's declaration that he, Wilton Fox Goins, only a boy, had the full anointing.

Tears ran down the Evangelist's face that day as he told the people of the power flowing out of his body into Wilton's, momentarily stunning him until he realized this was of God, that a prophet of a new sort had been raised up amongst them in the waters of baptism. A prophet of God, Wilton Fox Goins, proclaimed in their presence, a Tecumseh County man, still only a boy, anointed to live the Gospel in a new way, with signs and wonders following, signs and wonders of a practical sort, new wealth and influence for the people of God. He recalled that glorious moment, so clear today though almost thirty years in memory, wading from the water, glowing with awe and pride at what the Lord had done, trembling with holy tension under the jolting power of the Divine anointing coursing through him. And though God had chosen a career in business for him rather than the ministry as most people expected back then, it had never left him, the assurance of God's holy call, the will of Jehovah God directing his life.

But this afternoon had not been anything like that. The water, the minister, the robes, the hymns...all of it was the same or similar...the form was there, but not the substance, not the power. Still it was a necessary step to fulfilling the will of God for himself and Marva Ainsley, so in that way it was anointed, no matter that it lacked the power and the majesty. The people of God did not walk by feeling. It was good when you had that joyous emotion, but ultimately you walked by faith, you proceeded by obedience. This baptism was a step, perhaps in the flesh, toward bringing to fruition God's design for himself and Marva Ainsley.

God used whosoever He chose to institute His purpose. Even Harmon Hoheimer. The poor man had no anointing, was unworthy to lead the Church of Jesus in this community, was incapable of baptizing with power, let alone of being the vehicle of baptism with fire and the Holy Ghost. And still God used him. Education, position, ordination...all meant nothing without the Holy Ghost anointing of Jehovah. And yet, despite all that, God used this fat empty vessel, Harmon Hoheimer, to bring about His great and wonderful will on this sunny afternoon.

With the wet robes clinging to him, his hair dripping and sticking up in clumps after Olin enthusiastically rubbed it with a towel, Wilton smiled and shook hands, receiving congratulations from his new church family. After changing back into a dry suit, hanging his wet clothes and robes in Olin's wash-up room, and carefully combing his hair, he began working his way slowly through the crowd clustered around the tables piled thick with casseroles, meats and desserts, searching for Miss Marva Ainsley.

4
So How's Come You Baptized Him?

Olin Ainsley carried a glass of sweetened ice tea in each hand as he joined Reverend Hoheimer beside a tall lilac bush along the side of the house. "This'll be good, Reverend. I'll bet it's in the mid 80s. Summertime instead of Spring. But you know what they say about Indiana weather."

Harmon Hoheimer, who was sweating heavily, sipped at the tea. "My urge is to gulp it down, but Sister Hoheimer says that leads to headaches, and I suppose she's right. Like eating ice cream too fast. Of course they say the same thing about the weather in Kentucky...and Ohio for all I know...probably California. If you don't like the way it is just hang around a bit 'cause it'll change."

"Faster than you can blink your eye. You know, Reverend, you done good today. You really done good. I've been thinking about what you said...salvation and all...and despite any reservations you might have, I've known Wilton Goins since we were boys, and he is not only saved...more to the point...he will not let us down. There's a mile wide of difference between being saved and being reliable, and I'm not sure you preachers always appreciate that."

The preacher tapped Olin on the knee with the handle of his spoon. "Mister Ainsley--"

"To be fair, I realize you fellows are trained to get all involved in complicated theological issues, differences between this and that and so forth, but we're dealing here with practical matters. Dollars and cents when you get right down to it. Tea sweet enough?"

Hoheimer ran his handkerchief over his face and then blew his nose. "We're dealing here with the *Church*, Mister Ainsley. The *Church of Jesus Christ*. Jesus is the one who is reliable. Trust not to a man, nor to your own understanding."

Olin slapped his hands together hard enough to attract Belva Ainsley's attention.

"Don't get to fussing, you two," she cautioned.

"The church *is* a business," Olin whispered. "Now a lot of folks want to deny that simple fact, but there it is. You skip your mortgage payment and you'll see how fast you'll be recognized as a business. And if you want to put up a new building you better run things like a business. Look Reverend...sorry I raised my voice there... I'm a common, practical man and so is Wilton Goins. So let's forget all these reservations you have, and let's move forward with a successful building campaign."

"*Except the Lord build the house, they labor in vain that build it.*"

"Yes, of course. That's *Scripture*, isn't it? And of course that's all true and all well and good. But at some point a man has to set both his feet on the ground. Firm on the ground. Scripture's got an answer for however you want to go. You know that as well as me. A fellow can always find a verse. Now I respect the Bible and all, but my job is to raise the money to build us a decent sized church so we can spread the Gospel. And Wilton Goins is the man I need to help me do the job. So let's just drop all these theological reservations. They don't amount to a pile of beans. Not compared to a new building they don't."

Olin Ainsley made it only too clear, thought Harmon Hoheimer, that for the Church Board money, power and worldly fame were what really counted. Yet he and Sister Hoheimer had labored to build a life and ministry upon the firm foundation of Gospel truth, not fleshly glory. Furthermore, the church itself, *First Bible*

Baptist Holiness had been raised upon that bedrock. *For other foundation can no man lay than that is laid, which is Jesus Christ.* No compromise, no surrender. The spirit and the flesh were in fierce opposition, mortal combat...as were he and people like Olin Ainsley...or Mister Wilton Fox Goins for that matter.

"Are you asking me to compromise my deeply held convictions, Brother Ainsley?"

"No, of course not. But I feel you need to stand on your own two feet and take the consequences. I've told you that for years, so don't harp on me about compromise. Stand up for what you believe if it's all that important to you. But I also feel that men like Wilton Goins and me need to put up a new building if we're going to bring young families into this church. And a new building costs money. It don't fall out of the sky. God don't shower money on you. You got to go out and get it."

"Our church will be healthy only to the extent we follow Jesus. Your balance sheet cannot compare to the winding sheet in which they laid our Lord."

"What kind of nonsense is that? We need a new building. Period. We need money to do it. Period. And in case you haven't noticed, sir, getting hold of money is not your gift. Getting hold of money happens to be Wilton's gift. Now that's a fact, pure and simple. We need money to achieve God's purpose here in this town, Aschburgh, and Wilton can and will get us the money. All the money God requires for this job. Now if you have problems with that, well, it may be time for you to move on. Sorry...I probably shouldn't have said that...and it's not that we don't appreciate all you and Sister Hoheimer have done over the years...but we need for you both to be a help and not to be a hindering. And believe me right now we've got us a problem that has been a hindering. We haven't seen a new young person come in this church in years. Nobody gets saved, nobody gets baptized. Except Wilton Goins. And you're not even happy about that."

"It's just that I find it hard to accept Mister Goins' salvation. Saved men are not given to facial hair glory."

"So how's come you baptized him? My goodness, Reverend, I am not going to sit back and let some half-baked interpretation, for which you have no proof, no evidence, to stand in the way of a brand new building. A building which will give glory to God, and bring us in some young people. Wilton's mustache don't make no difference to God. For goodness sake!"

"*For the love of money is the root of all evil.*"

"Doggone it, Hoheimer, don't get me hot. I don't *love* the stuff, I plan to *use* it. For Jesus. There's a big difference. Plus Jesus wore a beard, didn't he? And a mustache last time I looked at His picture. What you call *facial hair glory*. Jesus had a big old bushy beard and a gnarly old mustache, plus long hair. *Plus* long hair on top of the beard and the mustache! And how often did those folks back then take a bath? Can you imagine the stink? So where's the big problem with Wilton having a clean and neatly trimmed mustache?"

"Mister Goins is not the Lord Jesus. Holiness calls us to be like Jesus in our spirit. Not in our appearance. It's not the same thing at all, and it's very complicated. In any event, I have my doubts, sir. I still have my doubts."

"Well, you know what you can do with your doubts, Reverend! Pardon my French as they say. Wilton Goins is a full member of our church, and I will see him on the Finance Committee, and I will see him on the Board, and I will see him on the Building Committee, and I will see him in the pulpit if that's what he wants. Period! End of discussion."

5
My Banker Beau Has Gone And Gotten Himself Sanctified

Marva Ainsley and Regina Winslow watched as Belva Ainsley pleaded with Reverend and Mrs. Hoheimer to stay for the meal…apparently to no avail.

"Daddy must have said something to him," said Marva. "He has a way of speaking his piece."

"Good. Reverend Hoheimer is a bore. Most preachers are. The man needs to be put in his place."

The cousins, holding hands and chatting, strolled away from the serving tables toward the large, gray gazebo which was set on the side of a hill some distance behind the farmhouse. From their childhood it had been a special sanctuary, dim and cool even in the summer heat, a place of privacy and security.

"I suppose I ought to be angry with the way they try to control my life," said Marva. "But what would be the point? Momma is Momma and Daddy is Daddy, and that's not going to change. Not until I have my own home. Which I will."

Dressed alike in long cotton dresses and small bonnets, Marva in dark blue and Regina in pink, with their long hair worn up in buns, the cousins liked to think of themselves as sisters, and most people around Aschburgh treated them as such. Neither of the girls was entirely happy with the *Holiness Way*, but neither of them was prepared to break with it either. Right after graduation from the *Women's Seminary* Marva raised the possibility of cutting her hair and studying art, but her mother had given her what Daddy called *that special look*. Belva rejected the idea out of hand, while Olin Ainsley smiled, shrugged and left the room. Stylish dresses, Paris and New York had never been broached.

"I hope you're not planning on doing something foolish," said Regina. "Running off? Maybe with your rich banker?"

They both laughed at the idea.

"It's hopeless, Regina. Even my banker beau has gone off and gotten himself sanctified."

"Sanctified or not he's still pretty nice. Do you think he's really interested?"

"In me? Not so far as I know."

"If you don't want him keep me in mind. Not really, of course, but…I mean he may be kind of old, but he's still good looking. I just love his hands. And well mannered and well dressed. And rich. O very rich! Don't forget rich. Have you seen his car? It's a brand new *Ford*. The best one they make."

"Now that's a holiness attitude if I ever heard one," said Marva. "Daddy would definitely agree with you on that."

The girls sprawled in big wicker chairs in the dim cool of the gazebo, Regina's feet resting on a bench, Marva's long legs slung over the arm of the chair. "Momma says he's made some sort of inquiries around town. He did that before we graduated so I don't know. It'd seem if he was interested he would've said something to me. I wish we were like normal people, so he could just take me out and we could have some ice cream and talk. I'm really not sure how I feel. I mean he's not really old. Not very old. Have you looked at him? The man is powerful. He has more vigor than any of those stupid boys at the church camp."

"Been looking at his muscles?"

"Of course not. Be serious."

"Maybe…Marva, for goodness sake. He was at the University before we were born. Mister Goins went to high school with your father. In the last century!"

"Daddy's not that old. You even said Mister Goins is still good looking."

"But to marry a man that age?"

"Could we talk about something else? Please!"

6

Bible Baptist Holiness People Don't Hold To Predestination

What with aimless chit-chat, iced tea and potato salad it was a while before Wilton was able to break away. Belva, noticing his growing unease and accurately assessing the reason, took him aside and asked if he had had an opportunity to speak with her daughter since she and Regina Winslow returned from the *Women's Seminary*. Without waiting for his response she pointed half-way up the hill to the gazebo.

"It's one of her favorite spots. Most girls have a place like that…kind of a girlish hide-out I suppose. Though I'm afraid all of that's soon to be behind her now that she's a woman."

"It seems a pleasant spot."

"Wilton, Marva was so pleased when she learned you were joining the church and were to be baptized in our little pond. I know she'd like to speak with you. The church is so important to her. As I know it is to you."

"Of course, Mrs. Ainsley—"

"Are you ever going to call me Belva? People I don't know, people I don't even like or respect call me Belva, but you...you act as though I'm a stranger. We've known each other a while, would you agree?"

Wilton grinned. "I suppose I can be a bit, well a bit stiff. Can't I? *Belva.* How's that?"

"I knew you had it in you, Wilton."

"*Belva.*"

"And it's only taken you...what...a little over twenty years? I know she's just dying to talk to you, Wilton. She admires you so much. As a mature man. A leader in the community and the church. Try not to be too formal. O.K? She's still a girl, only becoming a young woman. But quite mature, Wilton, quite mature. I was married with a child at her age. Still, she does like a little fun. That's normal. You realize that's normal, Wilton? A little fun?"

"O.K. Belva. I get the point. I'll try hard not to be my usual stuffed-shirt self." He grinned at her, and walked up the hill toward the gazebo acutely aware his heart was pounding. *Lord, this is Thy will*, he prayed. *I'm only doing what You want. Please give me steady nerves, and help me to be at least a little relaxed.*

Belva watched as he took long strides up the hill. There were very few women who could resist that boyish grin. She knew she couldn't.

Regina watched him approaching and signaled Marva to put her legs down and make herself presentable. Leaning casually in the entrance to the gazebo Regina waved to him. "Hi, Mister Goins. Congratulations again. It was a beautiful baptism."

"Why thank you. Thank you very much, Miss Winslow."

"Regina is just fine."

Wilton nodded, but wasn't sure he would take that liberty just yet.

"The turn-out for the baptism and the covered-dish is remarkable, don't you think?" she said.

"Yes, very much so. Just about everyone is here. And Reverend Hoheimer did a fine job. I was well pleased."

"I suppose he did. But people came out of regard for you. I felt the power of God, and frankly that's unusual at the Reverend's services."

"Well...."

"I probably shouldn't have said that, should I? Were you looking for someone?"

"Yes, actually I was. Mrs. Ainsley felt her daughter...your cousin...Marva, might be over this way."

Sitting in the shade of the gazebo Marva felt her cheeks warming. It would be humiliating if she kept quiet and he could see her. Which she was sure he could. He was just being polite. And Regina would tell him anyway. Marva stood and smoothed her dress and cap. It would all be so much better if she were properly dressed, not got up like something from another epoch. But then he might not see it that way. "I'm right here." She stood beside her cousin and smiled at him.

Dear Lord, You are perfect and Your will is perfect. As always. This girl is truly lovely, and truly meant for me. She is Your will for me, Father. I accept Your call to marry, and I rejoice in it. Please give me strength to overcome my fear, and faith to walk in Your plan even though it appears impossible.

"Miss Ainsley--"

"Marva, please."

Thy will be done.

"Marva."

"Do you have the time, Mister Goins?" asked Regina. "We were just wondering."

"Time? Pardon?"

"The hour. We've lost track. Do you have a watch?"

"The time! Of course." Idiot! he thought, fumbling in his vest pocket. "Three-fifteen. Fourteen actually."

"Goodness he is precise, isn't he, Marva? Well, that means I'm a quarter of an hour late. Fourteen minutes actually. My aunt and uncle will be annoyed. But, nothing to be done about that now. I'm on my way."

"Regina!"

"It was a beautiful service, Mister Goins. Just beautiful. See you soon, Marva."

"Regina!"

Wilton and Marva watched her walk quickly down to the house, stopping at the porch to turn and wave to them.

He stood by her side, happy but immobilized. She was like the painting he had seen on his recent visit to Professor Steele's studio at the University. A very pleasing picture. Of Steele's daughter. Done when she was this girl's age. Only Marva was lovelier, more delicate in her features, softer in the chin...but still determined and intelligent. Not a silly girl. The Lord had brought him this far, but now it was time for works to flow from his faith, and he found himself in the unusual position of being uncertain how to proceed.

"Would you like to walk, Mister Goins? I enjoy the walk behind the house, back away from the barns and toward the little woods. Daddy left the woods to remind us what this land used to be like. Momma doesn't care for it much. But I do." Marva found his smile charming. It seemed the aloof and forbidding banker, clothed always in somber black, also had a boyish side, simple and open. Only he wasn't a boy. She had to keep that in mind. He was a mature man...experienced and comfortable with the things of the world that were totally beyond her. Though she was interested. Very interested. In the things of the world. And in him.

"Yes, yes thank you. I would like that Miss...Marva."

They walked in silence on the soft grass, the sounds of laughter and children's games growing fainter. Wilton knew he would have to say something if only to cover the pounding in his chest. "Now that you've graduated, do you have some plans?"

"Not really. I had some silly ideas, but I've had to drop them."

"Silly ideas?"

"Well, for example, what do you think about holiness dress, Mister Goins?" Why had she ever said such a stupid thing?

"That's a good question. But look, Marva, before we get to that, let's settle this name business. Now if I'm to call you Marva, I think it's only fair you call me Wilton or Will, whichever you prefer. A few of my oldest friends, like your father, sometimes call me Will. Isn't that fair? What's good for the goose is good for the gander, so to speak. Well, perhaps a poor choice of proverb." This was going much easier than he had expected. It was actually pleasant speaking with her. Being with her.

"Fair enough, Wilton. Goose and gander. That's us," she laughed. He was a nice man. "But what about holiness dress?"

He hadn't forgotten her question, and he sensed where it was headed. "I usually try to avoid legalism, Marva. It tends to rub against the grain. Do you see what I'm saying?"

"Yes, but--"

"Let me finish. Sorry. I shouldn't have abruptly interrupted you."

"That's all right. I want to hear your opinion."

"Well, for one thing, I believe everyone has a right to make their own decision how they dress, what they eat or drink and so forth. Within limits, of course."

"Modesty."

"Yes, for one thing. Take myself. I like black. It's a no fuss color. So all my suits are black. But you know, if someone was to tell me I had to wear black, well, that'd be another thing. Then again, the way life is we sometimes have conflicting responsibilities. To ourselves, but also to others. And, of course, always to the Lord. So, for example, I can see a situation of a young woman, a very fine young woman I might add. And since she lives in her parents' home, and since they hold to holiness dress, she needs to be obedient to them and wear that type dress."

"Even though it makes her uncomfortable?"

"Even though she feels it's not right for her, even though in a little while she may choose to no longer dress that way."

"When she has her own home."

"Well, yes. She'd be free to make her own choices then. Assuming her husband didn't oppose her, of course."

"I'm sure she'd select her husband with care," said Marva. "She'd be looking for someone with a more open perspective. But you think for now she needs to be patient."

"And obedient. Yes. Do you think this young lady could? Be patient? For a little while?"

"As long as she knows it's not forever."

They reached the woods, and as neither wanted to head back toward the house, they walked along the edge of the trees toward the newly planted corn fields which flowed out from the far end of the lawn.

"Marva, I was also speaking of something else when I was talking about holiness dress and all that. Did you hear?"

"I heard. Yes, I heard." She looked straight ahead as they walked, but he felt he could detect her suppressing a smile.

"I don't think you have silly ideas, Marva. I suspect someone has criticized you for that, but I don't think it's true. Are you free to share any of your thoughts?"

"Wilton. That's what I'll call you if it's o.k. Wilton, sometimes I have ideas too big for my station. Have you ever hoped too big?"

"Not really. Occasionally too small. Never too big. And I don't believe you...I mean *you*, Marva...can have ideas and aspirations too large."

"O I'm sure I can."

"No. No you can't. My business takes me to many places beside Aschburgh, and over the years I've come to know a good many special and successful people. And not just in business either. In the arts, architecture, education. I was recently in the studio of T.C. Steele...at the University in Bloomington. A fascinating man. There are many things that people around here never even think about. And you have it within you to be one of those special people who thinks beyond the average."

"O for goodness sakes. I'm just a farm girl."

"That's not what I hear. Is that all you want to be? A farm girl?"

"No. I'd like to learn about art. Painting and drawing. Is T.C. Steele famous? I did some watercolors at school, and some people thought they were pretty good."

"You see. I've known you were special for quite some time. Yes, he's quite famous. And the Lord intends for you to have big ideas and big dreams. It's part of His plan. It's determined if you like, at least if you listen to Him and follow His will for your life."

"Goodness! Just for your information…so you don't get on the wrong side of Reverend Hoheimer…*Bible Baptist Holiness* people don't usually hold to predestination. Things being determined. At least not around here."

"Well, now whoever said predestination! Now *that's* too big an idea for either of us. But seriously, Marva, you are meant to have big plans. Dreams if you like, but I prefer to see it as plans, definite plans. But perhaps I'm speaking out of turn."

"No. No, you're not speaking out of turn. After all, we're goose and gander, you and me. You said so yourself."

"Birds of a feather."

"Same sides of a coin."

"Two of a kind."

"I've enjoyed our talk, Wilton. Sometimes I wonder if everyone is supposed to have the same ideas. Reverend Hoheimer seems to think so."

"O for goodness sakes, Marva! Don't let Harmon Hoheimer direct your life. What does he know? Forgive me, that's unfair. Sometimes I feel too strongly about things. But I suppose there are worse failings. Marva, people are meant to be different. Some folks around here consider that a dangerous idea, but it's still true. And some people are meant to be special. God has made them that way and there's no getting around it."

"Like you?" Whatever had possessed her to say that? She knew she was blushing, and wouldn't be surprised if he were too…

but she couldn't see his face without being obvious. "Have you ever been to New York City?"

Wilton glanced at her and smiled. He was pleased by the redness in her cheeks. Next time he was in Bloomington he would ask Professor Steele for another look at that portrait of his daughter Daisy. For comparison. It was pretty, he knew that…but not as pretty as this girl. "I was really thinking of you, Marva. And yes, I've been to New York City many times."

7
Discerning The Lord's Plan For Reverend Hoheimer

Olin Ainsley, short and thick, walked steadily toward his daughter and his friend. His suit jacket, which Belva insisted he put back on, was too warm and tight so he carried it over his arm, but his long-sleeved white shirt, heavily starched and buttoned tight at the neck, the way Belva liked it, without a necktie, irritated both his neck and his spirit. It would be good to get back into simple and comfortable work clothes. But that would have to wait because Sunday was a *day of rest*. What a joke that was. Sundays were work. Workdays were rest.

He really hated to bother Will and Marva who were obviously enjoying one another's company. As usual Belva was right. Ordained by God…at least by Belva …the relationship seemed to be a good one. Good for all of them. It was just that natural… or seemed to be. But this concern of his just couldn't wait…for he had probably gone too far with the preacher, and if so Will was the man to patch it up or to see the way to a solution.

Olin wiped his bald head and the back of his thick neck with a red bandana. They made a handsome couple, Will and Marva. Both tall and confident. Belva knew what she was talking about. Big people required big people. It had always bothered him that he and Belva didn't match up better. She towered over him, and while there was never any question of their devotion to one another, it just didn't look right. Unfortunately appearances made a difference in this world no matter what anyone said.

Olin glanced behind him toward the house and the crowd of people clustered around the food and drink tables. Belva made sure everyone was here for the baptism. Half the town. The better half of course. The half that counted. He grinned imagining her pushing and prodding folks. No one could stand up to her, not even Will Goins. She even got Joey Birdsall to give up his afternoon nap to come out here and see Will get dunked. Belva was plain and simple good at these things. She got what she wanted, and it was usually best for everyone else too.

What he really needed was to get out of this damned starched shirt. If you weren't allowed to wear a neck-tie, which if nothing else at least let you hide a loosened top button, then why button the shirt all the way up to your neck? What preacher thought that one up? What was so holy about that? Will Goins wore a tie and no one dared to say a thing. Will always did what he wanted, and no one ever dared say boo. Even when they were kids.

And now Belva...and she was sure another one...was planning a Christmas wedding. Of course it was all in her mind, but stuff that got in her mind tended to happen. And she was right that Christmas would be pretty, with the tree and the Winslow family candles and decorations, plus the snow. Belva was counting on lots of snow. But a six months engagement wasn't enough time and people were going to talk. Gossip was a factor you had to take into account in a small place like Aschburgh. Of course that didn't faze Belva. He'd never understood why it didn't, but it didn't. She was like Will that way. Didn't give a hoot once she made up her mind. A Christmas wedding would be pretty. And Will Goins as his son-in-law would be funny. He'd call him *sonny*.

"Warm enough for you, Will?"

"Olin. Miss Marva and I were only now wondering if we'd stayed away from the party too long."

"Daddy, Mister Goins and I were just beginning to talk about some important things."

"Will knows all sorts of things, doesn't he, darling? He's been everyplace and he knows everybody. Hard to imagine why he stays in Aschburgh. I'm just glad he does. Well, Marva my darling, I won't keep Will from you for long. But I do need to discuss some urgent business matters with him. I wouldn't have interrupted if it wasn't really crucial. Why don't you join Regina and your friends at the house?"

"Business on Sunday? At Wilton's party? Daddy!"

"I'll be sure to join you at the house, Miss Marva," said Wilton. "I'm certain this won't take more than a few minutes. Olin?"

"A couple of minutes, darling. No more. Fifteen tops."

"Why can't I stay?"

"Please, Miss Marva. Your Daddy has asked to speak with me privately, and we do need to respect that."

"Ten minutes?"

"As soon as your Daddy and I have finished."

"Darling, I am sorry. But we won't be long. Why don't you check with your mother? I believe she has plans."

"I'm sort of glad you interrupted us, Olin. There's a thing or two I feel a need to speak to you about."

"That's nice of you to say, but I realize this was a bad time. Let's wrap up my issue one, two, three so you and Marva can continue your chat."

"Our *chat* is something of which you and Mrs. Ainsley approve, Olin? We've always been frank with each other, and I'm feeling a little awkward here. Maybe in a bit over my head. All things considered. My age."

"You and Marva? We approve 100%. Couldn't be happier you and our daughter are getting along so well. Look, Will, age is a relative matter. Belva and I appreciate maturity. Very much so. So yes, we're pleased. We approve. And Will, she wants you to call her Belva, not Mrs. Ainsley. Do it for me. Please."

"Well that makes me well pleased. What you said about me and Marva. Well pleased. And yes, of course...*Belva*. Belva it is. I won't forget."

"Will, I'm afraid I've put my foot into it with the preacher. I'm not fond of the fellow...the man's an old woman...I prefer a real man in the pulpit, but....I just ought to have been more...what's the word?...discreet...no, tactful, that's the one I'm looking for."

"Oh?"

Wilton only half-heard Olin as he watched Marva walking back toward the house. Had he been too strong in what he said? Too much on her father's side? Confident though he was of his ability to deal with people, all of this was new. Men were easier than women, especially young women. Uncertain how to proceed he followed his instincts.

"Marva!" he called after her. She turned...he smiled and waved. Afraid she might not acknowledge his call, now he feared she would not return his smile and wave. But she smiled and waved back, and then continued toward the house. "I'll join you in a few minutes," he called after her. "Put your foot in it?"

"I'm really sorry about interrupting you two. Let's not mention it to Belva, if that's all right. My interrupting you. What I did was pretty much to tell Hoheimer to leave. The church, the pulpit. I mean I have no authority to do that. Plus we have no one to replace him."

"If Olin Ainsley doesn't have authority, who does? And don't tell me the Board. You're the power in the church. There'd be no church if it weren't for the Ainsley and Winslow families. And your money. Of course you have the authority. What did he say?"

"You know how he is. He hems and he haws. He's not a real man."

"Well, Olin, none of this is a problem as I see it. You've been straight-forward with him, and that's the end of it. It'd be a good idea if he left. In fact it's essential if the church is going to thrive. Now I'm new to the congregation, so I want to be careful here what I say, but Reverend Hoheimer is too comfortable in Aschburgh, and unless he's dismissed he might never leave."

"So you think we ought to dismiss him?"

"Better yet. Here's an idea. So as to avoid any conflict or disagreement within the congregation. If he was offered something better and even more comfortable I'm sure he'd resign in a heartbeat. All we have to do is give him the bait and he'll bite."

"So you think it'll be all right. I don't want Belva getting upset."

"Belva's a lot stronger than you think, Olin. We need to get rid of this man, and we need to do it quickly. All I'm suggesting is there's a clumsy way to do it, and there's a smart way. Belva will want for us to do the smart thing. Am I right in that?"

"O my, yes."

"Do you mind my speaking this way?"

"Will?"

"As I say, I'm new to the church. I have no authority."

"You have authority in this community. More than anyone. Plus you and I are like brothers, practically raised together."

"We need a young man, Olin. Either with a wife or ready to take one. We don't want someone that's not a real man. A young fellow full of energy and filled with excitement about ministering here. That's what we need. Our young families have a right to expect that, not a bored, frightened old fellow like Harmon Hoheimer. Your Marva and her cousin Regina, my goodness, Olin, Harmon Hoheimer bores them to tears. How will we ever keep them in this church? Before you know it they'll be off to the regular Methodists with their new Young Adult Group and you won't be able to blame them. But you get a young man with some spark, plus a willingness to work with and to learn from the Board...."

"I like that, Will. I like that. See, that's why we need you."

"And take my word for it, your dear wife...Belva...she'll stand 100% behind that sort of change. She wants the church to be here, to be alive, for her daughter."

"And grandchildren. Belva and I often talk about that. The future, our plans, our hopes. Grandchildren."

"Exactly. The way to do it, Olin, the way to please Belva here...is to avoid conflict. No firing, no termination, no angry words. That sort of thing always splits churches. No matter how you handle it, no matter how bad the preacher is, a firing will split the church. What we need to do, and I hope it's all right for me to say this since I'm so new to this, is to promote the man right out of Tecumseh County."

"I like it, Will. I like it. And frankly you are just the man to set it up."

"No. Not me. You. You and Belva just made a sizeable gift to the *Seminary* to honor Marva's graduation. Believe me the school is aware of that, and they have their eye on more. They're greedy so that makes them vulnerable…the kind of people we can work with. Gifts like the one you folks made establish a certain affection among men who understand how things work in this world. Do you see where I'm going?"

"I hadn't really put the *Women's Seminary* and Hoheimer together, but yes, yes of course. He'd love that, wouldn't he? They'd call him *Professor* Hoheimer… maybe even *Doctor*. And pay at least as well as we do…which of course isn't much."

"It's a simple thing, Olin. And everyone will be happy. You, me, Hoheimer, Marva…Belva. Just one thing. I want to see him gone by the end of the Summer. Come the Fall I want to be dealing with a different minister. A young man. Somebody I can talk to. Somebody I can deal with. Because we've got things to do."

"Consider it done, Will. Consider it done. I can't imagine why I didn't think of this myself."

"Now, if it's all right with you…you see, Olin…I'm seeking your approval here, as it were. I would like to go back down to the house and continue my conversation with Marva. But not without your permission. Do you understand what I mean?"

"Permission? Of course I understand. This is very much what we want. Belva and me. We want this, Will. It's more than all right. Way more than all right."

8

BELOVED PARSON MOVES TO HIGHER CALLING

Beauville Weekly Sun & Moon

Monday July 27, 1925

By: Menneth Reneau, Editor-in-Chief

The faithful congregants of Aschburgh's Bible Baptist Holiness Church struggled with strong emotions at yesterday's morning service. There was conflict within each Christian heart as they learned their beloved Shepherd Reverend Harmon Hoheimer would be all too soon leaving them to assume chaplain responsibilities at the Westbury Bible Baptist Women's Seminary For The Training Of Holiness Ladies.

Reverend Hoheimer and his faithful wife have guided the people of the church for several decades, and it will be a task perhaps beyond human capability to replace them. Church leaders Mister Wilton Fox Goins and Mister Olin Ainsley said the church had prayed over this situation long and hard, but in the words of Mister Goins, a leading citizen of Aschburgh and a well regarded personage throughout the State and Midwest, "Reverend and Mrs. Hoheimer have been called by the Lord Himself to assume a higher and a weightier responsibility, and as faithful Christians we must accept that, albeit with heavy hearts."

The date of Reverend Hoheimer's final sermon in Aschburgh will be announced when that date is available. Mister Goins said Reverend Hoheimer and the Westbury Seminary have graciously agreed that he will stay on in the Aschburgh pulpit until his replacement has been appointed. Though, in the words of Mister Goins, "Reverend Hoheimer can never be replaced."

CHAPTER 3
BIG CHANGES ACCOMPANY
YOUNG REVEREND POSTON

*A simple chapter in which little action takes place. Pastor
Hoheimer delivers his final sermon at Bible Baptist Holiness
and we hear of yet another variation of the sin of hair glory;
the Reverend Jeremy Poston of Rising Sun is introduced to the
congregation and a little later to Regina Winslow; Marva and
Wilton discuss deviled eggs and chocolate pie as well as the issue
of hard liquor at the Country Club.*

1
Hair Under The Nose That Stinks
Of Sweat And Unspeakable Filth

No one ever blamed Belva Ainsley for what occurred. The
consensus of opinion in Aschburgh was that odd things happened
to the minds of preachers who were allowed to hang around too
long.

According to Belva's plan, Sunday August 30th, Harmon
Hoheimer's final day in the pulpit of *First Bible Baptist Holiness*,
was intended to be a gala occasion. The morning service would
provide the old pastor an opportunity to bless his congregation

one last time before leaving to assume the position of *Professor of Christian Conversation* at the *Women's Seminary* in Westbury, as well as to introduce the new pastor, the Reverend Jeremy Poston, recently graduated from the *Switzerland Institute of Bible Baptist Holiness* in the southeastern corner of the State, not too far from Quercus Grove.

Afterward, following this historic service, Belva and several of the ladies planned for a festive luncheon to honor Reverend and Sister Hoheimer as well as providing the church a comfortable setting to meet their new Pastor. She could not have planned more carefully or with better intention, and she was as flummoxed as the next person by all that happened.

Pastor Hoheimer maneuvered his bulk behind the old oak pulpit, let his Bible fall open arbitrarily, and caught himself just in time to avoid running his hand through his sparse hair. Sister Hoheimer, after carefully plastering his remaining strands in place, warned him not to touch it lest it come loose and dangle along the side of his head in the peculiar way it sometimes did when he got too excited in his preaching. Looking around the old sanctuary at the small congregation he had preached to for so many years he no longer noticed the peeling paint, the cracks in the walls, the ugly pot-bellied stove in the center aisle, or the many empty wooden pews. As he wiped sweat from his thick neck he reflected that he had had a good ministry in this pulpit, even if some of the people insisted on holding onto ungodliness. And now that the Lord had raised him up to a higher position in the Church he was ready to move forward without any doubts or regrets about his ministry to the people of Jesus in Aschburgh or the rewards which would flow from his faithful service.

"You may rest assured, beloved holiness Church," he began in his oddly high pitched voice, "That as the Lord guides me in my endeavors to mold the young minds and characters of the women at the *Seminary, First Bible Baptist Holiness of Aschburgh* will be very much in my mind and in my prayers. I shall carry with me many fond memories of our fellowship in historic Aschburgh as I step out in faith endeavoring to do that new work to which the Lord has called me and for which He, in His wisdom, has anointed me."

As Reverend Hoheimer's opening remarks droned on, young Reverend Poston was observed to be taking copious notes. Belva, who sat beside Olin, Wilton and Marva in the traditional Ainsley pew, felt this was proper and respectful on the part of the new pastor, but she was hard-pressed to imagine what the young man could possibly be writing down. Now that Marva's engagement to Wilton was public and well received by the Church and the town, she was looking for an appropriate moment for herself and Olin to sit down with young Reverend Poston to fix the arrangements for a Christmas wedding. Pastor Hoheimer had never allowed weddings during the holiday season, but she was sure that would no longer be a problem.

"I leave our beloved Aschburgh with only one regret...that as diligent as I have been in my duties, I may...no, frankly it appears that I have failed to convince some of you of the necessity of holiness in the Christian life. It weighs heavy on my spirit that I have lacked in this. Yet I am lifted up in the knowledge that I have tried my best. Now as I assume my new responsibilities I am acutely aware that my teaching of *Christian Conversation*, of which more in a moment, will provide the foundation for spiritual growth in a life of holiness which will then be carried back to our congregations and communities by the young graduates. Indeed our own dear *First Bible Baptist Holiness* is so richly blessed by the presence of a recent graduate who is modeling, in our very presence, that life of holiness lived in and for Jesus Christ. I refer, of course, to Miss Regina Winslow. What an inspiration this modest young lady is to all of us."

A perceptible intake of breath spread across the congregation. Wilton smiled as he glanced at the floor and gently squeezed Marva's hand. Belva prodded Olin Ainsley who was beginning to drift off. "Did you hear that?" she whispered. "What?" "He intentionally failed to mention Marva. He mentioned Regina's graduation and deliberately omitted Marva's." "It's nothing, Belva. Nothing. An over-sight. He's getting old."

Wilton knew it was no over-sight, and prepared himself for more. When insignificant men like Hoheimer were given a position of authority they sometimes became confused and abused it, believing they had it by right. He expected Hoheimer to be more stable and cautious, all things considered, but clearly he had misjudged the preacher's arrogance and stupidity.

Marva wiggled her fingers at Regina who was sitting across the way with her uncle in the Winslow pew. "Regina's just so embarrassed," she whispered to Wilton. "I would die if he singled me out like that. Just die." He gently patted her hand. "He's done about all the singling out he's going to do. We'll just give him a little more rope. Then we'll give it a good jerk."

"Dearly beloved holiness Church, as I prepare to take my leave of you I feel the prompting of the Holy Ghost to speak frankly, even perhaps to the extent of giving a degree of offense to one or two. Let me caution you, however. What I say is not of me, but it is of the Lord. Remember there are times when the Spirit Himself rebukes and censures, indeed excoriates, and calls us to repent of our wicked ways."

Rebukes and *censures* brought most up short. *Excoriate* was just puzzling. They were always being called to repent, but *rebuke* and *censure*…and then *excoriate*…that threatened to get kind of close to home. That could get sort of strong. Was the man going to spoil a nice occasion by doing or saying something extreme? All had heard the tale of the young preacher who, in this very pulpit, back before it was called *Bible Baptist Holiness*, on a quiet Spring Sunday at the end of the Civil War, had divided the congregation into sheep and goats, ordering the sheep to go to salvation on the right-hand side of the sanctuary and the goats to condemnation on the left.

Sixty years later the good people of *Bible Baptist Holiness* lived in fear of a repetition of that day, or something even worse. Preachers were unpredictable and often unstable. Young Reverend Jeremy Poston, who was very stable indeed, put down his pencil, folded his hands in his lap, and prepared to listen to the Word from the Lord. Olin glanced at Belva who was nervously rubbing her hands together. Wilton looked coolly at Reverend Hoheimer and continued to hold Marva's hand.

"*Christian Conversation*, of which I have been appointed *Distinguished Professor*, refers not merely, as some would have you to think, to our speech... though that must always of course be above reproach...but in its broadest sense to the fulness of our life as Christians, which is to say, to the very life of holiness itself. And may I remind you, for some seem to have forgotten this basic fact, the life of holiness is the instant sign of our salvation. *It is written: be ye holy for I am holy.*

"If we do not see the sign, then there is no salvation present. If holiness and all its manifestations in our behavior and appearance be not present, then that person is striding on the road to hell. He or she shall never see God. Make no mistake. That one is on the road to hell!

"Dear holiness Church, allow me to be specific that even those with hardened hearts and closed ears might receive the Word. When we see a woman with shorn hair, and I refer of course to the so-called modern hair styles...styles we see even on the streets of Aschburgh, which used to be a Christian community but is so no more...when we see a woman decked out with rings and jewelry, like a common harlot, prostitute street-walker, then we do not see a saved woman, we see a woman prancing along the highway to hell! Now she may attend church, she may even be the head of the *Ladies Bible Holiness Society*, but in the eyes of Almighty God she is a painted Jezebel, a horror, an abomination, a prostitute on the way to eternal torment. And the instant sign of her condemnation is the ring on her finger, the bracelet polluting her wrist, the necklace choking the life of the Spirit from her.

"Now if I cause any pain here this morning it is because I am responsible for your souls. This is my final opportunity to see some of you saved. There can be no compromise. Holiness is holiness and sin is sin. When we see a man dressed with the frivolous and silly mind of a woman...I mean by that, dressed in an expensive tailor-made suit, purchased with what for a normal man would be six month's honest, hard-earned wages...when he has sought after these effeminate-minded garments in New York

City or some other place of riotous living...perhaps Chicago or even Indianapolis...when we see this so-called man bedecked in his finery, do not be deceived because you are told it is a *simple black suit.* It is an abomination in the sight of the Lord! *Be not deceived, God is not mocked.* His judgment will be quick and severe. This is effeminate finery, this is pride manifested in the rich cloth which covers the wickedness of the flesh."

"Is he talking about you?" Marva whispered to Wilton.

"No. He's just talking. Don't worry yourself."

"His hair looks so peculiar dangling off the side of his head."

"He's just gotten himself too excited. It won't last."

"When we see a man brazenly wearing a shirt so his arms are bared to all, we do not become confused and say, *Well, at least it is a white shirt.* No, because we know this is sin. We know that bare arms are a horror unto the Lord. Pure and simple. And so when we see a man whose shirt is open at the neck, or a man who wears that so-called la-de-da delicacy called a neck-tie, a gaily decorated and decadent and disgusting rag, which serves no purpose whatsoever. Just you tell me what it does. It gives glory to satan, that's what it does. Church, when we see these things we are gazing upon an unsaved wretch, a stench in the nostrils of God, an unrepentant worm of a sinner headed on a bee-line for hell."

"That's some pretty strong stuff there," Olin said to Belva. "A fellow working in the fields needs to roll up his sleeves and pop his collar button."

"Ssshhh! He'll be gone at the end of the day."

"When we see a man who flaunts facial hair glory, nostril hair that disgusts God, that turns the stomach of the Almighty... hair under the nose that stinks of sweat and unspeakable filth, hair that is an affront to the Scriptures of the Lord Jesus Christ, what shall we say? That man may have money, that man may have power, he may have fame, he may be in charge of the biggest business in town, but in the eyes of Almighty God he is a filthy, foul, stinking abomination."

The congregation was growing increasingly restless in the pews, many of the men nervously glancing around or staring at the floor, with one or two of the ladies wiping gently at their eyes. For her part Belva was pleased at her calm, surprised at how well she could deal with a vicious attack like this. Wilton was part of her family now, and the Ainsleys, Winslows and Goins could never be hurt by this terrible man. He could preach at them all he wanted, in the end he was the one who would be leaving, and God would judge him for his hatefulness. No matter how she might appear to others, this was the first time she could remember herself feeling so strong, so secure. Wilton, calm and gentle throughout Reverend Hoheimer's harangue, was good for all of them. Perhaps his strength rubbed off.

Marva, on the other hand, was angry and appalled. To have these feelings churning in her during a church service was a new experience, new territory. But this stupid, fat man with his squeaky voice was attacking Wilton. Her Wilton. She squeezed his hand tightly.

"I want to leave, Wilton," she whispered. "I'm so, so angry. I want to leave."

Just then Olin spoke out loud, so everyone could hear. "I've had enough of this nonsense. I'm ready to walk out, Will. What do you say?"

"Please, Wilton," said Marva. "Let's just leave now."

"No. I'm not going any place. This is my church," said Wilton, looking straight at Hoheimer and making no effort to mute his voice. "I'm staying and I expect all of us to stay put. Every single one of us. No harm is being done here. Not to us. It's just a tired, frustrated old man venting his spleen. Go ahead and finish your remarks, Reverend."

2
Deviled Eggs & Chocolate Pie

Following a terse benediction Reverend Hoheimer, with Sister Hoheimer firmly in tow, exited the building without a word, foregoing the traditional Aschburgh rite of *shaking the folks out of church.* As the congregation lingered in the sanctuary, uneasy with tension and unclear about how to hold a covered dish honoring the Hoheimers when the Hoheimers had just left in a huff, Wilton, urged on by Belva, stepped into the pulpit.

"Folks, why don't you just sit back down for a second? As the Hoheimers leave us, folks who have served with great faithfulness over the years, so now a new man of God has been brought to us by the Lord. A new man for a new day. This is a very special and joyous time for everyone here, and I think we ought to mark it with a few words before getting about the serious business of lunch."

"Wilton, I think some of the ladies will want to check on their dishes downstairs."

"Of course. Please forgive me, ladies. It'll be no surprise to you that I'm not much of a cook. You just go and do what you need to do. We appreciate you so much. People, these ladies are the backbone of the church. And I can tell you I'm really looking forward to this meal to honor our new Pastor." As several ladies headed for the basement fellowship hall and its adjoining kitchen, Wilton continued, "It's such a privilege to have Reverend Jeremy Poston with us this morning. Jeremy, you're about to find out *Bible Baptist* has the finest cooks in the County. No, in the State. Now I hope I'll not embarrass you, Reverend, but I think the folks ought to know a few things about your accomplishments up to this point."

"Thank you, Mister Goins," Jeremy muttered. Unclear as to the ins and outs of all that had taken place in the service, he was very clear that he ought to align himself with Wilton Goins and the Ainsleys, not with Reverend Hoheimer. "I'm afraid I really haven't accomplished much so far."

"Let's let the people of *Bible Baptist Holiness* be the judges of that. There's great days ahead. Many times the Lord sends wisdom with a young man, wisdom beyond his years, and I firmly believe that is what we are seeing right now, folks. We have been needing a bright young man who's not afraid to learn, and we have him now in Reverend Jeremy Poston. In case you are not aware, he graduated with honors. From the *Switzerland Institute of Bible Baptist Holiness.*

"Now that's not in Europe, that's down in the southern part of the State, in Switzerland County. So the Reverend is not only very smart and well trained in all the latest ideas for church teaching and evangelism, he is a Hoosier, born and bred. Actually from Ohio County. His people's still over to Rising Sun. Farming folks. Reverend Poston is smart, he's energetic, and he's also one of us. And with no lack of respect for Reverend Hoheimer, who was not from here but was from Illinois, I feel we've been needing a Hoosier touch."

"Amen to that!" bellowed Olin Ainsley.

"Now that's precisely why we're having this covered dish. To welcome our new Pastor, to have a time to chat with him over ham and beans, maybe over some tenderloin, green beans and bacon, you name it we've got it...Sister Dickensheet's cornbread too...just to enjoy some good Hoosier cooking and get to know Pastor better and give him a chance to get to know us. It's too bad Reverend and Sister Hoheimer couldn't stay for the meal and fellowship...I know they would have loved to...but things move on, and right now our focus has to be on the new man the Lord has sent to lead His people in Aschburgh. Reverend Jeremy Poston. Folks, Pastor Poston, I believe the ladies are ready for us, so let's head on downstairs, have a wonderful meal and get to know one another better. We've got a big job ahead of us to get *First Bible Baptist Holiness* moving forward again. But you just remember, the Lord's on our side and the Lord's sent us the man for the job. Amen?"

"Amen, Brother Goins."

Belva, who chaired the *Supper Committee*, was pleased to see everyone slowly filing downstairs into the basement for the luncheon. Though she had failed in her efforts to get the Trustees to paint the walls of the dining hall a pleasing pink, they did agree to apply a fresh coat of white-wash and that helped to brighten things up a bit. The five long tables they used for dinners were nicely covered with clean white paper, and each one had a graying wedding bell centerpiece. The centerpieces were left over from the Carlton wedding, held almost six years earlier.

Belva thought they had been discarded years ago, and was surprised to see them this morning. She needed to speak with the ladies about getting some fresh decorations. Fortunately Marva's wedding shower would all be catered so they wouldn't need to deal with these dingy things. The bells would be sufficient for this sort of event.

"Everything looks real nice, Sugar," said Olin.

"Adequate, not nice. We really need to spruce this basement up."

"The Trustees and I agree this isn't the time. Maybe when we've added a few new members. A couple more tithers."

"If it's left to the Trustees it'll never get done, and you know it, Olin."

"You can't spend what you don't have, Sugar."

Bowls of ham and beans steamed next to heaps of mashed potatoes...while a big platter of LaVon Dickensheet's corn bread sat in the center of the main serving table. At the end of the table were two platters of fried chicken, a bowl of green beans, three dishes of deviled eggs and a variety of casseroles. A smaller table set off to the side was packed with biscuits, cakes, pies and puddings. There had been a time, early in the Hoheimer pastorate, when these dinners were much larger, requiring three large tables for the main dishes and two for desserts. But Belva thought this quite a nice turn-out considering their decline over the past decade. A little heavy on casseroles and deviled eggs, but people brought what they could.

It was important to put on a nice meal to welcome Pastor Poston, but you didn't want so much festivity as to cause him to become puffed up. There was a fine line. Christian celebration ought not to become a source of temptation and even sin. Plus there was good sense in what Olin said. The church's budget for these events wasn't limitless. *You can't spend what you don't have.* She made a mental note at an appropriate time to speak with Reverend Poston about his cowlick.

Wilton carried a small wooden lectern to the front of the dining room, and asked Jeremy Poston to step up to it and lead his congregation in prayer for the first time.

Poston, not yet twenty-one, was short and thin with thick brown hair which refused all his attempts to tame it. Conscious that his face, scarred by severe acne, made many people uncomfortable, he tried to speak softly and be agreeable. Wilton had not cared for him from the first, and calling him to the pulpit of *Bible Baptist Holiness* had been a painful decision. Still, the time was short and although there were a few older men who applied, no other younger men were interested...the contract was only for one year at a minimal salary, and Wilton demanded and received a clause which allowed the Board to terminate Poston for any reason with two weeks notice.

The young man cleared his throat, smiled and began his ministry. "Would you bow with me as we ask the Lord's blessing on this food so faithfully prepared by loving hands."

As he prayed Olin thought his voice a little too high for a man, though not as jarringly high as Hoheimer's, and perhaps it would lower as the boy matured and got over his initial nervousness. This was a big undertaking for someone so young, fresh out of school. As the prayer went on, Olin slipped into his seat beside Belva. Marva and Regina had stepped outside the church after the service, and now stood quietly at the foot of the stairs to the fellowship hall waiting for the prayer to conclude.

"He looks scared."

"I think he's sad. He's all alone. His family's way down in Rising Sun."

"I'd be terrified."

"I just think he's sad and needs a friend."

Regina took her seat with Marshall Sevier Winslow at his table, while Marva sat between Wilton and her father across the way. As usual Belva was up and down, constantly moving around the room, making sure everything was just right. Marshall Winslow had been quick to the lectern with an invitation to join his table so Reverend Poston now found himself seated right across from Regina who was looking very embarrassed as her uncle...in his fanciest uniform...fussed over the young pastor.

Marva thought the fellow was very ugly, but she made a strong effort to drive the idea from her mind as being unfair and unworthy of a Christian. She was very much aware of Wilton's appearance and maturity, and very proud to be engaged to him.

She was still smarting under her mother's insistence she not wear her diamond engagement ring outside their home. At least not until the new Pastor made clear his position on engagement and wedding jewelry for ladies. Though her Daddy hadn't noticed, she and Belva barely spoke to each other at breakfast. The old pastor, Reverend Hoheimer, would have put her in hell for possessing jewelry, let alone a beautiful ring like her's. But Hoheimer was gone...part of the ancient history of the church... gone to torment the young girls still at the *Seminary*...and Wilton, though he insisted she obey her mother for now, said things were going to be changing under this new fellow. She'd be wearing her ring soon enough, no matter what Momma or the church said.

"It's just like you said it'd be, Will." Olin glanced around the room at the full plates of food and the happy conversations at each table. "Just like you said. A breath of fresh air. Wilton, you've always known how to get things done...keep folks happy but still get the job done. You've made yourself quite a catch here, Marva."

Marva reached under the table and took Wilton's hand, and to his annoyance he felt his heart starting to pound again.

Hopefully he would soon get this under control. He squeezed her hand lightly and smiled at her. "Should we get on line?" he whispered.

"Let's wait. If that's all right."

"Time to chow down, you two," Olin proclaimed.

"We're going to wait a few minutes, Olin. Let the line clear out a bit. But you go right ahead. Fill that plate up high. A farmer needs to stoke the furnace."

Olin ran his hand over his bald head and frowned. "Yes, yes that's for sure. Will, speaking of that…farming and cattle and so forth…there's something I've been meaning to seek your counsel about. But…I suppose that's best left for another time." As her father left the table to join the others on line Marva inched her chair closer to Wilton. "Business?"

"I would imagine."

Regina blushed when Mary Frances Winslow, uncle Sevier's oldest sister, sitting beside the new pastor, stretched across the table and cut up the large chicken breast on the Marshall's plate.

"Uncle Bill can cut his own meat, Aunt Mary Frances. Goodness."

"He'll leave it as big hunks if I don't cut it down to bite size."

Jeremy smiled at Regina. He thought she was about his height, 5'6…maybe even a little shorter. Which was so important. His father was two inches taller than his mother and always said it was one of the things which made their marriage strong. Regina's white cap was very becoming against her hair, but he was troubled by her pink dress, a color he had never seen before on a holiness woman.

"Pastor, have you been formally introduced to my niece?" asked Mary Frances. "Regina recently graduated from the *Women's Seminary* in Westbury. Along with her cousin Marva Ainsley. The Ainsleys and the Winslows are cousins. We're so proud of both girls, but especially Regina of course. Because she's our's. A Winslow. Though of course Marva's mother, Belva, is a Winslow too. We're all kind of close."

Jeremy started to rise, but the Marshall's big hand motioned him back into his seat so he merely continued smiling and nodded at Regina. "We don't hold much to fancy-dancy type manners, Reverend. Your basic straight-forward country courtesy is best. I like a man with dirty hands. Even a minister ought to get his hands dirty every now and then. Don't you agree? No high-fallutin, big time muckity-muck stuff. Now if you don't agree why feel free to say so. Everybody ought to be free to express his opinion. After all this is America."

"Sev!"

"Did you enjoy your studies at the *Seminary*, Miss Winslow?"

"Some of them. It's not as serious as the *Switzerland Institute*."

"Regina is a very skilled pianist," said Aunt Mary Frances. "And her cousin Marva...at the table across the way...the one who will be marrying Mister Goins, is quite a talented artist. I suppose it runs in the family. The Winslows."

"You're dreaming, sister," said Marshall Sevier Winslow as he mixed bites of chicken in with his ham and beans, mashed potatoes and hunks of tenderloin. "Not the Winslows I know. We've always been practical, down to earth people. Regina, do you think there'd be any of Lolita Lou's gravy left up there?"

"Marva likes to draw," said Regina standing and taking her uncle's plate. "I think there's still plenty up there, Uncle Sev. Lolita Lou knows how you favor it, so she always brings extra. You just stay. I'll get you some. Over everything. The way you like it. I don't actually play the piano all that well, Reverend."

"Only because Reverend Hoheimer didn't like instruments in the service," said Aunt Mary Frances to Jeremy. "I would hope that's something you'll be changing right away. The *Bible* has many good things to say about musical instruments."

"All a tempest in a tea-pot as far as I'm concerned," said the Marshall. "Regina's a good solid girl and that's what's important. She's seen me through since my Mrs. passed a while back. Always stayed close while at school. Piano playing might be a good thing, or it might not. I don't know and frankly I don't care. But I'll tell you this, Reverend, that girl bakes some kind of apple pie. Now she does, Mary Frances. Preacher, you be sure to get you a piece. I'll show you which one when you're ready for dessert. That girl can cook anything and make your mouth water, plus she sews all her own clothes, knows how to butcher, and has the prettiest hair in Tecumseh County."

"Uncle Sev! For goodness sakes."

"I'll be sure to have a piece of Miss Regina's apple pie, sir."

"*Marshall* is fine. Forget the *sir* business, son. We're simple people around here. She's a good girl, and she's going to make some man a fine catch."

"Sev!"

"I know it's not right of me, but I just hate these stupid dinners," said Marva. "All my life I've had to eat Susan Crowler's deviled eggs, and Brenda's ham and beans, and Hilda Harris' chocolate pie. I just get so tired of it. Always the same."

"Right now it's a necessary thing, dear. Once we're married I'll see that we avoid many of them if that's what you want."

"Really? We could do that?"

"Of course we can. Though Susan's deviled eggs are wonderful, and I'm very partial to Hilda's chocolate pie."

"O Wilton, you're so sweet. I think you know how to handle everything. I'll make you deviled eggs and chocolate pie. Will we be able to go to restaurants? Do you know I've never been to one?"

"Never? You're teasing me, surely."

"Never. Momma thinks they're sinful."

"O well. She's just concerned with your well-being. But we'll eat at lots of restaurants. The *Indianville Country Club* is quite nice, with excellent steaks. You'll like the fillet mignon, smothered with onions and mushrooms. In fact I'm sort of counting on having our wedding reception there. And I'll get you the *fillet mignon*. If you and your parents agree, of course. However, I warn you I do like a good home-cooked meal. We'll go to all the fine restaurants, but not all the time. And for the moment let's just keep this between you and me. Your Momma, Lord bless her, might not understand."

"That's for sure. Wilton, I make a better chocolate pie than Hilda. I should have brought it today. And my fried chicken is Daddy's favorite. Now that dish I did bring, and I hope you try it."

"You show me which platter is yours."

"Don't they serve liquor at the Country Club? In the back? That could be a problem."

"You don't have to go there. I rarely do. The Scripture calls for moderation. Did you realize that's what *temperance* means? In all things. Plus we need to have tolerance for people who see things a bit differently. But if we have the reception there I'll make sure they get the liquor out of the building for our party."

"Still, I wouldn't want gossip."

"Fair enough. I only want to please you. Suppose we eat in Indianapolis? Louisville? Chattanooga? Memphis? New Orleans? You'll like New Orleans. Might scare you a bit at first, but you'll definitely like New Orleans."

"You're teasing me."

"I want to take you to wonderful places, Marva. I love you very much, and I want to show you exciting things. And you don't need to worry about local gossip. We'll make some changes... changes you'll like and will be happy about. Very quickly after our marriage. But we'll keep all that to ourselves for now. Like the engagement diamond. And, Marva, there will be no gossip."

"I love my ring. I think it's the most beautiful ring I've ever seen. But there's always gossip in Aschburgh."

"I don't allow gossip, dear. I suppose I can't control what someone thinks, but gossip is another matter altogether. No one gossips about me or my family. Shall we join the others on the end of the line? I think we've held off as long as we can. People might start to gossip."

"Tease all you want, I still worry about it. I'll put an extra piece of Hilda's pie on my plate. Maybe two. For you. But be sure to take my chicken."

"And Regina's apple pie. And Susan's deviled eggs. And most definitely Mrs. Dickensheet's cornbread."

CHAPTER 4
LOVE RUNS AMUCK AMONGST THE BIBLE BAPTIST HOLINESS COMMUNITY

The reader is cautioned against allowing the title of this chapter to produce misconception. All this happened in a simpler time when love could flourish and yet be discreet and proper. Or at least appear that way. We see just such a relationship develop in the parsonage. As expected Marva weds Mister Goins, but questions are raised concerning the odor of alcohol. We also learn that Marva is well pleased to ride in Mister Penn's Rolls-Royce, of Marshall Sevier's pride in his uniform, one or two things about the Hoosier School, and of the shocking decline of the Hoheimers.

1
In Uniform

Town Marshall Sevier Winslow took pride in his trim waist and his speed afoot. Though very large and muscular, the Marshall, now in his forties, retained the 31" waist of his high school days and was still able to run down most of the town's ne'er-do-wells. There had been a moment, fifteen years earlier, when he was first appointed, that the Town Council promised to have a uniform designed for him. But after the Natural Gas Boom fizzled the fellows explained the uniform was a *frivolous fanciness*, and in any event, he could probably do the job better without having to worry about *puffed-up* clothes.

Marshall Sev, uniformed or not, was popular among the town's people, and over the years had been reasonably effective handling the occasional fight, public drunkenness and vandalism. Still the lack of a proper uniform was a sore spot. A white dress shirt, long sleeved and buttoned to the neck just didn't convey the sense of authority of a blue jacket and cap like they had in Fort Wayne. Even the guys in Giantown and Indianville had uniforms of a sort. His badge and pistol let folks know he meant business, of course, but somehow it wasn't quite the same. All this had been heavy on the Marshall's mind for years when Wilton Goins, who was practically a member of the family now that he and Sev's niece Marva, Olin Ainsleys daughter, were engaged, proposed to underwrite the cost of a uniform. While maintaining his dignity, Sevier Winslow had nonetheless jumped at the offer.

He soon drew up plans for a sky blue tunic and trousers. The tunic to be high collared, doing away with the need for a dress shirt. He saw it with scarlet piping on the collar and a broad scarlet stripe on the pants. Because Sev wasn't sure about the cap, Wilton requested images of headgear currently in use by major departments all over the country. The wait for all of it to fall into place had been difficult, but now it was done, the uniform delivered and declared perfect, sharper than any ever seen in Tecumseh or Stonewall Counties...finer even than the State Police.

It was in his dual roles as friend of Wilton Fox Goins and uncle of Marva Winslow Ainsley that Marshall Sevier Winslow sat in the drafty vestibule of the *Bible Baptist Holiness* parsonage in his new uniform, his dark blue cap with its scarlet braid stitched into the brim carefully placed in his lap, chaperoning from a discreet distance as Marva, accompanied by his niece and ward

Regina, met with young Reverend Jeremy Poston to put in place the plans for the Christmas Day wedding of Marva and Wilton.

In what was generally perceived to be an odd outburst, probably traceable to the stress of the upcoming wedding, Marva refused to meet with the clergyman at the Ainsley farm and scoffed at the idea that her mother ought to have any role in the planning. The whole situation was made even tenser...if not just plain embarrassing...when it became apparent that the groom-to-be had no intention of siding with the mother against his beloved.

Finally, however, Wilton did propose a compromise which relieved the tension a bit by satisfying the bride and providing the mother with a face-saving exit strategy. Marva, after receiving detailed instructions about her mother's plans for the wedding, would then be accompanied to a meeting at the parsonage by her cousin Regina, and the conference with Reverend Jeremy Poston, who was after all an unmarried young man, would take place in an open room supervised by Marshall Sevier Winslow, the widowed uncle of the bride and the guardian and uncle of Regina. These sorts of things had been much easier under Reverend Hoheimer when the rules were clear...the bride's mother was required to be present and Sister Hoheimer sat in on all her husband's meetings with women.

Marshall Sev, well aware of what actually was going on between many young men and women in Aschburgh, thought the whole thing silly, but agreed to participate when Wilton Goins not only made a personal request, but specifically asked him to wear his new uniform to the parsonage meeting. "Should anyone get the wrong idea about the young ladies meeting with the Pastor, the fact that you are there *in uniform* will put a stop to any gossip."

Young Pastor Poston smiled at the two young women sitting opposite him, their coats pulled tight against the parlor's Fall chill. Jeremy made a pot of tea for the meeting and set it on the small table his mother sent along with several other pieces to make the drafty old house a bit more comfortable. Despite a small fire the room was chilly as was most of the house on this damp morning in early November. His mother said the upstairs would have to be closed off within the next week if he were to survive the Winter, and this morning he could see her point. Unfortunately Jeremy had no more idea how to do that than he had about how to start this wedding conference.

"You've begun to settle in here, Reverend?" asked Regina. "I hope you're comfortable. That's a lovely tea pot. Would you like for me to pour?"

"If you would, Miss Winslow. My mother sent it. Perhaps the Marshall…." The freckles on her cheeks were charming, he thought. The freckles and her light hair, against the white of her starched cap, were so fresh and bright. Her cousin Marva, on the other hand, he found rather large and intimidating.

"Uncle Sev, would you like some tea?" Regina called to Marshall Winslow who was carefully tucked out of view in the entryway.

"No, darling, I'm just fine out here. Marva, did you remember your Momma's notes?"

Marva glanced at Regina and grinned. "Everything's fine, Uncle Sev. I remember everything she said." She pulled her coat tighter. "Is it always this cold in here, Reverend?"

"I'm afraid so. I'll build the fire up a bit."

"Please don't do that," said Regina who poured the tea. "We're not made of sugar and spice. Marva and I are country girls. Do you like a bit of sugar, sir?"

"Please." He decided he liked being called *sir*. "Hardly country girls. With you both being graduates of the *Women's Seminary* I mean. It has a very fine reputation."

Marshall Winslow, having changed his mind about the tea, walked into the parlor. "You'll need to do something about all these drafts, young fellow. Time to close off the upstairs. You'll be getting sore throats and be unable to preach. How did the Hoheimer's deal with it?"

Regina scooped four teaspoons of sugar into the cup and poured his tea. "Extra sweet. Just the way you like it, Uncle Sev.

Sister Hoheimer used lots of floor length drapes. That helps, but it makes the rooms terribly dark. And of course they closed off the upper rooms. I think the church needs to do something."

"O I don't know," said Jeremy. "It's just fine. Spring will be here before we know it."

"Not in this part of the State, Pastor," said the Marshall. "This ain't Switzerland County up here. You're going to see howling winds and drifting snow like you don't hardly get down along the River."

Marva studied her uncle as he stood in the center of the room sipping tea. He and her Wilton were the best looking men in town. But there was no comparison between a successful business man who traveled all over the world and a small town policeman who'd rarely been outside Aschburgh. "They get floods down there though. Your new uniform is extremely handsome, Uncle Sev."

"I'm more than a bit pleased with it, Marva. It's an excellent fit. Slip a little more tea in there, darling, and I'll just take my seat in the vestibule and be out of your way."

"Thank you, Marshall," said Jeremy. "I'm sure the *Seminary* was a deepening experience for both of you. Spiritually as well as intellectually. I found the *Holiness Institute* had an enormous impact on me."

"That's in Switzerland County?"

"Just outside Quercus Grove."

"Isn't that an odd name," said Marva. "Quercus? A Roman? Cincinnati was named after a Roman soldier wasn't it, Regina?"

"Cincinnatus. A farmer who became a great soldier and saved Rome. Or that's the story. It's probably just a legend. But I think Quercus is different."

"A farmer? A simple man of the earth," said Jeremy. "There's a moral there. There's great dignity in agriculture."

Marva glanced at him. The fellow was not only ugly, he was stupid and fawning.

"Did you enjoy the *Holiness Institute*?" asked Regina. "I imagine that's very pretty down there in Switzerland County."

68

"Very much. Quercus refers, I think, more to the type of trees in that area. It's quite close to the Ohio River. But I'm not sure. Don't quote me on that."

"I've never heard of a Quercus tree," said Marva. "Daddy said you approve of my wedding being on Christmas Day. You really have no problem with it I hope."

"I imagine it's quite serene down there," said Regina. She had no interest in discussing Marva's wedding. It was all going to be done Marva's way, so this was just so much wasted time. She loved her cousin, though she had no illusions about her. But Regina did want to learn more about Reverend Poston. "I think Quercus has something to do with oaks. It's a classification term. We studied it in *Botany*, Marva."

"*Botany* is the last thing on my mind."

"Very few people would know that, Miss Winslow. About Quercus. That's quite impressive. Yes, it is quiet down there. Though out on the River things are usually busy, and sometimes, in places like Vevay it can get plain and simple hectic. It can be a bit worldly. In Vevay."

"You have no problem with Christmas Day for my wedding?"

"I think Sunday is the 27th this year, so there'll be nothing else scheduled here on the 25th. It's a Friday. I had hoped to be home for Christmas though. In Rising Sun. That's where my family's from. Just a few miles outside it actually."

"I'm sure Mister Goins could get one of the other local pastors to officiate."

"O I didn't mean that. I'll be more than available. And looking forward to it. Very much so."

"There probably wasn't much to do down there but study," said Regina. She loved Marva...more than if they had been twin sisters...but sometimes her cousin approached rudeness. No, she was out and out rude. Sometimes. "It being so quiet around there."

"You'd think so, but we found ways to have fun. We had a lot of good times around Quercus Grove and those places... Bennington, Antioch, Searcy Crossroads, Lamb...places like that. There's lots of good spots. None of them's up to Aschburgh of course, but we still had fun. I don't mean rowdy though."

"Could we get back to the main point? There's a wedding to plan."

"I can't imagine you being rowdy," said Regina, smiling at him. "You have too much maturity and dignity."

"Study came first of course. But we did have lots of fun too. I'm sure that was the case at the *Seminary* as well. I'm looking forward to the wedding, Miss Ainsley."

"I hated *Seminary*," said Marva. "Uncle Sev," she called to the Marshall who was dozing in the vestibule. "I'm sorry we're taking so long. We'll finish up in a moment."

"Don't worry, Marva. Take as long as you need. I've got nothing scheduled."

"He needs to get back to work," Marva said. "The wedding will be small, and we won't be using the basement for the reception. I'll have two bridesmaids... maybe more...and my maid-of-honor. Regina, of course. Miss Winslow. Mister Goins' best-man is going to be Mayor Webster. Wilton wanted my Daddy...they're boyhood friends...but naturally Daddy needs to be with me, so that wouldn't work out. And then there'll be groomsmen...college friends, I think. College and business. But that's not settled."

"Webster...the Mayor of Indianville?"

"They're some kind of business associates. And they're both on the Board at the Club. What I have insisted on...and I won't budge on this...is for all of them to wear tuxedos."

"The Club? Tuxedos?"

"Formal dress. Apparently one of them has other ideas. Some friend of Mister Goins. But we'll get that worked out."

"I think Marva means the *Country Club* in Indianville, Reverend."

"Don't they serve alcohol there?"

"I'm not sure," said Regina. "I've never been to a place like that."

"There'll be no alcohol, Reverend. We're holiness."

"But tuxedos? As you say this is a holiness church, Miss Ainsley. Dark suits with white shirts would be proper and dignified. I don't mean to be rigid, but tuxedos would not be proper."

"What exactly do you mean if you don't mean to be *rigid*?"

"Why don't we step back for a moment, and think this through," said Regina. In a moment Marva was going to walk out in a huff. "Is the problem the bow-tie that goes with the tuxedo?"

"For the most part. But it's all finery. Frivolous."

"A simple black bow-tie is hardly *frivolous*, Reverend," said Marva. "I'm not going to have my wedding ruined by a brand new preacher and his dead legalism. We're living in the 20th century."

"Surely you agree the bow-tie has no function but frivolous decoration. It's all display."

"If you try to ruin my wedding--"

"Now just wait you two," said Regina. "There are other ways to approach this. I saw a photograph of a wedding party where the groom wore a sort of strand of black ribbon or lace. It ran from the collar down the front of his white shirt. I thought it looked quite nice."

"*Lace*? Surely Miss Winslow."

"A thin piece of *black* lace, Reverend. I thought it was very respectful, sir. Not at all frivolous."

"I want the traditional bow-tie. Mister Goins expects it as well."

"I do want to be agreeable, but I cannot allow bow-ties in the church. And I know you mean well, Miss Winslow, but lace on a man is just out of the question."

Marva sat back in her chair and yelled. "Uncle Sev!"

Startled, the Marshall rushed into the room. "Girls? Reverend?"

"He's trying to ruin my wedding, Uncle Sev. I'm not going to put up with this any longer."

"Now...."

Despite the chill in the room sweat was running down Jeremy's thin neck. "I'm not trying to ruin your wedding, Miss Ainsley. That's the last thing I want to do. You'll have a lovely wedding.

It's just that a holiness church has to have some standards, and bow-ties are simply not allowed."

"So all this is about bow-ties?" asked the Marshall. "That's quite a bit of heat building up in here just over some bow-ties. Which by the way I doubt is in the *Bible*. Is there something else going on here?"

"I'm sure we can work out a compromise," said Regina. "All of us are mature. And we all want the same thing. A beautiful wedding for Marva and dear Wilton. The simple strand of black lace still seems a good idea to me."

Marshall Winston rubbed his chin. "Lace? On a man?"

"Uncle Sev, please take me out of here," said Marva, already on her feet. "Regina, I want to talk with Mister Goins."

"Please, Miss Ainsley," said Jeremy. He could see himself out on the street in the snow. *He lasted three months in his first pastorate* would be plastered on his file at *Bible Baptist Holiness* headquarters.

"Mister Goins is far too busy for this, Marva," said the Marshall. "There's no need to bother him about bow-ties."

"Miss Ainsley, let's try to work something out," offered Reverend Poston who was startled that things had gotten so out of control. All he had done was try to apply some basic rules, and the idea that a young woman raised in the holiness church and schooled at the *Seminary* would rebel against holiness standards and a holiness preacher was beyond belief. But being brand new to Aschburgh he knew he couldn't afford a battle with Misters Ainsley and Goins. And maybe Marshall Winslow too. "Surely there's a way. If we both give just a little we'll find a way."

Marva stood by the door, beckoning to Regina and glaring at the Pastor. "Uncle Sev!"

Regina whispered to Jeremy, "I'm sorry for all this," before joining her cousin.

"I'll be right with you, Marva, Regina," said the Marshall. "Reverend, I'll be back in an hour and we'll get all this settled. Man to man. I don't like a fuss and Mister Goins certainly don't like a fuss. And we don't care...neither of us...for our ladies being upset. There'll be no problem. I'll be back in an hour. You be here."

2
Friday, December 25, 1925

That a local wedding, held unusually late on Christmas Day, would command the presence of Mayor Webster of Indianville, and that he would willingly play second fiddle to their own Wilton Goins, was considered a great coup by all the people of Aschburgh. Now the strange little white haired fellow from Indianapolis, apparently a great friend of Mister Goins from his college days, all decked out in blue velvet or whatever, well now…that was quite an odd choice to be part of the wedding party, especially with his trousers tight at his ankles, wearing some kind of black leather slippers. And no socks. As near as could be told, no socks!

But the bride was beautiful in her Grandmother Winslow's wedding dress, the groom impressive in his black tie and tuxedo, and young Reverend Poston kept himself muted and in the background as was fitting. All in all most agreed it was a majestic occasion and a feather in the town's cap. Invitations to the reception, for obviously not everyone in town was invited, were highly prized. Most were saved, later to be pasted into family scrapbooks.

Needless to say, a reception at the *Indianville Country Club* had not been in Belva Ainsley's plans. Not that the facilities were less than ideal. Wilton arranged everything just right…perfectly. As she understood it this was the first time the *Country Club* had ever been open on Christmas Day, and even now it was a one time event, only for Marva's reception. Apparently Wilton and the Mayor had the whole thing set up. There was even a lovely view of the frozen pond, lighted especially for them.

Earlier that Christmas morning, having let themselves in with a key provided by Wilton, Belva and Olin looked over the *Country Club's* dining room. "It's nice. Very nice. But do you think it's a little too much, Olin? The church basement could have been fixed up quite adequately."

"I think Marva is going to love this, Sugar."

"Please call me Belva when the guests are here."

"Everyone knows I call you Sugar."

"This is going to be an occasion, so let's treat it that way."

Wilton had everything exactly as she demanded, and she had to admit he had gone beyond what she expected. Somehow he got the *Club* open just for their wedding party and guests, the old liquor bar very tastefully hidden or at least disguised, and the entire reception area scrubbed and disinfected.

"Can you still smell liquor? I detect cigarette odor."

"Not a bit."

"What are we going to do about this enormous dance floor?"

"Ignore it. Or dance."

"Don't be ridiculous. There is some cigarette sense in the air. Be sure to tell Wilton."

"Will has other things on his mind, Sugar. Just let it be."

"I'm afraid some of the ladies are going to be hurt we had the reception here instead of at the church. Brenda Fernung was surprised we were having a dinner at all. I could tell she felt we were *putting on*."

"Because she wasn't invited. She doesn't even come to church. Shoot, it's none of the woman's business."

"The Fernungs go to the Methodist. Don't swear."

"Methodist? That'll be news to Tom Fernung."

"Brenda pointed out people around here generally just have punch and cake. At the church. Which ought to be sufficient. Wilton's been rather extravagant, and I'm not sure it won't give a degree of offense. A special *Fillet mignon* dinner for Marva!"

"And one for you too, don't forget. And the rest of us will be having top quality roast beef or chicken. We won't exactly be suffering. Don't forget Will's paying for this out of his own pocket...which you know perfectly well he didn't have to do. I've never known you to get so worked up about what people think.

Let them worry about their own kids. Once they get a bellyful of the roast beef they'll forget all about church basements."

"We certainly don't want people to know Wilton's paying. It's not the way things are done. And I really think Marva and I ought to have the roast beef like everyone else." She thought the whole business must have cost a pretty penny. As the father of the bride Olin offered to pay of course, but Wilton was emphatic. Graciously emphatic, naturally. Not that all of this wasn't wonderful, and a tribute to Marva and their family, but the church basement would have been more in keeping. The Ainsleys and Winslows had never been people for show. "I'm serious, Olin. We'll have folks from all the churches, so I'd like for you to sort of get the word out that all the cigarette smell has been removed from the premises."

"But it hasn't been removed, Sugar."

"It's been nicely hidden. Is the cake here yet?"

"All taken care of. Will gets things done."

"I still think we should be paying for this. We are the parents of the bride."

"I spoke to Will about it. He said please don't even think of it. The way he sees it he's a good deal older than Marva and lucky to have her, and then he points out he's well established in life, and then he also said he wants to do it. So I didn't know what more to say. Did we get them a nice gift?"

"About the best china I could find in Giantown. I suppose we ought to honor his request. But still."

It *was* all very nice. Nicer than her reception had been. If you could speak of a *reception* on a farm stinking of hogs and cow manure, with flies falling in the punch, and the men leaning on their wagons, talking about the weather and prices. Wilton had gone to the extreme of having the wedding cake prepared in Indianapolis. It could have been baked in Giantown or Indianville at a third the cost. But she was sure it would be the most beautiful cake any of them had ever seen. No one in Aschburgh ever had a wedding to compare with her Marva. Tecumseh and Stonewall Counties for that matter.

"Are you sure?" Marva asked him as the *Rolls-Royce* pulled up to the *Country Club* entrance. "It seems an unnecessary extravagance. We'd better go right in. People are already waiting."

"I want you to have one that's yours. All yours. The people are fine. They'll be fine. Designed especially for you. Exactly the way you want it."

"But there's nothing wrong with the house you have."

"The house *we* have. Look out there, Marva. There's already a crowd waiting to catch a glimpse of you. The beautiful Mrs. Marva Ainsley Goins. Mrs. Wilton Fox Goins. After we get back from the South I've set up an appointment with Greg. At his offices in Indianapolis."

"Mister Penn? The architect friend of yours? He's a little... well, different isn't he?"

"Judge for yourself. He did a good job as a groomsman. Be fair. Take for example this automobile of his. Loaned to us for tonight. We're not looking at a *Ford* here, Marva. I've known him all my adult life. We were room-mates and fraternity brothers at the University. If I have any kind of taste it's because of Greg Penn. Just touch this upholstery. Does he have good taste or not? The fellow will give you a *Rolls-Royce* of a house. He's different, yes...but Greg's no fool, and he's one of the best architects around. Definitely the best in Indiana."

"He didn't have any socks on."

"Greg doesn't wear socks. Never has. Not even in the Winter. That's just the way he is. You get used to it after a while. My goodness, Marva, the man's feet are clean. Just accept him the way he is. And he's always had his pants made with those tight ankles. As long as I've known him. Take him or leave him. That's Greg Penn. But he'll give you a house that will take your breath away, designed just for you, designed to meet your every wish.

Anywhere you go…New York City or New Orleans…Berlin… where I do some business…people know who Greg Penn is."

"This *is* a beautiful automobile," she said, running her hand along the leather upholstery. "I imagine it's tremendously expensive." Marva glanced out the window at the crowd of family and friends waiting for them to enter the *Club* for the reception. "We do need to go in, Wilton. They're waiting in the cold. But let's talk more before you have Mister Penn do anything."

"They can wait. They'll be fine. Now I can see you're not well pleased with what I've done. About the architect and the house. I ought to have consulted you. I'm sorry. I've got some learning to do. But it won't be a problem. I'll just cancel the appointment."

"O no, don't do that. I'm a bit…it's all a bit too much, so soon…quickly. That's all. A *Rolls-Royce* and then an architect. Why do we need to meet with Mister Penn? Doesn't he just draw up plans, blue-prints or something? This car is only on loan, right? We can't afford anything like this. Can we? He could do that…draw up the plans…and then bring them up to Aschburgh. Or mail them for that matter."

"No…it's not quite like that. He doesn't work that way. Greg Penn is an artist…he's very sophisticated in his approach to plans and even to construction. It's not just a matter of banging in some nails with a hammer. Why don't we sit down with him tonight? At the reception. That way you'll have a sense of the way he approaches things."

"At the reception? Plan a new house?"

"No, just get to know him. I know the way he operates. Eventually he'll want to sit down with you, probably over coffee, maybe breakfast or lunch, and find out all that you want in a house. He'll achieve whatever you want. But it could take a couple of days. To find out your dreams. *Precisely* what you want."

"You'll be there too, won't you?"

3
Edifying Conversation Rather
Than Drinking & Dancing

After opening the top button of his shirt and attempting to disguise what he had done by tugging at his bow-tie, Olin made his way back to the Ainsley-Winslow table. Wilton had done the best he could with this reception, but the Birdsall's always threw a better party because they weren't so tied-up in knots about music and clothes and stuff Jesus never even thought about. Some nice music, even polite dancing, would have turned this reception into a fine time. But that was too much to hope for. *Good* people, *Bible Baptist Holiness* people would spend the evening gossiping, free from the sinfulness of wine and waltz.

The new pastor had joined the Ainsley-Winslow table in Olin's absence and, seated next to Regina, was laughing at something Marshall Sevier Winslow said. The preacher boy was ugly, but there wasn't all that much to select from in Aschburgh, or the whole of Tecumseh County for that matter. Thank goodness Marva was all settled with Wilton. The Birdsalls had some smart, good-looking fellows who were Regina's age, but Birdsalls almost always married within their own. With so many cousins of all kinds of degree it rarely caused any scandal for them. Plus everyone knew that's just the way Birdsalls were.

"Marshall Winslow was just asking which denomination was looked down on by the *Bible*," said Jeremy Poston to Olin. "It's a joke of course. No one got it until he told us. Explained it. Marshall, why don't you tell Mister Ainsley?"

"Kind of a riddle?" asked Olin. It was good to be able to breathe again so he chose to ignore Belva as she made buttoning motions under her chin. "Some say the Bible's full of riddles."

"Not if we allow the Holy Ghost to guide our understanding," said Jeremy Poston. "But I'm sure you were referring to Samson."

Olin was again grateful Marva had a husband. Somehow preachers weren't real men. Not with all their quibbling and namby-pamby concerns. Plus they didn't make enough to support a wife and kids.

"It's the *Church of the Brethren*, Olin," said Marshall Winston. "You know why?"

"There's not many of their churches around here," said Belva. "So it's not something Olin would normally be thinking about."

Olin noticed the preacher whispering something to Regina. The fellow was clearly interested. Hopefully Sev would have enough sense to invite the young man for supper. He noticed Belva picking up on the whispering too. And Regina was smiling. Maybe he and Belva could have a dinner to honor Regina for something, and invite the preacher out to the farm. The more they could bring the two of them together the more likely things were to click. With Regina's mother as good as dead, off someplace in Louisiana, and who knew anything about her father…and the Marshall a widower and unlikely to remarry and have children of his own, it was important to get on with this business. The Winslows needed some babies. Even if the man was ugly and poor. Plain and simple. Babies. Sugar was right on target about that.

"What's that Bible citation, preacher? Tell Olin what that one is," said the Marshall. "He'll pick up on it right away."

"*Romans* 1:13."

"Afraid it's not ringing a bell."

"Olin's not one for memorizing Scripture," said Belva. "It's more important to live the Word. We've always believed that," she added, continuing to make occasional and none too subtle motions toward her throat.

"*I would not have you ignorant brethren*!" shouted Sev Winslow, slapping his heavy hand on the table. "Do you get it? *Ignorant Brethren*!"

"Of course the punctuation in the original Greek makes it clear the Apostle's not really talking about the denomination," Jeremy Poston said to Regina. "But it makes for a good joke."

"Are they the ones who wear the funny hats? Like Pilgrims?"

"The ones with the silver buckles on their shoes?"

"I have no idea. Here's another one for you. You'll know this one for sure, Olin." Olin thought the Marshall, splendid in his blue uniform, was an ignorant ass, but family was family. You didn't get to choose very often, and a man had to settle for what was available and what he got. *"America's legions are armed not with the sword but with the cross.* Who said that one? Now this one's not a riddle."

"How do you memorize all these things, Uncle Sev?" asked Regina.

"It's a wonderful gift, Marshall," added Pastor Poston. He wanted to touch Miss Winslow's hand, just lightly, but was afraid it might be misunderstood.

"Clue," offered the Marshall. "It's an American president. Olin?"

"Don't have a clue. Abraham Lincoln? George Washington?"

"Not even close."

"Do you detect the smell of cigarettes?" Jeremy whispered to Regina.

"I don't know what it smells like."

"Of course. Of course you don't. Isn't that stupid of me!"

"Anyone else want to take a stab at it?"

"I believe it's President Coolidge," said Belva.

The Marshall stared at her with his mouth open. "How did you ever come to know that?"

"I thought it was memorable when I saw it in the paper. The ladies used it for our theme at the *Send The Light Conference* this past Summer. We gals know a few things, Sev."

"But we each have our separate and special gifts," said Jeremy as he brushed the side of his hand against the side of Regina's. "Men and women. The politicians and suffragettes can say what they want."

"I believe that," whispered Regina. "But I think the vote for women is a good thing. Don't you?"

"Perhaps," said Jeremy who was trying to be careful. This was no time for politics.

"I don't care for political discussion at the table," said Belva.

"Don't take a genius," said Olin. "Bulls ain't heifers, mares ain't stallions."

"There's a lot of wisdom in that."

"I think that is about enough."

"Unfortunately a whole bunch of us guys is mules!" said the Marshall, slapping his hand on the table so that Belva's *fillet mignon* bounced.

"Shall we talk of something a little more edifying?" said Belva.

4

New Horizons

His white hair was both curly and fine, and somehow...Marva couldn't imagine how...it stood out a good four inches all around the little man's head. Greg Penn, just at five feet tall, his loose-fitting dark blue velvet shirt open at the collar, leaned forward and kissed her hand.

"Thank you so much, Marva, for allowing me to participate in your wedding. I wish you all zest and joy and lots of goodies."

"It was a fine service, wasn't it, Greg?" said Wilton quickly joining them. "Marva's intrigued with the way you prepare for a new job. Thinking of her house."

"Now, Wilton," protested Marva, "I didn't say that. Zest and joy. That's nice. And goodies! Just like chocolate. I like that. It's just that all this is a little confusing to me. All these things at one time...Mister Penn...."

"O don't I know it! Don't say another word, my dear. Please call me Greg. It's just too much. Far too much to digest at one sitting. Of course it is. Willie is always overwhelming people. He did it when we were at the University, and he's never let up. He's a charmer, of course, and he has all that money and power...don't try to deny it...but he comes on so strong he just overwhelms people. Did you know we were room-mates at Bloomington? Can you imagine? He's so tall and I'm so small. Tall and small...that's what the fraternity comedians use to call us, if you can believe it. And Willie was stuffy even then. Hasn't changed a bit. No, we'll just wait until you've had time to digest all this newness, until you're back from your honeymoon...don't be blushing now...and then we'll get together at my place and proceed at a leisurely pace to line out the entire plan. I hope you're excited about it. It's going to be so much fun."

"The old house seems more than adequate."

"Not for you, Marva. Not for Mrs. Wilton Fox Goins. Isn't that a grand name? We'll completely redo the house...start all over. Your home needs to reflect you, who you are and what your aspirations are...but it also needs to lead you forward, bringing out the deeper truths of where you are going and what you will become."

Wilton grinned and squeezed Marva's hand. "Don't let him bamboozle you, darling. He's a talker."

"Now, Willie, don't be turning Marva against me. You'll break my heart."

"I want to keep the country flavor of the house, Mister Penn," said Marva. "We are farming people. The Ainsleys. And the Winslows, my mother's people. The Goins for that matter. Prior to Wilton. We've never been *town*. That's important to me."

"Precisely. You see? You see, Willie? This is why we need to spend time with each other. This is how a creative reality develops. I can't create in a vacuum. You don't take it out of some book. It's living, it's breathing. Isn't this exciting, Marva? Now I'm thinking of a studio designed along the lines of a barn...the exterior for sure...in keeping with that rustic, agricultural look. The *Winslow Studio*, in honor of your mother. And possibly the interior. Authentic to the spirit and life of a farmer's barn. But without the smelly cows. Resplendent, Marva, resplendent."

"Easy now, Greg, easy," said Wilton, smiling at his old friend. "You're in Aschburgh now, not Indy. We move at a more modest pace. Marva's only started thinking about painting. Not that she hasn't done some fine work at school. But don't go getting her all tipsy with your notions about studios and whatnot."

"No, seriously, Willie. I want you to catch the fire. Imagine this. Branching off the large central studio, with its white walls and towering ceiling and skylights, we'll have smaller rooms, with a rougher finish, something like the stalls you'd find in an old country barn. But artistically- pure and also functional. By the way, Marva, I believe in white walls in a studio. All these drapes and dark furniture you see in traditional studios…it's all wrong. You'll see that kind of old-fashioned set-up when you meet Professor Steele. But you need light and more light. Northern light…o all that's fine…but mostly you need light… north, south, east and west…light. Light for a painter. And these smaller rooms, stalls…we'll use for storage, smaller studios, that sort of thing. Now this is exactly what the three of us need to be doing…sharing, thinking, creating. Over a sumptuous meal, with a pleasant wine. O, I forgot! No wine. I think it's so sweet that Willie ordered the special *fillet mignon* for you. Makes me jealous."

"Wilton's right, Mister…Greg. I've never actually done any painting. Who is this Professor Steele?"

"Willie will tell you about Steele. The most famous painter of our time and place …notice I didn't say the best. The point is your desire says *all the more reason to get started*. I know you desperately want to paint. I can see it all over you. So paint. Be an artist. The point is you need a studio. And I will give it to you."

Marva squeezed Wilton's hand and smiled at the little man. "It was kind of you to let us use your automobile."

"You may keep it as long as you like. As long as you like. Friends will pick me up later this evening and take me back to Indianapolis. But I must have my chauffer returned. Absolutely I must have Bob back. Bob is very special. Bob is very important to my operation. To my life. We've been together for years."

"He seems a nice person," said Marva.

"He has a sharp and impudent tongue. But yes, I suppose he is nice, in a way."

"We won't need the *Rolls* after the reception, Greg," said Wilton. "We'll spend a few days at the *Old Goins Place* before heading South. My *Ford* will work fine for now, and we'll see about things when we return. It sounds like you've got lots of plans and ideas brewing."

"I love New Orleans. And Memphis. The coloreds, you know. The coloreds are magnificent. And to be fair, lots of the whites too. Just decadent enough. Can you believe him, Marva? You'd never know he's been to Paris...and Prague...and Berlin...how we love Berlin, don't we, Willie? *The Old Goins Place*! Wilton Goins, I must have your word that once I've transformed that old farm into a suitable residence for your dear Marva you'll change the name. Please. *The Old Goins Place*! And you cannot be driving Miss Marva about in a *Ford*. For goodness sakes, Willie! It's 1925, you're a wealthy man, and the world is filled with beauty. Now that Marva is part of your life things will have to be different. It's time to give up your black suits and get a little color in your life. *Brooks Brothers* will survive quite nicely without you."

"O the *Ford* will be fine, Greg," said Marva, laughing. Once she got over his size and peculiar dress she realized he was quite handsome, with sharp and fine features and beautiful teeth. Unusually beautiful teeth. And perfect hands. With a clear polish on his nails. Like Wilton. Surprisingly he was fun. It was fun talking with him, just listening to him and the flood of his ideas.

"Get rid of the *Ford,* Willie. A *Ford* is not a proper vehicle for you, Marva. Now I have taken some liberty in reflecting about your studio, and I hope some of my ideas will meet with your approval. But we'll talk much more when we meet at my place."

"I'm really not sure about this studio business. Let's be frank, Mister Penn. I--"

"Greg, please."

"Greg. I have no ideas about architecture, I have no ideas about art or artists, I certainly have no ideas about painting. I've only done a few watercolors, for goodness sakes. It all sounds exciting, but I don't know...I have no reason to believe I have any talent."

"I want you to have a place to pursue your dreams," said Wilton, concerned that Greg had brought all this up prematurely.

Marva needed more time to digest things and begin the transition. "Let's talk about this later."

"Fine, fine," said Greg. "Anyway, I just want you to know what I've done thus far. And let me be clear about one thing, Marva. I know artists. Not *about* artists. I *am* an artist and I *know* artists. And you are an artist. I can see it, I can feel it. You resonate *artist*."

"I *resonate* artist. My goodness! Mister Penn…Greg, I have never even thought about myself as an artist. Let alone with a studio. What would I do with a studio? As big as a barn! I've done a few watercolors. That's all."

"I know an artist when I see an artist."

"I think we ought to discuss all this later," said Wilton. "You're overwhelming Marva, Greg."

"That's not my intention, Willie. Dream, Marva, dream. Don't be afraid. Be filled with courage. I have taken the liberty of consulting about your studio with Professor T.C. Steele. Not the best painter, but you can't do better than that when it comes to studios. Although his own is rather 19th century and stuffy. But Steele knows how it ought to be. And Willie knows I'm right, Marva. When you talk with T.C. Steele you are, as they say, in the big leagues."

"Professor T.C. Steele?"

"Professor T.C. Steele. The Hoosier master. Not up to Forsyth, but very impressive. He's old fashioned, but he has the touch. And very indebted to your husband, very grateful and looking forward to meeting you."

"Me?"

"I have done him some favors, Marva. I'm helping the Professor with a project he has at the University," said Wilton. "Some ideas for an expansion of their Art Department."

"Some ideas, indeed! A whole new *Arts Building*, Marva. Filled with studios…everything modern and the best quality. Professor Steele hopes to see a renaissance in American painting, emanating from Bloomington. Of course Willie recommended me. I would have loved to be involved in a project like this, but I just couldn't find the time. Can you imagine? And all of it is being made possible by Wilton Fox Goins."

"There's no gift involved, Greg. It's all business. Plus there are others in the picture. But you'll have time for Marva's project, am I right?"

"I'll make time. Berlin and Vienna can wait. It's not a thing to cause worry."

"Greg, you don't seem to understand I'm only an amateur. A beginner."

"Please stop repeating that. Not so far as T.C. Steele is concerned. He's looking forward to meeting you, Marva. Steele is sound, very sound, and he'll have lots of encouraging ideas for you. For advanced training Steele is the man. Very sound, a little formal perhaps...not especially creative...but very friendly and pleasant. The man's been quite ill...a heart attack I believe...but he says he's much better and eager to meet you."

"Me? Professor T.C. Steele is eager to meet me?"

"Yes. Haven't we been over this ground a second ago? But he'll wait until you're ready. The Hoosier *master*. Back from your honeymoon. Now, if I may, on a different matter. I was thinking. I hope this is all right. That I don't over-step myself and make Willie so angry he beats me up. Why don't you get your hair cut and styled while you're in the South? Something more up to date. Just a thought, but you are such a beautiful woman."

"Greg!"

"Have I insulted you, Marva? O I hope not. Tell me the truth. Are you furious with me?"

Marva laughed and touched his hand. "No, not at all. I've been thinking about it. Do you think I could do that, Wilton? Would you approve?"

"I think it would be nice. Though I love your hair the way it is. But if that's what you'd like I think it would be fine. Plus we'll get the dresses you've been wanting. And I'll speak with your mother after it's cut."

"Do it, Marva, do it. Consider getting it curled."

"Momma will be furious."

"Willie's up to the task. He'll charm your Momma. You'll be so lovely, so gorgeous."

Before he and Marva left the reception to return to *The Old Goins Place,* Wilton excused himself to meet with Marshall Winslow and Olin Ainsley. Everyone had heard the rumors from the *Seminary* in Westbury, but no one spoke of what they heard... for the reports were far too dreadful. If a fellow had nothing good to say, it was best to say nothing.

"I've been meaning to tell you how sharp that uniform looks, Sevier," said Wilton. "It's important for the town that you look truly fine. When visitors come by you represent Aschburgh to their eyes. Plus it makes our business people feel more secure. I'm well pleased with the look of the uniform. Is it comfortable?"

"Couldn't be more so. The only thing is, Wilton, it's hard to keep it proper looking and clean when it's the only one I've got. I was just wondering if you could be speaking to the Town Board about a second one. Would that be over-stepping? I don't mean to over-step."

"I might be able to see my way to that, Sev."

"I'd like to see some gold stars on it," said Olin. "That new fellow over to Matthews has them on his sleeves, but I was seeing one or two on each side of Sev's collar. The way the collar's way up high like it is seems made for gold stars."

Sevier Winslow fingered the high collar of his uniform and considered Olin's suggestion. "It might work. Just might. It'd be more professional. There'd be more authority there."

"I might be able to see to these things," said Wilton. "Now, Sevier, I hear you've got some accurate information from the *Seminary.* Not that we want to pry."

"And I've double-checked it for its accuracy," said Olin.

"About Reverend Hoheimer?"

"Who else?"

"You've heard what they're saying?"

"I don't care about that," said Wilton. "What's really going on?"

"He's out, Will," said Olin. "Harmon Hoheimer is out. Dismissed by the *Seminary* and he'll lose his *Bible Baptist Holiness* credentials for sure."

"These things happen. Even in the Church," said the Marshall. "I mean it's a shame, but hardly that big a deal. Police see it all the time...even here in Aschburgh."

"Perhaps so," said Wilton, "But the fellow's ordained clergy. That's different from some town drunk."

"I thought he was a bit tight the way he acted in the pulpit before the retirement banquet," said Olin. "And then just walking out. Of course it's hard to tell with a man like him, but given the things he was saying I thought you handled yourself very well, Will."

"The Reverend was never what you'd call an *easy* person. But I seriously doubt he had a snoot full at that service." Wilton, holding onto an empty punch glass, glanced around the room. All the tables were still packed, a throng of holiness surrounding and ignoring the lonely dance floor. No one seemed to want to leave. Always a good sign. "I hope Belva was well pleased, Olin. And Regina had a good time, Sev?"

"With the new preacher giving her so much attention, the girl's tickled pink. Too bad he's ugly as a goat. I like him well enough, but that's just not right for a pretty girl like my Regina."

They looked on while at the Ainsley-Winslow table Jeremy Poston whispered to a giggling Regina.

"The boy's not a beauty, that's for certain," said Wilton. "But you know, Sev, they say beauty's only skin deep. The scarring on his face tells nothing of the measure of the young man. And his teeth's not bad. In all of the planning for this event I found him mature beyond his years. Marva commented how agreeable he was to work with. Went along with everything she wanted."

"I'll bet he did," said Olin. "Now Hoheimer wouldn't have. That's for sure."

"Hoheimer was a difficult man," said the Marshall. "Very touchy about his dignity."

Olin motioned them closer. "I heard three open bottles were found in their quarters. Now what disturbs me is not the booze...

it's wrong and it's illegal and all that, but we've all been around a bit, the three of us…no, what it is that's so bothersome is the Hoheimers live right next to the girl's dormitory. I mean, for goodness sakes, fellows, that's where Marva and Regina slept when they were down there. Now those are our girls…well, actually your wife, Will…and my daughter, and your niece, Sev. Drinking that stuff right next to where our girls used to be sleeping. That's just wrong. Just plain wrong."

"No question about it," agreed Sevier Winslow. "What I hear is they both denied knowing anything about it. Reverend and Sister. Insisted they never took a drink. *Liquor has never touched these lips.* That sort of stuff. No repentance at all."

"Well, what would you expect them to say?" said Olin. *Good riddance to bad rubbish.* So you're going to spend a few days here before heading South?"

"Out at your place? That's nice," added the Marshall. "Say, be sure to tell Marva I got those boys that disturbed the cemetery. In case she was worried about it. Being on the way out to her parents' place."

"We thought we'd rest up before the trip," said Wilton. "Local kids?"

"No, no. I don't think any of ours would dare. They might step out of line once, but not twice. They'd never do anything like this destruction. These're from over to Gaston. Busted up a bunch of Pefley stones. Which ain't going to go well for them."

"It's a good idea to take that time, Will. Marva will have a chance to be…to have adjusted a bit, if you know what I mean. Before leaving and everything. Sugar and me couldn't be more pleased. Having you in the family. It's a dream come true."

"So it's not just the Ainsleys and Winslows anymore," said the Marshall, "Now it's Ainsleys, Winslows and Goins. The Birdsalls will have to sit up and take notice."

"I'm sure they already have," said Olin. "Joey and those boys can see the handwriting on the wall. There's no stupidity in the Birdsalls, whatever else anyone may say about them."

"I suppose," said Sevier. "For sure Joey's not dumb."

Wilton waved to Marva who was standing on the other side of the deserted dance floor with Regina. "Fellows you'll have to excuse me. My lady is waiting. Too bad about the Hoheimers. But I'm afraid the fellow is gone. Which is a tragic thing. Just remember he may be a difficult man, even a fallen man, but he's still the Lord's anointed and we need to be lifting him and Sister Hoheimer up in prayer. Daily."

"That's for sure."

CHAPTER 5
A RUSHING, MIGHTY WIND
BLOWS THROUGH ASCHBURGH

Wilton and Belva wrestle with anxieties, but in the final analysis Sunday dinner will continue to be at the Ainsley table. Marva and Wilton chat, Olin Ainsley's secret problem is brought up, and Wilton heads off in a snowstorm in his Tsarist fur coat. Reverend Poston is made aware of significant changes, while the Town Board, led by Millard Craib, is inspired to be the unknowing instrument of God's will.

1
Changes, Changes, Changes

Belva's outburst as she shoved her way past the head teller and strode into Wilton's office was unusual behavior for an Aschburghian lady. Stepping around her as she stood in the middle of his office Wilton motioned to the tellers to get back to work and shut the door. He gestured for his mother-in-law to take a seat as he resumed his place behind his desk.

"Fortunately there was no one here but the tellers."

"Is that all you've got to say, Wilton? *That's* what's important to you?"

"No. I mean no disrespect, but first of all, don't ever come here and create a commotion again. I'm serious, Belva. I'm not some little boy you can push around."

"Marva is *my* daughter and you're not taking her away from me."

"Take her away from you? Just sit there and listen. No, be quiet. Just listen. You burst into my bank shouting about *your* feelings, *your* standards, *your* rights. Well, Mother, those are not *my* standards, not the standards of *my* home, *my* family. And Marva happens to be *my* wife."

"Marva is *my* daughter, and you're trying to change her and turn her against me."

Wilton leaned back in his high leather chair and ran his hand over his face. "We have been friends for many years, and now we are family, so I'll not say the obvious."

"I didn't come here to be your enemy or to embarrass you, Will. I want to be your friend, your mother, but you…and I suppose Marva too…are moving too fast, changing too much. She's breaking my heart, Will. Everything I taught her, everything we've had together…it's all gone. I don't even recognize my own daughter. Do you have any idea how that makes me feel?"

Belva took a small embroidered hanky from inside her sleeve, wiped her eyes and dabbed at her nose. Wilton refrained from smiling.

"I'm sorry you feel that way, but frankly I think you're over-reacting. Marva loves the Lord as much as she ever did. Nothing of any significance has been altered. The only thing that has changed is the length of her hair, and I suppose the style of her dresses. Goodness, Belva. What a fuss over nothing. I need for you to stop."

"You need for *me* to stop! This is not going to be as easy as you think, Will. You are not going to push me around the way you do everyone else in this town."

"What does Olin think?"

"I don't care what Olin thinks. I want you to stop."

"Belva…please. Marva and I are very happy, and I intend for it to stay that way. She loves you and Olin, and surely you know how much I care for both of you. I don't know what more I can say."

"*Your* being happy is not enough. Other people have feelings too."

"Has it occurred to you that we will have children? Belva, has it dawned on you that you will be a grandmother? You have thought about that, haven't you?"

"You're far too old."

Wilton took a deep breath and rubbed his hands together. "I am not too old. And you will be a grandmother. I know you would like that. Am I right?"

"This is embarrassing to me. We are talking about my daughter."

"My wife. Would you like to be a grandmother? Yes or no?"

"I suppose. But just because I would like to be a grandmother... and what woman wouldn't?...that doesn't give Marva a free pass to do whatever she wants."

"You haven't lost Marva. She loves you and you know it. Belva, you can be happy or you can be miserable. It's entirely your choice. I want all of my children ...and I expect to have a number...to be close to their grandmother, but that really depends on you."

"You threaten everyone in this town, but you will not threaten me!" Belva stood up and glared at her son-in-law, but made no move to leave. "You are not going to push me out of Marva's life."

"Marva and I will be consulting with Greg Penn, the Indianapolis architect. Very soon. He and I were room-mates at Bloomington. I've asked him to create a new house, a home, especially for Marva."

"There's nothing wrong with the one you have. You don't need a new house." Belva sat back down and wiped at her eyes.

"Please. I'm ready to sell. And let me lay this out for you so we're clear. I want my new house to be here in Aschburgh where my family has lived for close to a hundred years...where my parents and grandfather and others are buried. But, and this is not what I want and certainly not what Marva wants...if I am forced to do it I am prepared to leave. Placed on the market my bank would be a lucrative prize, easy to move. And there are many, many other things I would like to do."

"I see. So you are giving me no choice."

"I'm asking for you not to force me out of this community. My roots are deep here, as are Marva's. But I will do what I have to do. Please don't force this on me, Belva. I want and I need for you to be a loving grandmother to my children. God has shown me a large number of beautiful children. He has said He will make of us a great family. Many girls...a few boys perhaps. But the power will be with the girls. I don't understand that, Belva, but that is what He has said to me, and that is how it will be. God is bringing change. The Father is giving us these children, beautiful children, and I need for you to teach them, to guide them. Only a grandmother can do that."

Belva breathed deeply and composed herself. "You realize how upsetting it is to see my daughter giving up things I cherish? *My* daughter."

"Of course. But think how much beauty and joy my wife is going to give you."

Belva knew she was committed to holiness, and that simply could not change. But were hair and dress lengths all that important? She knew only too well that holiness preachers differed in their interpretations. This new young pastor had a different view from Reverend Hoheimer. And Hoheimer, no matter what he said from the pulpit, had turned out to be a drunk so you couldn't trust his view of holiness. Things were changing and changing fast, but as long as righteousness was maintained she knew she could live with the changes. Still, Wilton Goins, with all his talking with God, was not going to push her around. He was just not going to have his way that easily.

"I've always felt you were bull-headed, Wilton. And I don't accept all you say about you and God having these talks. But Marva's happy with you, and I suppose that's the main thing. As long as you two continue in holiness. I've never felt you fully understood the importance of the *Bible Baptist Holiness* way.

You're a decent man. I don't mean that you're not. But you're not perfect. You think you are, but you're not."

"I have a lot to learn, Belva. But I do want for all of us to be happy. All of us to be a family. And to do that we need to accept that we're living in new times and things are changing. In the town, in our family, even in the Church things are changing and it's futile for us to try to stop it. *Bible Baptist Holiness* itself is likely to see some dramatic modifications in the next year or so."

"*Likely to see*? You see yourself in charge. Don't you? Isn't that how you see it? You've only just joined the Church but you see yourself in charge."

Wilton stepped out from behind his desk and sat opposite her on a small leather sofa. "God has touched me...shown me He wants to use me as a businessman, as a Christian. And yes, naturally as a leader. But ultimately He is the leader, not me. The Lord wants fresh air, the wind of the Spirit, to blow through Aschburgh."

"Please, Wilton. You must think I'm an idiot."

"Hardly. Belva, let's work together. I want to remain in Aschburgh with Marva and our children. You want a happy family and beautiful grandchildren. We can have it, Belva. We can have all of it."

"I expect you to think of my concerns. If you will stay close to our family, visiting regularly, consulting before you make some of these changes of yours, and especially if you will not keep my daughter away from me, perhaps something can be worked out. I'll have to think about it. And see what Olin thinks, of course."

"I believe it's all going to be fine. I know it will. Belva, I'm well pleased with our discussion. Really I am."

"But whatever I decide, Sunday dinners will continue to be at my house."

"Of course they will. Marva so looks forward to that. And to helping you. That time together with you...just you two...it's very special for her."

"She still has a lot to learn. Whatever she may think."

"Definitely."

"I'll expect you and Marva this Sunday. Immediately after church. Do you object to my inviting the minister?"

"I defer to your wisdom on that. Olin's too, of course. I had thought though that maybe just family this time would be nice. Enjoying each other's company. Our family. Sharing some of our plans."

"I'll see."

"That's all I ask."

2
Tension Release

Heavy snow was falling, and that made the old farmhouse with its two big fireplaces all the more cozy this morning. She poured a second cup of coffee for him and joined him at the kitchen table. He looked strong and dignified in his vest, white shirt and black tie, but she noticed dandruff specks on the collar of his jacket which was draped over another of the chairs.

"Isn't it pretty, darling," he said. "I'm going to take the team in this morning. The fellows are getting the horses ready now."

"The sleigh?"

"Even in the middle of Winter I rarely use it anymore. But this looks like it'll be at least a foot or more so it'll be the only way to get around. Even Greg's *Rolls-Royce* would be worthless today."

"Is it warm enough in that old cabin for the boys? That's pretty exposed out there. They're barely old enough to shave."

"Working for me is one of the best jobs in the County for a young fellow. I pay well, and they're well provided for. Whether they're old enough to shave or not. And if they do their jobs well there's a future. They'll be coming into town today a bit behind me, in my father's old sled."

"That heavy old thing?"

"The horses pull it fine. It's slow of course, but they'll get there eventually. And I'll know they're coming up behind me, just in case. It's safer that way, plus there's some clean-up at the bank and at a few of our in-town properties. It's a good day to get those things done. The boys really can't do anything around here right now. You know, Marva, it gives me pleasure to think of you warm and comfortable out here, protected from this fierce storm."

"But you're still set on a new house?"

"O yes. Definitely. It'll be much better for you. Even though this is quite nice in its own way."

Marva stepped to the stove and cracked an egg into a frying pan. "Two or three?"

"Two will be fine. And perhaps another piece of toast. Perhaps two. Could you serve the eggs on top of the toast?"

"Wilton, I think it's really odd what you told me, and I'm a little worried about Daddy," she said while brushing flecks of dandruff from the back and shoulders of his jacket. "I have been since I learned he did that."

"Stop, stop. Just leave the jacket alone. I'll take care of that. You know, I'm sure he's not the only farmer who does it. Plus he's trying to put a stop to the business. Is there more buttermilk? It is a problem of course. Olin has a problem. But let's not make a big thing of it. I do like the way you make the coffee. You've told me, I know, but I've forgotten. You put some spice in it."

"Cinnamon. Just a pinch or two. Regina told me about it."

"You know, I've talked with Olin about this several times over the last couple of years. It damages the Ainsley property and the livestock, so it's bad for business. Just he and I. He sought my counsel. Do you think we could have biscuits with supper? Your biscuits are terrific. It's a long-standing issue. I realize it's unpleasant but…it's related to all the tension he feels."

"Tension? Daddy has no tension." She poured him a glass of buttermilk, set it beside his coffee, and continued to brush dandruff from the back of his vest. Walking over to the window she realized she felt unusually good, protected. "Why would he feel tension? This is all so peaceful, and the *Old Ainsley Place* is just as nice."

"Marva, farming is filled with tension. Leave that, please. Please. It's embarrassing. The dandruff. It's a problem for me, but I'll take care of it."

She served his eggs atop his toast and sat opposite, pleased to watch him eat, his back to the window, the snow falling outside.

"Your Daddy has just kept the pressures hidden from you over the years. You never know about the weather or the pests and you can't control the markets. You make some educated guesses, plant and tend your crop and hope for the best. So much of it's outside your control. Personally I couldn't tolerate the uncertainty."

"I guess I've never thought of it that way. The snow is pretty for us, but for Daddy it could mean a delay in getting things done for Spring planting. Do you think *Pinkhams* or *Father John's* would help with your dandruff flakes? Daddy always keeps both around."

"Your Daddy is bald, darling. Those are mostly for colds and strengthening."

Wilton smiled at her, reached across the table and squeezed her hand.

"When he had hair. He used them then."

"Olin is trying his best to get his problem under control. He will. He realizes it's affecting the value of his operation. I suggest we let him be. Let's focus on us and our life, our family. I'm in Giantown tomorrow, assuming there's no big drifts and I can get through, and I'll check on what's recommended for dandruff. You know I'm still surprised you didn't like New Orleans."

"It was just a little too much for me, I'm afraid. I want to do new things, but sometimes I get a little overwhelmed."

"That's understandable. Aside from being beautiful, you're young. But I hope you know I won't let anything harm you."

Marva smiled and touched his hand. "Colored people frighten me, Wilton. I've never seen so many colored people as there were. Even in Memphis, which I liked very much. They talk so fast I can't understand a word of it. They're just not like us."

"Hmm. You know there's colored over in Weaver in Grant County. Quite a few nice families too. Clean and well dressed. High School graduates. I was able to work out a nice financing package for the extension on their church building. *AME* they call it. Derived from the Methodists I think. And you know they paid the whole thing off within a year. Remarkable. These eggs are delicious. I had no idea you were such a good cook."

"Momma's a good teacher, I guess. And Regina helps me a lot. When our aunt died Regina had to take over all the cooking for Uncle Sevier. Of course he missed that the years while she was at *Seminary*. She's going to show me how to make a Dutch Apple pie."

Wilton wiped his mouth and hands and stood up from the table. Marva quickly cleaned the table and helped him on with his suit jacket, carefully wiping at the dandruff.

"You're just not used to being around different kinds of people. Meeting with Greg Penn and then with Professor Steele will be good for you. I sort of thought that artist fellow in New Orleans would interest you."

"The little man at the hotel? He said he was a writer, dear, not an artist. And who knows how much of a writer. To me he seemed mostly interested in airplanes and whiskey. I never imagined anyone could drink that much whiskey. In fairness though, he had very fine manners, and he was interesting when he talked about his home State."

"Gave us some good tips on the University down there, didn't he? The minute he opened his mouth you knew he was from the deep South. And as you may have noticed I'm rather partial to Southerners. They're good people, the better class of them…and I've always known them to pay their debts. A lot like Hoosiers."

Marva brought his heavy fur-lined coat from the closet. "I left your fur gloves and hat in the hall. You want to be sure to pull down the flaps and tie them under your chin. There's quite a wind. Will the fur lining leave hair on your suit?"

"Never has. It's excellent quality. From Russia. Fur outside and inside. It even pulls down over my forehead."

"Russia?"

"Before the Bolsheviks. Under the Tsar they turned out some fine products. Before everything got all fouled up. Socialism is the worst thing ever invented."

Marva helped him on with the heavy coat, rubbing her face in the soft fur. "That'll keep you snug. Wilton, do you absolutely have to go to that silly Council meeting tonight? With this snow and cold. I'm sure if you just told those men what you want they'd do it without your having to be there."

"Perhaps. But I can't risk that. I have to work with those men, Marva. That's just a fact of life in places like Aschburgh. They may be called the *Town Council*, but most of them are laborers. Not a one of them knows a thing about business. Most of them can barely read. With that kind of person…insecure you know… you can't push too hard or you'll get their backs up against the wall."

"I suppose. But I'll miss you, and I'll worry."

"I'll be half an hour late. No more. Marva, the Lord has shown me that this must be done and exactly how to do it. So I'll be there and I'll get it done. Darling, everything I have…that *we* have…all the authority, the integrity, the power in the Goins' name, our financial security…such as it is…all of that comes from listening to the Lord God and faithfully carrying out His will."

"I've never known anyone like you, Wilton. When you say God is real, you really mean it. But please be careful. I'll have lots of biscuits with your supper. With that blackberry jam you like. Steak and mashed potatoes. Will green beans and corn be all right?"

"Excellent. This meeting shouldn't take me long. An hour at the most. And the boys will follow me home in the old sled, so there's no danger at all."

3
Promises of More Chickens to Come

Wilton arrived at his office on time, but the boys took forever, fooling around in the snow no doubt…but eventually, in mid-morning, they showed up at the Bank with their cargo of Reverend Jeremy Poston. They brushed him off, shook his hand, and ushered him into Wilton Goins' office. "Mister Goins keeps it nice and warm," they assured him. "You'll thaw out in a second."

Wilton leaned back in his chair and smiled at the chilled clergyman. "Sorry to bring you out on a day like this, Reverend, but there are things of which I must speak to you. Just couldn't wait, I'm afraid. Can I offer you some coffee or tea? The tellers always keep a pot on in the back."

"No thank you, sir. The ride on the sled, while brief, was quite interesting. I don't think I've ever done anything quite like that before. We rarely see snow like this. In Rising Sun. Or Quercus Grove for that matter. This is a very nice office, very nice. So large and bright."

"Reverend, I'll bet that sled's seventy-five years old or more. My father bought it from the Devers people, the Claude Devers, when their operation went belly-up. That was forty years ago, when I was a small boy, and it was considered an antique back then. But it still gets the job done when it comes to hauling. Actually they...the Devers family...tried to buy it back recently. We only use it to bring wood up to the house, but as I say it does the job, and I'd hate to dispose of something like that. Part of the Goins' family now. Won't change your mind about the coffee?"

Pastor Poston, who had no idea why he had been summoned and was afraid to ask, wondered where all this was going. "No thank you, sir. I don't drink much coffee or tea I'm afraid. Mostly just milk. Your office simply amazes me. It's so spacious."

Wilton swiveled around and pointed to a small bookcase in the corner near the large window facing *Apple Drive*. "There's not a book there I don't look to at least once a week. Everything in that bookcase has a purpose. Casual reading, that sort of thing, I leave at home. The office is for work, nothing else. I like to keep it simple. Not puffed up. The only thing I do here other than banking business is to pray. Because of the simplicity of the room it's the best place for me to speak with the Lord and to hear from Him. Early in the morning, before business hours. You have established a prayer closet at the parsonage I hope."

"O yes. That's very admirable, sir."

Wilton, surprised at how much about himself he had already disclosed to this young man, decided to move into his own agenda. "Jeremy...I may call you Jeremy I hope?"

"O yes. Of course, sir."

"Jeremy, I've asked you to stop by because there are some things that will be happening, some changes that I want you to know about. Well in advance. As far as I am concerned, and I speak for Olin Ainsley and of course the Winslows as well, you are the spiritual leader of our community and need to be consulted every step of the way. And despite your youth I intend to do just that."

"I'm pleased to receive your vote of confidence, sir. It means a great deal to me."

"By the way, before I forget, Mrs. Goins asked me to say hello and to express our thanks. She and I are deeply appreciative of the beautiful job you did for our wedding. You helped to make it a truly memorable occasion."

"Thank you, sir. I only just did my job. It was a great honor for me to share the day with you and Mrs. Goins."

The boy was genuinely homely. *Ugly as a coyote* to quote Olin. But for some reason Regina was clearly taken by him, and it was entirely possible things could proceed to a serious pass. So that had to be considered. She was Marva's closest friend as well as her cousin, and he needed to keep that in mind. And then, much as no one would ever admit it, in a small Church, with its abundance of loud, vulgar and often insecure husbands, a homely non-threatening parson was something of a prize. A married homely parson would be even better.

"Jeremy, as I'm sure you are aware, changes are being proposed for our Church, and those changes, which will occur, believe me, will make all the difference for the Church and Aschburgh. You're an educated and perceptive person, so I know you can see that. Changes for Aschburgh...not to mention for your career. And to be quite frank, man to man now, for your salary."

Jeremy, who had no clue what Wilton was talking about, felt he needed to say something. "I'm very happy with the Church and with Aschburgh, sir. There's a lot of good people here."

"Look, Jeremy, I realize you didn't become a minister for the money. You were called. It's a genuine calling or it's nothing. Quite different from business in a lot of ways. Though not completely. God has called you and that's reward in and of itself. I believe the ministry is the highest estate a man can aspire to. There's no question about it. And the Lord will provide."

"He's so faithful, sir."

"So money is not an issue. But a little extra bacon on the breakfast table never hurts. When you choose to marry...and that may come about much sooner than any of us thinks...you're a very eligible and presentable young fellow, if you don't mind my saying...the ladies especially enjoy a few new odds and ends around the house. Am I right or wrong in that?"

The Reverend Poston, who sensed he was blushing, allowed himself a slight laugh. Still unsure how a minister ought to conduct himself he leaned toward a certain humble, if not fawning stuffiness. But he felt if he did make a mistake around Mister Goins it would be understood and forgiven. He liked and respected Wilton Goins, and having been made aware by the other preachers that five was the going rate for a wedding in Aschburgh, and having received exactly that from the best man, the Mayor of Indianville no less, Jeremy was deeply touched by the extra twenty-five Wilton slipped him after the wedding.

"You've been more than generous already, Mister Goins."

"I'm not going to bore you with the business details, Jeremy. That's my bailiwick. The point is the Church needs to be fully modernized...building, status in the community, youth programs, role of the ladies, even doctrine. The whole ball of wax, as it were. Even the name needs changing. If we're going to grow and spread the Gospel of the Lord Jesus Christ we need to appreciate the fact that this country is hurtling into the middle of the twentieth century, and it's not going to wait for us. We've got to leave the nineteenth century behind. We've got to change and we've got to change now. In the Lord's will and in His timing, of course."

"Of course. But doctrine is fixed, Mister Goins. It's right from Scripture. To modify or change it, that's very difficult, if not impossible. Don't you think?"

"No, Jeremy, not at all. That's a myth. Like anything else doctrine needs to be brought up to date or the Church dies. My father did business with a handshake. If I tried that I'd be out of operation in a month. Times change, practices change, doctrine changes. Jeremy, Christians used to believe and teach the world was flat. Some still do! Can you imagine? The world is round, not flat, Jeremy. Am I right in that? Another thing that's been tugging on my heart. Right now we're paying you five hundred a year. That's about it, isn't it? That's what it is?"

"Five hundred and twenty, sir. Ten dollars a week. Plus the parsonage, of course. That really makes it quite a bit more. Fairly generous, really. And folks have been so good with vegetables and things. Some are bringing canned beans and corn now we're into Winter. Even a chicken last week."

"Aschburgh people are very thoughtful. Especially in our Church. Look, Jeremy, I'm going to propose twelve hundred. One hundred a month, twenty-five a week, more or less. There's a little more than four weeks in a month, if you follow. Effective immediately. Retroactive to last Sunday actually. Unless you stand in the way the treasurer will start next Sunday. I've already told him. And if that's not sufficient, if you need a little more, I expect you to let me know."

"I don't know, sir. Can the Church afford that much?"

"I understand the ministry's not about money. It's about serving the Lord and trusting Him. But your authority and standing in this community need to go way up, and they will with the changes we're making. I've checked around, and you'll be the best paid minister in Aschburgh."

Jeremy, his heart beating faster, grasped the armrests of his chair. "It seems too much, sir."

"Perhaps for a less spiritual man. But not for you. You won't be puffed up. And as far as I'm concerned you're worth every bit of twelve hundred plus housing…a whole lot more…but unfortunately the Church can't afford more than that right now. Later on, as we move ahead with these changes, as we grow and take on greater influence in the town and the County it will be another story altogether. Would that be satisfactory,

Jeremy? Twelve hundred for now, considerably more later on as we modernize and grow. Plus the manse...parsonage, as it were. And of course special gifts...vegetables, hogs, chickens and so on. I'll make sure all that is forthcoming."

4
Tending To The Lord's Business

Wilton arrived at the Town Building, which was also headquarters for the Volunteer Fire Department, ten minutes late. He disliked being late, but found it made no difference this evening since Millard Craib, the Town Clerk, hadn't arrived, and the meeting couldn't begin without him. Millard's sore feet often caused him to be late, and with this snow storm no one was surprised to see his chair empty. The other four members of the Town Council sat gossiping behind a long table at the front. Each greeted Wilton as he entered the drafty room.

He sat in the front row next to two members of the *First Methodist Church* who also had business before the Council this evening. The only other persons present were Gathel Reneau, who along with her husband Menneth was owner, publisher, editor and reporter for the *Beauville Weekly Sun & Moon* – "A Small Town Paper For Small Town Folks", and the cleaning lady who wasn't going to be able to start her work until the meeting was finished.

One of the Council members gestured toward him with a pencil. "Wilton, are the Gosnells from over to Matthews, out there south on Wheeling Pike...are they the ones related to Mike Gosnell over west of the State Road? We was just wondering."

"Distant to both actually. By marriage, I believe. Actually Wilma Gosnell is a Craib, so in a way they're closer to Millard Craib's people than to Mike's people. Have we heard from Millard? I'm a little pressed. And with this snow it's going to take me a bit to get home."

"Still coming down?"

"Was when I got here."

The Lord had shown him the *Ainsley-Goins Cross* from his office window, and now even though the prophecy of his marriage to Marva had been fulfilled, the *Cross* still needed to be erected as a sign of God's reality and power in his life. There was a calling, even a destiny, and the street signs were to be a testimony of the Lord's immediacy in him and in Aschburgh's future.

Jehovah God wanted him here tonight. Demanded it. The snow storm was an obstacle in his path, an attempt to turn him from obedience, but he was here, his presence a testimony to his faith and his passion to obey the Word of God. And that was the only reason he would be here. Wilton knew all these people, including the cleaning lady, knew their parents and often their grandparents, knew their family histories and their finances, such as they were.

This was definitely not where he wanted to be spending a cold, snowy evening. But the *Cross* changed everything. It was the plan of God and Wilton would either work to achieve it or God would get someone else. The Lord's will would be accomplished one way or the other. With him or without him. He really had no choice if he wanted the Lord's blessing on his marriage, children and business. And so he had already spoken to all five of the Council members this past week. Preparing the ground was a Biblical principle. Wilton was confident there would be no problem, but still, he had to be here to see it through. The *Ainsley-Goins Cross* would become a reality. In truth it was a spiritual reality now, but the Lord wanted it manifested in the physical, and for that he needed the Council's approval.

The Council members continued to chat among themselves, and Wilton and the representatives of the Methodists exchanged pleasantries as Millard Craib, the Town Clerk, entered the room. Crippled with Plantar's Warts on the soles of both feet, he hobbled slowly up to the front table, brushing snow from his hat and coat, acknowledging no one, and declared the meeting open for business.

"How's the feet, Millard?"

"More of the same. No need for a roll call. Everyone's here." He glanced at the agenda which had only two items. "Gathel, you want me to send you my notes on the meeting? I can slip them under the door of the newspaper on my way home. I know Menneth's not been well. Figured you might want to get back to him."

Gathel, the publisher-editor-reporter, was delighted to be given an excuse to leave. On the way out she stopped to shake Wilton Goins hand. "Menneth and I are so sorry we haven't stopped by the house, and of course we couldn't be at the wedding. Him being the way he is. We heard from everyone it was a lovely occasion. Marva's a wonderful girl, and you're such a fortunate man to have her. It's no excuse, Wilton, but with this tumor Menneth's got now there's been no time for anything."

"We missed you both, Gath, but we certainly understand. Hope Men's feeling better soon. We've been missing his column."

"I'm afraid it doesn't look so good. It's growing again. Anyway, I hope Marva was pleased with the article about your nuptials. Menneth tried to make it all real special…not just an announcement, you know."

"She was well pleased. As were the Ainsleys and myself. We're most grateful for your thoughtfulness."

"Folks, we need to move along here," said Millard Craib nervously tapping a pencil on the table. "I'll get you those notes, Gath. Didn't mean to interrupt you and Wilton, but…we're all sorry about Menneth. You give him our best. We've got two items on the agenda so let's get it done and get home to supper. I see you've got your team outside, Wilton."

"Easiest and safest way to travel in this storm."

"The old ways are the best ways."

"A lot of the time."

"They worked good when we was kids and they still do."

The representatives of the *Methodist Church* stood to request an easement so the Church might use a portion of an adjacent vacant lot for a playground for their children's Sunday School classes.

"It's too cold to have the kids outside."

"They want it for the Spring and Summer."

"Why don't you just go ahead and use it when the weather turns better?" asked Millard Craib. "It's owned by some Giantown people. Haven't maintained it and haven't paid any taxes on it, so you might as well say it belongs to us. Go ahead and use it. It's for the Church, for the Lord, seems to me."

"Nobody's going to complain about that. For the Church."

"Well, the preacher would sort of like for it to be legal and all. Especially since he's thinking about buying some equipment and stuff."

"See, if we start down that path we'll have to refer it to a lawyer. That's going to take time and money and who knows what all. You just go and use it. Some problem comes up we'll deal with it then. If it ain't broke, don't fix it."

"Well, I don't know. Pastor feels it should be legal and all."

"You just go and use it. It'll bless each of us. No need for Council action on this. Just tell the preacher that's how we do things. He's pretty new but he'll learn after a bit. Wilton, your concern's up next. It's always good to see you. Married life agreeing with you I hope? What do you got for us tonight?"

Wilton adjusted his tie and smiled tightly. They all knew perfectly well why he was here and what he was going to say. *Father, give me wisdom and give these fellows a bit of courage to do Thy will even though they have no comprehension.* He remained seated, one leg crossed over the other. "It's a small matter, Millard. Hate to even waste your time. A small matter, but one on which I must have your approval."

"Fire away."

"I'll be to the point. At my personal expense…my expense now…nothing to the town. At my personal expense I am proposing a change in the names of two of our thoroughfares. *Apple Drive*, which for as long as I can remember a lot of people call *Small Alley*, needs to be renamed. Nobody calls it *Apple* anyway, and *Small Alley* …which was its name in the last century…is not the kind of name we want for one of our major streets. It's not good for business. And the thing is, except for the street signs the bank put up by our building, there's no signs on the street at all. It's not a good business situation."

"The Bank paid for them signs? I always wondered."

"Yes. And as I say, we're concerned about the image problem of having no street signs and having backward names like *Small Alley*. It just doesn't sit well with the business community. *Main* is the same thing. Many folks just call it *Downtown*...which again is its real old name...and except by the Bank there's no signs."

"And the Bank paid for those signs too?"

"Every single one of them. And happy to do it."

"Those signs don't come cheap, Wilton," said Millard Craib. "The town can't spend what it don't have."

"Be that as it may, fellows," countered Wilton. "It speaks poorly of Aschburgh, especially when you men are working so hard to bring major industry back into the community."

"It's a lot harder to do now than when we had the free gas to offer."

"We've got lots of good workers, but the companies don't care about that. They just want the free fuel. Which we ain't got no more."

"Right. I hear what you're saying. So let me offer something that will bless all of us. I will pick up the cost of the signs and the posts and the installation. It won't cost the town a penny. Now that's me, not the Bank. Let's have no confusion on that point. What I'm proposing is to rename *Apple* to *Ainsley Avenue* in honor of one of the town's oldest and most distinguished families."

"Marva's people? And you'll pay the whole thing?"

"Mrs. Goins family, yes. I personally will pay everything."

"Don't we need County approval?"

"*We* make the decisions for Aschburgh!" said Millard Craib. "Not some County bureaucrat who don't even know how we do things."

Wilton nodded in agreement. "And at the same time we need to rename *Main* or *Wide Street* after our town's founding family, from which I am honored to be descended."

"No offense, but some would say that'd be the Gibbs."

"Well *some* would be wrong. The Goins founded Aschburgh in 1867. My father, Louis Fox Goins, traveling with a Birdsall established this community. As I understand it his Birdsall guide went on to the area of Power City, but my father settled east of the present town and began marking out the plots which to this day make up our town. I still live on that land, fellows. I'm proud to own that property. My family's sweat, and a bit of our blood, is in that soil. Now the Gibbs, who're good people and always have been...I'm not speaking here against the Gibbs...they came almost ten years later. And when they got here they blessed this community with their hard work and honesty, but my father, Louis Fox Goins, put in many a crop before those good people arrived."

"So you'd like it *Goins Avenue?*"

"*Goins Boulevard. Ainsley Avenue.*"

"So the Bank would be at the corner of *Ainsley* and *Goins.*" Millard grinned despite his aching feet. "Still, Wilton, the cost could be an issue. I know you're going to pay for everything, but there's future maintenance to consider. Plus replacement costs if they're damaged. I don't see where we can commit the Town to those expenses. Not the way things are right now."

"I will bear all costs, Millard. Everything. I'll have the papers drawn up. And again I'm talking about myself, not the Bank. When you approve this, my boys will start putting up the posts. As soon as we can clear the snow. And I'll have all the signs up within a week or two. Lord willing."

"Those the boys riding around town on the sled? And it costs us nothing?"

"Costs you nothing. Not a red cent. I'll even maintain the signs. And replace badly damaged ones. On those two avenues. Those two only now, let's be clear. Not the whole town. Just those two streets. Spruces up the heart of the town, making it more presentable for industry representatives, plus two distinguished families will be well pleased with your efforts. You can be sure that'll make a difference too."

"Sounds all good to me," said Millard Craib. "No need for a motion and all that nonsense. We're all agreed. You get those new signs up and it's a done deal. Let's go home and have supper."

CHAPTER 6
THE PEACE OF A
PROPERLY KEPT SABBATH

*Considerable talk relating to the Church and theological issues
in which we learn Mister Goins and Jesus have similar ideas
concerning unity, and Reverend Poston hears of some startling
ideas about Apostles and Bishops. Following a discussion of
Olin Ainsley's sin, and a pause to learn of the death of Menneth
Reneau, both Olin and Wilton settle down with the family for a
Sunday dinner and some wide-ranging conversation.*

1
The High Priestly Prayer Of Jesus
And The Future Of Aschburgh

All along *Ainsley Street*, energized and resplendent with its new
street signs, church services drew to a close, preachers shook
their folks out of the buildings with a handshake for the ladies
and back slap for the guys, so that up and down that recently
renamed thoroughfare there was a sense of good people, who
having done their duty, were now set free to enjoy the day that
the Lord hath given.

However, it must be admitted the Sunday morning service at *First Bible Baptist Holiness* was dreadful, the congregational singing dreary, the piano out of tune and poorly played. The Reverend Jeremy Poston read his sermon, read it incompetently, and ran twenty minutes long. But afterwards, as folks lingered in front of the church, enjoying the unusually warm February sunshine, chatting about preparations for planting, children and grandchildren, everyone seemed quite pleased with the way the Sabbath had begun.

Further down *Ainsley Street*, at its intersection with the paved half of *Big Circle Road,* the bells of the new *First Methodist Church* chimed the noon hour as that small congregation, which took a quiet pride each Sunday in worshipping longer than the Baptists, slowly filtered out onto the dirt street. Five years after the dedication of this new sanctuary on *Ainsley* their old church building on *Epworth Street* remained vacant, beginning to decay, and some had questioned whether it had been wise to take on the debt of a new building which was rarely more than one third filled on Sunday. A vague sense of dissatisfaction loomed over the congregation. There was even talk of finding a new pastor, someone who would be able to attract young families and children. Still, all things considered, the Methodists of Aschburgh were delighted to be sharing one another's company on this glorious Lord's Day.

At the other end of *Ainsley Street*, not far from where it intersected *Goins Boulevard*, the *First Christian Church* had long since concluded their forty-five minute service and gone home. Unlike the Methodists and Baptists, Christian Church people, who were rather unclear just what to call themselves since *Christians* seemed a bit presumptuous, held only one service a week. They tended to feel anything more than that smacked of fanaticism and would hardly be fitting for people who were better bred than most of your typical Baptists, Methodists or even Friends for that matter. Why good families like the Birdsalls, Winslows, Ainsleys and Goins tended toward the Baptists remained a mystery.

Though related by blood and generations of close ties, though separated by no more than a hundred yards along *Ainsley Street*, the Baptist, Methodist and Christian Church people of the town rarely acknowledged one another of a Sunday morning. No hostility was expressed...little was felt...the others were Christians, not Catholics, Jews, Mormons or atheists after all. It was rather more a sense of peacefully and lovingly sticking with one's own kind. There would be plenty of time for contact with people from other believing churches during the week. For the moment the Baptists and Methodists standing out on *Ainsley Street* separated by a hundred yards of dirt and gravel, and the Christian Church people snug and unbuttoned back in their warm homes, existed quite comfortably, thank you very much, in their separate theospheres.

Reverend Poston lingered at the periphery of a group of Baptist men who were clustered by the side of the church steps eagerly discussing a projected late winter hunting trip to Brown County. Jeremy, who knew a bit about hunting, and very much wanted to be included, was excluded by the men without a thought. He was the preacher, the new preacher...not one of the men. In five years perhaps, once he had shown himself to be even a tiny part of Aschburgh, he might be included. In a small way. But not now, not yet...it was way, way too soon. Plus, in a sense that was difficult to define, preachers were not really men.

Wilton Goins, with Marva silent and happy by his side, moved around the various clumps of *Bible Baptists*, chatting here and there with several elderly couples, and slowly making his way toward the preacher. He never permitted himself the luxury of spending too much time with any one clique from the Church. Folks would try to use these casual relationships later in the week when they had business with the bank. So it was better to appear friendly, to smile, share greetings, and keep moving, slowly, circulating and eventually drifting away.

Marva had no desire to talk with anyone other than Regina, and her cousin was fully engaged with several young men Marshall Sevier Winslow had steered her way. Daddy punching harmless cows in the face was dreadful no matter how Wilton tried to explain it away. Punching cows was not a natural thing. Certainly not like hunting. It was abuse, pure and simple, and she didn't see how you could do that and claim to be a Christian. True, Daddy always repented of it...at least that's what he told her...but then he would go and start socking them again. She supposed everyone had odd spots. Even Momma, who was certainly a balanced person, said that one morning she saw her Papaw, Hiram Winslow, dead fifteen years at the time, sitting in their parlor reading *Pilgrim's Progress.* Everyone had their quirks. But punching harmless cows was a lot worse than seeing a ghost one time. Tension was a ridiculous excuse. She loved and respected Wilton, but tension was no reason to excuse what Daddy did. Wilton had a special relationship with the Lord... so he often saw things from God's perspective...everyone knew that...but the fact was Daddy had no real tension in his life. He just beat up poor cows because he wanted to...killed them every now and then apparently...and there was no getting around the fact of his cruelty and sin.

Wilton shook Reverend Poston's hand while Marva stood close by smiling, still unsure after six weeks how her hair and dress were being received by the congregation. Everyone was polite, but that was most likely because of their regard for Wilton and Daddy. She was sure they really condemned her and would like to order her to leave the Church. It would be much easier if she and Wilton lived somewhere else. But New Orleans had been terrifying, and even Memphis...though she liked the shops Wilton took her to, and she admired the way the salesgirls dressed...even Memphis was intimidating. As were Louisville and Indianapolis for that matter. She supposed she was, as Wilton liked to joke, a country girl, an Aschburgh girl. But then again she knew she wasn't...she needed and wanted more. How it was all going to work out she had no idea. Marva lived with a growing conflict between a desire to break free and a desire to find a place in the community. In danger of finding herself *neither fish nor fowl, a square peg in a round hole, odd woman out,* the potential pain lurking down the road troubled her.

"We appreciated your remarks, Pastor," said Wilton. "Very timely and to the point. Mrs. Goins was just saying she thought it was a wonderful service."

"Thank you, sir. Thank you, Mrs. Goins. I know I still have a great deal to learn."

"There's plenty in the pulpits around here who can't hold a candle to you. Did you get the right amount? The new figure we spoke of?"

"Yes, sir, I did. I really appreciate all you've done."

"It's only right, Jeremy. You deserve every penny. Did the treasurer give you the extra amount for last Sunday as well? That was the agreement."

"Yes, sir. Every penny."

"Good. You know, when it comes to business I like things to be on the mark. And, Jeremy, never forget that the Church is a business. A lot of preachers can't accept that, but it's true. A different type business for sure, but still a business. You're selling the best product in the world…eternal salvation…and most folks are happy to pay a tithe for something like that. A place in God's kingdom. Still…and Jeremy don't ever let yourself forget this… when the day is done the books have to balance."

Wilton glanced down *Ainsley Street* toward the Methodists, and waved to two of his cousins who cautiously returned his greeting and then resumed their Wesleyan conversations. "Does it make any sense to you, Reverend, that the *Church of Jesus Christ* should be separated this way every Sunday? We've got three Churches right here on *Ainsley Street*…three churches in a row…not to mention the others scattered around town. You join just these three together, consolidate their finances, and you'd have a powerful impact on Aschburgh, not to mention Tecumseh and Stonewall Counties. Just these three, not even mentioning the Friends and the other sects. You bring them in…I'm talking about those other sects…you'd have another seventy-five to a hundred right there. Maybe another hundred dollars a week if you treat them good. Use some of their peculiar language. Not much, but just enough. Isn't that what Jesus was getting at in His prayer? What is it? *Luke* 16 or 17?"

"The *High Priestly Prayer*? Is that the one you mean? In *John*?"

"Where He says He wants His Church to be one. Not a bunch of ineffective, squabbling denominations. The way it is now is like having six or more general stores in town. No way they can survive."

"I think you mean *John*, sir."

"*John* then. Fine. *John* is good. That's why you're the preacher."

"Chapter 17. I think verse 20 or 21. That whole section is what's sometimes called the *High Priestly Prayer* of our Lord."

"You really do have a fine education. On these matters. Regina, Miss Winslow, was telling us your school is in Quercus Grove. In Switzerland County?"

"Yes, sir. A bit outside Quercus Grove actually."

"But the point is, Jeremy, He wants His Church to be one Church, not a thousand. The Lord will not tolerate disunity. For one thing it makes no economic sense, and that is one thing God is always emphasizing."

"I'm afraid doctrinal differences will always stand in the way, sir."

"No, no, no. Jeremy, as I told you before, doctrine is over-rated. Nobody *really* cares about doctrine except some small-minded old preachers. You're too big for that, son. Once things get serious all that doctrine business falls by the wayside. Jesus wants His Church to be one, Reverend. One, not a hundred or more. One. Huge and powerful. Able to make a mark in this world. Do you realize a united Church could call the shots in Indianapolis...even Washington?"

"I don't think the Lord means for us to ignore false teaching, Mister Goins. Surely we can't allow the wolf to devour the sheep."

"One, Jeremy...*one* Church. Who knows what's false teaching and what isn't? Or who's a wolf and who's a sheep for that matter? Back years ago my family was Quaker, Friends as it were, and water baptism was the worse thing a fellow could do, if you follow. Did you know that about the Friends? They won't baptize...most of them. No matter what the *Bible* says. In any event, in obedience to the Lord's will, and maybe even a bit beyond that, I've had myself immersed twice because the Lord has shown me we need to get beyond all these ridiculous doctrinal and denominational barriers. That's the will of God, Jeremy. The sovereign will of God. One preacher says short sleeves or a mustache will send a fellow to hell, but then the next preacher turns around and says those things are no big deal but you'll go to hell if you use hair pomade. That sort of inconsistent thing just won't do. It's not acceptable and it's not fitting, Reverend. Suppose I just up and changed interest rates right in the middle of a contract? Said I just changed my mind. Folks wouldn't accept that kind of unsteadiness. The Lord Jesus has called us to be one Church. And He's spoken that to me as well. One Church. Just one. *The Church of Jesus Christ at Aschburgh,* though the exact name is unimportant. And I for one will be well pleased to see that happen, to see that day."

"A new Church? *Bible Baptist Holiness* headquarters would never accept that. I don't know, sir. I mean...each congregation is independent...afterall that's the Baptist way...but too much independence just...well, it just wouldn't be acceptable."

"Surely you see my point, don't you, Marva?"

"I think you're very clear, Wilton. But I also think we need to give Reverend Poston some time to consider what you're saying. You're suggesting a major change."

"It's going to happen no matter what we do or don't do."

"I think you're being too emphatic," she whispered. "You need to give Jeremy some time."

"You do? Really? Well, you just think about it, Jeremy. I don't mean to push my position. I don't believe in shoving a man. One congregation of two or three hundred instead of ten tiny churches with twenty-five old folks nodding off during your sermon. I see one Pastor, with one or two of these other fellows around here as his assistants. No more than his hired help. Hired and fired as that top man sees fit. Now I can see you in that top position as Senior Pastor. I can see that clearly. But Mrs. Goins is right. I've learned that Mrs. Goins is always right, Jeremy. She has a sharp mind *and* a kind heart. I need to let you have time to give it some thought. I can see several large churches like that, covering the whole of northern Indiana, maybe the entire State. With maybe a Bishop or Apostle overseeing the whole lot of them. Such a man would have national power and authority. Could you see yourself in that role?"

"Wilton," whispered Marva. "You're overwhelming the Pastor."

"Bishop or Apostle? Baptists don't--"

"Bishop or Apostle, or even both, Reverend. You just think about it. Mrs. Goins and I need to be off for Sunday dinner with the Ainsleys. Her mother...my mother too really...God bless her. She left Church early to go and prepare the meal. Now that's faithfulness. Belva Ainsley is a woman with a *Martha-heart*, and I respect that."

"She's a fine lady. The Lord's blessing on you and Mrs. Goins, sir. I'll think on what you've shared. I'll be praying about it. I'll be praying about it a lot, sir."

"And I'll be praying for you, Jeremy. That you have the wisdom and the discernment to see how the Lord wants things to move around here. Especially for you. God's got some big plans for you, Reverend. Bishop, Apostle...maybe five hundred tithers in your congregation...some monumental plans. Several of these local preachers working for you as assistants...at your beck and call."

As they walked arm in arm toward their *Ford* Marva sensed the other women of the Church staring at her. And it wasn't just because she was wearing stylish clothes and had an automobile. They had become cool and distant, totally different from the way they had been only a few months ago. All her life really. Like they wanted her to go away. Disappear. Only Regina, who still wore her bonnet and long dresses but had an open heart and mind, was friendly and accepting. Regina was the only one of the lot she could trust. The only one she wanted to trust. "They dislike me, don't they, Wilton?"

"No, not at all. They're simply starting to fear you. And that's not a bad thing. They can see you're growing beyond their timid little lives and it frightens them. So you're becoming intimidating. Which is good. Very good. You're much, much better than any of them. Ignore the bunch of numbskulls. Let them squirm."

"Wilton!"

"They're not your equals, Marva. Get used to it. They never were, and they're certainly not now. Intellectually, spiritually, socially. It's important for them to realize it. And for you to realize it too. So don't let them get too close, and don't do anything to try and make them feel better. Never do anything to make them feel better. You're going to make new friends, people with a broader vision. I realize you grew up here, as did I, but these folks are not our equals. I try never to treat them that way. In her heart mother understands what I'm telling you."

"My mother?"

"Belva. She's my mother too, you know. One flesh as they say. Ainsley/Goins. Ainsley/Goins is who we are. God's anointed. Mother knows how to maintain distance. She always has. You can learn a great deal from Belva Ainsley. Anyway, Marva, you and I have bigger fish to fry. Am I right or am I wrong?"

"You're right, Wilton. You're right, I suppose."

"On another matter, I'm getting a strong feeling you'd really like to keep our present house and not build a new one. Am I misunderstanding? I don't want to be overbearing. I want you to be happy."

"I would like to keep our house. Yes. But only if you want to. I'll do what you say is best."

"You know I want you to have what pleases you. But I think there are changes which need to be made to meet your needs. Suppose we discuss it with Greg Penn when we see him in a couple of weeks? He knows the house and he knows something of our plans. He'll be able to give us a pretty good idea of what can be done with it. If anything. It must be modified to meet your needs. I can't accept something that fails to meet your needs."

"It's a beautiful old house, Wilton. It just needs some paint and some care. And maybe a few modifications. You're right... Greg will know just what to do."

"I hope so. I really do. But it has to be *your* house. Not my parents house, not my house. My parents had no sense of anything but farming, and I've been so wrapped up in my business I've never paid any attention to the place. Until now. It must be *your* house. Maybe Greg can show us how to make that happen. Would you like that?"

"I like Mister Penn. He's odd, sort of different, but I like him."

"Even if he doesn't wear socks?"

"I worry his feet must get very cold in the Winter."

2

Four Legged Chickens, Beans, Biscuits & Yellow Gravy

Mother and daughter, Sunday dresses protected by large gray aprons, moved easily around each other as they shuffled pots and pans on the large wood burning stove which filled the center of the enormous Ainsley kitchen.

"He's got this stove too hot as usual," said Belva. "This is the sort of thing I mean about men. They may be smart about lots of things, especially business, but there's a lot they don't know. Stuff they were never meant to know."

"I think it's sweet that Daddy carried all that wood in here for you and started the fire. That's exactly the kind of thoughtfulness Wilton is always showing."

Belva grabbed a rag from her daughter's hand and wiped up a spill on the edge of the hot stove. "What I've been trying to get at, and I'm certainly not intending to interfere between a husband and wife...I've never liked that sort of thing...but what I'm asking is just a simple question. Do you think it's right to give up wearing your bonnet outside the house? Do you think that's right? Does it seem proper?"

"I think it's fine, Momma. I know you don't, and that does bother me a bit. But I'm happy about things, and Wilton is well pleased."

"You're even talking like him now."

"That's not fair, mother."

"*Momma*. I just think it's not the way you were raised. It may be fine for Wilton's peculiar friends in Indianapolis, but you weren't brought up like that."

"I'm a married woman. I'll get the beans, you check the chicken. I'm still your daughter and I always will be, but now I live under my husband's covering. And you know that's Scriptural."

Belva easily removed the chicken pieces from the large pot, and began straining the broth for the yellow gravy. "How are the beans?"

"Wilton likes a stronger flavor, so I added some extra bacon and a bit more salt."

As she scraped the bottom of the pot Belva cast a sharp glance at her daughter. "I think it's only right when it's dinner at *my* house he eat them the way your father likes them. Take the biscuits out. They ought to be ready."

"They both like the gravy thick."

"I think I know how men like gravy. Take this and keep stirring. Don't let it get lumpy. How've you been feeling? In your stomach."

"Fine. We're getting a few lumps."

"Well, just break them up good and stir more. No one likes lumps in yellow gravy. Neither men nor women. Not even your precious Wilton. What do you mean *fine*?"

"Fine. Good."

"Everything's normal then? Cover those biscuits with a rag. Don't let them get cold."

"I can't break up the lumps, stir faster, and cover the biscuits all at the same time, Momma. Plus season the beans the way you like them."

"The way your Daddy likes them. It's too late now for the beans. They'll have to stay the way Wilton likes them." Belva reached around her daughter, shoved a wooden spoon into the gravy and quickly broke up all the lumps. "Like that. You'll have to learn these things if you're going to keep your own kitchen. Or is Mister Wilton Goins going to get you a maid?"

"I'll do fine and I'll run my own kitchen. Though a maid would be nice. We've talked about it. Maybe after our first child."

"O I'll bet it would be nice! First child? Are you getting sick to your stomach in the mornings?"

"I'll let you know when that happens. A maid would be nice to have around then too."

"Marva, all of this is amusing now, but it's different when you have a family. Once you have children running around it's different. Believe me. You can't just be worrying about Mister Wilton Goins and how he likes his beans once you have babies to care for."

Marva grinned, covered the biscuits, and resumed stirring the gravy. "I'll make a good mother."

"In God's time. Yes, yes you will. Things are all right? Between you two? Private things?"

"Fine. Goodness that's a big chicken."

"Two. It's two. Chickens don't have four legs, Marva. Sometimes I think you're a town girl. We've got big men, Olin and Will. Four legs on a chicken! I'll finish the gravy. They went over by the old barn so you'll have to ring loud and long for them. Four legs on a chicken!"

3

Alongside A Pile Of Muck

Wilton placed his large, well tended hand on Olin's shoulder. The childhood friends, pleased now to be family, stood behind the old barn, far from the house, beside a piss soaked muck pile of manure and straw.

"I think it really bothers her, Will. I'm afraid I've really hurt her this time."

"She loves you."

"But it really upsets her, doesn't it?"

"Yes, I suppose. But Marva's not a sentimental girl about these things. She was raised here on the farm after all. It's not the animals that trouble her. It's you. She really believed you about repenting and stopping. You and me, Olin, we're grown men, we understand these things, we can make allowances, but women're different. And frankly it's affecting me too. She was crying the other night, and I don't want to see my wife crying. And I know you feel the same way."

"O God, Will! She's my baby. I wish I could stop, and I really meant it when I told her I would. I know it's wrong, and I know it's stupid. Three cows this past year...that's a loss I can't afford to live with. No farmer could. But, Will, I just get so damn angry!"

"At what? Belva? The town?"

"No, no. None of that. Belva's the same as she ever was. We've learned to get along. Sort of stay out of each other's way."

"Things seem to be going well for you, buddy. Harvest was good, prices are looking up...for now anyway. Should be a good Spring."

"Just stuff, Will. Just stuff. It's hard to put your finger on it."

"There's got to be a cause, Olin. Things just don't happen for no reason. And I don't see you stopping these outbursts until you take the time to figure them out."

"I wish I did know. Then I really would put a stop to it. But it just comes. Happens and then it goes. Like a darkness. Like night, only fitful. Fitful and fearful I guess. It just comes. The whole thing is stupid. I mean it doesn't make sense, does it? You know more about these things than me. You went to college."

"You understand more than you say, buddy."

"Willie, I know some things, and I know I shouldn't have had to butcher three weeks ago. That animal wasn't ready for butchering, and that made no sense, no sense at all. And it wasn't right. But I just had to do it. Beat the damn thing. Beat it 'til it couldn't hardly stand. Totally wrong time to butcher that animal. So I had to do it myself...which I never do anymore...

it's wrong for me. But I couldn't call on anyone else...not under those circumstances."

"It's getting out of hand."

"I know. I know. I'm strong, Willie, I'm strong. It's costing me. Cost me a bunch. Belva and me don't need that meat. I thought we'd give some to you and Marva."

"We'd appreciate that. We'd appreciate that very much."

"But don't tell her where it come from."

"No, of course not. The meat's still good no matter what the reason."

"I can't stand for her to be ashamed of me, Will. I can't bear that. It's too much. Belva, she knows me, knows my moods, but it's different with your own child. It's different, Will, believe me, when your own child, your baby...when even she's ashamed of you."

"You've got to get a grip on it, Olin. Otherwise it'll destroy you. It'll kill you, fellow."

The clanging of the triangle called their attention back to the farmhouse, to Sunday dinner, to the presence of their women in the kitchen.

"Better get back and wash up a bit. I need to get this pile of muck out of here. Belva don't like it, even this far from the house. Truth be told she really wants it off in Kentucky or Ohio or someplace."

"We need to talk more, buddy."

"Maybe. Another time. I don't know. Talking like this doesn't go down quite right. You know what I mean? Even though we're old friends, a man's got to handle his own stuff. I appreciate your listening to me, your concern, don't get me wrong. But I know I can handle it. I have to handle it, Willie. I just have to."

4
MENNETH CLAUD RENEAU
1875 – 1926

Menneth Claud Reneau, prominent local newspaperman, entered into eternal rest at his Beauville home this past Friday morning,

February 19th. Surrounded by his loving family Menneth passed peacefully from this life.

Menneth Claud Reneau was born May 3, 1875 to Maurice and Nahomi (Frazee) Reneau in Beauville. He and Gathel Speece were married by Reverend Xen Peacock at the parsonage of First Friends Church on January 3, 1907.

Recognized by his teachers at Beauville High School as a go-getter, Menneth left his home community to attend Indiana University at Bloomington. After he completed his studies there he went on to further renown at Harvard University and later at the University of Chicago. His studies completed he returned home to Beauville where he assumed the editorship of the family newspaper from his father Maurice Reneau. Joined in his endeavors from 1907 until his death by his worthy spouse Gathel, Menneth was known throughout the area as a newsman par excellence.

Menneth, always the literary man, published his own poems as well as at least one novel and a book of essays. He took special pride in having established THE BEAUVILLE HIGH SCHOOL FUND FOR LITERARY EXCELLENCE which each year awards a college scholarship of $100 to the boy or girl born and raised in Beauville and attending Beauville High School who writes the best original essay or poem in praise of Tecumseh County and its delights.

Preceded in death by his parents, Menneth is survived by his wife Gathel and two sons, Willard of Beauville and Dannis of Aschburgh.

Visitation will be at the Birdsall Home in Aschburgh on Sunday from 6 until 9 p.m. and on Monday from 10 a.m. until 4 p.m. and again from 6 p.m. until 9 p.m.

Services will be on Tuesday at 10:30 a.m. at First Christian Church of Aschburgh with Reverend Harley Noffsinger officiating. Interment at Winslow Cemetery.

Memorials may be made through the Birdsall Home to THE BEAUVILLE HIGH SCHOOL FUND FOR LITERARY EXCELLENCE.

5

Tearing Down The Walls Over Sunday Dinner

"Olin. We're ready. Please."

"Dear Father, we thank Thee for this day and for all this good food, lovingly prepared. Bless those who have prepared it, and bless the meal to nourish our bodies. And keep us ever close to Thee as we have entered his new year. Amen."

"Amen."

"It's so good to have our family all together around the table at this time of year."

"The yellow gravy just looks delicious. The best ever, ladies." Wilton tucked a large napkin under his chin and ladled gravy onto his chicken, a little on his green beans, and slathered it over his biscuits. "Speaking for myself, I am delighted that we can be together like this. Well pleased with the delicious meal, and pleased as a ripe peach to be received into this loving family."

"Flattery may just get you someplace," said Belva, laughing. "Eat your fill."

"And I'm honored to be the husband of such a beautiful woman."

Marva grasped his hand under the table. "Eat your dinner."

"Beans are a bit sharp though, Belva." Olin began to push them to the side of his plate, but catching the look on his wife's face pulled them back with his fork, and focused his attention on the chicken.

"It's the way Wilton likes them. Marva prepared them special." Belva smiled at her son-in-law. Still the best looking man in Aschburgh, even if he was stubborn and opinionated. "Marva made the gravy too, Wilton. I had no idea she was such a gifted cook. She learned a lot at the *Seminary*, that's for sure. And love will work wonders. More biscuits?"

Wilton Goins grinned at his young wife who was staring down at her plate and blushing. He supposed she'd shared the good news of morning sickness with Belva, but it was best to remain discreet in what he said until he was certain. The Lord said they would have mostly girls, but he was certain this first would be a boy. Named after him, but different, with *Ainsley* for a middle name rather than *Fox. Junior* was an uncomfortable tag to carry all your life.

"Two more of those biscuits will be just fine. And I'll just help myself to some more of Marva's gravy, though I'm sure you had a hand in it too, mother."

"We're both too old for me to be *mother*, Wilton."

"Never too old for love and affection. And deepest respect. Plus now that I've got Marva I've shed twenty years. At least."

Olin ripped a biscuit and used the pieces to sop up the gravy. Preoccupied with his problem, he paid little attention to their banter. He needed to repent properly or he was surely condemned. Not just to Marva or Will, but before Jesus, on his knees, at the altar. Still, he could no more do that with Reverend Poston than he could have done it with old Pastor Hoheimer. The preacher leading him at the altar needed to be a man of sanctification, not just words and an ordination certificate.

"Marva'll make him fat, don't you think, Olin? With all that good food."

"Chicken and biscuits is good for sure, Sugar" Olin agreed. "And the yellow gravy's remarkable. Not a lump in it. But the beans are a bit on the sharp side."

"Just eat your dinner. We need to finish up by 2:30 so Marva and I can clean up the dishes and have things ready for dessert and coffee at 3."

"Why 3, Momma?"

"I've invited the Marshall…Sevier…and Regina for dessert at 3. And Reverend Poston will be coming too. So we'll need to finish here by 2:30. It gives us plenty of time for a leisurely dinner."

"Reverend Poston?" Wilton glanced across the table at his mother-in-law. "I didn't think the preacher was being invited today."

"Not for dinner. Frankly, Wilton, you being new to the family probably don't realize I have a heavy responsibility for Regina. Her mother is my sister…her father was a third cousin or something…but since my sister won't care for her own child, I'm the one who has to be attentive to Regina's needs. Unfortunately

Sevier is incapable of that. The man is a good fellow as far as that goes, but he has no conception of what's required."

"But Reverend Poston, Momma?"

"Regina seems quite taken by him. She has a right to see him at Sunday dinner. At least for dessert. She has a right to that opportunity. And having both of them here for coffee and pie seems appropriate. At least it does to me. But if anyone has any objection...."

They ate in silence for a few minutes, Marva amused at the quantities of food her husband devoured. Normally Wilton ate sparingly, often skipping the afternoon meal. So this afternoon's performance was a labor of love, and she was both pleased and impressed.

"I thought this morning's service went pretty good," said Olin, breaking the silence. He knew he ought to have kept his counsel about the beans. Now he'd get them sharp for the next month or more. "It takes a while, but the Pastor's catching on."

"I can't stand him *reading* his sermons. Reverend Hoheimer never did that."

"But then *he* turned out to be a drunk."

"Daddy!"

"Hoheimer probably was so *stinko* he couldn't see to read them."

"That's so unfair, Daddy. You don't know if any of that's true."

"Sorry, darling. You're right. I shouldn't have said that about a minister."

Wilton took another biscuit and wiped up the last bit of gravy from his plate. "Personally I believe Jeremy...Reverend Poston... is going to be the finest Pastor Aschburgh has ever known. I know some might consider that a bit of a stretch, but I believe it. I'm looking forward to sharing some of mother's apple pie with him, as well as with Regina...and the Marshall of course."

"Will! You're dreaming. Marva, did you put something strong in your husband's water?" Belva clutched her napkin and stared at her son-in-law with mock open-mouthed amazement. "The boy's so nervous he can scarcely remember his own name."

"Wilton and I think he's very nice. I just wish he wouldn't read his sermons--"

"He can't even read them well."

"We were well pleased with the way he did our wedding service. Weren't we, Wilton?"

"You were *well pleased*? How nice." Belva smiled at her daughter. "Doesn't that sound like someone else I know?"

"Let me have a few more of those beans, would you, Will?" said Olin.

"Tease all you want, Momma. Reverend Poston did a wonderful job."

"I didn't mean to say he's not well intentioned. And I'm sure he'll learn. And he'll get over that nervousness as soon as he gets to know us."

"The Reverend will mature fast, Belva," said Wilton. "You're quite right, he's got a lot to learn. But I intend to see that he learns it and learns it well and learns it quickly."

"You do?"

"I do. Yes, I do. Olin, you've been very quiet. I hope I haven't sounded too radical and given offense," said Wilton.

"Marva, would you begin to clear the table? I'll help you in the kitchen in a moment."

"The Lord has shown me a great truth, Olin. And I believe Jeremy is the young man to bring it to fruition."

"The good china for dessert, Momma?" asked Marva who remained seated at the table. "Should I start the coffee? I'm going to need your help."

"Fruition? Hold off on the coffee. I'll make that myself. The china is already out on the counter. Second best china. Why don't you clear the table?" said Belva. "The Lord has spoken to you about Reverend Poston? Sometimes you carry things a bit to the extreme, Wilton Goins. I suppose the Lord told you about *fruition*?"

"No offense, mother, but I favor the way Marva prepares my coffee. She uses a little spice in it. Changes the whole thing."

"I doubt we have the spice."

"Just a little cinnamon, Momma," said Marva, squeezing her husband's hand.

"I suppose we could try it once. But wait for me, dear."

"Bring it to *fruition*?" said Olin. "I knew I should've gone off to college when you did, Willie. I've always figured the plain way is the best way to say something."

"Do you remember the Lord's prayer for the church, Olin? Not the *Our Father*, but the one in *Luke*. Chapter 21, I think."

"*John*, dear," whispered Marva, who was determined not to leave the table until her mother did.

"*John*. Yes it's *John*, not *Luke*. I keep making that same mistake."

"Pretty much one of a kind to me," said Olin. "You know I'm not much for *Bible* reading. A little bit goes a long way. I believe it, of course…it's God's *Word* and all of it's true. But a fellow can get too big a portion of it. We just need to be square with Jesus. If we're not we're in trouble. If we are we're o.k."

"What Jesus says is, *That they all may be one*," said Wilton.

"*John* 17, verse 21, I believe," said Belva. "It's a beautiful thought. I prepared a lesson on the *High Priestly Prayer* for the *Dorcas Circle*. Marva?"

"I've always thought that was an odd name. The woman was stone cold dead. Why name your group after a corpse?"

"I'll go back to the kitchen when you do, Momma. We'll have time to get it done. I'm interested in what Wilton has to say."

"I've told you before, Olin," said Belva. "Dorcas was raised to new life by Peter that she might continue almsdeeds."

"Almsdeeds?"

"It's more than a beautiful thought, Belva. The call for the Church to be one. It's really a command," said Wilton, pointing toward her with his fork. "In my quiet times with Him the Lord has shown me He's going to fulfill that prophecy, or maybe it's a command, or maybe even a promise, but whatever it is He's going to fulfill it starting right here in Aschburgh. Walls are coming down. Denominational walls and squabbles are out of touch with twentieth century America, and the Lord is going to tear them down, Olin. Believe me, it's true."

"Less squabbles would be a good thing. That's for sure."

"This country, under God's blessing, is moving forward in the next seventy-five years to be the greatest power the world has ever known. A Christian power, a nation for Christ by the end of this century. I truly believe that. The growth of our economy…and I don't mean the Stock Market speculation that's going on…that's all hyper-inflated puffery…no sensible person should be putting his trust in that …but the solid growth of our national product plus our industrial expansion …especially the capital investment in heavy machinery…all of that gives glory to Jehovah God."

"My goodness, Will!" said Belva. "You sound like Billy Sunday."

"In America the Lord expresses His will through the power of industry and business, Belva. And you better believe I'm enthused about that. Just like Mister Sunday is. By the way, I doubt that's really his name. Anyway, any sane person would be enthused to be a part of it. And the Lord's going to do that in Aschburgh if we sweep all this denominational clutter out of the way and get serious about honoring Him. We'll see this town come back to new life…and more."

"You think the Lord's going to make us some money?" asked Olin, grinning.

"He will. But that's not the point, Olin. Money and all that is a by-product of God establishing His kingdom on earth. And I know from my quiet times with Him that America is where He desires all this to be. God is comfortable with us, with Americans."

"You're married to quite a man, Marva," said Belva. "You better keep your eye on him. But we need to get this table cleared."

"I'm very proud of Wilton."

"Belva, it's not a joke. The separation of the *Church of Jesus Christ* into all these little self-important denominations makes no sense. Frankly it's an out and out sin because it violates God's will. And I truly believe, no matter how it may appear to the world, Jeremy is going to be God's man to help bring the walls down. It has to start someplace, and Aschburgh is going to be that place because He's got His man here. And don't forget...it's not Jeremy, it's God."

"Jeremy? Reverend Poston? Who can't even *read* his sermon intelligently? And you don't think you're being *extreme*?"

"You're the one who's invited him for dessert, mother," said Wilton, smiling at her. "To be frank though, extremism is not in my nature. The God who shares with me is a God of order, not some Holy Roller nut. I've never voted anything but Republican, and I never will. I believe the Republican party is God's way. But regardless, all these things will come to pass. Because God desires it. And it'll begin with the *Bible Baptist Holiness Church*. I see us becoming *First Church. The First Church of Jesus Christ in Aschburgh, Indiana*. And it'll move on from there like a snowball. Because it's God's plan...not mine. *That they all may be one*."

"Now that's something," said Olin. "That there's really something. A fellow could sink his teeth into a Church like that. A Republican Church. There'd be some substance there. Some action, not just talk."

"Well, my goodness," said Belva. "Marva, we need to get moving. You stack the dishes while I make the coffee...with a bit of cinnamon. The Reverend and Regina will be here in a few minutes. And Sevier, of course."

CHAPTER 7
A WORLD TURNING
UPSIDE DOWN

Indianapolis traffic congestion delays a fabulous luncheon with a world famous architect and an unusual view of racism. Wilton and Marva meet two men, one of whom will change their lives. Reverend Polson dazzles Regina, though Belva doesn't understand. All this concludes with a distinctly American position on the Power of Perfect Placement and the need for Large Blobs.

1
A Delightful Little Luncheon Atop A KKK Rally

The huge limestone obelisk at the center of the City towered in the distance, with motionless lines of black vehicles stretched before it. She had never seen so many automobiles...all of them jammed together so tightly Wilton was unable to make any progress. Marva and her new husband sat in the right lane on *Meridian*, staring at the automobiles...and the occasional horse drawn wagon...surrounding them. For some reason drivers were sounding their horns, making the horses nervous. Wilton tried to ignore the noise, and told her Greg Penn's offices were down there ahead of them on *Monument Circle*.

Why were these men sounding their horns? It was absurd. No one could move. Until now the drive down from Aschburgh had been delightful. She and Wilton chatted all the way about his plans for the house and tomorrow's trip to the *University*, and the whole drive had been so gay she was actually looking forward to lunch with Mister Penn, peculiar though he was. But now she could see Wilton was becoming tense because of all this noisy confusion.

"I'm going to see what this is all about," he said. "This is ridiculous."

"Wilton, please don't leave me here. I can't drive."

"I'll only be a moment." He hopped from the car and approached a large man who was rising up and down on his toes on the sidewalk trying to get a glimpse of what was going on down at the *Circle*.

"Some problem?" asked Wilton. He couldn't see anything but the line of cars and wagons stretching to the *Soldiers and Sailors Monument*.

"Big mess I'd say."

"That's for sure. Can you see anything? Any idea what's going on?"

"Not really. It's a big rally. At least that's what they say."

"Not an accident? A rally?"

"Big one. The Klan's pretty upset. First that set-up of D.C. Stephenson, and now...seeing how they got away with framing him...the coloreds are acting up."

"Right there on *Monument Circle*? Blocking everything so no one can move."

"Some colored hit someone yesterday. Something like that. Maybe shot him. Knifed him. A man's got to draw the line. At a point like that."

"The Klan? Right there on the *Circle*? You're sure?"

"That's why everything's backed up. Framing D.C. Stephenson was just the last straw. It's so packed you can't get through the *Circle*. Hardly any room for a white man in this city anymore. Coloreds are taking over everything."

"Any telephones around here?"

"Might be, but not so far as I know."

"Well…thank you."

"They've even got the Mayor down there. John Duvall. That's what they say, and I hear Governor Jackson'll speak later. The whole place is packed. Everybody's together on this one. You want to be fair, but there's a point, if you know what I mean."

Marva looked frightened when he came back to the car. "I heard a man say we'll be here for hours, Wilton. He said they're killing someone at the *Army Monument*. That the Mayor himself is lynching a group of colored people."

"No, no, it's nothing like that. Don't get upset. *Soldiers and Sailors Monument*. That's the big white tower you see down there at *Monument Circle*. Don't be afraid." He smiled at her and touched her hand, then slowly eased the *Ford* onto the sidewalk, and pulled off onto *Allegheny*. "I think we should park here and walk down to the *Circle*. Will that be too much for you? I don't want you to strain yourself, but it's no more than five or six good blocks. Not much more than that. Greg's right on the corner of *Market*. Do you think you can handle it?"

"I don't want to go. Really. They're killing people, Wilton."

"No, no, Marva. No one's being hurt. It's just a stupid rally. They make a lot of noise but there's nothing to it. The Klan is in serious trouble right now so they're making some noise. They're always having a rally about something in this city. But believe me no one's being hurt or lynched or anything like that. No one's being hurt."

"A Klan rally?"

"So I gather. Hoods and all that nonsense." He pulled the car behind a warehouse and shut the engine off. "I feel terrible about all this. I ought to have foreseen the possibility of this sort of thing the way things are right now."

"There's no way you could have known."

"Do you think you can walk several blocks? I mean are you comfortable enough? Are your shoes right for that? You're not having any discomfort?"

135

"I'm fine. I'm a country girl and I've walked all my life. But that's not the point. Let's turn around and go home, Wilton. I'm afraid. I'm sure we can meet with Mister Penn another time."

"If you're sick I'll turn around. Otherwise I can't."

"You know I'm not sick. I'm pregnant, but I'm fine."

"I'll see to it we have no problems. I always do, don't I? We'll walk down *Pierson*. It'll be empty and it runs right into *Market* down by the *Circle*."

"They'll be there."

"Marva, this city, in fact the entire State is jam packed with these cretins. We even had them in Aschburgh until I got it straightened out. Reverend Hoheimer was with them until some of us told him to stop it. We can't let them decide our future. People like this…if they're allowed to have their way…create a terrible environment for business."

"No matter what you think these people can be dangerous."

"We'll walk slowly. Do you feel all right? If you don't we'll turn around right now."

"No, no I'm all right. I'm fine. Are they only against colored people?"

"Plus anyone with half a brain. They're not our sort of people, Marva."

As he expected *Pierson* was deserted. Stores were closed for the rally. Most people were already down at the *Circle*. That a businessman would close his store to go to this spectacle was beyond him. But that's exactly what they had done. No wonder they were going bankrupt left and right. He walked slowly so as not to tire Marva, yet determined his plans were not going to be upset.

Market was packed with people shoving to get onto the *Circle* to see the Klan officials and to hear the speeches of Mayor Duvall and Governor Jackson. Telling Marva to stay right behind him, Wilton, his forearm raised in front of his chest, drove straight ahead through the crowd. Marva clutched the back of his topcoat with both hands and tried not to look at the angry people as Wilton smashed a path through the mob.

Greg Penn, more than a foot shorter than Marva's six foot one, clasped her hand between both of his and looked up into her eyes, all the while talking to Wilton. "It can be so terrifying to find yourself surrounded by people of that low level. Especially for Marva. Especially for a sensitive woman. But you're both safe here. Klan or no Klan, it's all one to us, Willie.

"From this haven we'll just look down on the *Circle* and laugh at them. Won't we, Marva? I'd forgotten how tall and lovely you are. We'll just laugh at them, and have ourselves a delightful luncheon. Which by the way, will be here shortly. Did you notice the restaurant downstairs? The *Wien, Wien.* It's not authentic Viennese, or even Austrian, of course, but it's good, hefty Germanic stuff. With an unfortunate Hoosier edge, but what can you expect? I adore everything Teutonic.

"We'll sit right over there. By my windows. We'll lunch by my magnificent windows. Atop the rally. Towering above their silly ranting and raving. I just heard the Fire Department is asking them not to burn that hideous Cross they've stuck out there. Apparently Mayor Duvall is afraid to light it. But I'll bet when Governor Jackson shows up he'll light it himself. That's the reality in which we live, Willie."

"It's very nice here," Marva said, pulling her hand free. They stood in the brilliant white central room of Greg's offices, the one he reserved for his private workspace. He wore a loose fitting red shirt, open at the neck, dark blue flannel trousers which were pulled tight at the ankles, black patent leather dancing slippers, and, of course, no socks.

"We won't be disturbed. My secretary will keep the hordes at bay. Even the ones in gaily colored robes." He led her over to the large window...a single sheet of glass stretching the better part of the wall. "I want you to savor my gorgeous view. Even though all we can see is those people. Just feel the sunshine! I designed this myself...the windows...so you don't have all those tiny panes breaking up your view.

"The way Forsyth does. Yet it's unbelievably stable. Reinforced in several different ways. Isn't it remarkable? Have you met Forsyth yet? William Forsyth the painter? Willie's told me how much you love painting. I've got some remarkably vigorous ideas for your studio. You'll love it."

"No," she said. "I mean about Mister Forsyth. He's a painter?"

"O my goodness!" said Greg. "Don't ever let him hear you call him *Mister.* Unless of course he's in one of his *democratic* phases. Every now and then he falls in love with the masses. For the most part Forsyth likes to be called *Professor*, much like Steele. You've met the old gentleman? Steele?"

"No. Not yet."

"Willie! What's going on here? Let's get on the go, fella! Let's advance the program."

"You're moving too fast, Greg," laughed Wilton. "Slow down, slow down, buddy. Not everyone's got a firing rate as fast as yours."

"Metabolism, *Wilton.* Some things are simply exciting. There's no other way to put it. I've known these men most of my adult life, but to be part of introducing a young painter to them... that's so tremendous. Seeing a new career take off. Marva, these are great painters. Forsyth and Steele. A little old fashioned perhaps, but great painters. Though as far as being entitled to be called *Professor*, neither one... Forsyth or Steele...has academic credentials that I know of. Still, that's what they want. Most of the time anyway. And one needs to defer to genius. Who am I to challenge them? Certainly I expect that same courtesy. Though of course I've *earned* my degrees."

"Calm down, Greg, you'll convince Marva you're a madman," said Wilton who had taken a seat at the table and was studying the crowd far below. "I'll bet there's ten thousand down there. Look at the size of that Cross! That's Mayor Duvall right in front of it."

"Where did you study, Mister Penn?" asked Marva.

"Lots of different places. Even in Europe. Of course I was at *IU* with your precious Wilton for my initial studies. But as for advanced architectural work ... have you ever heard of *Notre Dame*? It's in South Bend. That's where I began my preliminary work. It was a nice gentle introduction. So peaceful. Nothing

but young priests and cows. Of course it's never completed...
architectural study, that is."

"Catholic?"

"O that had no impact on me, you can be sure. But *Notre Dame*
was where I got my start. My introduction. Catholics have built
some fine buildings over the years. Mostly in Europe, though. All
the flummery up there in South Bend was nothing more than a
light amusement so far as I was concerned. After their fashion
they're good people at *Our Lady*, but I had to move on to other,
to bigger things of course.

"*MIT*...that's the *Massachusetts Institute of Technology*. And a
decisive stint at *Harvard*. Plus a bunch of other places hither and
yon. Some charming spots in Europe as I mentioned. It's all just
preparation, Marva. And contacts, of course. Helps you get in
the front door...but ultimately no matter where you study or who
you know you have to get out there and actually do your art. Get
your hands messy. Never forget that as your career develops.

"But back to what I was saying, Forsyth took the small studio
directly above these offices. He heard I was here, plus he wanted
the view, you see. He was desperate for the view. And the light,
naturally. But he can't get it. The view. Not with the fragmented
windows up there. A million and one panes of glass.

"You can't have a view that way. Your eye goes off in a thousand
different directions. It's subtle...you don't realize it at first...but
that's exactly what happens. He's furious. Forsyth. I actually
think he hates me because I have the view and he doesn't.

"But I designed these windows just for myself, and I don't
intend to share the design. At least not without handsome
remuneration. Which he can't provide. *Professor* Forsyth. But
he is a great painter, Marva. I do not disparage him. A truly great
painter. Somewhat in the 19th century style."

"Forsyth really gets under your skin, doesn't he?" said
Wilton.

"Goodness." Marva immediately regretted it, thinking it was
a stupid response to either Greg's outburst or Wilton's remark.
Greg was more peculiar today than he had been at her wedding.

And still with no socks and those odd black dancing shoes on his tiny feet.

Accustomed to people being nonplussed by his appearance and antics, Greg beamed at her. An unruly mass of white curly hair topped his ruddy face, blue eyes and classically chiseled features. He knew women, once they accepted his size, were struck by his dramatic good looks. Women often fell for him, though as a rule he had little interest in women…or men for that matter. Life was too wondrous to complicate it with entanglements. Willie was an exception. Greg loved Wilton Goins …had loved him since their days in Bloomington. Willie had a fierce dollars and cents integrity. He never really gave a damn about Greg or anyone else, and Greg found that charming. Willie did what Willie wanted to do, never showing anything but amusement at Greg's appearance and style. And of course what Willie always wanted was to make money and more money and more money.

"What are you looking at down there, Mister Goins? A mob scene, a riot? A crazed Governor? Let's join him by my wonderful window, Marva. Let's share the sunshine. What's going on?"

"Nothing to compare with your showing off for Marva," said Wilton. "Have a look."

The three of them, their faces close to the window, studied the crowd massed below. "Look over there. See? On the podium," said Greg pointing to a row of hooded men seated in front of the large wooden Cross. "I'll bet they're going to set it ablaze."

"Fire Department says no."

"They don't care about the Fire Department. They own the Fire Department. They own the Mayor and the Governor."

Marva wasn't sure just what she was supposed to be watching, and safe twelve stories above the Klan rally she was no longer very interested in it. Once you got over Greg Penn's size he was rather pretty, she thought. In a bizarre sort of way.

"Tell us what's catching your eye, Greg," said Wilton. "What could you possibly like about a Klan rally? You realize, I hope, they'd string you up in a heartbeat."

"True. Quite true. And worse things. Nonetheless, look at those robes, Marva. Just look at those robes. With an artist's eye.

The colors, the texture of the fabric, the folds." Holding her hand he glanced over at Wilton and mouthed *She's precious*. "Willie has always been a *stick-in-the-mud* type. I love him, I'd die for him, but that's just how he is. When we were at school...I'm embarrassed to say this was back before they had paved roads in Bloomington...Willie wore the same drab black suits. With a vest! Always with a vest. I think he came out of the womb with a vest. Needless to say, my dear, I was the one to add a little color, a little zest. O sometimes I wore a vest too. But not a black one. Never, never a black vest!"

Even from Greg's office, far above the Klansmen, the roar of the crowd was unmistakable. A piercing cry of victory, a shout of angry triumph. Greg pressed his face against the window. "O they've set it ablaze! I told you, Willie. I told you! Screw the Fire Department!" Flames leaped from the creosoted wooden Cross, while hooded figures grabbed their chairs and scurried to the front of the platform, putting space between the real threat of the burning Cross and their combustible robes and bodies. "O Marva, please forgive me for that outburst. Please."

Marva glanced uneasily at Wilton, not certain how he would take all this.

"Greg, between your bantering and the Klan's rabble rousing you're making Mrs. Goins uneasy."

Penn bit at his lower lip. "How could I? Of course I'm disturbing you with all my carrying on. Not to mention those morons beneath us. Please forgive me, Marva. I'm so stupid, so dense sometimes." He mouthed *Sorry* toward Wilton, and gently took her hand in his. "Did you know I spent several days in Aschburgh a while back? Not at your wedding. I mean you would remember that! I mean before your wedding. At Willie's place. *Your* home, I beg your pardon. It gave me an outstanding opportunity to pull together some ideas for our renovation. Really a new creation. I have some wonderful ideas I want to tell you about. But first I want you to see this."

As they were talking and glancing out the window at the burning Cross two beefy waiters from the *Wien, Wien*...in the building's lobby...busied themselves arranging the table and the food, gracefully working around the trio who were straining for a better look at the bacchanalia below.

"Professor Forsyth envies my view. He really does. But he'll never have it unless he commissions me to redesign his windows. I'd gladly take several of his paintings, eight or ten say, in lieu of cash, but he won't even consider it. The fact is his light is fine, as good as mine, and ultimately that's what he wanted…though it's northeast, not pure north…but fundamentally his view is fragmented. Marva, Willie, just look at the power of that green… the big shot's robes."

Greg pointed out one of the Klan leaders, swathed in forest green robes with a red Cross on his chest, who was walking across the platform toward the microphone. "The Cross…the fiery one and the one on his robe…it's way too much, I think you'll agree. Don't they call that *over the top*? But that green! Can you see me in trousers like that? What a powerful statement that would make. That would truly be something. Well, anyway…let's turn to our lunch. The boys have done a remarkable job serving it under decidedly abnormal circumstances."

"Sounds good to me," said Wilton, holding the chair for Marva. "We can talk some business over lunch. Let's just leave Forsyth and his fragmented windows out of it. You really need to let go of that issue. We'll be taking off for Bloomington as soon as we finish."

"Surely you'll stay until that horrible rally is over? I've got another meeting in an hour, but you're welcome to stay here until that mess downstairs is cleared up and the riffraff dispersed. I don't want you heading out into all that confusion. All that smoke and filth. Bloomington?"

"We've got reservations at the *IMU*," said Wilton. "We're to meet with Professor Steele in the morning. At his *University* studio. He's very impressed with several of Marva's watercolors."

"O Wilton," she said. "That's just a girl's work. From school."

"I'll have Bob drive you to Bloomington. In the *Rolls*. Now I took the liberty of ordering the *Schnitzel a la Holstein* for all of us. I do hope that's all right. I have a passion for everything *Deutsch*.

It's all so wholesome and sturdy. I just adore it. Forsyth shares that passion with me. O…I forgot. No more Forsyth."

"We have our *Ford* downstairs, Greg. But thanks for the offer."

Marva eyed the egg atop the breaded veal with some reservation. "It looks…remarkable. Wholesome and sturdy. Sort of like Hoosier cooking. Like a tenderloin. Except for the egg. I hope it's not runny."

"Not runny, dear," said Greg. "But not too firm, and certainly not hard. You'll love it. *Schnitzel* and tenderloin are worlds apart. Worlds apart."

Wilton lifted the egg off the veal and dropped it onto his *Deutsch Hash Browns*, broke the soft yolk and mixed it and the runny whites into his potatoes. "Down home cooking. I'm not sure this is really what the Viennese eat, Greg. Maybe a Hoosier variation."

"Dig in," said Greg, laughing. "I love it! I absolutely love it! The heavier the better. The only place that makes a better *Schnitzel a la Holstein* is the *Inn* at Batesville. You know the one, Willie? We eat there whenever Bob drives me to Cincinnati. My synagogue is being built downtown, Marva. Downtown Cincinnati."

He reached over and sliced open Marva's egg, grinning as the yellow yolk and runny whites flowed over the brown *schnitzel*. "Bob is my chauffeur. And one of my best friends. I can't stand the artificiality of social class partition. Enjoy, Marva. Enjoy. Frankly the *Union's* a little too *collegiate-collegiate* for my taste, if you know what I mean. But you'll find the rooms quite nice, and the staff polite if not elegant. Meeting with Steele is good, but you really ought to talk with Forsyth. Begging your pardon, Willie. But Forsyth's the one, not Steele. He's over at the *Herron Art Institute* right here in town. Perhaps on your way back. Do you think you'd like to study at the *University*, Marva?"

"I'm not sure. We want to hear what Professor Steele has to say. Wilton would prefer for me to study at home. But I don't know if that'll be possible."

"Of course it is," said Wilton. "The *University's* too far away. Try the *schnitzel*, Marva. Delicious."

"I doubt Steele would agree to travel up there, Willie," said Greg. "No offence, but you're rather remote. Willie likes to say Aschburgh's not the end of the world. But in fact it is."

"Sure he will. If I ask him."

"O Willie. Well, don't get me wrong. Professor Steele is a nice man and has done truly remarkable work in the style of Munich in the last century. In fact I own one of his better early sketches. *Bavarian Peasant.* Quite nice. Both he and Forsyth studied in Germany, you know, and have great regard and respect for Germanic culture. But, as I say, Steele's old now, and I'm afraid passé. Plus I very much doubt he's healthy enough to make that trip, Willie. No matter how you squeeze him."

"Do you have that sketch here?" Wilton asked. "So Marva can see it."

"Afraid not. Try a bite of the red cabbage, Marva. You'll fall in love with it. So earthy. The sketch is at my home. Did you know I'm planning to build a new place, Willie? Out by that reservoir Clarence Geist is putting in. It'll take a few years for things to be ready, but I'm in no rush. It's going to be beautiful out there. Isolated, but only half an hour from *Monument Circle.* You couldn't ask for anything better."

"Really? By the new reservoir?"

"The property cost me a bunch. A bundle of bunches! I mean the price was wildly inflated. Someone's making a handsome profit on that land," said Greg, fully aware Wilton owned the land surrounding the vast reservoir project.

"I'm sure it's worth every penny you paid and then some," said Wilton. "So you prefer Forsyth to Steele?"

"Steele has seen his best days. Plus he's not well...not at all. Forsyth is the man. But suit yourself. Do you think a fellow could get a rebate on some of the excess profit that's built into the price of the land out there, Willie? What I'd really like would be to add on the acre or so just to the north of the lot I'm building on. That land is useless right now because of the digging and construction, but later it would guarantee me total privacy on the reservoir. That would be so nice. For me and for my guests."

"I suppose friends can always work things out. Problems can be resolved with a little give and take on both sides," said Wilton. "As they say, everything has a price. It's just a matter of meeting that price, and lots of times the price is often not a question of money."

Marva nibbled on the veal, but the yolk and the whites of the egg smeared all over the meat revolted her, and the red cabbage was disgusting. "Will we have time to talk about our house? In Aschburgh?"

"You're absolutely right," said Greg. "Time is flying. *Tempis fugit* or something like that. Why don't we move over to the conference table and talk about your house, Marva? We can have our coffee there if we're very careful. It's going to be so, so beautiful. And will meet all your needs, my dear. Everything will be predicated on meeting your needs." As Marva moved to the conference table, Greg whispered to his old friend, "Willie, you're aware I don't normally do houses? There's not enough scope for my imagination, plus the return for all my time is negligible. I haven't bothered with a tiny job like this in at least ten years. Let alone barns."

"I'm aware. And I appreciate all that you're doing for us, Greg. The extra mile you're willing to go. It's worth acres to us if you understand what I mean. And perhaps we ought to think more seriously about Professor Forsyth. I appreciate that tip as well, buddy."

"He needs the money. He'll be more receptive than Steele to having to travel a bit. Now my efforts are all strictly a labor of love. I would never touch this job were it not for Marva. I mean that now. I really do. A wedding present for Marva. It's all for you, my dear. All for you. I can't get over how delightful and gorgeous she is, Willie."

2

With His Hat At A Rakish Angle
& A Cigarette Dangling

A pleasant breeze blew across the empty campus. High dark and heavy trees pressed against the walls of the *Franklin Library* where Professor Steele had his studio. Marva looked forward to meeting the great artist, though not at all confident she had any talent for drawing or painting. After the initial shock of the KKK rally, and overlooking the awful meal, it had been great fun spending time with a creative person like Greg Penn, and she wondered if a world renown artist like Professor Steele would be as flamboyant. Wilton implied not, telling her the Professor was an older man, gracious but set in his ways...even a bit unworldly. But Wilton had not fully prepared her for Mister Penn, so who could tell what she would find this morning.

Marva carefully selected a loose black wool dress, not too short, no jewelry, and simple shoes for walking. The morning sunshine was cool enough that she carried a light sweater. Deserted of students for the early Summer...its magnificent old trees full and rich, the campus was at its best...she found it exciting and promising despite the lack of students. For his part Wilton seemed bored with it all.

He wanted to take the *Ford* from the *Union* building to the Library to meet Steele. She probably should have done it his way, but it was a short walk and a lovely day...and how could she have foreseen the padlock on the door of the artist's studio after they climbed all the way to the top floor of the Library?

"They say he's over at *Kirkwood*. At the *Observatory*. Can you imagine? This is no way to conduct business."

"He's an older man, so possibly he just forgot our appointment. Is *Kirkwood* far?"

"Age is no excuse. And he's not that old, you know. We were very clear about 10 a.m. at his studio. I mean, Marva, I'm not being unreasonable about this. An appointment is an appointment. It was *his* idea to meet at the studio. Not mine for goodness sake. I would have preferred to meet in comfort at the *Memorial Union*.

The heat is going to build up...no matter what you and your sweater may think."

"Well, there's nothing to be done now but walk over to the telescope. It is a telescope? The *Observatory*?"

"*Kirkwood.* Yes. By *Dunn's Woods.* It's a ways though. Evidently he's painting. Out in the open."

"*Plein Air* it's called. That will be fascinating. Let's go."

"I'm not pleased about having you traipsing all over the campus after this silly old man. Are you comfortable? Why don't you let me carry that sweater? You're not going to need a sweater. Why don't I get the car?"

"O don't be silly. I'd rather walk, and my shoes are comfortable. It's a beautiful day, Wilton. Let's not spoil it with anger. We'll rest if I tire. But I'm not going to."

"I'm not angry. I'm just annoyed. This is no way to conduct business."

"He's an old man. Wilton, for goodness sake, he's in his seventies, maybe his eighties from what Greg said. And he's been ill. He's simply forgotten. How far is it to the *Observatory*?"

"Right over there. You can see it. The domed building."

"Well, my goodness, Wilton Fox Goins. Let's get a move on. It'll take us five minutes, no more. Mister Penn has some excellent ideas. You had obviously let him know we wanted renovation. About our house. Don't you think?"

"Perhaps. I'm comfortable with renovating...instead of a new house. But I have to consider his proposals carefully."

"He is a little different though."

"He works hard at it. Being different. He enjoys shocking people. Are you sure about feeling o.k? But don't get me wrong. Greg is very smart. Always has been. In an artistic way, if that's what architects are. Why would Steele want to paint outside this time of year? If he'd wait a couple of months everything would be pretty and getting cool. They're different...architects...at least Greg is. Practical but sensitive...visionary almost. It's a strange combination."

"His ideas for a nursery make a lot of sense. I really hadn't thought about it. As far along as I am you'd think I would have. And the kitchen. Updating it and glamorizing it that way. Momma will love it, though she'll say she hates it I bet. With all that storage space, and such a big work area."

"He's a good businessman. Not like Steele. He may dress peculiar, but he knows the value of a dollar. Greg never gives anything away without getting more in return. I respect that... but even so."

"The land? By the new reservoir? Will that be an obstacle?"

"It's expensive land he wants, Marva. Very expensive. Plus he's not giving up his fee. It's the land *plus* his fee. And his drawing for your studio? I mean that wasn't anywhere near up to standard. No more than a bunch of squiggles."

"He said he'd redo it. It's only a preliminary sketch. I thought you were a little harsh. I mean he is one of your oldest friends."

"And still is. And will continue to be. But this is a business matter, Marva. I told him what I wanted, and he simply ignored me and did what he wanted. That's not acceptable, and friendship has nothing to do with it. I'll be the one paying the bill."

"You know he doesn't do houses anymore. The fact is he's doing this especially for us. For you really. I think he's being very gracious."

"Gracious? What with the land *plus* his fee he'll end up clearing more than enough to buy himself a new set of tires for his precious *Rolls Royce*."

Fifty yards ahead of them two old men were gesturing before a small canvas on a *plein air* easel. The smaller man was not much taller than Greg Penn though his movements suggested strength and toughness. His hat was set at a rakish angle and a cigarette dangled from his lips as he poked his finger aggressively toward the face of his distinguished looking companion who held a palette and a small paint brush.

"That's Professor Steele in the long top coat with the scarf," said Wilton. "We'll see what's going on. He must be sweltering."

As Wilton and Marva approached, the two men stopped their animated discussion and turned in apparent surprise. The small man, his cigarette now in his hand, took several strides toward them and held up his other hand, signaling them to stop. "This is the Summer vacation. For your information the *University* is shut down. What are you doing here? Can't you see Professor Steele is busy? Do we have to put up a sign? Post a guard? Go away!"

Wilton easily stepped around him, leaving Marva to confront the angry little fellow. The taller painter, though really only of average height, was inappropriately if formally attired in black fedora, long black top coat over a black suit, heavy starched white shirt, winged collar and broad black tie...with a heavy scarf looped about his throat against some imagined chill. As Wilton came closer he realized how frail the old man was and how badly his left hand shook. Despite what he had been told it was clear the heart attack had taken a heavy toll.

"Professor Steele. Our appointment, sir?"

The old man stared at him, embarrassed by his inability to remember. "I...."

"Wilton Goins, sir. We had a ten o'clock appointment. At your studio. We spoke just last week."

"I must have forgotten to jot it down. I'm needing to do that more and more now. Goins? Do I have that right? Were you a student of mine?"

"Leave the Professor alone, you goddamn idiot!" shouted the short man, shoving himself between them and scattering ashes on Wilton's suit. "I'll get the police if I have to. Who the hell do you think you are?"

Marva stood off to the side twisting a tiny embroidered handkerchief. "Wilton, perhaps...."

The problem with Steele was obvious, thought Wilton. Greg was right, the grand old man was finished and would be of no use to them. But he rather liked this feisty banty rooster. He brushed the ashes from his jacket, and extended his hand to the little man who ignored it. "I'm Wilton Goins of the *Aschburgh Bank and Trust.* Professor Steele and I had an appointment this morning, but it seems to have skipped his mind in the press of business."

"The *press of business* my ass! You don't bother a painter when he's working. Are you an idiot?"

"Mister Goins, the banker?" said Steele. "How could I forget? You've been so helpful in the past. We were to discuss the new studios, wasn't that it? More and more I'm forgetting. Names and dates, sometimes even faces."

"The financing for the construction, sir. Among other things. Actually the financing is in place. President Bryan and I have taken care of that, so it needn't concern you. And the studios will be well underway within the year. May I present my wife, Mrs. Goins. Marva is quite an accomplished water-colorist and has been looking forward to meeting you."

Steele took a couple of steps toward Marva, moving with difficulty. The short man, clearly still annoyed by this interruption, went to take his arm, but Steele waved him off. "Mrs. Goins, my pleasure. I am Professor Theodore Steele. It appears my failing memory has caused you inconvenience. I am so sorry. A water-colorist? Perhaps you brought some of your work with you?"

Marva wanted to protect him, and took his hand in part to steady him. Theodore Steele seemed from an earlier age, ill prepared to deal with Wilton or this angry little man. "Mister Goins is exaggerating about my water-colors. Really. And you've caused me no inconvenience. The campus is so lovely. It's my first time here."

The short fellow smiled, his cigarette back in the corner of his mouth. "Lovely? Young lady, look around you. Open your eyes if you're supposed to be a painter. Without students the place is depressing. It's almost like Winter's on the way. No life. No life at all."

"Sir! Watch your tone when you speak to my wife."

"That's uncalled for, Forsyth," said Steele. "It's a beautiful day. Introduce yourself to these good people."

"I'm not a banker, that's for sure. William Forsyth. *Professor* William Forsyth of the *Herron Institute of Art*. Professor Steele was at work when you interrupted him. I hope you realize that. The creative process is not the same as money grubbing."

"All this tough male talk is not for you, my dear," Steele whispered to Marva, as she continued to hold his trembling hand. He led her over to the easel and the small canvas. "I've done the

Observatory before. Some fine work I think. But never under these circumstances. A little chilly...for me. I'm recovering, you see. From a little episode. And I wanted to see how it would go. I'm afraid Bill doesn't care much for it. But I've only just begun. It's barely a sketch at this point."

The dome of the Observatory was fairly well defined, but the rest of the canvas looked to Marva little more than smudges. "It's lovely."

"No it's not," said William Forsyth. He and Wilton were standing a short way off, their attention focused on the old man and the young woman. "In any event, painting needs to be a lot more than *lovely*. It's no good. As it stand now, even as a beginning, I can tell you, Steele, it's no good."

"Now, now, Bill. You're in one of your moods when nothing's any good. I'm afraid you're going to frighten Mrs. Goins."

William Forsyth pushed his hat to the back of his head and removed his rimless glasses to clean them with a handkerchief. He stepped away from Wilton Goins and joined Marva and Steele in front of the canvas. "Professor Steele has done this scene before, young lady. But with verve, with a power punch. This on the other hand," pointing to the canvas, "This has a long way to go, and I'm not sure it'll ever get there. There's no punch, no fire. It may be an early sketch, but I still expect to see some fire. Do you grasp what I'm getting at?" he asked Marva. "And Steele, if you ask my opinion I'm going to give it. Let's be clear. No beating around the bush. Right now this canvas is a mess, it's hopeless. Sorry, but that's all I can say on the matter."

Steele smiled at Marva. "Well, I didn't have to ask him, did I, my dear? Have you met Professor William Forsyth? One of the foremost painters and teachers of art in the entire world. I believe that's a fair assessment."

Marva nodded at the little man. Forsyth intimidated her, seemingly always ready to pick a fight. Still she could see that Professor Steele took him very seriously and had great affection for him.

"I'm afraid as usual you're right, Bill. Let's call it a morning. I'll try again tomorrow. I must honor my commitment to Mister

Goins. I'm afraid I've let him down this morning. He's been a big help to us in the past, Bill. A big help. And now he's arranged for the new studios. Set it all up with President Bryan. Can you imagine?"

"Money talks."

Steele placed his arm on Forsyth's back and moved him away from Wilton and Marva who were looking at the canvas. He leaned down to whisper in the smaller man's ear. "Of course it does, you goddamn fool. You are going to need this man more than I will, so cultivate him. Control yourself and cultivate him."

"So this is just a beginning, Professor?" asked Wilton. "Sometimes it's difficult for me to see where a sketch is heading. Mrs. Goins and I were just discussing that deficiency of mine. We've been spending some time with Gregory Penn, the architect, and he's provided some preliminary architectural sketches that we're having a tough time interpreting."

"Penn!" shouted Forsyth. "You know that pipsqueak? He ought to be locked up in an asylum."

"You know better than that, Bill. Gregory Penn's an outstanding architect," said Steele as he placed several brushes back in his painter's box. "Different but nonetheless outstanding. And well respected by his peers."

"If he were a real artist he'd help with the lighting in my studio. Instead he treats it like a joke."

"He expects to be paid, Bill. Just like we do."

"Don't believe it. It has nothing to do with money. The man likes to torment people. It's the way he handles his own inadequacy."

Pointing to Steele's canvas Marva said, "It's really only a beginning. I think it's too early to judge it. Don't you think that so often the beginning is the really difficult part?"

"Yes it is, dear. A beginning. And difficult to assess. And who knows, perhaps an end as well. Mister Goins, Bill will take the canvas and my paints and brushes. If you would be so good as to carry the easel? Be careful not to get paint on your clothes. My automobile is just off to the left there. Bill will drive us back to my studio. Mrs. Goins and I will lead the way, walking slowly. Very slowly, my dear."

3
Tea, Mormons & Holy Rollers

There could be no doubt that Wilton Goins was God's man, and Belva Ainsley had come to see his plan was all for the best. An expression of God's will. That was the point. Her son-in-law wanted these changes, believing them to be the path to the future for their town and their Church…as well as for their family. And they were in fact one family now. With Wilton at the head.

Confused and depressed as he was, her Olin certainly wasn't providing any leadership. *Ephesians 5* might as well not exist as far as he was concerned. It would be a miracle if he could even put out a crop this year. There really was no choice other than to follow Wilton's lead. Belva, having settled these matters for herself, was now prepared to step out in faith.

Encouraging the bond between Regina and Reverend Poston was one of the things on which Wilton smiled, though at first it had really been Belva's idea and he had merely approved. Wilton had plans for a great Church to develop in Tecumseh County… *The First Community Church of Indiana*…and having Regina in place in the parsonage to encourage the process would be a tremendous advantage. The thing to do, he told Belva, was to guide these local changes so they benefited the Ainsleys, Goins and Winslows and at the same time fulfilled the Lord's plan.

Belva saw her role as providing an ever deepening faith to the inevitable process of change. Faith wasn't some abstraction for her, and in her experience very few ministers had a good grasp of it. Faith was first and foremost a matter of family, grounded on the security of the hearth. If God's foundation of family was lacking, faith would fail to grow. But a strong family, Biblically nurtured, provided a firm base upon which to step out in trust. Which was why God created family in the first place. Abram would never have made his faith journey of fifteen hundred miles if he had not been able to bring his entire family along. Joshua would never have had faith to conquer Canaan without the family he boasted of at the end of his book.

Faith produced change, but all the same, faith was based upon a family structure rooted in the past. Belva liked that Wilton was very clear on that score... family was critical for the changes ahead of them, though at times the complexity of the whole process caused her great confusion. Changes in the Church, in Aschburgh and Tecumseh County, in their life-style and even in their family...at times it was hard to accept. But when she considered that Olin was no longer of any help to her, no longer a husband, that for all practical purposes she was alone, Wilton's direction was indispensable.

And in Wilton's mind the uniting of Regina and the Reverend Poston was useful if God's plan for all of them was to be realized. In any event, the marriage would be a wonderful thing. Good for the family and good for Regina. The fact was there were very few young men available to her niece. Other than a couple of the Birdsalls. And that was really no choice at all.

And difficult as some of these changes might be for her and for others in the community, Wilton would see that they came to pass. That was the reality. Her son-in-law always got what he wanted. Belva struggled at first...it seemed so drastic... but now she could see the changes would work for the best. *All things work together for good to them that love God, to them who are the called according to his purpose.* And the Winslows, Ainsleys and Goins had been among the *called* for generations upon generations.

That her son-in-law did in fact walk with God was clear. Like the renaming of the streets and the peculiar *Ainsley-Goins* street signs. What he called their *Family Cross*. It was easy to misunderstand that, to think there was a process of puffing-up going on there. And people in town might smile about the signs when Wilton wasn't around, but everyone knew the *Bank* was on the corner of *Ainsley & Goins*. And in their hearts everyone knew it was the will of God.

Belva sat close by the fire while Reverend Poston and her niece Regina sat together on the sofa, sipping tea. Regina was a lovely girl. A good and faithful girl. She wore the holiness dress so well, and her little starched white cap set off her light hair brilliantly. Hopefully Regina's example would help Marva to come around where she could see the beauty of some of the old ways. No matter what Wilton thought, holiness dress was worth keeping.

But if Regina was a delight, Reverend Poston was another matter altogether. The least the young man could have done for this special meeting was polish his shoes. Dirty scuffed shoes, worn with a black suit, jumped out to the eye. Holiness didn't mean you had to be sloppy. That Regina fancied him had to be a sign of the wondrous working of God's grace.

The acne flowing over his face and neck was not his fault, of course, but his mother was certainly to be blamed for allowing so much ugliness to come upon him. There was neglect in that home without a doubt. Belva recalled how carefully she had smoothed back Marva's ears, how much effort had gone into shaping her daughter's infant head. And she had never hesitated to go over to the Winslows to be sure the same attention was given to Regina's features. Ugliness in a child reflected a lack of love and dedication in the mother and it reflected poorly on the entire family.

"I enjoyed your sermon last Sunday, Jeremy," said Regina. "It's true that drinking is the great sin of our time. Don't you think, Aunt Belva? I thought Jeremy made that point so forcefully."

"I put a lot of effort into that sermon. Tying the temperance theme into the story of Paul's salvation was unusual, but I think very pertinent. A great man once said, *Tea is the drink that refreshes without inebriating.* To my mind that's still true."

"You know so many things. Jeremy's thinking about studying for an advanced degree at the *Holiness Institute.*"

"In Switzerland County?"

"Quercus Grove."

"Not right away I hope," said Belva. "There's work to be done right here in Aschburgh, and I know for a fact Mister Goins is counting on having the Reverend's leadership. Advanced study may be for later. After you settle down and have a family, Reverend."

"Jeremy and I have been thinking about that too," said Regina, squeezing the minister's hand and causing his face to turn redder than usual.

Belva sensed she hadn't been paying enough attention to what had evidently been going on. But whether she was up to date or not, apparently the process was heading in the right direction. Wilton would be well pleased.

"I've started reading Doctor Charles Carter's little book on some of the odd groups popping up all over the place. *Gibberish, Tongue-Talking And Assorted Cultisms.* I think it's absurd the *Mormons* won't even drink weak tea. Have you heard that, Reverend?"

"I'm afraid I don't know much about their theology, Mrs. Ainsley. Do you know, Regina?"

"No. No, not at all. I was wanting to show Jeremy the old gazebo, Aunt Belva. I think this would be a good time. He and I can head up there. There's no need for you to bother, and we won't stay too long. I just want him to see it."

"It's too hot and dusty, dear."

"I agree. I think it's too warm for you to be going outside," said Jeremy. "We can see it another time. The *Mormons* are a cult though, Mrs. Ainsley. Of that I am certain. Much like the *Holy Rollers.*"

"O, Jeremy. The sun is nice, and I'd like for you to see the gazebo."

"Is there actually a group with that name? You'd think they could come up with something a little more dignified than *Holy Rollers*. It's all so strange to me," Belva murmured, more to herself than to the young people. "You'd think Scripture wasn't perfectly clear with all these wild groups popping up. It used to be just *Methodists* and various types of *Baptists*. But I'm sure Doctor Carter said it's caffeine the *Mormons* choose to take exception to. In both coffee and tea. Can you imagine? We've been drinking tea and coffee for generations. I suppose they drink lemonade or pop. It seems an odd foundation for a religion, if you ask me."

Regina glared at her aunt, and squeezed Jeremy's hand. "Let's go outside for just a bit."

"I've always thought *Bible Baptist Holiness* was the clearest presentation of Gospel truth," said the Reverend. "For a precise exposition of God's will there's nothing to compare with the *Bible Baptist* insight."

"Mister Goins told me some of the coloreds in Giantown practice this *Holy Rollerism*. I suppose whatever it is it meets their needs. Are you comfortable in the parsonage, Reverend? The Hoheimers didn't take very good care of it, I'm afraid. What you need there is a feminine touch to make it more comfortable."

"Aunt Belva!"

"Yes, Mam. My mother has provided some nice items to make it more homey. But I'm quite happy there. I've closed off most of the rooms during last Winter, and I bought a sharp knife for the kitchen yesterday."

"Perhaps Regina could help you fix things up a bit. You could do that, dear, couldn't you?"

"I suppose, Aunt Belva."

"By the way, Reverend, Mister Goins asked me to check with you about the increase to your salary. He wants to be sure the treasurer is continuing to give you the extra money. He told me he had it increased significantly. That's so like Wilton. To just go and do it. No fuss, no beating around the bush, just go and do it. Is the extra money helping?"

"Aunt Belva, this is not the time...."

"Very much. I'm very grateful to the Church."

"It's Mister Goins you want to thank, not the Church. He's always thinking ahead for the Church. He just mentioned to me that some people in town have commented that our old name, *Bible Baptist Holiness,* sounds rather like a cult. Like *Holy Rollerism* or *Mormon.* He feels it's time to change the name of the Church. Of course I've grown up with the name, but I think he may have a point. Don't you? He'd like for us to change to *First Community Church of Indiana.*"

"Jeremy, I'm really feeling a need for some air. Perhaps if we took a short walk around the house?"

"But we're *Baptists.* Just because some people--"

"And always will be *Baptists.* It's just a name change. Don't you agree, Regina? Mister Goins only asks that you think about the change before we actually adopt our new name."

"But he intends to change it?"

"Evidently. I think he's pretty much done it. When Mister Goins makes up his mind, especially when God has spoken to him, there's really no way to change him. And he's always right. Just like when he increased your salary. Would you both like some more tea?"

"I'm going outside for some air." Regina got up and went to the door. "It's too stuffy in here."

"Regina!"

"I think I'd better go with her, Mam," said Jeremy, carefully putting down his tea. "I'll make sure she's all right and doesn't get too much sun."

4

The Power Of Perfect Placement & The Theory Of The Large Blobs

Wilton Goins leaned the easel against the wall of the stairwell, and grasped Professor Steele under the arm to steady him for the final steps up to the studio door. Once at the door he backed off as the old artist insisted on opening the padlock unassisted.

"Sticking you up here practically on the roof is a travesty, Steele. You ought not to put up with it." William Forsyth ground out his cigarette under his shoe. He removed his hat and wiped the sweat from his brow. "It shows how the Trustees and President Bryan have contempt for great artists. They'd never put students up here. Let alone other faculty. Only artists. Imagine if there was a fire! For Christ's sake, Steele! You'd never be able to get your work out."

"It's really an excellent place for a studio," Steele said to Marva. "Superb light. And nice and quiet. Try to be patient, Bill. Remember that damp barn we used for a studio in Schleissheim? Now that *was* a travesty. And we were delighted with it, weren't we?"

"May I help, Professor?" Without waiting for the old man to respond Marva guided his shaking hands to slip the key into the padlock.

"Schleissheim was Germany. In the last century, damn it. This is America. Indiana, for Christ's sake. You're the foremost painter in America."

"Don't forget yourself, Bill. When you get to ranking. You're right up there. And then again maybe Otto Stark is top dog. What would you think of that? Don't be too severe. Remember Otto's not doing very well from what I hear."

"Don't be ridiculous. We're all going to die eventually. Stark's no different. Aside from myself, in my best work, you've always been top man in America. Everyone knows that."

Once out of the stairwell and inside the studio Marva found herself agreeing with Professor Steele. It was charming in an old-fashioned way. Late morning sun poured in through the large windows onto a sitting room carefully furnished with an abundance of comfortable arm chairs, tables and a large sofa. Plants were scattered around and Oriental rugs covered the floor, except for the small section where the Professor's easel stood. She supposed all his indoor painting took place in that corner. As Wilton and Professor Forsyth set the brushes and paints in the proper spots, Marva walked about the room and fingered several brightly colored woven pieces hanging on the walls.

"Those are from Selma's collection, my dear. Very old woven scarves. Selma also takes care of the plants. I'd never remember. Do you like plants, Mrs. Goins?"

"Selma?"

"Mrs. Steele," said Forsyth. "A lovely lady. But I must say, Steele, every time I'm here it seems Selma's taken a bit more of your painting space for some new jimjam she's found at a local sale."

"That's the wrong word, Bill. You know that perfectly well. You just like the sound of it."

While Marva and Wilton looked around the studio Forsyth flopped onto the sofa and stretched out his short legs. "Ought to be. Actually I'm pretty sure it is. *Jimjam's* a good American word."

"*Gewgaw* is the one you're searching for. *Jimjam* has to do with palsy, the shakes, things like that. Mrs. Steele has done all the decorating for me, Mister Goins. I often have students and faculty here of a Sunday afternoon. For tea and talk. Delightful times. Hasn't she done a masterful job, my dear?"

"Simply gorgeous. This is very, very nice, Professor. Don't you think, Wilton?"

"Very. I'll bring the easel in."

William Forsyth, his hat now back firmly in place at the preferred angle, took the easel from Wilton and set it against the wall in the painting area. "*Gewgaw*? You're sure about that? I'll bet this area has been cut down by a third since I was last here. We could use a little ventilation, don't you think? Frankly, Steele, if you don't keep a close eye on Selma she'll toss your easel. Come to think of it, aren't *jim-jams* pajamas? I'll get a couple of windows open. Grab a couple of sticks from over there, Goins. It is Goins isn't it? To prop open these old windows. We used to know some Goins over toward Valparaiso. Not very nice people."

Wilton smiled as he stooped to pick up the sticks. "Sounds like my cousin Hobart's family." He liked the little man and was amused at the way Forsyth scurried about getting everything set up. "Must be a challenge in the Winter to heat this place with all these old windows."

"That's one of the reasons I prefer my smaller panes to the monstrosity your friend Penn has in his place. That's strictly a British usage though, isn't it? For pajamas. It costs him a fortune to heat in the Winter."

"All studios have that problem," said Steele. "Greg Penn tells me his window's really quite economical. Though in my opinion for an American it's peculiar. A bit pretentious."

"Penn would say that. But this one's impossible to heat too," said Forsyth. "And then the *University* shuts down the steam heat the first day of April! Do it every year. Or when Easter vacation starts. Whichever comes first. Got to save some coal. Doesn't matter what the temperature is. That's why we got him this old pot-belly. But then the great man here didn't bother to clean it and almost asphyxiated everyone this Winter. Just coming back from heart problems and they stick him up here. You think you'd ever get William Lowe Bryan up these stairs, Steele?"

"We're in the Summer, Bill. Let's not worry about Winter heating. Why would Doctor Bryan be trudging up these stairs? The man has better things to do, Bill. The President is the reason I have this position at the University. And this studio for that matter. He's been very good to me. And he's never flinched from spending for the arts. Like the new studios Mister Goins is financing."

"Damned bunch of ingrates," said Forsyth to no one in particular. "Greatest painter of our time crammed up in an ice cold attic every Winter."

"I'm afraid I can't offer you any refreshments. Selma brings them in special for our Sunday gatherings. I wish you both could be here for one of them. The students here are so gifted. And polite. But do sit down, and let's make ourselves comfortable. Bill, please, please. You'll get your suit filthy scurrying around. Alice will never forgive me if you've managed to ruin your pants. You know she'll blame me. Bill can do no wrong in Alice's eyes. Mrs. Forsyth. A charming lady."

"Alice has enough concern with the girls. She doesn't need to worry about my trousers."

"That's another one. *Trousers*. I'm sure that's a British usage. Americans say *pants*, don't we?"

"Trousers, pants, who gives a damn. All Alice cares about is that I get back in time for supper. She's gotten very particular about that. Personally I'd rather stay here and go back tomorrow. But...once a fellow gets married he loses control of his own destiny."

"Well, you're always welcome to stay at our cottage, Bill, but if you have to return to Indianapolis today perhaps you could drive back with Mister and Mrs. Goins. You will be heading that way, sir?"

"Yes, we'd be delighted. We thought of stopping at St. Elmo's for a bite. Would you honor us with your presence, Professor Forsyth? Our treat, of course."

"St. Elmo's? It'd be a pleasure. Of course I'll need to let Alice know. Not to ruin her plans."

"O yes," said Marva. "That would be delightful. I love their baked potato."

"Do you live in the City, Professor?"

"Used to, but now we're off to the east a bit. Irvington. Just another village on the *National Road*. Out in the country and fresh air, where a man can breathe and do a bit of painting as well. I'd appreciate the lift. Tell me, Steele, this meeting of yours today, would it be all right if I hung around? It's o.k. to say *No*. No hurt feelings. I'm not the sensitive type."

"We'd love to have you stay," said Steele. "Wouldn't we?"

"Marva is interested in studying painting," said Wilton. "Becoming an artist."

"O not an artist, Wilton. Don't exaggerate. I've only done a couple of small things. In school."

Wilton was bored with Steele, whom he considered an ancient fusspot. Forsyth would be a more interesting teacher for Marva. But of course Steele had to be deferred to. "Mrs. Goins is always too modest, Professor Steele. She's quite talented. She and I would appreciate your assistance in arranging a program of private study. Of course we would need for her teacher to travel up to Tecumseh County on a regular basis. Staying over with us on those regular visits. In comfort of course."

"Mister Goins, you've been so helpful to me over the years. I only wished--"

"Travel up Tecumseh! Are you out of your mind, Goins? Steele has been seriously ill, and he's in no condition--"

"Perhaps you'd let Professor Steele speak for himself? The travel would be difficult, I recognize that. But it's up to Professor Steele to evaluate how taxing it would be for him."

"Bill, Bill, Bill. It's all right." Steele got up from his chair with some difficulty, and stood beside Forsyth with his hand on his friend's shoulder. "Professor Forsyth is sometimes a bit over-protective of me. But I'm sorry to say he's correct this time. My health is not what it ought to be, and I'm afraid travel is out of the question."

"You're certain?" asked Wilton. "I would provide private transportation, and of course you would be well compensated. I realize it's a long trip, and of course our climate is a bit rougher than it is down here, but I had hoped...well, I suppose a fellow can't have everything he wants."

Since they had arrived in Bloomington last night Marva had misgivings about Wilton's notion that she should study in Aschburgh. It would be exciting to live on the Bloomington campus. Even with the students gone for the early Summer she sensed the excitement present at *Indiana* since the end of the *War*.

New buildings were going up all over the campus, and President Bryan was well known for hiring famous artists and scientists. To be on this campus would be thrilling, so unlike the *Holiness Seminary*. Unfortunately she was expecting. And Wilton would insist on having her at home in Aschburgh. Actually he would insist on that even if she weren't pregnant. No matter what she wanted painting would have to be at home in the studio Greg Penn was planning, and now that she'd seen how old these great artists were it seemed unlikely she would ever get to study with either of them.

"Wilton, do you think it would be possible--"

"That's so kind of you, Mister Goins," said Steele. "But I'm afraid it's out of the question. My health simply will not allow it. I wish my situation were different, but unfortunately that's how it is."

"I'm sorry as well, sir." Wilton shrugged in resignation. "But Professor Forsyth, your health is good and you're fairly close to the *Inter-Urban*? Am I right? It's a direct shot up to Aschburgh." He leaned forward and smiled at Forsyth. "An hour, hour and a quarter at most and you'd be right at our door."

"Wilton--"

"One second, dear."

"Bill used to ride it up to Fort Wayne to teach. All the time. Didn't you?"

"And I stopped teaching up there because of the traveling. You can be sure I'm not about to get myself into that again."

Wilton took a pad and pencil from his breast pocket and rapidly sketched a line labeling one end *Indianapolis* and *Fort Wayne* the other. He held it up for everyone to see, and then making an X in the middle of the line declared, "*Aschburgh*. I can see where going all the way up to Fort Wayne would be too much for anyone. But Aschburgh's no ways near Fort Wayne. It's not the same thing at all, Professor Forsyth. Aschburgh's not the end of the world.

"You'd be surprised, sir, how easily problems like this can be worked out. There's nothing that can't be solved, no difficulty that can't be overcome. It's merely a matter of putting our minds and our wills to work."

"Wilton, do you think it would be possible for me to study down here? Maybe if there's a later Summer semester."

"Please, Marva."

"Absolutely impossible!" said Forsyth. He walked to the window and stared out at the trees. "I have too many responsibilities at the *Heron Art Institute*. In Indianapolis."

"Professor, I don't question that. A mind and a gift like yours is always going to be in demand. But believe me things can always be worked out if we're willing. Would you do me a great favor?

Indulge me by not shutting the door? I'm not asking much. Just be willing to listen to me and to think about what I have to say. We can talk more later on. Believe me I'm more than willing to hear you out, to compromise, to bend over backwards if that's what it takes. Just leave the door open for now."

"Sounds reasonable, Bill," said Steele. "There's no commitment on your part, and to be frank, Mister Goins has been very helpful and generous to me in the past. I owe him a great deal. A great deal."

Forsyth continued staring out the window, an unlit cigarette dangling from his lips. "I have studied with the masters and have progressed from there, Mister Goins. Over forty years of work and thought. Frankly I'm not a teacher for a beginner." He turned back to the room, and looked to Marva. "Please don't take offence, Mrs. Goins. Everyone has to start someplace. It's just that I'm not a teacher for starting out."

"I understand," said Marva. "Have you really been an artist for forty years? That humbles me. I was wondering about eventually studying here on the campus. It might be more appropriate."

"Forty-eight years is more like it."

"Give us a chance, Professor," said Wilton. "For reasons of health Mrs. Goins cannot stay down here to study. Plus I need her by my side in Aschburgh. But I can promise you she will prove a diligent and gifted student. And your services will be greatly respected and very well compensated."

Steele, who could see some of the funding he needed evaporating if Forsyth continued to be stubborn, turned to his old friend. "Light your cigarette, Bill. Light it for goodness sake. I hate to see you just sucking on that thing. Only be careful about ashes on Selma's carpets. Perhaps you'd share some of your thoughts on painting? I'm sure the Goins would like to hear that. It'll help us all to evaluate. Use that tin over there for your ashes."

"Please," said Wilton. "Some of your thoughts on art... perhaps the special teaching techniques you've developed over the years. Your philosophy, as it were."

"I do need a teacher," said Marva who could see the option of studying down here was no option. "Perhaps you could recommend someone."

"Bill is the best teacher around. No one else comes close," said Steele. "Are you comfortable, my dear? The best in America as far as I'm concerned. There is another good fellow in New York City. We saw him last year. When Selma and I were out East. Bill, I can't remember his name. This is so frustrating."

"Henri," said Forsyth. "He's good but slightly over-rated in my opinion."

"William?" asked Steele.

"Robert. Robert Henri," said Forsyth. "He writes well, but writing's not teaching. The man gets a fortune for each of his paintings, and I've never been able to figure that out."

"I have a sense no one can hold a candle to you when it comes to either painting or teaching," said Wilton. "Professor Steele excepted, of course."

"I'm recognized as one of the best certainly," said Forsyth. "Not to brag on myself, but no one's better on composition, that's for sure."

Wilton repressed a grin. "Professor, please be open to us. I believe you're the man we need."

"Come on, Bill," said Steele. "Be a good fellow."

"We'll leave the door open. Nothing more than that," said Forsyth.

Like most of the painters working in the Midwest Forsyth had a family to support and had never known anything approaching financial security. Working with Mrs. Goins once or twice a week could make a big difference, but the thought of the time wasted traveling and the days away from his family depressed him. "But I can assure you, Goins, much as I like you and your dear wife, the door will eventually be shut. Firmly."

The little man lit another cigarette and began pacing the studio, scattering ashes about him on Selma's rugs. "Painting is the most serious of the arts. You need to realize that first off, Mrs. Goins. Before you ever commit yourself to the life of an artist. We're not speaking here of a pastime for dilettantes. Not everyone would agree with me of course, but that's the way it is." He paused and tugged at the brim of his hat while his audience of three watched him attentively. "Let's be clear I am not traveling off to the boondocks. I am merely sharing a few of my ideas. Period."

"Understood. But please don't shut the door."

"First of all then, Marva, Mister Goins, anyone who enters into a course of study with me must make a total commitment. I'm serious about that now. No half-ways. I've tossed more than one from my classes. Let's be very clear on that."

"Fair enough."

"Now, Mrs. Goins...Marva if I may...do you grasp the difference between a desire to be a painter and the desire to paint? There's no relationship between the one and the other."

"Professor?"

"Be clear, Bill, be clear," said Steele. "Strive for clarity."

"Everyone...everyone!...at one point or other wants to be a painter. To live the artist's life. Free and full of drama, loaded with adulation. The problem is it's not like that at all. It's plain and simple hard work. Hours and hours of drudgery, and then some half baked lout tells you your work is no good. Laughs at you and tells you you've wasted your time. Can you imagine? That never happens to a banker, does it Mister Goins?"

"I'm listening, sir."

"Some critic mocks you, but you have to go ahead and paint anyway because you love to paint. You live to paint. It doesn't matter what anyone says, you are a painter. Do you see what I'm getting at here?"

Marva leaned forward in her chair, watching him intently. As he talked about his art he seemed to fill with energy. She imagined she was seeing him as he was at his easel. "I think so, but I'm not sure. I've done nothing yet, but I know I want to paint. I think I've always wanted to paint. But it's not the only thing I want. I want a family too. I want children. I want a home. But I do want to paint."

"Children? Yes, children are fine. I've three. All girls," said Forsyth, removing his rimless glasses and cleaning them carefully with his handkerchief. "Forget being a *painter*, Marva. Put it out of your mind. That's for the dilettantes. Being a *painter* is nothing. Trash! Am I right Professor Steele? Am I on to something here?"

"You need to clarify, Bill. Be more precise. In your enthusiasm you sometimes make yourself difficult to understand."

"The *act of painting* is what you want. The pure *act of painting*, the business of creating color and shape, that's what you want. Messy, smelly. Paint. That's the real stuff. If you have the gift then that's what you want. Paint and paint and paint."

Steele smiled and tapped Wilton on the knee. "He's a master, a true master. Bill, you always manage to make it sound like the ministry, like going into a monastery, taking vows."

"*Priesthood*. That's for sure. That's precisely what it is. Now mind you, Mister and Mrs. Goins, I've no interest in religion. I don't get into that business. Mine is the *priesthood of painting*."

"But how would I even begin? I mean--"

"Exactly the point," said Steele. "I think you need to be more precise, Bill. Spell things out more clearly."

"Perhaps," said Wilton, "But I think we're getting a very good sense. I believe you're the man we're looking for, Forsyth. And I think we can come to a very comfortable accommodation."

"I tell my students...and mind you, Mister Goins, I am not traveling outside my area...don't be confused because I'm sharing ideas with you...I tell my students to be certain they are of the priesthood of painting. Be certain of that as though it were life itself. For it is. It is. But having established that...and be advised it will take time...you must be certain...then with brush in hand focus on what I have called the *Power of Perfect Placement*."

"O my goodness, Bill. Dear goodness, please go easy on all that philosophy business or you'll scare Mister and Mrs. Goins off," said Steele. "My dear, painting is achieved with a brush not a philosophy. Don't let him frighten you."

"O no," said Marva, sensing that she liked this little man. He really was a banty rooster. "I realize I know nothing. But I would like to learn. I want to paint... that much I know for sure."

"Well, there you have it," said Wilton.

"Marva, the *Power of Perfect Placement* is where you must place your focus."

"For goodness sake, Bill, Mrs. Goins needs to learn how to hold a brush." Steele was accustomed to his friend's bluster and philosophizing, and it amused him to yank Forsyth's feet back to earth. At the same time he was worried Forsyth was going to offend Wilton and drive him away. The Art Department needed the man's know-how, not to mention his money. "I always begin my instruction with the brush and its bristles, while Professor Forsyth prefers the *Great Idea* as his starting point."

"We both end up with the painting though. And that's the point, isn't it, Steele?"

"*The Power of Perfect Placement*?" Marva looked at him intently. "What exactly does that mean?"

"Getting it right the first time. No half baked, stumbling efforts ever survive. Getting it right. The first time and every time. Precision in the placement of paint. In time you'll see, Marva. Excuse me," said Forsyth, lighting another cigarette.

"You smoke a great deal," said Wilton. "Mrs. Goins isn't used to that I'm afraid."

Ignoring him, Forsyth puffed deeply and went on. "I believe in time you'll see it exactly, Marva. Now I'm not making any commitments here, Goins. But for the moment, just for purposes of demonstration, think of a portrait of Mister Goins, let us say. Any such painting starts with what I prefer to call *Large Blobs*."

"Now you've lost everyone for sure, Bill," said Steele. "Why must you insist on using this inflammatory language?"

"It's good American talk. *Large Blobs*. You immediately get what I'm saying. Straight-shooting, nothing fancy. American. Large areas of color. There's your background. Here's your major focus. His nose will come later. Stop fretting about the nose. There's your shoulders. There's your head. Frankly, Steele, I'm pretty sure *jimjam* is the word. *Gewgaw* doesn't sound right to my ear. You can be sure I'll look it up when I get home. Are you getting my point, Marva? Proceed with the *Power of Perfect*

Placement. **Get your large blobs in place. In the *right* place. Once you get these essentials you'll be able to move forward."**

   "*Jimjam* suggests a drinking problem. *Gewgaw* is correct. You go ahead and look it up if you like. *Gewgaw* is the word."

CHAPTER 8
AND A LITTLE CHILD
SHALL LEAD THEM

The notion of University study is set aside. Skoot enters the world and is dedicated to the Lord, Olin continues to struggle, while a Springfield Silver Ghost Closed Limousine snakes its way toward Aschburgh. Greg Penn admits to being wrong about curtains as Professor Forsyth falls in love.

1
Talking Things Over

"I think I should make an appointment for you with a specialist in Indianapolis. This is our first child. Goodness...I mean who knows...no one can say exactly how you will react."

"I'll react fine. I'm more concerned with what you thought of Professor Forsyth."

"Marva, when you go with the local man everything is fine as long as there are no complications. But if you do run into any difficulty, then you're going to want the more experienced fellow. But it may be too late to get him at that point."

"Doctor Aiken will be fine. He delivered me, and our family's doctored with him for years. Aiken is fine."

"I've nothing against the man. If I've got a cold he's the one for me. But when I'm seriously ill I want someone whose skills have been tested. You said yourself the man is wrong about how far along you are. He doesn't have the skills. I don't see how you can trust his judgment."

"He's the one for you. What's that supposed to mean? You're never sick. You don't even get colds. Wilton, you're sweet to worry about me, and really I do appreciate your concern. But I'm fine and I don't need another doctor. I know pretty well when I'm going to have this baby. Way before what the Doctor thinks, but it'll all be fine. Anyway, how would I get down to Indianapolis every time I needed to see the doctor? What did you think of Professor Forsyth?"

After they dropped off a well fed William Forsyth at his home in Irvington Marva had moved back to the front seat of the *Ford*. Now as Wilton drove through the mild warmth of the early Summer evening, past mile after mile of newly green fields Marva leaned her shoulder against the door and stared straight ahead.

"It's just that if…and it's just an if…there were a problem I'm not sure Aiken could handle it."

"At that point we can see a specialist. I'd prefer to go to Chicago anyway."

"What do you know about Chicago?"

"Regina's Aunt Venetta…the Marshall's wife…Uncle Sevier… she was treated up there for cancer."

"She died for goodness sake!"

"Uncle Sevier said she had excellent care. It had spread too far, that's all. Anyway there's not going to be any problem. What's that noise? Do you hear that?"

"All automobiles have noises. It's nothing."

"Are you sure it's running all right? We don't want to get stuck out here in the middle of the night. Why can't we have something better? Something like Mister Penn's vehicle?"

"Forsyth's a good man. The *Ford's* running fine. Personally I'd prefer having you study with Professor Steele…he's certainly the old master…but it's obvious that won't be possible. I doubt he'll last much longer. The old fellow's in terrible shape."

"Perhaps I could live at the *University*. Like you did. For just a little while, you know. Until I have a sense of how to go."

"That's unrealistic. You need to be at home with me."

"I could travel back and forth. Maybe stay at the University for two or three days at a time. Just for a while. I'm sure that could be arranged. Then I could study with Professor Steele."

"Greg is going to be with us after a bit. We'll both need to devote our time to him once we get the schedule set. Which is going to mean some sacrifice. Can you imagine he's giving us the best part of a full week? It's just a question of figuring out when he can fit it in. Of course he'll charge an arm and a leg. But I want all the changes in the house to be exactly the way *you* want them. I want the house to be *your* house even if we have to tear it down and start all over again. Seriously. I mean that has been my plan from the first."

"It'll go fine I'm sure. But Greg's *only* with us for a week. And we don't even know when. There's plenty of time for me to enroll. They're starting a new Summer semester. I checked before we left. So that would work fine. Just for one semester, and then I'd have a clearer sense. And being in Bloomington maybe I could see an Indianapolis specialist like you want."

"You're going to have our son, Marva. Indiana University is no place for that."

"I'm very much aware I'm going to have a baby."

"I want you at home with me."

There was no point pressing the matter. Not now anyway. Wilton was right. Wilton was always right. Doctor Aiken said around Thanksgiving, but it was going to be much earlier. In any event the *University* wouldn't want her on campus if she was expecting. And the truth was she was needed in Aschburgh. Momma had her hands full with Daddy having more and more of these fits. Even Wilton didn't know the extent of the problem. At least she didn't think he did. Wilton didn't tell everything.

"Wilton?"

"Hmmm."

"The *Large Blob Theory*. What's that all about do you think?"

"Sounds peculiar, doesn't it? Of course that's exactly what Forsyth wants. An aura of mystery. He's a good fellow though. Don't let his artist ways scare you off. I believe he'll make you an excellent teacher. To be honest about it, I'm quite well pleased with him. All things taken into account."

"He doesn't want to be my teacher."

"O he'll come around. Actually he already has. Didn't you see how relaxed he was on the drive back to his place? He really enjoyed that steak. I'll bet he hasn't had one in a while. O he's made up his mind. The man's not stupid. Forsyth knows how the world works, and he can see the advantages to himself, especially for his position at the *Heron Institute*. There's been some problems there. His job's not as steady as it used to be. From what Greg tells me."

"You spoke to Greg about him?"

"When we had lunch. In the Men's Room. It was good of Greg to make time to join us at the restaurant. Though I'm not sure Forsyth appreciated his being there."

"O he was fine about it. Professor Forsyth did enjoy that lunch didn't he? I don't think he'd ever been there before. Greg acted like he owned the restaurant."

"St. Elmo's? Of course Forsyth enjoyed it. Probably the best steak he's ever had. Greg says the fellow is virtually out at the *Art Institute*, and he's not exactly rolling in money."

"Do you think we'll be able to go back there? Sometime. You and I. I love the baked potato."

"Green rules the world, and it's not beans I'm talking about, darling. William Forsyth understands that. He may be an artist and all, but he's also a practical down-to-earth fellow. He'll come around. The man has a family to support. You saw how crazy he is about those girls."

Daddy's fits were definitely getting more frequent and more intense. And harder to disguise. Apparently Momma was so upset she'd even asked Doctor Aiken about them. In general terms, of course. Not that he was of any help.

"Forsyth is your classic *Little Man*. Needs to be always throwing his weight around…a little loud…that sort of person. The kind of fellow who thinks he knows everything. Which can be an annoying trait. But I've checked him out a bit. Greg respects him…seems to like him actually…despite all that nonsense about the windows. You know, Greg said that Klan tie-up in the center of town cost a quarter of a million in lost business sales. Try to get that back from the *Imperial Dragon*! Not to mention scaring off new business down the road. No investor is going to be eager to put his money into that situation. They really need to put a stop to that nonsense."

"They didn't hurt anyone I hope."

"But getting back to Forsyth, Greg knows his wife Alice too, and he says Forsyth is the best. As far as Greg is concerned he's a better painter than Steele. Personally I find that hard to believe. Steele is the old master. Dresses well, conservative, and never without a tie. Just too sick, way too sick. It's sad, but that's the way life is."

"That *Large Blob* business doesn't sound very conservative, does it? If I'm going to study I'd rather study with someone sensible. That's why I thought studying on the campus might be better. With Steele. For a little while."

"O Forsyth's sensible, Marva. He's very conservative. I'd never let you be around one of those peculiar artists. Don't worry about that. Forsyth may try to shock you with his terminology and such, but he understands the bottom-line. He's every bit as conservative as I am. Don't worry about that."

"I really wasn't."

"And as far as the *Large Blob* business, as I was saying the man just likes to shock. It's all because he's only five feet tall."

"O he's more than that."

"A couple of inches maybe. Greg Penn says all that *Large Blob* nonsense means is *Big Areas of Color*. Paint, you know. Blocking in the major areas of a painting. Putting the colors on the canvas that way at first. Head, torso, background, all that sort of thing. Greg says it's just common sense, and I tend to agree. I mean you can't start a portrait with the tip of the nose. You have to know where the entire head is going. And so forth. It's just plain common sense."

It would've been nice to live in Bloomington for a while. To be around some young people who had different ideas...maybe more experience. Young people who had traveled and seen some things. Being around Regina wasn't the same. Even Wilton...who had traveled...was basically just Aschburgh on a higher rung. Unfortunately being married and pregnant had a way of setting the agenda. Not to mention Daddy's fits.

"Are the farmers expecting a good Summer?"

"As I see it, Marva, Forsyth's ideas are no different from the way a businessman looks at things. You always have to see the big picture before you can make a local decision. These fellows will most likely plant as much corn as they possibly can, totally ignoring what the market is likely to be this Fall, let alone next year. No wonder so many of them have trouble staying in business. I tell you, Marva, there's plenty of them out there...good local people...buying and selling, going into debt, deep debt, way over their heads, buying the most expensive machinery with no idea where the money's coming from, and paying absolutely--"

"Professor Forsyth will be fine."

"Of course he will. I'd more or less thought we agreed on that."

"So you think painting is like a business?"

"I get the feeling you don't really care, Marva."

"Of course I care. I always care what you think. But sometimes I get the feeling that what I think isn't very important to you."

"Now that's plain and simple ridiculous. That's just out and out ridiculous. Marva, you're going to be the mother of my son, and you're the most important thing in the world to me. Surely you know that."

"*Thing?*"

"Person. Goodness gracious, don't be so touchy. You know what I mean."

2
The Dedication Of A Baby & The Birth Of A Church

It was on the first of September 1926...in the middle of the week...about when Marva, Belva and Regina expected...and without the assistance of Doctor Aiken who was on a fishing trip in Michigan...that Marva gave birth to the first child of her union with Wilton Fox Goins. The baby, a healthy eight pound girl with ten fingers and ten toes, was a surprise to Wilton who had never doubted the birth of a son. Marva, Belva and Regina were delighted, and entered upon a festival of hope and plans for this adorable heir to the maternal heritage of the Winslows. For his part Olin Ainsley went through the motions of grand-fatherly joy, but as he descended ever deeper into the darkness of his demons and furies he was scarcely touched by this new life in the family.

The contented baby...named Wendy Winslow Goins...was dedicated to the Lord on Sunday October the 17th, a sunny crisp morning, at the first worship service of the newly incorporated *First Community Church of Indiana*, just a few hundred yards from her father's office at the *Aschburgh Bank & Trust* by the blessed intersection of *Ainsley Street & Goins Boulevard*.

As Wilton...solid in a brand new three piece black suit from *Brooks Brothers* ...hovered protectively over the family group clustered at the front of the crowded sanctuary, and as Regina and Belva fussed over Wendy, who was bundled and asleep in Marva's arms, the Reverend Doctor Jeremy Poston...splendid in new Doctoral robes with blue velvet chevrons...which Wilton had purchased and the Board publicly presented...offered a spontaneous prayer of praise and rejoicing which had taken him three days to memorize.

"Dear Lord, we give thanks to Thee for the birth and the health of little Wendy Winslow Goins as we lift her up and dedicate her to Thee on this beautiful Fall morning. We thank Thee for her wonderful family, for the love of her mother Marva, her dear, dear and precious Aunt Regina, her proud grand-parents Belva and Olin, and we especially thank Thee for the commitment, dedication, guidance and leadership of her father Wilton Fox Goins. We thank Thee for his loving attention to his family and for the spiritual direction and generosity he has repeatedly demonstrated to this congregation. We give thanks to Thee, O Lord, as Thou hast led this body into a new dawn as the *First Community Church of Indiana*, we look forward to our new building and to the capital fund drive which will make it a reality within the near future, and we especially thank Thee for the perseverance and generosity of the Winslow, Ainsley and Goins families which has made all this possible. Finally, Father, we thank Thee on behalf of little Wendy for the wonderful family with which Thou hast blessed her. And we pray all this in the powerful, mighty, and wonderfully strong name of the Lord Jesus. Amen."

Regina wiped her tears and blew her nose and then took little Wendy in her arms so Marva could wipe her own tears and blow her nose. Belva fussed with the baby's blanket, and Wilton, grinning broadly, slapped a solemn Olin on the back and shook the soft hand of Doctor Jeremy Poston. "Let's have everyone process up to see the baby, Doctor," he whispered. "The service will run a little long, but just for today that'll be all right."

Jeremy watched his fiancé and Belva Ainsley cooing over Wendy, and he wondered where all this gush and fuss came from. Babies were not attractive even if everyone pretended they were. He was grateful they had not asked him to hold the child. "Dear people, I know you all wish to congratulate the new parents and the proud Aunt, as well as Mamaw and Papaw, not to mention our precious little Wendy. So let's just take some time for that. If you would just form a line up the center aisle, and after you've had your moment, proceed back to your seats...*those of you lucky enough to have seats*, he joked...by the side aisle. That'll work nicely. Isn't this a glorious day in the history of our congregation, and won't it be wonderful when we have our new sanctuary and expanded seating for celebrations like this? If you would now just take your moment, and remember to proceed back along the side aisles."

The beauty of the day was only slightly marred as Belva confronted Olin on the steps of the Church, grabbing him by the arm and causing him to lose his balance as he pulled away from her. It was no secret to the town that Olin had been failing rapidly for some time, though most felt he had really always been a bit that way. It was part of the Ainsley nature, though fortunately there was no sign of it in Marva and hopefully the baby would be spared.

"Don't talk nonsense. You know I'd never do anything to hurt Marva. Never."

"Then get back in there and have your picture taken. You couldn't hold your grand-daughter? You couldn't wait for the photographer to get set up? Your time is so invaluable? What is so important you couldn't stay for Marva? Regina's crying because of you. Olin, pull yourself together."

"Don't push me. What you don't know would fill a book. A library. I don't want to be around anyone. I've had enough. No one. Not you. Especially not you. Just let me be, will you?"

Though for years she had known about the cows it was only now she felt incapable of dealing with her husband's strangeness. For the first time she was really afraid. Something was inside Olin, something she didn't even want to consider, something which threatened the stability of her family. For as long as she could recall Olin had punched cattle. It was just a part of who he was. She could usually see it coming as a dark mood slipped over him, he pulled back from everyone, and then exploded in the barn or field. Then it would be over, normally for months, and their life would resume its slow rhythm. But recently it was different. He was actually maiming the cattle...had in fact killed three she knew of. And the darkness wasn't lifting.

Doctor Aiken had been of no help. Not to hold that against him. Aiken had always been a good and faithful friend to her, and a fair enough family doctor. This was over his head and he admitted as much. He tried referring him to some Indianapolis doctors, but Olin wouldn't listen. She'd looked to Wilton, Olin's oldest friend, but he was preoccupied with his new family, not to mention his plans for his business, Aschburgh and the new

Church. And while no one could question Marva's love for her father, she was still only a girl, and with a new husband and baby she had no time for Olin's foolishness.

She followed him across the street to the lot where he left their automobile. "Olin, please listen to me."

"Have I ever struck you?"

"Struck me? Don't talk crazy. Olin, we can't afford to be losing cattle like this."

"Don't call me crazy! What do you know about it, about cattle? What do you know about crazy? Just shut up about cows. Talking about things you don't understand. You're making everything worse, creating problems where none exists."

"You know I'm right."

"People are staring at us, but you don't care. You have no regard for our family name. You're always right. You know everything. That's the problem right there in case you didn't know."

"Olin, you know this has to stop. We all want you to be happy."

"Who's this *all*? Nobody's complaining but you. As usual. Complaining and complaining as usual."

"We want you happy. The way you were."

"The way I was? What do you know about the way I was? The way I was is the way I am. There's no difference. And nobody cares except you. You've got to stick you nose into everything. You can't leave anything alone. You've always got to meddle."

Belva rubbed her hands together as Olin started the *Ford* and drove away. She turned at the sound of Reverend Doctor Poston calling her name. "Mrs. Ainsley, Mister Goins wants you and Mister Ainsley for the photograph."

3

On The Way To Visit Wendy Winslow Goins In A 1924 Springfield Silver Ghost Closed Limousine With Coachwork By McNear

Alerted by the Indianapolis *Knights* the Elwood branch of the *Klan* was quietly waiting for the *Rolls Royce* as it slowly passed through town. To Professor William Forsyth, annoyed at having been coerced into making this journey and now feeling uncomfortably on display, it seemed the entire population of Elwood was lining the town's main street as Greg Penn's dark green 1924 *Springfield Silver Ghost Closed Limousine*, driven by Bob, Greg's handsome blond chauffer processed at 15 mph.

Assured by Bob that the crowd did not appear violent Greg Penn ignored the scene outside the vehicle. Attired in Kelly Green trousers gathered tight at the ankles, with a loose fitting black velour jacket over a dark blue shirt open at the collar, and as usual wearing patent leather slippers with no socks, he ran his hand through his hair, fluffing up the mass of white curls, wondering if it would be possible to have the *Rolls Royce Company* install curtains or nice shades for the windows.

"I ought to have listened to you about the curtains, Bob. You were right, I was wrong. One of these days I'm going to learn. I'm very sorry for not paying attention to you."

"You were thinking of the economy of it all, Mister Penn. No one can fault you for that. As is often said, *You can't spend what you don't have.*"

"Of course in the real world you frequently spend what you don't have. But I can see where I was wrong. Penny wise but pound foolish."

"It can be attended to, sir."

Greg placed his fine hand on Forsyth's shoulder. "I realize it's a long trip and may seem bothersome, William, but it's imperative you see my plan for the renovation of both the house and the studio in their natural setting. Alice was so kind to allow you to come along."

"Alice has no say in the matter," said Forsyth. "I'm very uncomfortable about this whole project. We'll be giving these people false hope that I will accept the teaching position."

"Without the personal feel, the local touch if you will, my drawings will appear dry as dust. Surely you, as a painter of repute, can see that. An atelier in Montmartre is simply not the same as a studio in a barn in Aschburgh. There's no getting around the influence of environment."

"Why do these people choose to live in such barbarous conditions? Have you even bothered to glance at these drooling boobs? Right out there. Lining the street. It's the whole town. I hope Bob is right and they're not dangerous."

"It's best not to look at them, Professor. You'll only give them cause for optimism. Have you decided to do something about the fragmentation of your studio windows? I realize it's perhaps too costly for you. I ought not to have even mentioned it."

Forsyth studied the people lined up along the sidewalk, a few in robes, but most of them in the scruffy, grab-bag attire of the agricultural poor. Here and there a suit, a top coat, the occasional sign of civilization. A young boy in torn knickers held up a sign declaring, *Queers and Bolshie's Out*!

"Once we're there you'll see how I've used the agricultural *Gemutlichkeit* as the primary influence for the Goins' studio."

"*Gemutlichkeit*?"

"The *ambience*. There's nothing like it outside these little Hoosier villages."

"Your German's always been shaky. *Gemutlichkeit* doesn't mean *ambience*. How far are we from Aschburgh?"

"How much longer, Bob?"

"Another twenty miles, Mister Penn. This is all Madison County. Tecumseh's on a bit. Did you notice those placards back there, sir?"

"I did, I did. Take no heed of them, Bob. They're nothing to us. These poor souls are experiencing the greatest moment of their lives as they watch us go by. This is it for them…it's downhill after this moment. No need to speed. Fifteen is fine. We don't want trouble with these dears." Greg turned slightly to face William Forsyth, tucking his short legs under him on the soft fabric and grasping the leather strap for balance. "I'm sure it has an aura of *ambience*. I hope you're comfortable, William. It's about twenty miles. You realize, of course, we're journeying through a hotbed of the *Klan*?"

"No, I would never have guessed. I just assumed they wore those sheets to plow the fields. These are not my kind of people. Is Aschburgh like this too?"

"No. They're not this sophisticated in Aschburgh. Did you hear that, Bob? I said they're not this sophisticated in Aschburgh."

"You've a good sense of humor, Mister Penn."

"Up here, William, it's pretty much localized in Elwood. The *Klan*. At least the leadership is. *Imperial High Potentates* and all that secret lodge nonsense. That's what Bob was referring to...the Klan signs back there a bit. They'd burn a Cross on my head if they could. Foaming at the mouth, the poor darlings. The Indianapolis branch has been sending me love letters for years. It's pretty much like getting personal mail from the Mayor and the Governor. They're both in the *Klan's* pocket. Did you know that? You'd think they'd have more important things to attend to what with all the indictments against them."

"Threatening?"

"Indictments are always threatening."

"The letters, damn it!"

"The letters? Very much so. They called me a *degenerate male organ sucking dwarf*. Can you imagine? Of course they didn't actually say *male organ*, but I'm trying to be delicate. Lovely people. Bob and I had a good chuckle about it. By the way, I don't want you to worry. I don't do that. Do I, Bob? Not my cup of tea, as they say. Getting back to your studio windows, I think less fragmentation would transform your light, and personally I believe it would have the effect of lifting your work to a whole new level."

"There's nothing wrong with my light or my work. I don't need any *lifting*." Forsyth glanced out the window and was shocked by the gestures some of the children were making. "I hope you contacted the police."

"The notes were probably sent by the police, Professor. After being proofed by the Mayor and the Governor. Let's be realistic."

"I hear D.C. Stevenson is talking to the prosecutor. Cooperating."

"Really. That could be interesting."

"If there's any justice the whole lot of them will go to prison."

"Don't fret over it. There's no justice."

Penn had snatched Forsyth from his *Monument Circle* studio early that morning, and after a brief stop in Irvington to see Alice and the girls, they had taken off on this wild excursion. Forsyth felt uncomfortable and out of place sitting in this magnificent automobile in his paint splattered suit. Especially with Penn decked out like a *Bird of Paradise*, and insisting Forsyth sit on a tartan lap robe so as not to damage the upholstery. "I'm not dressed for this. Mister Goins is rather fastidious in case you hadn't noticed."

"Willie has always dressed like a prosperous undertaker. Yes, I have noticed. For the last twenty-five years I've noticed. He's a hopeless case, but I believe the young Mrs. Goins is going to bring some light and some lift into his life. In spite of this new baby she chose to have. I really wish she hadn't done that. By the way, lest I forget later on, you are never to call him *Willie*."

"I wouldn't call a dog *Willie*."

"It could be misconstrued as intimacy, if you see what I mean. Would you agree with that, Bob?"

"Absolutely, sir. *Mister Goins* is always safest."

"But your dress, your attire...that formal suit and tie...really surprises me, William. Is the tartan comfy? I had expected to find you in farmer's overalls. What with your reputation for he-man outdoor painting and all that." Greg twisted his torso away from Forsyth to stare at the locals...two and three deep in places...who were gawking at the brilliantly polished *Rolls-Royce*. "They're really a different species, aren't they? Please slow down, Bob."

"We're already crawling, sir. I'd like to put this behind us."

"We're in no hurry, and the last thing we want is trouble with the local *Keystone Cops*. Turn up the heat a bit, would you, Bob? My feet are feeling a bit chilled. You would think if they can design a magnificent vehicle like this they ought to be able to come up with a better heating system. We shouldn't need to transport all these lap robes. Of course I suppose the average person's automobile doesn't have *any* heat. Am I right about that, Bob?"

"I believe you are, sir."

"The *average person*, as you put it, can't even afford a *Ford*."

"More's the pity. Did you know Willie drives a *Ford*? He's a multi-multi millionaire, and he drives a *Ford*. The man owns half the land surrounding Indianapolis and he drives a *Ford*."

"Put some socks on, Penn! Wrap yourself up for Christ's sake. You must be fifty years old so stop pretending to be a kid. Of course your feet are cold. It's November! I don't see why we couldn't have handled all this back in Indianapolis. My God, man, it's only a dilettante's studio we're talking about here."

"Don't be a snob. I absolutely abhor snobbish talk. And I'm only in my forties, and in remarkably good shape. I've given up most heavy Germanic food, stopped drinking dark beer and wines, and am restricting myself to a gluten-free diet which has transformed my life. Now if only Bob would follow suit."

"I prefer a nice steak, sir. With baked potato and sour cream. Or mashed and gravy."

"Fine, fine, if that's what you want. We'll buy you steaks, pork chops, chicken, or whatever you insist on. But I do care about you, and I wish you would at least try some gluten-free cuisine. Professor, what I've discovered is if you restrict your diet to non-glutinous vegetables and fruit, age becomes irrelevant. You can live forever. Literally. Meat...especially red meat...but chicken's about as bad... potatoes and to a lesser extent turnips...those are the things that bind you up... clogging your vital aqueducts. Also squash."

"I agree with Bob."

"Thank you, Mister Forsyth. *Professor,*" said the chauffeur.

"For your information, Forsyth, my hair turned white when I was still at *University*. And…listen carefully to me now…I know you and Bob think you're very funny…don't interrupt…but my old college chum Willie…*Mister Goins* to you, Professor…would not appreciate that *dilettante* remark of yours."

"I certainly meant no disrespect to your friend. How much do you have tied up in this ark, Penn?"

"Very funny. *Ark*. Did you hear that, Bob? Please remember that Mister Goins has money, a lot of money, plus the ability to get lots more. Sometimes I think he prints the stuff in the back of his bank. I'm joking of course. It's all from that Natural Gas Boom. Well, the land, really. There isn't any gas anymore. Buying and then knowing when to let it go…when to buy, when to sell, and how to reinvest. It's a gift. The stupid bank has next to nothing to do with it. As far as this vehicle, the fact is it cost me an enormous amount of money, and even more to keep it running properly. My annual costs would leave you stunned, Forsyth. And I'm not even talking about the costs inherent in *Penn Enterprises*. Most people have no idea. They think that because my gross income is large…as in fact it is…that I'm swimming in money. Nothing could be farther from the truth."

"You sound like some old Hoosier farmer."

"Tell the Professor a little bit about this vehicle, Bob."

"Not necessary. I was only inquiring about the price. Nothing more. So you've become a vegetarian."

"Vegetarianism is not the issue."

"I could have predicted it. That sort of cultic stuff has your name written all over it. Meat and potatoes is the name of the game so far as I'm concerned. With lots of thick country gravy."

"Why am I not surprised? Hopefully you'll learn before it's too late. It wasn't until I stumbled upon *The Gluten-Free Way* and actually spent some time with Doctor Waymire that my eyes were opened. Go ahead, Bob, enlighten the Professor about the *Silver Ghost*."

"Exactly what kind of *doctor* is this Mister Waymire?"

"Well, Professor, the *Ghost* is the top of the line. No question about that. The *Springfield Silver Ghost*, if that means anything to you, sir. 1924. Your *Closed Limousine*. Or *enclosed* if you're partial to that distinction. You'll hear it both ways. The *McNear* people did all the coachwork. They're not as big an operation, but superior to *Barker* in the solidity of their craftsmanship...in my opinion that is. Some would of course disagree, and that's their prerogative, as the saying goes."

"Doesn't he have a powerful command of this, Forsyth? Bob is a remarkable person."

"The leather grasps back there...very soft and agreeable to the touch...I had all that specialized for Mister Penn. He relishes a firm softness, if I may say."

"Lord! What does something like this cost?"

"Perhaps we'll have a chance to test our strength against each other, Forsyth. There are all these misconceptions about the effects of a gluten-free diet. The fact is I can take you in arm wrestling with no difficulty. You'd be surprised at my upper body strength. Which was not there as long as I restricted myself to a more Germanic cuisine. I've taken down men twice my size."

"What's that got to do with anything?"

"And as far as my hair, it would be nothing to dye it. But *most people* find my white curls quite striking the way they are."

"My God, man!"

Hanging onto the leather grasp, Greg leaned forward toward the front seat. "You were right, Bob. I was wrong and I sincerely apologize for what I said and the way I acted. We ought to have ordered curtains or shades. One of these days I'll learn to listen to your wisdom. That was a major oversight on my part. Major. One of my typical false economies. Please forgive me."

"You were only thinking of doing the right thing, sir. The way you always do. It's hard for a busy man like yourself to keep track of everything. Especially with all these clients being so dependent on you. It's very taxing, and I worry about your health. Even with this new diet. And I'll give it a try if you really think I should. But if you would like some curtains, sir, it can be easily arranged. I can have them sent over from England, or perhaps from the agent in Boston. I'm sure my brother-in-law can install them quite nicely. I'll see to it personally if you like."

"Since you were Goins' roommate you're at least close to your mid-forties. Am I right? But no matter. That's your business. In round figures, Penn, what did you have to lay out for this rig?"

"That's thoughtful of you, Bob. That's so kind."

"Just trying to be helpful, sir. May I speed up a bit?"

"Unless I'm mistaken, William, you have very little money, and need a lot more for your operation at the *Herron*...not to mention your advanced age...so.... Do you get my drift? I'm trying to break through to you, Professor. I'm trying very hard to ignore your nastiness. The way I see it you've probably got medical problems...other than your addiction...which leave you bad tempered. I mean, for goodness sake, around Mister Goins...who can help you out...please watch your mouth and your smoking and behave yourself."

"I don't need you to tell me how to comport myself. Jesus Christ!"

"That swearing for example. That's a good case in point. Mister Goins has some taste...it's limited of course...but good Lord the man graduated *Indiana University*. Bob, is it *graduated* University or *graduated from* University? Bob takes an interest in these things."

"I prefer the simple *graduated*, sir. I believe *graduated from* is more typically American."

"Well, for Christ's sake we are Americans," said Forsyth.

"Thank you, Bob. *Graduated* University then. Very sharp." Penn waved to a group of children on the sidewalk. "Aren't they cute at that age? There's a lot to be said for living in the country."

"That's why I've been *kidnapped*, isn't it? So Goins can put the screws to me ...force me to come up here and teach his dumb wife."

"Pull yourself together, William. I detest melodrama. Wait until you see their new baby. Wendy Winslow Goins. Cute as a bug. I gave her a solid silver bowl. From *Tiffany*. Just imagine! And please, please don't so much as allude to your feeling that

Mrs. Goins is *dumb*. You can speed up a bit now, Bob. I'm passing no judgments, but O my God, what a disaster that would be! Calling her *dumb*. We'd be tossed onto the dung pile. Is that what they call it?"

"That's what this is all about. Putting pressure on me. What *addiction*?"

"Nicotine, Forsyth. Nicotine is as addictive as morphine."

"Nonsense. You have no intention of telling me how much this car cost, do you?"

"None. But to get back to my earlier point, isn't a three piece suit, starched shirt and tie just a bit over-doing it? For splattering paint around in your studio? No, of course I'm not going to tell you something so vulgar as the cost of this car. Let's just leave it at more than you earn in ten years. Fifteen…maybe twenty."

"Which is no skin off my nose. The suit and tie, that was Steele's damn influence. Shortly before his death. He got Mrs. Forsyth, my Alice, insisting on it when I go to the studio. For my *image*!"

"God rest his soul."

"For Christ's sake, you don't believe in God, Penn."

"Professor Steele was a good and a kind man. If a bit fussy. But wearing a business suit in the studio seems *excessive*. To me anyway. Now the fact is you are addicted to nicotine. It's a glutinous substance which clogs the lungs and the sinus cavities. Anyone who spends ten minutes around you knows you are and senses your lack of balance. But listen, dear friend, if your nicotine addiction is no big deal for you, it's no big deal for me. Don't you agree, Bob? Life can be difficult. What I'm trying to say is this… simple dress in the studio would be more appropriate."

"I like a good cigar every now and then, Mister Forsyth," said Bob. "Though I think the Cubans are over-rated."

"Penn, will you look at yourself? You don't even wear socks. Who are you to talk?"

"I don't need socks. Bob drives me wherever I want to go. And makes sure I'm dry and warm. He's *very* solicitous of my welfare. Isn't that right, Bob?"

"I try to do a good job for you, sir. You deserve the very best."

Forsyth didn't want to hear anymore from Penn or his flunky Bob. He was growing more and more irritated over not being permitted to smoke in the car. "You're going to sit there in that *court jester's outfit* and criticize my work clothes?"

"This court jester's outfit, as you call it...well, best not to say anymore. Bob, are we out of that dreadful town yet?"

"It's just behind us, sir. Another seventeen miles, eighteen at the most. Right to the front door of *The Old Goins Place*. Though if you recall, sir, it's a bit out of the way. But very comfortable. Not too far once we enter Tecumseh County. On our last visit I found Miss Marva to be very kind, and she keeps her home nice and cozy."

"Yes she is and yes she does. Willie did very well for himself there. Do you realize she's almost thirty years younger than him? How about that? And the girl worships him, Bob. She's rather gawky, but she absolutely worships him. I'd give anything to have someone adore me that way."

"She can't be thirty years younger than him. She'd be in high school."

"It's not so difficult to imagine, sir. Someone adoring you."

"Bless you, Robert. Now for your edification, *Professor*, my *court jester's outfit* has over eight hundred sunk in it."

"I could paint for a year on that."

"Two at least."

"You're an arrogant s.o.b., Penn."

"If you clean up your language and behave yourself, *Professor*, your money troubles will be behind you. But say *goddamn* once to young Mrs. Goins and you'll be hawking your paintings outside Union Station. On the sidewalk, three for ten dollars."

"Shit! I need a cigarette before we get there, Penn."

"Bob, please pull off the road when you can. Somewhere where there's no danger to the *Silver Ghost*. The *Professor* is beginning to shake. He has *needs*."

4
The Provocative Nature Of Scootums

"I would never have anticipated this, Greg," said Wilton. "Which is not to say I'm less than well pleased. Truth be told I am very well pleased indeed."

"I sensed this would happen. Once he'd seen her. I just knew it. This is going to resolve everything, Willie. Move our entire relationship with him to a new plane." Greg and Wilton lingered in the hallway, glancing into the nursery where William Forsyth and Marva were playing with little Wendy. "Frankly though, and I hope you take no offense, I think it appalling how adults...even gifted people like Forsyth...behave around babies."

"Not you though." Wilton smiled and slapped his old college roommate on the back.

"Definitely not me. Of course the Professor's got three of his own. Three! Can you imagine? Show a little restraint. My God!"

"Any girls?"

"All girls."

"Girls are wonderful. I'm delighted about Wendy, but our next one will be a boy."

"*The next one.* Suit yourself, Willie. Forsyth takes his along on his painting excursions. I suppose you'll take yours to the meetings of the *Mortgage Committee*."

"He does? I rather like that. Painting trips with his daughters. That's another side of Forsyth I couldn't have guessed. A side I like very much."

"My God, what is she doing now? O Willie, let's step away. She's changing it. I don't want to see this."

"Let's go to the kitchen. Marva is delighted with your plans for the nursery. You've turned that depressing bedroom of my parents into a bright little room, full of fun. I know it's less than small potatoes for you, but you've pleased her and that pleases me. I'm very grateful. Indebted to you."

Greg acknowledged his friend's praise with a slight nod. "Don't say anything until you've got my bill." He stepped away from Wilton to peek into the nursery where Professor Forsyth and Marva were huddled over the crib. "What're they doing? O my God, he's got some of it on him! And he's laughing about it. I'd puke, Willie. I'd absolutely puke. I just may puke right now."

"It's a natural thing, Greg, and Forsyth is obviously an experienced hand. The man's moved way up in my estimation. Way, way up. Why don't you and I grab a cup of coffee, and have a sort of preliminary run through about Marva's studio? Maybe take our coffee and your plans and stroll over to the old barn. She and the Professor can join us when they finish cleaning up Wendy."

"And wash their hands. They will wash their hands, Willie? My God, I hope so. Do you have any idea?"

"Will your feet be warm enough in those pretty little slippers? I have some *Wellingtons* and lots of thick wool socks."

"You always were a riot, Willie. I'm sure you'll wear your vest to the barn. Did Marva like the bowl I sent for Wendy?"

"She loves it. We both do. It's right up there. On the shelf over Wendy's crib."

"Is that a safe place? It's from *Tiffany*. New York. 5th Avenue."

"I know where *Tiffany* is. Don't worry. It's a very safe place."

Wendy Winslow Goins clasped her tiny fingers around the index finger of the old painter and grimaced at him.

"She's smiling at me. Look, Marva, she's smiling. Isn't she the cutest little bunny? The doctors will try to tell you it's just gas, but don't ever believe that. Don't give in to that scientific claptrap."

Marva hovered around Forsyth and Wendy, concerned the old man might be too rough, and at the same time embarrassed by the odor of the bowel movement they had just cleaned up. The diaper pail wasn't adequate when you had company.

"Professor?"

"They'll try to tell you her sweet smile is merely a physiological response to gas. Nonsense."

"Would you like to wash up?"

"Wash up? No, no I'm fine. We'll take care of that in a bit. The smile is real, Marva. 100% genuine. Isn't it, you little rascal? You little Indian. You little rapscallion. Pooh, pooh *skootums* to you too. Authentic, my dear. A precious response to the adored face of her beloved Mamma. And then, of course, over time that response, Wendy's love response to you, gets transferred to the face of her dear Father, and then to others. Myself for example. But never with anything approaching the degree of love she feels for her Mamma. Isn't that right, *skootums*? Pooh, pooh to you too. You sweet little *skootums*."

Marva wanted to pick Wendy up to smooth out the sheet in her crib, but she couldn't get around Forsyth. "She's such a good baby. Wilton thinks so too. Shall we straighten up her crib?"

Forsyth continued to lean over Wendy, wriggling his index finger up and down to her delight. "*Skootums, skootums, skootums.* That's what Alice and I called our daughters when they were infants. All babies like the sound of *Skootums*. It's the soft flowing *oooo* followed by the firm *ummm*. Sounds silly I know, but there's something about that combination that delights them."

Forsyth's fascination with Wendy charmed Marva. The Professor was odd, and so opinionated, but she couldn't help but like him. Wendy needed a grandfather ...all children did...but Daddy was so preoccupied...about something...who knew what?... that he paid no attention to her precious Wendy. He hadn't even stayed for the Dedication photos. Her eyes misted as she realized that later on, when Wendy showed those pictures to her own children, there'd be no Papaw Ainsley in them.

"*Skootums*? You really feel there's something soothing about *Skootums*?"

"No, no not at all. That's a very common misconception. Not *soothing*. Unless you're putting her to sleep you don't want to *soothe* Wendy. What you want to be doing is stimulating her, even provoking her."

"*Provoke* her?"

"In the most positive way, yes, *provoke* her. *Skootums* does just that...the soft followed immediately by the firm. It's jarring to the baby, but in a pleasant, stimulating way. What we want to be doing is to lift Wendy's thought processes, to trigger her creative powers."

"And you believe *Skootums* does that?" She made no effort to mask her smile.

"I know it seems remarkable, but give it a try. You'll be amazed. I've always taken an avid interest in child development. Even before I was married. Before I had children, of course. Studied a bit of it while I was in Germany. As in most things the Germans were way ahead of everyone else."

"Then you've actually been to Europe?"

"Lived there for six years. Studying painting. And babies. Always was fascinated by babies."

Marva was certain the smell from the diaper pail was permeating the entire house. "I'd like to hear about Europe. It's someplace I've always want to see. Wilton and I went to New Orleans and that was different. But it's not Europe. But right now, Professor, Europe is going to have to wait while I wash out that dirty diaper."

"Let me help. Or better yet, you watch Wendy and I'll take care of the diaper. I think we're going to learn from each other in our studies, Marva. I'm really looking forward to getting started. You know, Germany and Austria were a paradise for me as a young man. Not home. Not Indiana, of course. But the next best thing. Here, let me have that diaper pail. By the way, Marva, Alice and I have found it's best to go a little light on the talcum powder. Otherwise it tends to clump up."

CHAPTER 9
MEN IN QUEST OF A VISION

*The Giantown Town Dump is home to a genuinely good man.
Perhaps a bit quirky. Olin Ainsley struggles with his sin, behaves
badly at table, and blames the paltry number of Bible Baptist
Holiness salvations on the Bolsheviks.*

1
2,000,000 Souls Set Free For Christ

Ordained twenty years earlier in Nova Scotia by Brother
J. Robert Clamder who himself had hands laid upon him by
Evangelist Aimee Semple McPherson... herself only a child of
twelve at the time...though a fire-baptized child...at a meeting
in Toronto shortly after the turn of the century...Evangelist
John Patrick William Carrigan was a pure Holy Ghost man...a
driven but humble soul who bore a simple and direct call from
the Lord Jesus Christ. That call, joyfully received and so much
in evidence during the early meetings he and Brother Clamder
held throughout eastern Canada, had been mightily yoked upon
his shoulders in a vision of Christ which came upon him later,
during a cold Huron River baptism just outside Ypsilanti in the
great State of Michigan.

And it was that gloriously yoked vision that even today remained the driving force behind his hard-scrabble ministry. *2,000,000 Set Free For Christ,* the call spoken during that yoking near Ypsilanti, was hand-painted in red on a board leaning against his home-made pulpit, while in the midst of the Giantown Dump the vision was proclaimed to the people of Indiana on a banner waving atop his *Glory Tent.*

It was a Sunday evening when Olin Ainsley, his eyes sparkling with tears of remorse and anguish, parked his *Ford* fifty yards from the patched and water stained *Glory Tent* of Evangelist Carrigan. Olin learned of these meetings from one of the boys at the Gaston Elevator, a fellow who made fun of the Evangelist's simple faith which had led him to erect his tent in the center of the Giantown Dump. But it struck Olin that there might be something to it, something beyond the dull services they endured in Aschburgh. Not that he didn't respect the Church and the new Pastor, but especially during planting and harvest times it was hard for a man to stay awake on Sunday mornings, impossible Sunday evenings and just forget it during the mid-week service.

He had heard people went to evangelistic meetings like these and got saved and healed and had really bad problems solved. Things that never happened in your typical Church. And Olin knew he needed something powerful like that, something to help him handle the dark moments, the headaches and the awful burden of shame he carried. It was said an evangelist like this fellow could put his hands on your head and just suck all the devil out. Surely it was worth a try.

Plus being out where it was, in the middle of less than no place, square in the heart of the Town Dump, and then being the kind of tent meeting it was…Olin figured he was unlikely to run into anyone he and Belva knew. Pain or no pain, he couldn't afford the humiliation that would follow if someone from Aschburgh saw him here.

Somewhere in the *Bible* it said God's Word was a boulder blocking the path of the devil and foolishness to many people. And there was a lot of truth in that. But there was also healing in the Word of Jesus, and he needed it. He sighed and forced himself to lift his heavy, powerful body out of the front seat of the *Ford*. Belva would never understand this, but it was something he had to do for Marva. He was so ashamed that she knew about his weakness and sin.

A hard-times wagon was tied up right beside the tent with what seemed to be a house full of pitiful furniture in the bed. As Olin walked along Brother Carrigan's hastily constructed path that weaved among the heaps of smoldering trash he could hear through the canvas of the *Glory Tent* a woman's voice as the Evangelist led his tiny congregation of three in an acappella rendition of *Leaning On The Everlasting Arms.*

This was the first of Evangelist Carrigan's *Giantown Glory Crusades*, but his plan was to make them an annual event. It wasn't the best time given the Fall harvest and the unpredictable cold and wet weather, but it was God's will spoken to him... and that settled the matter. Although Carrigan experienced rebuff upon rebuff when he tried to find a place in town for the meetings, he was now clear that the Lord had led him to this field far to the north of Giantown's business district, in an area deserted after the gas wells dried up fifteen years earlier, and now used for dumping and burning garbage.

It was precisely the sort of place Jesus would select to share the Good News. A Hoosier *Valley of Gehenna*. With smoldering fires to cover the stench of rejection. *The base things of the world, and things which are despised, hath God chosen, yea, and things which are not, to bring to nought things that are. That no flesh should glory in his presence.* Encouraged by the Word of God, Carrigan cleared trash, drove tent stakes into the clay, and with great difficulty raised the *Glory Tent* in the cold rain of the Hoosier Fall, fully aware that few would likely come to his first meetings, but warmed by the conviction that God wanted him in this place at this time. *Because the foolishness of God is wiser than men; and the weakness of God is stronger than men.*

Bald before forty, with strong reddened, cracked and calloused hands, his wrinkled face and hard, lean body spoke to the life of an itinerant preacher in the Midwest. Not for Brother Carrigan the admiring crowds, wealth and adulation of the Billy Sundays. The Evangelist was a simple Gospel man. At his ordination Brother J. Robert Clamder whispered a verse into his ear and urged him to live by it. Many nights cold and hungry, tearing down his tent after meetings at which few if any showed up, he would recall those terrible words. *Our God is a consuming fire.* He tried to preach a message of the love of Jesus, of redemption, salvation and the wonderful grace of God, but the call upon his own life was fierce, often bitter.

Sister Carrigan, a Georgia country woman he married ten years earlier and dearly loved, had left him almost twelve months ago. Frantic for the lack of food and clothing for their children, despairing that Evangelist Carrigan would never stop his wandering and settle down to the normal life of a small town pastor, she left him in tears, taking her three sad boys back to her parents in the South.

"You're a good man, John Patrick William, and I love you dearly and have followed you faithfully, but your call is too strong a fire, too hard for my babies." That's all she would say to him as she and the boys boarded the train in Oskaloosa. He wanted to go with them, he recognized the terrible burden his call placed upon them even though they had not been called, but he remembered the Scripture he had been given and the vise-hard grip of God upon him. There had still been a week of meetings in Oskaloosa...more if people opened their hearts to the Word... plus a *Glory Crusade* planned for East Dubuque...and after that he would trust in the God who called and held him close. It broke the evangelist's heart to see his poor boys and his precious love leave him on the train, but his call was fierce and his vision of *2,000,000 Set Free For Christ* drove him forward.

Olin pulled back a flap on the side of the tent and slipped into a wooden chair at the rear. Evangelist Carrigan stood behind his rough pulpit, stocky and wrinkle-faced, his cheap black suit stained from sweat, the knees of the trousers clumsily patched, his gnarled hands gripping the thick wood. Anchored in his faith, steeled by suffering…he was not a man to play church.

He glanced at the young father and teen-age mother in the front row…the smiling girl with a baby in her arms. He looked up and saw Olin seated in the back of the tent. The Lord brought those who were supposed to be here, he thought. Opening his *Bible* to *1 Corinthians* he paused to set the loose pages of the book back in place, and then announced his text, *1 Corinthians 2:1-5*.

Olin opened his *Bible* randomly to *Malachi* and placed it on his knees. He would listen, he prayed he would hear, and if he could hear then he would surely remember. This sermon would be for him, it would change his life if he could only force himself to hear it. Having been in church every Sunday since childhood, having attended several revivals a year with Belva, he understood how God worked …though he had never allowed the Word to touch him…and he was certain that tonight he would meet the Lord in the power of His Spirit for the first time. Tonight God was going to save him, heal him, make him whole. This very evening.

"Before I try to read these words God has written down for us I want you to join me as I pray for myself. I know that sounds bad, kind of puffed-up and smelling of self-delight, but it's not that way. I just need help to read these words." He smiled at the young father. "I don't know, but maybe you've had it hard trying to read. I surely have, and though I'm getting better I'm still not easy with it. But see, I try hard because God's given us a *Book* and it needs to be read. God's done His part, so now I've got to do mine even if it's hard. So I've read this big book through a bunch of times, and you know that's not easy when you can't figure out a lot of the words. I know I haven't gotten a bunch of it, but I've got a pretty good sense. And I'm still trying, I'm still working at it. I'll read it all my life. And one of these days, with God's grace of course, I'm going to be able to read it easy. But not yet. It's still hard for me. So I need His help tonight. And I need yours too."

"I'll pray with you, Evangelist," said the young mother. "Me too," said Olin. "I know how it can be when you had to work as a kid and you didn't get to go to school much."

"God bless you for your compassion. Let us pray. Dear God, bless these good people who've come tonight because You called them. And bless my mind and my eyes and my tongue so I will read this passage pretty good and not make too many mistakes. There are some long words here, Father. Help me to read them right so the folks will understand. And again, Lord, bless these people and this baby, meet all their needs, and bring them to know Jesus. To know Jesus tonight, that's my prayer. Amen."

Carrigan then read the five verses aloud. In truth he read poorly, faltering on *excellency* and *trembling*, and done in by *demonstration*. Even after years of struggling he had trouble with many of the longer words. Though his voice was not impressive he did quite well when he recited from heart, for he had memorized large portions of the Scripture, carefully listening to Brother Clamder and later to his own Sister Carrigan read the passage aloud to him, and fixing it in his mind even as they spoke the words.

But now Brother Clamder was gone to be with Jesus and his beloved Linda-Cheri was gone back home to Georgia, so he was forced to rely on God to insure that the power of God's Word came through to the people despite his own failings. He often recalled the huge presence of Brother J. Robert Clamder intoning God's truth as that great servant had done so many times in moments of despair during cold and empty meetings in the Maritimes.

So shall my word be that goeth forth out of my mouth: it shall not return unto me void, but it shall accomplish that which I please, and it shall prosper in the thing whereto I sent it.

It had been difficult to memorize that verse. Somehow, in the early days of enthusiasm, it seemed beside the point. Fortunately Brother Clamder insisted he get it down perfect, and in years to follow it had sustained Evangelist Carrigan at his own cold and often empty evening meetings. The *Gospel Truth* revealed in Jesus the crucified was the compassion of God for His weak and stumbling people, and especially for this poor, ignorant preacher.

"Dear darling people, I'm going to try hard to get right to the point and be as brief as possible this evening. I know you young people are traveling and we want you to get a good night's rest right here in the tent, so I'll get finished quick. Mister," he called to Olin. "Would you have a couple of dollars for this young family? I hate to put you on the spot like this, but I don't have but twenty-five cents …which I will give them…but they need a little something more to travel down to Kentucky in the morning. I won't be taking any offering, so whatever you might have put in for my ministry, why you can give it to them. God has showed me they're the ones who have the need this evening."

"Well, I suppose I might have something in my pocket," said Olin, knowing he had at least thirty, but annoyed at being singled out. "I've got a couple. Well, three I can spare." He was surprised at himself. This was the house of God. He ought to have better sense.

"God bless, you sir," said the Evangelist. "Would you bring it up here right now? And take a seat by these young people so we can be together as a family before the Lord."

Olin stepped up before the pulpit and held out three dollar bills toward Carrigan.

"Would you hand it to the young father, sir?"

Olin turned and gave it to the young man who stared at the ground as he shoved the bills into his pocket. The young woman mouthed *Thank you*, as Olin sat down at the end of the row.

"Dear ones, the Lord has showed me some have come tonight with a terrible burden. There are some here who can already feel the noose of satan tightening around their throat. If you are one of these, perhaps even that particular one…for He has not showed me a number…if that one is you then be comforted for He knows you are here, and He is going to meet your need. I believe He is going to set you free. I really do believe that. If you will trust Him you're going to be o.k."

Olin fumbled in his back pocket for a handkerchief to wipe the sweat from his forehead. His heart was pounding and here the Preacher hadn't even got started. The man was right...God had called him here tonight. Called him here to deal with this shameful situation, and this pounding he felt was that Holy Ghost power he'd heard about all his life but never known. As he wiped at his face his *Bible* dropped to the floor. "Shoot!" he muttered loudly as he leaned over to get the book.

Evangelist Carrigan smiled at him. "God loves you, sir. The Lord has His hand on you this very minute, and He's got peace for you. I can feel that, so you be sure to listen carefully. God is going to whisper in your ear and give you some ease."

And I brethren, when I came to you, came not with ex...cell...ency... excellency...of speech or of wisdom, declaring unto you the testimony of God.

"Now that *brothern* in there, that sounds like God is just talking to men, but sister, take my word for it He is speaking to women as well. The sisterns are loved like the brotherns. *There is neither male nor female: for ye are all one in Christ Jesus.* Now that's just the way it is whether some folks like it or not. God works through women the same as men. Listen dear ones, I was anointed by the Holy Ghost through Evangelist J. Robert Clamder, and Brother Clamder received his Holy Ghost anointing through the hands of Sister Aimee Semple McPherson when she was little more than a baby herself. All this was way up north in Canada. So I'm telling you tonight God loves everyone of us, men and women and babies, those who can read and those who can't do it so well, those with a job and those without, the ones settled down and the ones on the road. God's love and God's grace are for all of us. So please pay attention to what God is whispering.

"You know I don't have a single one of those...what they call *degrees*...to hang on my wall. I wished I did. I really do. But I'm an ignorant man who has learned to speak half-way decent because the Lord has showed me how. So I have more than a degree and I have more than an education...I have the Holy Ghost. And believe me that's more than a paper degree.

"The Holy Ghost has already...just a few minutes ago... showed me things about every one of you and about myself as well, and He's even showed me things about that innocent little precious baby. Sister, I'd like to pray over him after the service if you'll permit it. I have three wonderful boys of my own, praise God. Though they're not with me just now, I'm ashamed to say. Be sure to pray for them ...and for their mother and me. We're apart right now but I know the Lord wants us together, and I sometimes feel real confused about what God wants me to do.

"Forgive me, dear ones. But this weak and worn out Preacher...I haven't got any of those learned papers that are so prized by some ministers and Catholic priests. The only certification paper I've got is Holy Ghost wisdom, and the only office I've got is a tree stump where I can sit to read the Word of God the best I can. I have holes in my shoes and I have holes in my trousers. And that's the Gospel truth. But brothern and sistern, I am a blessed man. Praise God. I know only Jesus Christ and Him crucified. No honor but the Cross of Jesus. No wisdom but the Word of God. No power but the Holy Ghost."

"Amen, sir," said the young woman. "You're a good man, Evangelist."

"Thank you, but remember it's all Jesus. All Jesus. This is all true, dear darling ones. I wouldn't even know how to lie to you. I've got no cause for that. I'm just honored to share in the Cross of Jesus and Him the crucified. By the power of the Holy Ghost I'm schooled in the wisdom of the simple Gospels...all four of them. Plus the *Book of the Acts* and a bunch of Paul's writings that I can pretty much understand.

"I can't understand them all...like say the *Book of Hebrews*. That's one that's too high up for me right now. Maybe always will be. But the ones I can understand...at least a bit...now these are all common books, written for common folks like you and me. Folks needing no other book but the *Holy Bible*. You understand I hope, I'm speaking here of the *King James Bible*, the Word of God, not some of these so-called revised standard modern translations. King James got it right when God spoke to him. So there's only one *Bible* and that's the *King James*. I do truly believe that."

"My mother has the *King James* at home," said the young woman. "When Billy and I got married the pastor at my home church, he used that *Bible*."

"Billy," said Evangelist Carrigan to the young man who continued to look at the ground, "Because you honored God and His Word in your marriage, He's going to bless you and your family, son. I know things look tough right now, but believe me, when you get to Kentucky He's going to bless you. You just stay strong and take good care of your lady and your little baby." John Patrick William Carrigan lifted his battered black *King James Bible* high above his head. "Lift them high, brotherns and sistern. Your *Bibles*. Don't be shy now. We're friends here. Thank you, Sister. Sir," he pointed to Olin. "Please lift high your *Bible* if you would."

Olin felt holding his Bible in the air was unseemly, but so were the stupid tears running down his face. No one would ever know, and he had to do the right thing if he was going to get help, so he slowly raised the book to shoulder height.

"Thank you, sir. Thank you. I can see the Holy Ghost at work this very minute. Don't be embarrassed, my dear brother. It's the Holy Ghost. No wisdom but by His touch, no wisdom but by His Book. I'm so glad I went to the *College of Hard Knocks*. How about you? I'm so glad I went to the *Seminary of the Gospel* not to the *Cemetery of Human Learning & Vain Philosophy*.

"O how I love Jesus! I stand here before you with no power of money or of family fame or of political corruption. I've only got the power of the Holy Ghost. But let me tell you there's no greater power. When the wind blew into the Upper Room that first Pentecost Sunday there was none of those folks ever went to one of our big city colleges.

"See I'm talking about Harvard University in Boston or Saint Francis Xavier or McGill or Dalhousie. Those are from where I'm from…in Canada. A long time ago. Makes no difference. Though I suppose I'm a full American now. My wife, God bless her, she's from Georgia. She and I met while we were both at a Church Conference in Tennessee. A place called Cleveland. But not Ohio. Some powerful meetings we had there. Mrs. Carrigan…she's just the best woman in the world. I truly believe that. And I want you to know I miss her and boys so very much. Anyway, Canadian or American, it doesn't mean a thing. All are one in Christ Jesus. Neither slave nor free. He will bring us all together in His time. Praise His holy name.

"Anyway, not a one of those folks that first Pentecost went to Harvard University. Or Dalhousie. Not a one of them. Those first saints, they all went to the *College of Calloused Hands*. Just like you and me. And they got…let me get my English correct here… they *received*…that's the word the *King James Bible* uses… they *received* the Holy Ghost in power just like I have, just like God wants all of you to have. *Received* is the word. Like *received* a gift, for that's what it is. A pure and a good gift. *Acts chapter 1 and verse 8*.

"Now I know this is not where we started out tonight…we were in one of those writings of Paul…but it's so important and it's where the Lord has led. Look it up when you have a chance. I know how busy you are, but when you have a chance. *Acts chapter 1 and verse 8*. O bless the Lord! He is so good, so very good. Some scholars want to say God is awful…o yes they do…and I say yes, He is *awful* good. Just plain awful good. And He wants all of us… common folks…God's kind of people…He wants all of us here tonight to receive His power, to walk in the strength of the Holy Ghost. Whatever you've done, He knows how tough it is, and He's not holding any of it against you.

"Listen to me, Billy, I realize you're down on your luck… look up here at me, son…but Jesus was down on His luck a lot worse than you. You may think your sin is the worse thing that ever happened. But it isn't. Not to God. He knows the sin of powerful people hating and murdering His beloved Son. Believe me, brothern He loves you and forgives you and wants to bless you. Now isn't that something? Isn't that a good package He offers? Love and forgiveness and blessing and then more love. O glory to His name. The Lord is so awful good and fine."

Olin Ainsley heard very little of what the Evangelist said for the Spirit had touched his heart and all he could hear was the pounding…all he could feel was the burning of his sweaty face… all he knew was he needed to get it straight with God. He needed this Holy Ghost power, however a fellow got it. No way he was going to get his problem under control without it. No way he was going to win back Marva's respect. He needed that power. Before he went home he needed that power. The Evangelist was speaking…still speaking…and Olin struggled to focus, to hear the words that would heal him.

Carrigan never moved from behind his pulpit. He had never believed flashy preaching was for him. His gnarled hands gripped the wooden lectern as though glued to the top of the pulpit, and occasionally he would…without thinking…lift the entire hunk of pine off the dirt floor and drop it down a few inches closer to his congregation.

"Not in the wisdom of the world, brotherns. That's not going to get you what you need. The doctor with all his fancy education, he's not going to heal that hurt that's gnawing. He'll take your money, he'll smile and send you home…but the hurt will still be there. Isn't this the way it truly is? Now you can give your money and your time and your hope to the doctor…that's up to you…but for my part, I'm putting my trust in the Holy Ghost."

"You're right, sir," said the young mother. "That's what my preacher back home says too."

"He's a godly man, your preacher. You listen to your pastor. And you listen to your husband. Billy's a little down right now, but he's getting up…right Billy? … and he's going to be fine."

Olin knew the preacher was right. It was true…Doctor Aiken told him to *calm down*! How could you calm down when that devil power came all over you? He didn't need to calm down. He needed to get right.

"Dear darling ones, you don't need no doctor. You don't need the vain and worldly philosophy so many are offering. What you need tonight is the power of God. What you need is Holy Ghost power. And God is here this evening…right this very minute. The Lord is here for you with His love and His forgiveness. You need the power and He has the power. You need the forgiveness and He has the forgiveness. He's offering it to you tonight, whatever it is you need. God's got the answer for you. Come to the altar of the Lord and receive His cleansing, receive His salvation, receive His Holy Ghost power."

Is thy heart right with God,
Washed in the crimson flood,
Cleansed and made holy,
Humble and lowly,
Right in the sight of God?

The young mother, clutching her baby, knelt before the pulpit as Evangelist Carrigan sang the invitation hymn. It would be so much better with a piano…even a guitar…but the Lord provided as the Lord saw the need. "Jesus is calling to you, dear ones. Every one of you. Jesus is calling and offering you cleansing and power this very evening. Come forward and see your life changed for the better. Praise His precious name."

After praying for the young woman and her baby, Evangelist Carrigan patted Billy and Olin on the shoulder for encouragement in their battles, and as was his practice in good weather or bad, he walked alone outside the tent and looked to the night sky. "Dear Father," he lifted his hands and prayed aloud, "Please be with my Linda-Cheri and with my boys Johnny and Billy and Pat, and help me to find my way home to them, Lord. But only as Thou willest, only as Thou willest. Mighty One, Thou art in truth a consuming fire."

"Reverend, may I have a word?"

The Evangelist turned to see Olin Ainsley standing behind him, his jacket draped over his arm, wiping sweat from his face with a red handkerchief.

"Forgive me, sir. I was having my private time with Him, but I ought to have attended to your need first. You have a need tonight?"

Olin's face was reddened, he felt his body afire, his chest tight. "Reverend, these meetings you're holding…."

"Have you come before? I'm afraid I--"

"There's something…something a bothering me. But maybe this is not such a good time."

"There's no better time, Mister." Carrigan was familiar with the signs of conviction. This poor soul was in torment. One more toward the two million. He could not be certain, but he suspected he would not be allowed to see Jesus until the full 2,000,000 had been brought in…until his personal harvest was complete. Thumbing through his book last night had humbled him and left him in fear. Fewer than fifteen hundred for twenty years of faithful effort. 1,500 of the 2,000,000 demanded by the Lord. He really did want to see Jesus. But the work needed to go forth, and he supposed he would see Jesus when Jesus was ready to see him.

O the Holy Ghost was pouring all over this dear man. "There is no better time, sir." Once God got hold of a sinner's heart He wasn't going to let up. He'd squeeze and squeeze. Torment time was upon this poor fellow, and the only solution was for him to fall on his knees and repent…and maybe repent over that pitiful three dollars too. "This feels like God's time for you, Mister…I'd like to pray for you by name, sir."

"Thomas. Ernest Thomas." Olin was shocked even as he heard the lie come from his mouth. He'd done lots of things…that miserable three bucks for those poor people…but lying wasn't one of them. He never lied. Lying meant you were weak and afraid. So he never lied. Sometimes he might have kept quiet instead of saying what he knew to be the truth. But he never actually lied. He certainly never lied to a preacher. Still, he heard himself lie, lie to a preacher…and he let the lie stand.

"Mister Thomas. Ernest Thomas, what is it you'd like for Jesus to do for you tonight?"

How could he just look the Evangelist straight in the eye and point-blank lie? "This doesn't seem a right kind of place to be holding meetings." Where had that come from?

"God has put us here, Mister Thomas. In the Town Dump. And He's going to send us 2,000,000 souls for Jesus. And you are called to be among them. Of that I'm certain."

"Not in a dump. A dump is no place for meetings." He didn't care about the Giantown Dump. Why was he saying these things?

"The Lord has His ways. Jesus will meet your need. Even in the Town Dump. I know God is speaking to you, Mister Thomas. I know the Dump is not really troubling you. God has just shown me it is something about an animal. Isn't that right?"

Good Lord! Forgive me, Jesus. Forgive me, Jesus. "I don't think any of this is right. Do you realize you didn't even take an offering? How do you know those people are going to Kentucky? I'd think you'd be more responsible." Why was he speaking like this to the preacher? He needed God's cleansing, he needed God's power. Why couldn't he just ask for it?

"Mister Thomas, the Town Dump is fine. And the Lord has promised to meet all my needs, so I have no fear. But sir, the Spirit of Discernment is showing me there's something very dark troubling you, something about an animal that's in your care. Maybe seeking your protection. What is it, sir?"

"It's the Dump. It's just the Town Dump. It isn't right. Not for the Gospel."

"When God is moving you need to be listening and you need to obey. Truly. This is a most serious matter. Don't fiddle around about the Town Dump."

"I'm listening. I've heard everything you've said, Preacher. But you ought to listen too. You could get disease out here in this place. That baby could get sick. Well look, I've said all what I had to say. So I've got to go. Thanks for your time."

Olin stepped around Carrigan and headed for his *Ford*, stumbling through a pile of garbage before he located the path. His heart was pounding, his collar wet with sweat. He felt ashamed, angry, furious that some two-bit Evangelist would dare to speak to him this way. He'd been honest and told the man what was on his mind. He'd have been willing to offer help if the preacher had been open. After all he had the money. Money wasn't the issue. Instead he'd practically been accused of lying… he'd been treated like some damn criminal.

"Good night, Mister Thomas. I hope you'll be back tomorrow evening. God will be here for you."

"Don't hold your breath."

2
First Methodist Repeats Fete
Pads & Pies Promoted

Each year about this time the ladies of First Methodist Church of Power City touch hearts in Tecumseh County as they sponsor The Bandage & Bake Festival. According to Wauneda Bazzler, Chairman of the event, "We provide more cancer pads than any other group. Plus our pies are real good." This year Mrs. Bazzler's Dutch Apple Pie will be one of the features. Those locals who have experienced more than a few turns of the calendar can perhaps recall to memory the days when the Church Ladies produced bandages for the men of the Grand Army of the Republic at the Soldiers Home. Nowadays, with fewer needs for bandages the need of the older soldiers at the Home for cancer pads has been impressed upon the ladies. All the pads are made with love and are donated completely free of charge to deserving but needy veterans suffering the ravages of this cruel disease. Pies, cakes and other goodies are on display and all are for sale. All are home-made, and available to the public at a reasonable cost. The Festival will take place this Saturday afternoon at First Methodist from 1 until 4 p.m. All members of the community are cordially invited to attend.

Entry to the event will be via the side door of the Church.

3
A Wonderful Assemblage Of Family,
Friends & Church Leaders

Belva Ainsley, unusually tense, stood in the doorway between the kitchen and the dining room while Marva, holding Wendy at the table and sensing something wrong between her parents, squeezed Wilton's hand. Olin, in place at the head of the table, wondered aloud why Belva told everyone to be seated. There was nothing to eat but some rolls. He glanced around the long table where his daughter and son-in-law and baby granddaughter sat on one side, and the newly engaged Reverend Jeremy Poston and Regina Winslow on the other.

"Regina made the rolls," said Belva. "Don't they look simply delicious?"

"Belva, why don't you just sit yourself down so the preacher can lead us in prayer? Once we get that out of the way I'm going to devour Regina's rolls since there's nothing else on the table."

"I would prefer you lead us in prayer, Mister Ainsley. Since you are the head of the household," said Jeremy.

"Just a simple prayer would be fine," added Regina. "It doesn't need to be fancy."

Olin stared at his niece and her fiancé as he grabbed a roll and stuffed a hunk into his mouth. "I expect the preacher to pray. That's what he does. The rolls are excellent, Regina. Try one, Willie."

"I'll wait until we pray, thanks. Did you hear Tom Mooberry's retiring? Getting out lock stock and barrel. After that heart attack. There should be a good auction coming up out there in the Fall. Plus his fields will likely be up for sale. Though I don't believe he's a hundred percent made up his mind on that."

"I've got all I want," said Olin, taking a second roll and smearing it with butter. "Mooberry's land's no good anyway." His stomach had been upset ever since the meeting at the Giantown Dump four days earlier, and he didn't feel up to a meal or rolls or prayers or company for that matter. But this was Sunday dinner. And he was determined to enjoy his Sunday dinner. There was no excuse for Belva telling everyone to come to the table when the meal wasn't anywhere near ready. Was this her way of embarrassing him? Trying to get even?

Belva wiped her hands on her apron and sat on the edge of her chair. "I'll need to get right back to the kitchen. Once we pray. The roast took a little longer than I expected."

"I'll help you, Aunt Belva," said Regina.

"Thank you, dear. It's nice to know someone cares. And Marva, if you could. I know you're not feeling well, but I do need your help. Wilton can surely hold the baby for a few minutes. The roast was just so much larger than I anticipated. We've had to do some unexpected slaughtering recently, and there's just all this meat to deal with. Regina, I've so much, I hope you can take some with you for the Marshall. And you too, Marva. Wilton loves a good roast. I know that for a fact. Please, girls, I do need your help."

Olin shot a glance at his wife. Why was she bringing this up in front of the preacher? In front of Marva? "We haven't prayed, preacher."

"Perhaps we should wait for the food before we pray. If that's all right, sir?"

Jeremy Poston, oblivious to the tension around him, was very hungry. The sooner they got the women back into the kitchen, the sooner he could eat. "We missed you and Mrs. Goins at the prayer meeting last week, Brother Goins."

"No, it's not all right. We need to render thanks now," said Olin.

"It's always good to be missed, Reverend," said Wilton. "Mrs. Goins and I have enjoyed your recent sermons very much."

"Thank you, sir."

"Let's pray now, Preacher. I don't want to wait any longer."

"Why not take a moment, Olin," said Belva. "I'm afraid I've rushed everyone to the table, and I apologize for that. We'll have everything ready in a couple of minutes, and then we can pray. Regina, Marva, I have aprons for you in the kitchen. We don't want to get anything on your new dresses. Doesn't Regina's dress look lovely, Marva? You might consider some like that. Come, girls. Please. Olin, I'll have everything on the table in a minute. It'll only take us a minute. Now, Wilton, if you have a problem with Wendy you call."

"Sit back down, Belva. Reverend, let's pray now."

"Olin," said Wilton, "You're pushing it a bit, buddy."

"This is my house and I want the Preacher to pray. Now."

Reverend Poston glanced around the table, and noting that even Wilton had decided to bow his head, began the blessing. "Our gracious heavenly Father, we thank Thee for this food--"

"Yet to be served," mumbled Olin.

"And we ask Thee to bless this wonderful assemblage of family, friends and church leaders. In the strong name of Thy Son Jesus we pray. Amen."

"Amen," echoed Belva. "Girls. We'll only be a minute, Olin, Wilton. I'm sorry."

Marva touched Wilton's arm and brushed the baby's cheek as she stood to go to the kitchen. She would have liked to go home, but accepted the impossibility of ignoring her parents' squabbling. It would have to be endured.

"Before you step into the kitchen I want you ladies to know how much we all appreciate you," said Wilton. "Your labors at home, and also your efforts at the Church are well appreciated. What a blessing the three of you are."

"O Wilton, you are something," said Belva. "Girls, please. I need your help now or we'll never get this meal on the table."

"Sorry, Willie. No offense intended."

"None taken, buddy."

As the women left the table Jeremy looked to Olin who had begun aimlessly shifting his silverware around on his bare plate. "So you had to do some unexpected slaughtering? Why was that?"

"What? What business is that--?"

"There's really no set time," said Wilton. "More a matter of preference. It's not like planting. Reverend, on another matter of concern, I had hoped to see us well accepting of the new name for the Church, but as near as I can tell some don't really understand the change yet. Is there something I need to do to help move this along? Help the people grasp the significance? Jeremy?"

Olin tapped his finger on his empty plate and glanced out the window. *Community Church*? Is that what you're thinking, Willie? Belva mentioned that... something about changing it. Sounds good to me. A Church for the whole town. You've got my vote on that. I'm really sorry for what I said before. To you. I was completely out of line."

"Sometimes it just builds up in a fellow. That's what friends are for."

"It's not really a matter of a vote, Mister Ainsley." Jeremy Poston ran a finger around the edge of his plate. "I have some reservations about dropping the name *Baptist*. And some others are bothered by that as well. Frankly it's--"

"*It's*?" Olin looked up from his silverware reverie. "*It's* what? Wilton just told us he thinks it's a good idea. Period. If you think it's good, Willie, then I think it's good. Reverend, let me tell you something...you'd be advised...and these *others* too. Just who are these *others* with their fancy *reservations*? I've got no reservations, Preacher."

Wilton smiled at his old friend. Olin was losing control, but he was still loyal. "I see it as a matter of mission for the Church, Pastor. We need to lift up our eyes and see as our Lord would have us to see."

"I can't fault any of that, sir."

"Well yes, but we're not doing it. You see, Jeremy, Mister Ainsley and I have watched over the years as the town, and the Church for that matter, have grown more and more provincial and inward in our focus."

"Provincial?"

Olin got up from the table. "I'm going to check on them in the kitchen."

"Please let them be, Olin. We need to respect our ladies. They'll serve the food when it's ready. That's their role, not ours."

Sitting down Olin ran his hand over his bald head and grinned. "Can't live with 'em, but can't live without 'em."

"There's a lot of truth to that old saying, buddy. Reverend, no one new ever moves into Aschburgh. Now it wasn't always like that. This used to be a thriving community, son. But businesses have been shutting down for the past ten years 'til now there's hardly anything left but Churches and the *Birdsall Home*. You can't build an economy on a funeral home. No new plants have opened up since the wells went dry. I mean for goodness sake this just can't go on. There's going to be no one but a bunch of graybeards. Which'll be us. We never have a visitor at the Church. Never. Unless it's a relative visiting for the holidays. Now I'm not an alarmist, Jeremy, I'm a positive, progressive person. I like to think of myself as a forward looking businessman. A Christian and a strong Republican. But do you know the last time anyone was saved at our Church? Olin, can you help us out?"

Olin looked up at Wilton and pursed his mouth as he considered the question. "That'd probably have been the very old Mister Birdsall, Willie. Don't you think? Esterton Birdsall. He's long retired and dead now. Of course he was from a different group of the Birdsalls from ours. He was never in the funeral business like Joey. They all farm over to Mooresville. Josephuston's his actual name, but he's usually called Joey. Not Joey...he's not from Mooresville...but Esterton's family was. His son was Steventon who was killed a couple of years ago over by Brooklyn."

"Pinned under his tractor wasn't he?"

"Mushed is more like it. Lay there all day before anyone found him. Said he didn't have a drop of blood left. And of course they held the funeral over here, at the *Birdsall Home*, so a lot of folks thought he and his father, Esterton, were local Birdsalls because of that. But they're really a whole different group from Joey and his bunch. Though you know all of them lean to that *ton* business...have those sorts of names. Plus they're a clannish people. And I suppose when push comes to shove you'd have to say they're all from around here. The men, not the women. On the *ton*. They all favor that *ton*, and it sets some in town against them. Seems a little... well, *partial to themselves* I suppose. So anyway that was Esterton, the old man, who got saved. And Steventon, the son, the one that got killed. He went forward in any event. Esterton. It could've been just his wife insisting. She was always like that. All over a fellow."

"You can never know what's in a man's heart."

"And Esterton was a man, sir? I mean the name is like a woman's."

"Preacher, if you'd known him you wouldn't ask something like that. Those of that generation had an integrity and straight forward honesty about them that you just don't see. Not any more. They were common and they stood forward and they stood hard. You don't see that much these days. I don't mean to call attention or to embarrass him, but Mister Goins here, he's still got those same old-fashioned qualities."

"Now, Olin, you're laying it on pretty thick."

"It's true but I'll drop it. People these days aren't willing to accept responsibility for anything. They got their Unions and their Democrat Party always making excuses, and they're expecting a hand-out every time you turn around. There's no real Americans around here anymore. You can't get anyone to give you a decent day's--"

Belva stood in the doorway to let them know dinner wouldn't be much longer. "The girls have everything almost ready. Regina's just fixing the gravy. They are such a help to me. Is Wendy being good, Wilton? I don't know what I was thinking to take so long."

"Is there anything we can do? Perhaps carry things in?" asked Wilton.

"Just be patient with us, Will. I believe the meal will please you."

"I'm sure it will. But we'd be glad to help."

As she returned to the kitchen Olin muttered, "Dinner used to be on time around here. That's another thing. Times are changing. And not for the better either."

"Now, now, buddy. We don't have to catch a train. That wasn't when he was actually saved, was it? Esterton?"

"No. I suppose you'd have to say no. No one gave much credit on that one. Especially Reverend Hoheimer. The old man was pretty much forced. The real one was at *Indianville Memorial*. The hospital, Reverend. Just before Esterton finally died. He'd been coming and going for over a month. Every day they said was his last. So Reverend Hoheimer told him he wasn't saved and he was going to hell...just put it to him like that...I think that's what finally put a stop to the coming and going ...but he got him saved that morning. Reverend Hoheimer. Esterton died that day. He may have had a weakness for whiskey…the Reverend…but I've always felt he was a good man. Sister Hoheimer sang at the funeral. Not much of a singer, but it sure touched a lot of folks. Do you remember that, Willie?"

"O yes. Not too high, not screechy like she sometimes did."

"Alto?" asked Jeremy.

"More or less I suppose. In that general area."

"And that was the last salvation at *Bible Baptist Holiness*?"

"Last one I can remember," said Olin. "Didn't have time to get him baptized of course. Immersed. So some always questioned if it stuck. But see it's not just the *Baptists*. There's no salvations in any Church around here so far as I know. Some of these preachers don't even believe in it anymore. Anybody wanted to get saved they wouldn't know what to do. Not that I would know everything, of course. You'd figure some kids would get saved in Sunday School and all. But I've never believed most of those salvations are stickers either."

"If you're *saved* you're *saved*."

"Not if the first salvation wasn't real."

"It's not for us to judge, Mister Ainsley."

"I know a salvation when I see a salvation. Believe me, Reverend, if there's one thing I do know it's a salvation that's not real. Somebody that says he's saved and then he's drinking and…well, he's up to stuff."

"Who can say?" offered Wilton hoping to get his friend off the subject of Esterton Birdsall. "But you see what I'm saying, Reverend? I'm not pointing the finger. We're all to blame. But the fact remains no one's been saved around here for at least ten or fifteen years. You've got businesses closing, you've got families breaking up and kids running off to who knows where, you've got able-bodied men joining unions, and you've got no one going to the altar. It's a doggone shame."

"No profanity, please," Belva called from the kitchen.

"A lot of it is because of the Bolsheviks," said Olin.

"Now that's absolutely true, buddy. From what I hear most of it's due to that. But the issue is what can we do to turn it around here in Aschburgh?"

"But I'm sure people around here are growing spiritually, Mister Goins. Church people."

"Yet that's not what the Word of God demands, Jeremy. We are called to go out into the highways and the byways, to all the world...my goodness...and to bring them in, to get them saved. Even the Jews. All the world, Jeremy, all the world."

"Well yes, sir, but--"

"Changing the name of the Church is a small thing, son, but it is step one in the process of changing our focus. Getting *God's Vision*. Making the call of Jesus our call. *First Community Church of Indiana*, Reverend. With mission Churches all over the State...then all across the Midwest."

"I like that, Willie. Now that's a big idea. That's a really big idea."

"And our Pastor, our Aschburgh Pastor, totally in charge, really in an apostolic role, developing and over-seeing all these assistant Pastors all over the nation, and later all over the globe itself. That's the vision right there in a nutshell. Is that the kind of thing you could handle, Pastor? Because I believe you can. I believe you have that in you. The vision of the Lord Jesus Christ. Hundreds being saved every week for starters. Eventually thousands. Thousands upon thousands. Not one old man on his deathbed every ten years. I'm sorry for going on like this, fellows, but I get excited just thinking of it. I believe you have it in you, Reverend Poston. I really do. Apostle. Reverend Doctor. I can see that. Reverend Doctor with a whole staff of assistants."

"Reverend Doctor?"

"Would we have authority to do that, Willie?"

"I can see that. I can see it. I really can. Of course we have the authority. We'll just take the authority. Who's going to tell us otherwise? *Reverend Doctor* and all that that would mean."

Marva and Regina carried steaming plates of beans and corn and mashed potatoes in from the kitchen. "Dinner is served," said

Marva. "No more starving men," said Regina. "Watch the baby around those hot plates, Wilton."

"We really would have the authority, Mister Goins? Where would we get it?"

"Son, let's not even talk about it again. I said we have the authority. End of discussion. We have the authority. We get it from God."

"Belva, corn and beans and potatoes is fine, but let's get some meat on this table."

CHAPTER 10
THE FELLOWSHIP OF BELIEVERS
MUDDLES THROUGH THE
WINTER OF 1926 – 1927

A long chapter leading us through the muck and the mire.
Physical and spiritual. The architectural party explores rot and
Greg endures suffering, finally concluding the situation calls for
an alternative strategy. Summoned to the Cincinnati synagogue
Greg refuses to ignore the plight of Marva and Forsyth. The
Professor lectures on the virtues of the Hoosier pioneers, but
Greg finds a good cup of A&P more to the point. The name of
Norman Overbeek pops up again as Wilton and Bob discuss cars.
Curiously it turns out that attendance is taken at the wedding of
Regina and Jeremy. Many other things of interest are recorded.

1
A Nice Hot Cup Of Earl Grey, Or Even Better,
Lapsang Souchong

Freshly shod in heavy woolen socks and green *Wellingtons*,
Wilton, Greg and Bob stumbled in the heavy mud around the
outside of the old barn, poking at the rotting wood. Bob wore one
of Wilton's old black topcoats, while Greg clutched an oversized

moleskin jacket around him, its bottom flapping inches below his knees.

"These socks and galoshes are killing my feet," said Greg as a piece of board snapped off in his hand. "It's so bitterly cold, Willie."

"The mud would have sucked your slippers right off," said Wilton. "You'd be barefoot in all this icy slime."

"O God, I don't even want to think about it. Willie, this is terrible. I had no idea of this condition. You should have warned me when we were up here earlier. I don't want to lose any of the rustic charm...the potential that is...but the rotted innards will have to go. It's just a disaster. I'm so disappointed."

"Hasn't been used since years before my father died. We rent out most of the land, but the barn's not been used for well over twenty-five years. We keep a couple of young fellows on...mostly to maintain the house and lawns and so forth, but I'm sure they haven't bothered any with the barn."

"It's a good old country barn, sir," said Bob. "With a little work it could be quite nice again."

"Maybe for cows. I had no idea it turned so cold up here. And it's not even Winter yet. Did you know that it did, Bob? The wind just blows and blows. I didn't notice it on the drive from the city, but it cuts right through you. It just drives full force from the Rocky Mountains. There's not a thing in the way, you know. Even with this gargantuan coat you've put me in, Willie. It's a monster. Chills you to the bone. My God, it's like living at the North Pole. Bob, make a note that my sense is most of the supporting timbers are good...no, write *adequate*. But I'm so upset about the exterior. Don't you agree? Willie, I had counted on you to take better care of things."

"The old barn has never been high on my list of priorities."

"Don't be glib. I'm trying so hard to help you, so don't be glib. Marva needs this structure, but look what a mess you've made of it. I hope you realize you have responsibilities. With a wife...and now on top of that she's chosen to have a baby. I hope you have at least some realization what you're putting me through. This is going to absorb much, much more time than I have to give. I'm

221

being brutally honest with you, Willie. The Cincinnati synagogue has to take precedence. I owe that to the Hebrew community there. They've been more than gracious to me. Plus there's a good chance for an international award. And the Hebrew community has never had me traipsing about in the rain and mud, and that's the truth, Willie. They've been very kind. Isn't that so, Bob?"

"I certainly don't want to take you away from your obligations to Ohio's Chosen People."

"What do you mean by that remark? Don't be smart, Willie. I really want to help. For Marva, if not for you. I've always cared for you, but this time you've let me down. I'll just have to work out a plan for a temporary studio in the house. Not the ideal solution, but it will be only stopgap. It must be below zero out here, Bob."

"Thirty-nine up at the house, sir."

"That's *inside* the house, surely."

"Zero is quite different from this, Greg. Your nose falls off at zero. Why don't you just head back to the house and get warm. As far as a temporary studio, Marva and I can work that out."

"No. Absolutely not. We've got Forsyth involved in this, and frankly my reputation is on the line. I'll work something out. I'll get Marva a superb studio. Don't worry."

Bob leaned toward Wilton and whispered, "Mister Penn can be extraordinarily creative in a situation like this. He responds well to pressure."

"It'll be a stopgap…only a stopgap. Until I can straighten out this mess you've made. Bob, give some thought to your brother-in-law for this job. Norman. The rough work. Willie, you ought to be ashamed to have let the barn deteriorate this way. If you'd taken just a little care we'd have a gem on our hands. I could envision it in major magazines. Major. Marva's studio. Marva's studio would have been a gem. A sapphire. Instead I have to work with a rotten hulk."

"I am sorry, buddy."

"You ought to be. Shame on you, Willie. Shame on you."

"Don't be so hard on Mister Goins, sir. After all carpentry's not his field."

"I'm sorry, but it's *shame*. That's what I'm left to deal with. *Shame*."

Marva and Forsyth, amused, watched as Wilton, Greg and Bob burst into the unheated changing room, the architect flapping his arms and rubbing his ears, and quickly completing the process of pulling off over-sized coats and boots and rushing into the heated house. Greg, bare-foot…clutching his slippers and stumbling…was the first one in. Marva grabbed two of Wendy's crib blankets from the laundry room and double wrapped them around his thin shoulders. "You look so cold, so very, very cold," she whispered.

"O Marva."

"Toughen up, man. This is Hoosier country," admonished Forsyth. "Our ancestors laughed at frost-bite."

"I didn't see you out there, Professor. It's way below zero."

"Thirty-nine by the kitchen thermometer. Marva and I have been tending to more important things than mucking about in the mud. We need a studio, Penn. And it needs to be warm, to be suitable for Skootums."

"Skootums?"

"The baby, man. Baby Wendy. Marva and I have decided to get to work next week-end. And the baby will be with us as we work. So we need a studio. At least an acceptable area while you get that rotten barn ready. And make sure it's properly insulated."

"O Marva, I'm so cold."

"Let's go into the kitchen. I'll pour you a nice cup of hot coffee. Let me help you slip into your shoes."

"*Prima Dona ballet slippers* is more like it. Anyone who wears ballet slippers and no socks in late October deserves to be cold."

"A nice cup of *tea*, please. *Lapsang Souchong*. Or if you don't have that available, *Earl Grey* will be very nice."

Marva tucked the blankets tightly about him and smiled. "*A & P?*"

Wilton steered Bob into his study to learn more about the operation of the *1924 Springfield Silver Ghost Closed Limousine With Coachwork By McNear.* "Do you think it's up to these rough country roads we have around here? I've considered getting one, but I'm not sure I want to put that kind of investment to the trial of all these ruts. I'm working with the Town Board on paving, but it's still a couple of years off. At best."

"The *Ghost* will stand the test and give you real satisfaction."

"On these roads? Invested in the *Company* are you?"

"Wish I were, Mister Goins."

"What about maintenance? Repairs? We're really out of the way up here."

"Now that could be a problem. You might want to consider a chauffeur/mechanic sort of individual. Perhaps someone who would also have other duties around your estate, sir. As he mentioned, Mister Penn sometimes employs my brother-in-law Norman Overbeek. The fellow knows these vehicles inside and out. I think he could very well be your man. Perhaps something could be worked out."

"Your brother-in-law?"

"He's more than capable, sir. And he's a very hard worker. He's young, but he's an old school sort of fellow. You could get rid of the young guys you keep around. That would level out some of your expense. I'm sure Norman would agree to a trial run, as it were."

"Chauffeur, mechanic, handyman? Interesting. I'll think about it. Norman."

"Overbeek, sir. Norman Overbeek."

"Let's warm up with a cup of coffee...or I guess it's going to be tea...and then I'd like for you to pull the *Ghost* into my garage. Not that I know much about engines, but I'd like to take a closer look."

Greg Penn, with Wendy's blankets still draped over his shoulders, eased off his patent leather slippers and vigorously rubbed his feet. "Thank you for the tea, Marva. *A & P*? It is so good. The quality is superb. I'm very pleasantly surprised. Many times it's the humble things that provide the deepest pleasure. What does *A & P* stand for?"

"Now you just sit right there until you're all warmed up. We don't want a chill setting in. I need to check on Wendy, and then I'll be right back." He was probably twenty-five years older than her, but even so he was so tiny and frail. Like a boy. She wondered who took care of him when he was in Indianapolis or traveling all over the world on his projects.

William Forsyth sat across the kitchen table critically eyeing Penn. "We're going to need a studio of some size, and we're going to need it quickly. That decrepit barn's not going to do for Marva, and you know it. She'll want to have Wendy near her side as we work. That's only reasonable. Can you imagine having a tiny little baby in that damp, cold cavern?"

Greg Penn pulled the slippers back on his feet, sipped at the tea and sighed. He reached out and took Marva's hand as she rejoined them. "It was so, so cold out there, Marva. I didn't feel it at first. I suppose I thought it was going to be a little lark in the country. But how wrong I was…how very wrong I was. Isn't it too cold to be having babies up here?"

"Wendy's sleeping fine."

"Professor, I realize you have no sympathy for me, but I've never claimed to be a he-man like you."

Forsyth eyed him with contempt. "Hell, Penn— I beg your pardon, Mrs. Goins. Please forgive me."

Marva reached out and touched the back of the old painter's hand. "It's all right, Professor. I'm not all that delicate."

"I'm very sorry."

"You were saying to Greg about a studio…."

"Yes, of course. We need something right away, Mrs. Goins. It needn't be large, Penn. But a warm, cozy spot. Bright. Bright, warm and cozy. Like what you've done so effectively with Wendy's nursery."

"The nursery is only temporary. It's nothing like what it will be once we've had time to actually renovate. I'll transform this farm house into an estate."

"Mrs. Goins, I am sorry. That's not like me. Using language like that around a lady."

"Professor, please. It may be temporary, Greg, but it's also very nice. Don't be so modest. You have more than talent, you have a gift. You are a very great artist. And I know you can do wonderful things for my temporary studio."

Feeling much better now, Penn lowered the blankets a bit, though he still kept them wrapped about his lower back. He ran his free hand through his white curls, fluffing them out the way he liked. "I think maybe if I'd worn a hat."

"It's not even November, man. Do you have any idea how cold it gets out here in January?"

"I don't even want to think about it. Dear Marva, please don't be afraid. It's true the barn is a mess. Willie has disappointed me, to say the least. I can't remember another time when he has done that. But in spite of my personal disappointment, I won't let you down. You'll have a beautiful studio with northern light, high ceilings, skylights, whatever you desire. And in the meantime I'll arrange something, as you say, temporary...I think in terms of *stopgap*...something at the very least suitable for your initial artistic studies before Bob and I head back to civilization later today. I need to be at my synagogue in Cincinnati for several days at least. Unfortunately the *AIA* hasn't shown any interest, but I'm hoping *RIBA* will be open to us even though the synagogue is an American design. I believe the British are making a concerted effort to be more receptive to Hebrew things. Up until recently *RIBA*'s had a rather poor record that way...as I'm sure you know. But you'll be pleased with my stopgap studio, Marva. You'll be pleased, so don't be afraid. I'll meet your need."

"*RIBA*?"

"Thank you, Greg," said Marva. "I have total confidence in you."

"*The Royal Institute*, Professor. Your trust means so much to me, Marva."

"Institute of what?" Forsyth stood up and rinsed his coffee cup at the sink.

"British architects, of course. I hope you're not going to leave your cup there like that. Someone may come in, think it's clean and use it."

"It is clean. Let's have a look around, shall we? British architects! What do you think about the attic? My Lord, that's the spot. Mister Goins says it's well insulated, and it's got a couple of medium sized windows, so that may well be the logical place. Mrs. Goins and I will be getting to work next week-end, and we need a spot. At this point northern light isn't going to be a big issue. I think the attic's just right, but if not, we need some place and we need it right away. A nice well lighted place for Skootums too."

"Wendy will love being with us as we work."

Greg lifted the blankets higher on his back and flipped one end around his neck. He stepped over to the sink and filled Forsyth's cup with water. "That way, Professor, it's clear to everyone that this is a dirty cup. Clean means *carefully washed with soap*. You know, Marva, though I still intend to pursue the barn studio, this attic atelier of ours could be quite charming."

"I would like the barn. Eventually. Something completely my own. Separate from the house."

"Of course you would. We all would. You deserve it. The artistic pursuit requires a clean separation from the mundane. And you'll have it for sure. But for now our charming attic atelier will be quite nice."

"Well, let's have a look, shall we?" said Forsyth. "The way you're moving you're going to dawdle the whole day away. Sipping tea and draping yourself in blankets."

"Would you have a little more hot tea, Marva? The *A & P*, with perhaps a touch of cream, would be magnificent. There's a lot to be said for grocery store tea, but I wonder if you've ever sipped *Earl Grey*, or even better, *Lapsang Souchong*?"

2
ATTENTION
TAX-PAYERS & PROPERTY OWNERS OF ELWOOD

Who paid for extra police protection for the

FAGGOT RED DWARF

When he traveled our streets coddled by our own police???

YOU DID!!!

You paid out hard earned dollars so your cops could protect the Queer Fag Pervert GREGORY PENN. This character is well known to our Christian leaders who are working hard to keep our nation safe on account of his sick interest in little children and BOLSHEVIKS!!!

Did the Mayor or Police Commissioner worry about your kids???

NO!!!!

About your property taxes???

NO!!!

Are they all in the pocket of this BOLSHEVIK QUEER???

YOU BET!!!

SUPPORT

THE UNITED BROTHERHOOD

OF

THE MADISON COUNTY
KU KLUX KLAN

DEFEND MADISON COUNTY

&

OUR BELOVED ELWOOD

from

KIKES, JIGABOOS & FAGGOTS

KEEP AMERICA

FREE, WHITE &

CHRISTIAN

3

A Moment When Truth Is Spoken To Power

Finding a minister Doctor Poston would accept was difficult, but once they settled on the Reverend Doctor Bartlesharm, President of the *Switzerland Institute of Bible Baptist Holiness*, all obstacles to the wedding fell by the wayside. Jeremy assured President Bartlesharm the change in the name of the Aschburgh Church in no way indicated a repudiation of *Bible Baptist Holiness* principles...so that cleared that obstacle. Jeremy's uncle, who was both the honorary mayor of Quercus Grove and a member of the Switzerland County Council, assured Doctor Bartlesharm that certain alleged violations in the electrical wiring at the *Institute* would evaporate... which removed yet another roadblock. Finally Wilton Goins, badgered by his wife, assured the success of the entire operation by sweetening the honorarium discreetly handed to President Bartlesharm several weeks prior to the sacred nuptials.

First Community Church of Indiana was packed that first Saturday morning in December of 1926 as Regina Winslow, tresses blazing against the simple white of her dress, taking the arm of her uncle Marshall Sevier Winslow, who was himself in full constabulary glory, processed down the aisle to become the bride of the Reverend Doctor Jeremy Poston.

As cousin and best friend of the bride, Marva Goins, who only that morning began to suspect she might be pregnant again, was Matron of Honor, with all three of Jeremy's sisters serving as Bride's Maids. The groom's selection of Wilton Goins to be his Best Man had been something of a shock to the Poston family when they learned of it back home in Rising Sun, but each of his three brothers graciously agreed to step aside and to serve as humble groomsmen.

Virtually every respectable soul in Aschburgh, Rising Sun and Quercus Grove...plus a number of good people from Giantown and Indianville...were invited to the ceremony, though only a highly select group were to attend the reception at the *Lions Den*. Busy with his duties as Best Man, Wilton directed the two tellers from the *Aschburgh Savings & Trust* to take note of which Aschburgh residents failed to make an appearance at the wedding. Fortunately only a handful failed to pay their respects...several clergy and the local grocer...and Wilton felt only the grocer was of sufficient significance to require a reprimand.

Naturally, the next day being Sunday, and it being the Christmas season, Reverend Doctor Poston was in his pulpit in the morning and Regina was at the piano at the front of the Church. But early the following morning duty was left behind as they took off... in a *Ford* borrowed from Marshall Winslow...for five glorious days of honeymooning.

After staying overnight in Richmond at the home of one of his cousins, Jeremy proudly drove his bride to Rising Sun early Tuesday morning where she was bid welcome by the entire Poston family, several of whom traveled over from Madison and even Louisville for the occasion. All that week Regina met new relatives, toured the family farm, and cooked on the old wood burning stove under the supervision of her mother-in-law.

She and Jeremy broke this routine...fascinating though it was...with two short trips to Quercus Grove where she was introduced to various faculty and she and Jeremy were privileged to have tea with President Bartlesharm. By Friday afternoon as they headed back north toward Aschburgh...though Jeremy thought the visit a immense success and regretted leaving so soon...Regina was delighted to wave good-bye...prepared to settle into her new home and to begin the domestic process of caring for her Jeremy and bearing his children.

They had been home but ten days, and she had just begun to get the parsonage looking half-way respectable, when she learned that Reverend Franklin Tuyter, the elderly pastor of the *First Methodist Church* had insisted on a meeting of the local ministers and that Jeremy had agreed to host the gathering of divines in their parlor that very afternoon. After several hours of deep cleaning she answered the door to greet Pastor Tuyter, a man the Winslows and Ainsleys had disdained for as long as she could recall, as well as Pastor Warren Warburton of the *First Friends Church*, a quiet cleric she scarcely knew though he had been in town for many years. Apparently the Pastor of the *First Christian Church* had been too busy to attend. She noted that not one of them had been at her wedding or sent a gift.

Regina stood in the doorway to the parlor with a serving tray full of cups and saucers, a pot of hot tea, napkins and fresh baked cookies, but she was reluctant to interrupt the rather intense conversation between Jeremy and Reverend Tuyter.

"To my mind...and I say this in love, young fellow...the very name of your group is presumptuous. Who has declared you the *Community Church*? As though the rest of us are interlopers. You still have a lot to learn. A minister must guard himself against spiritual arrogance, my boy."

"It can be a fatal defect," agreed Warren Warburton. "Prayer is the great protector."

"God showed the name to Mister Goins in a sort of revelation," said Jeremy.

"Elucidate that for me in the Bible, son. *A sort of revelation*? I think not. Young lady, why don't you just come in and put that tray down. We can help ourselves when we're ready," said Reverend Tuyter, the elder statesman of Aschburgh's clergy. "You elucidate that for me with chapter and verse, young man. Just show me where God ever speaks to the town banker rather than to the Gospel minister. I'd like to see that."

"Well, surely Matthew was *like* a banker, don't you think?"

"No I don't *think*."

"That's unfair," said Regina who though she had put the tray down, had not left the room. "Anyone with half a brain knows Matthew was too like a banker."

"Now dear," said Jeremy. "This doesn't concern you."

"He was more of a tax collector than a banker, but there are similarities," said Pastor Warburton. "God often speaks to those who don't seem likely to be chosen. He does have a heart for the outsider."

"Young lady...I believe you were a Winslow...am I right?" said Tuyter. He was a lean, hard, wrinkled man with large, bushy white eyebrows. His efforts, years earlier, to bring the Winslows and Ainsleys into the *First Methodist Church* had proven fruitless, and he had never forgiven the slight or the families.

"I *am* a Winslow, and I am closely related to both the Ainsleys and the Goins. Which you know full well, sir," she said, glaring at the old man.

"Be that as it may, this is a discussion for ministers of the Gospel, not for their wives. I'm sure you understand. And remember no matter who you are related to *God is no respecter of persons*." He turned his attention back to Jeremy. "Matthew was a saint, my boy, he was not *like a banker*. You and Mister Goins need to repent of spiritual pride and consider the truth of the Gospel. As far as I'm concerned your little group has no reason for existing. If you wish to post a claim as Baptists, well that is within our local tradition...but the last thing we need around here is yet another bunch of schismatics claiming to be a *Community Church*."

Regina, who had not budged, knew she was losing her temper and that there might well be consequences. "For your information we are not a *little group*. We are the largest Church in the area, with close to two hundred of a Sunday morning. Hardly a little group! I believe you have about thirty. If that."

"Now, now Regina," said Jeremy. "No offense was intended."

As was frequently the case during meetings of Tecumseh County clergy the tension between the spirit of brotherly Christian love and the bloody tooth and claw of congregational and denominational competition hovered menacingly over the chairs, sofa and doilies of the parsonage parlor. Franklin Tuyter, now red in the face, fingered the gold lapel pin, a brightly colored rose, which had been presented to him by the Chamber of Commerce of Giantown for his efforts on their behalf. He considered either storming out of the house or slapping the nasty girl, but decided neither action would be to his advantage. *"Not by might, nor by power, but by my spirit saith the Lord of hosts,"* he said with his head bowed.

Until recently Reverend Tuyter had always been invited to offer the blessing at the monthly *Lions Club* meeting. This had been the case for so long that many in the community...and even some within the ranks of the *Lions*...believed him to be the official chaplain of the *Club*. But for the last three months... at the insistence of Wilton Goins...the Reverend Doctor Jeremy Poston had been sought out to say the prayer...and the Reverend Tuyter had been left to sulk over his chicken and noodles. Frank Tuyter could recall when *First Methodist* had been the largest, most influential church in town. In those days they had their own orchestra and choir, and even now he stored their rotting choir gowns in an unused and locked Sunday School classroom for the day when the Church would once again taste of that glory. In fact they would still hold their position of *first among equals* if it hadn't been for the preposterous *Bible Baptist Holiness* sect and now this mutation calling itself the *First Community Church of Indiana*.

And behind it all were the Winslows, Ainsleys, and nowadays the Goins. Pushy arrogant people. Poston was too stupid and too wishy-washy to have thought this up on his own.

"Wasn't it our Lord Himself who cautioned us not to pay too much attention to the quoting of Scripture?" asked Regina. "Didn't He say that all sorts of riffraff could quote the Bible? Something like that?"

Reverend Tuyter sipped tensely at his tea and kept his counsel. He was a man who knew how to bide his time, who intuitively sensed how best to survive and come back from an attack. Despite facing insurmountable legal and moral problems shortly after the turn of the century, when the Police Chief of Indianville caught him peeking into bedroom windows and the Stonewall County Prosecutor had charged him with *Indecent & Unnatural Acts*, Franklin Tuyter, through a calculated process of marrying well, investing his wife's money wisely, and cultivating those in high places, had survived and surmounted. By patiently working his way back into the community's good graces, he had even in time become a powerhouse within the *Indiana Methodist Convention*.

"Jeremy, it's not attendance figures, or for that matter dollars and cents in the offerings, which concerns us so much," said Warren Warburton of the *First Friends Church*. "It's the decline of the principle of Scriptural love and unity we see in the local Christian community." Pastor Warburton believed once Jeremy Poston saw himself guilty of sheep-stealing he would ease off, and relations between the Aschburghian congregations would return to the natural balance of harmony and peace which had existed as long as anyone could recall. Competition and the agitation that followed were not in anyone's interest.

"It's not that we're worried about money or numbers. Not at all. Our concern is about *Agape* love and cherishment, about the joy of brotherhood which has reigned in Aschburgh long before any of us were called to this blessed place. Money is not an issue. The Lord provides."

"I appreciate your concern," said Jeremy who had very little understanding of what this was all about, but was a bit frightened by the tone of the meeting.

Regina knew that the *Bible* and the Church taught that she was to be submissive to Jeremy, in fact submissive to all men in authority, and especially ministers, but the Winslow women had never paid much attention to those ideas, and Town Marshall Sevier Winslow had often been amused by the way she would speak her own mind no matter what he cautioned.

Now she found it impossible to remain quiet in the face of this nasty old hypocrite and his ridiculous companion. Everyone knew Tuyter had been arrested as a pervert and had spent six months in jail, but no one would ever say anything for fear of his connections with the local judges and politicians. She knew Jeremy would just sit there and put up with all these insults and innuendos. But she would not. She had had enough of the Reverends Tuyter and Warburton...especially Tuyter.

Regina was proud of all that Jeremy had achieved. *First Community*, under his leadership, and with a lot of help from Mister Goins of course, brought new life and enthusiasm to the Christians of Aschburgh and Tecumseh County. Men like Tuyter and Warburton wanted to be left alone, in comfortable command of their little fiefdoms. They wanted everyone to remain asleep. These hirelings were terrified and threatened because power was being restored to the local Church by her Jeremy.

"God is moving in the life of *First Community*," she said, afraid they would hear the quiver in her voice. "You two may not like it, but God is empowering Jeremy's ministry at *First Community Church of Indiana*."

All three ministers turned and stared at her. "Pardon?" Reverend Warburton was puzzled, Tuyter furious, Jeremy intimidated.

Unconsciously Regina kneaded her apron and bit down on her lip. "Our Church is doing important things. God is blessing my husband's ministry and wonderful things are happening. People are coming to the Lord and are being saved and baptized and filled with the power of the Spirit for a life of holiness." She could feel the tears on her cheeks but was determined to go on. "And people in the community recognize it too. That's why they're coming our way. They want to experience Jesus, and they can't do it in your dried up old Churches." It was embarrassing to say these things, but she had to do it.

"Now, now, Regina," Jeremy cautioned.

Reverend Tuyter glowered, his face red, his white eyebrows seeming to jump out at her. "Reverend Poston, may I remind you of the Word of God? *For if a man know not how to rule his own house, how shall he take care of the Church of God?*"

Warren Warburton rubbed his palms together and then ran them through his hair. "That's a good point, Reverend. I can feel the move of the Spirit."

"Regina, would you bring us some more hot tea?"

Regina was certain her damp face was reddening and that everyone could hear her pounding heart and her strained breathing. But she could not and would not let this go on. She wiped at her tears, and resolved to speak what needed to be said. Sometimes truth had to be spoken to power…and certainly to pomposity. This was her home and she was not about to let this dreadful old man insult and demean her husband and quench the Holy Ghost.

"You're afraid because you're losing your power over people in the community. You're losing money and people and influence. That's what this is about. I've lived here all my life and I know about you, Mister Tuyter. I know about your past and all that you've done and gotten away with. And I'm not the least bit impressed by that absurd rose lapel pin you think gives you the right to lord it over folks. Jeremy is an honest man, a man of simple holiness. My husband is a stranger to sin, unlike you."

"How dare you! You're going to regret this. *Both* of you."

"Could we have a word of prayer?" asked Reverend Warburton.

"We all need to calm down," said Jeremy. "Please. Can't we all just get along?"

"People are leaving your churches and coming to *First Community* because they sense the presence of God in our midst. And because Jeremy gives them the good teaching they need. And because they know of your past perversions. It's as simple as that. Up until now people have been afraid of you, sir. Because of your money and who all you know. But that's over. Everyone knows what you've done, the disgrace you've brought on yourself and on your Church. And it's you, not Jeremy, who's arrogant and filled with pride. Everyone can see that too."

"Control your wife, Poston! Order her to be quiet!"

"My goodness."

"Regina, please."

4
A Touch Of Honey & A Dollop Of Grape Jelly

Late that afternoon, in response to Jeremy's rather incoherent telephone call, Wilton Goins stopped by the parsonage. He was more than well pleased with *First Community's* rapid growth, and satisfied with the way Jeremy was handling himself. At least until now. Hysteria in a man was not something which he readily abided. Still, Jeremy's personal limitations were the main reason he was so useful.

Much of the Church's growth resulted from Goins' own efforts, a word here a word there, well thought out and well placed, subtle but not so subtle they wouldn't be understood. And slowly there was a flow of new families attending, first from Aschburgh of course, but increasingly they were seeing a better class of folks traveling down from Giantown and even a few up from Indianville. One family had actually traveled over from Muncie last Sunday. That kind of growth was unheard of in the history of Aschburgh.

First Bible Baptist Holiness probably never had more than sixty on Sunday mornings, and now, restricted to the same building for the moment, they were packing out the sanctuary. One seventy-five was standard, and that first Sunday back in October, for Wendy's dedication, they had been forced to go to folding chairs borrowed from *Giantown First Baptist*.

Borrowing chairs from the Methodists was the old Baptist joke, but this time the local Methodists, really dirty old Frank Tuyter, refused the loan request. Of course one seventy-five would be tops on average…until they built a bigger church. But that would happen soon.

Jeremy Poston sat on the sofa across from Wilton, head down, rubbing his hands together, while Wilton slowly and rhythmically rocked back and forth in the rocking chair which as he recalled used to be in the parlor of Regina's grandmother, Zula Winslow, a rather difficult woman who tended to slam her cane on the floor when thwarted. Regina came from the kitchen with tea and a plate piled high with freshly baked chocolate chip cookies.

"Good afternoon, Mrs. Poston. Now those are going to spoil supper, but there's no way I can resist."

"*Regina* for goodness sakes. Mister Goins. Please."

"The word's out that you gave old Parson Tuyter what he deserves and a bit more for good measure." He grinned and turned his chair to face her. Tucking a large white napkin into the top of his vest he took four cookies onto a small plate. "You make the best chocolate chip cookies in Tecumseh County. Or Stonewall for that matter. Jeremy, for years Regina's cookies have been tops. Back when you were in *4-H*…I remember them even from then. Now don't you tell my Marva I said that."

"County Fair actually. I won the blue ribbon two years in a row. How are Marva and little Wendy? I hope *they* had a good day. I've been planning to stop by to visit. We've never been apart this long, Marva and me. Not in our whole lives. Absolutely never. We've hardly seen one another for more than a minute. And I haven't got to spend any time with our little Wendy."

"They've been fine. Marva's been missing you a lot too, though she understands. She's been real busy getting her studio all set up, and getting into a painting routine with Professor Forsyth. The artist. Her teacher. They seem to be striking it off real well. Which is kind of curious, they being so different in lots of ways. Of course Wendy's the center of attention. *Skoot* they call her now. Did you ever hear of such a name? I believe she's going to turn out some fine paintings."

"I'd like to see her and the baby. Skoot? That's a nice cute-name. I've been missing her."

"She'd be well pleased to see you. Where'd you ever find such a good wife, Reverend?"

But the Reverend Doctor Jeremy paid no attention to his wife or to Wilton's banter. He continued to run his fingers through his hair and to stare at the floor. "Is there some way we can make amends to Reverend Tuyter, sir? I'm more than willing to seek his forgiveness. I just don't know what to do. Some way we can patch this up? I do want to continue here at *First Community*. I don't want to have to resign."

"Forgiveness? Resign?" Wilton munched on a cookie and sipped some tea. "Is this a special tea, Regina?"

"Like that *Lap Sioux*? O you men! The last time I saw her Marva said Mister Penn wanted her to serve that. Whatever it is."

"Sounds like him. He's what they call a *connoisseur*. I do admire your chocolate chips, Mrs. Poston."

"*Regina*. It's *A & P*, just like Marva serves you. She picked it up in Giantown for both of us."

"Simple and straight forward. That's always best. Pastor, what are you talking about, seeking forgiveness, retiring? Patch things up with Tuyter? Why would we want to do that? The man's a terrible bully who's always had to have his own way. A dirty, nasty man. I can't abide people like that. Forget him. What we need to do is finally drive him out of town like we ought to have done years ago."

"We've offended him, Mister Goins. And probably the *First Methodist Church*."

"Him yes, the Church no. They've been trying to get rid of him for years. I don't know how he ever survived that mess he got himself into years ago. Connections and money, no doubt. It's not fair, not right, but money tends to rule the roost. Do I detect a touch of honey in these cookies, Regina? Just a touch. Am I right?" Wilton helped himself to two more cookies.

"How did you know that? That's amazing. I wouldn't have thought you could taste it. Does it take away from the chocolate taste? I like a light chocolate."

"Quite the opposite. Delicious."

"You know that little friend of yours made quite a stir with his fancy car," said Regina. "I've never seen anything like it. I'll bet it costs more than most houses."

"It looks more expensive than it is. A fellow can afford one if he sets his mind to it. Marva's thinking about one, but I'm still partial to our *Ford*."

"She is! Wouldn't that be something? More tea?"

"We've made a powerful enemy, sir," said Jeremy. "It's so discouraging. I mean I've worked so very hard, and now that we've begun to grow we don't need an enemy like Reverend Tuyter."

"Tuyter's a blowhard, Jeremy. He'll be ancient history in no time now that you've stood up to him. Regina, did you know Greg designed the *Opera House* in Giantown? Right after we graduated from college. Before he went off to *Notre Dame*. Long before the *Institute of Technology* and all those fancy places in Europe. Years and years ago now, I'm afraid. Of course since then he's gone on to do major stuff all over the country. All over the world really. I think there's even a job coming up in Vienna or Germany or someplace over there."

"Isn't *Notre Dame* that Catholic school up by South Bend?"

"Didn't seem to bother him none."

"He's so tiny."

"He's got lots of friends who watch out for him. I just hope he finishes my job before he takes off for Europe. And then he's still got to finish that Jewish synagogue or temple in Cincinnati. But back to what we were saying, I think the way you use the honey brings out a slight change in the texture. Gets you away from the brittleness you get in so many chocolate chips. It's not so much an issue as to taste…though perhaps there is a subtle difference."

"Softer you think?"

"Pliable. That sounds odd doesn't it? About a cookie. May I have one more, and then I'll stop."

"Pliable?"

"Now Marva uses some mixture of light and brown sugar. I don't know the details, but I imagine it's more or less traditional. She got that from Belva, and Belva probably had it from Zula. She was a character, your grandmother Zula. For the most part that mixture...whatever it is...does the job quite nicely. When I was a boy my mother liked honey. Quite a bit of honey actually. Back then my father used to keep bees. That's how I come to know about it. But then she always overdid the rolled oats which dried things out. Yours are so delicious I won't want to leave."

Regina offered the tray of cookies to Jeremy who waved it away. Wilton started to reach for another but pulled his hand back. "Too many, too many for me. Jeremy, you ought to try one."

"Do you see anyway around this, sir? I really don't want to have to resign."

"Stop fretting, Pastor. You can't offend a man like Tuyter, you can only threaten him and beat up on him. The thing is once you've started beating him you've got to finish the job. Otherwise he'll go for you as soon as you turn your back. Like a cornered copperhead. Anyway, Regina gave it to him good from what I hear, and I'm sure not going to get my britches all twisted up about that. I hear he was angry as a wet hen."

"I appreciate your saying that, Mister Goins," Regina whispered.

"Wilton, please. Pastor, you're a well blessed man to have a wife like Regina. Truly well blessed."

"I can't help but worry about the whole thing."

"Take no care for tomorrow, for tomorrow's gonna take care of itself. I think I have that a little wrong, but there's a lot of wisdom there. We're fine, just fine. I'll have a little talk with Warburton and Tuyter. Threaten them in a friendly way. Everything will be settled just as we want it. The honorable way. Our way. The best way."

"Mister Goins is right, Jeremy," said Regina. "Fretting's not going to help anything."

"I suppose."

"Now here's something for you to fret about, Pastor. I want to get started on the plans for a new church. Not an expansion. A totally new church building. Maybe outside Aschburgh on the main road. Would you put together a sketch...your own ideas... for a new building? What you think we'll need. You've got to think in terms of what the architects call *function*. The things we do, the things we're going to need as we continue to grow. Then the appearance of the building will follow on those things. I want us big...very big. Bigger than anything else in Tecumseh or Stonewall Counties. So you can start right there. And as I say, probably located just outside of town. I hear the State's going to pave that gravel highway real soon...and once that happens I want to be ready to branch out.

"I want that report by Sunday so you'll need to really rack your brains. Make sure we have your input too, Regina. Fair enough? I can see a lot of opportunity for you, Jeremy. Somebody's going to have to lead our growth, and you're the logical man. In no time at all we're going to start other churches, missions of *First Community Church of Indiana*. All over the State. I've told you this before and now it's about to happen. And we'll need a Bishop to supervise the work, the expansion."

"A new church building?"

"We'll have it to you on Sunday, if not before," said Regina, pushing the cookie plate toward Wilton. "I have never heard anything so exciting. Such vision."

He helped himself to an eighth cookie. "One thing my mother did make well, and that was her molasses cookies. She always put a dollop of grape jelly right in the center. Made a little indentation, you know, with her thumb. I remember a couple of times she let me do it, but my fingers were pretty small back then, so usually she did it herself. Simple and straight forward. Always the best way. *Scrumptious* my Daddy used to say. He was a lot like me that way. He loved a good cookie."

"*Scrumptious*! That's so sweet."

"She died when I was quite young. But her cookies were scrumptious."

5
Pulling The Gospel Banner Back To Earth
& Folding Up The Battered Gospel Tent

Four evenings in a row...faced with a freezing tent filled with empty chairs... Evangelist John Patrick William Carrigan had fallen to his knees on the straw and sawdust covered dirt floor and begged for a sign that he was free to pack up and go south to rejoin his family. But there had been no sign, only the nagging realization that God often left His prophets in the desert until was He was ready. *In the fullness of time.*

So Carrigan stayed...a hard, unsmiling, balding man in a stained and patched black suit, a tattered canvas coat tossed about his shoulders, with a large black *Bible* in his gnarled fist... striding daily through the deserted Giantown Dump on his way from his scratched and dented truck, a converted Army ambulance, to the empty *Gospel Tent.*

The cold, sharp morning cheered him, and he resolved he would devote the morning and afternoon to prayer and study, preparing for his evening service. He knew he couldn't expect many to turn out when the temperature was hovering in the low-20s...but he felt certain God was getting ready to move and His servant had to be prepared for that precious moment.

As he walked around a ten foot high pile of smoldering trash the old graying *Gospel Tent* came into view. With its patches and stains, its tens of thousands of holy travel miles...worn with authority...it had come to resemble the Evangelist himself. One end of the Gospel Banner proclaiming *2,000,000 Set Free For Christ*, normally secured along one side of the tent, had broken loose, and its large hand-printed red letters soared and dived in the crisp wind, its divine prophecy snapping twenty feet above the faithful tent.

Olin Ainsley had arrived at the Dump an hour earlier hoping to catch the Evangelist before the holy man began his morning routine. It had been many days since he had slept...a long time since he had been able to speak with Belva or anyone else for that matter. But there were many things which needed to be said, needed to be done, needed to be resolved. And it seemed all of that led him back to the *Gospel Tent* in the Giantown Dump and to the ministry of Evangelist John Patrick William Carrigan. *2,000,000 Set Free For Christ.*

As Carrigan drew closer he saw twenty yards from him, a powerfully built man of average height, balding like himself, dressed in farmer's overalls and canvas jacket stained with oil, pulling the loose end of the banner back to earth and securing it in place along the side of the tent.

"Thank you, sir," he yelled into the wind.

Olin glanced over his shoulder at the Evangelist, but said nothing.

"Much appreciated. Very much appreciated, sir. Fewer and fewer will go out of their way to help. I believe it's a sign of the Lord's soon coming."

"That wind would've tore it all up," Olin said, extending his hand. "I just thought I might stop by again. See how things were going for you, you know."

"I'm sorry, I'm afraid...."

"Back a bit. I stopped in one evening. There was only a few here. It must get hard trying to do your work in this place. Can't be many stop by."

"And you came forward?"

"We talked after the meeting. One time. Just a few minutes."

"Mister...?"

"Vinson."

"Mister Vinson. Well, sir it was good of you to stop by this morning to save our banner. Perhaps the Lord has sent you. I sense Jesus working in you."

"Jesus in me? Well, Preacher, I don't know about that. But I believe He has sent me, though not about the banner. God's got bigger fish to fry than the banner or me for that matter...don't you think?"

"No, Mister Vinson, no I don't. Nothing's too small for the Lord's love and attention. His eye is on the small, cold bird…don't you know? The Lord's concerned about the mosquito, the worm, the cottonmouth down south where my children are staying. You name it, God cares for it. Doesn't matter what we think. That's just the way He is. He's a Lord who can't love enough. The *Bible* says that's His very nature, Mister Vinson. *God is love* it says. Did you know that? You just can't out love the Lord. He's--"

"Reverend, I'm not sure just how to say this, but would you have time this morning to talk to me? I've got some…well…."

"Something loading up inside you? Some kind of problem?"

"No, no…not really a problem. Things are fine and all that. Just some things…things that maybe could be talked over."

"Well, that's what I'm here for, sir. Why don't we go inside? Not that it's not chilly in there too, but we're both men used to weather…and at least we'll be out of the wind."

Olin and the Evangelist tied up the tent flap away from the west wind…letting in the bright morning light…and pulled up a couple of wooden chairs to face one another. The farmer sat down and stared out to the northeast at the blue sky against the horizon of mounds of smoking trash. This was not where he thought he'd be perhaps…definitely not where he wanted to be… but the Preacher was right, something was loading up, something in his chest or a little lower, something signaling the *Gospel Tent* as where he needed to be this morning.

"Sorry that I don't remember--"

"You talk to lots of folks, Reverend. No offense."

"Yes, but each person is special. There's no excuse."

"A lot of regular folks look alike."

"Common folks are the Lord's star-spangled people. That sounds kind of fancy, but I've always preached that. I do apologize for my forgetfulness. But however that may be, let's talk about what brings you here this day."

Olin sighed, stood up and ducked just outside the tent. "I think I need a second, Preacher. I'm about ready…about ready. It's just not an easy thing. Just give me a second." After pacing back and forth in the wind he came back in, blew his nose and sat down across from the Evangelist.

"It's often not easy, sir, but that's o.k. Take your time. Sometimes these things are just not smooth and there's no rushing them."

"O.K. Let me just spill it out. Do you feel death is the end of it, Reverend? I know you can't say that sort of thing from the pulpit, but man to man right here this morning...do you think once we die it's all over...there's nothing? Sometimes it seems to me that's how it'll be. Maybe a time of pain and then that's it. Like with a sick dog. Now I can handle pain. I'm not afraid of that. And the peace would be good. A fellow over at the elevator, the grain elevator, he calls it the *peace of death*."

"No, no, no, sir. I don't mean to speak against your friend, but Satan's talking through that fellow. You listen to me carefully. I've got nothing to gain by lying to you, Mister Vinson. I'm going to tell it to you straight. After we die we all face eternity and then the judgment. Every single one of us. Eternity either in heaven... if we've trusted Jesus and lived that way. Or in the torment of hell if we haven't."

"And that's fire, right? That's what the *Bible* says, isn't it?"

"Yes. I'm not going to sugar-coat it for you. That's what it says, Vinson. More pain than any man can bear."

"Vinson's not really my name. So that's a lie right there. I'm sitting right here lying into the face of a man of God. That's some way to get started. Some way!"

"I don't need to know your name, sir. Jesus knows it. And that's enough."

"But I don't see why I've got to lie."

"Do you lie all the time? Something you can't help?"

"No. Definitely not. That's the thing. I'm not a lying kind of man. Never have been. To be honest, I can't stand that trait in a fellow. You lie to me...we're finished. And yet here I am I can hardly say good-morning to you without lying to your face. Bare-faced filthy lying. Totally dishonest. Contemptible."

Evangelist Carrigan stretched out his heavily muscled arm and grasped Olin by the shoulder. "Sir, you're a working man, same as me, so I feel I can talk straight, no pussy-footing around. Mister, both the Holy Ghost and the devil's got ahold of you good, and you're in a life or death fight. *For we wrestle not against flesh and blood , but against principalities, against powers, against the rulers of the darkness of this world.* That's the *Bible.* You understand what it's saying there?"

"I'm fighting the devil. Right?"

"That's it. You got it right there. But with the Holy Ghost on your side. See, you can't fight the devil alone. *Wherefore take unto you the whole armour of God, that ye may be able to withstand in the evil day, and having done all to stand.* Now, Mister you're staring the *evil day* right in the eye. The devil's trying to kill you."

"You got that right, Preacher."

"Listen to me. Ain't no turning back, no stepping aside. I'm speaking simple here because that's all I know. We're just common type men, you and me. I'm talking a spiritual battle, I'm not talking flesh and blood here...but Mister, it's your eternal life that's on the line because the spiritual controls the fleshly. It's a straight on nose-to-nose fight to the death...fists, knives and guns, nothing ruled out...axes and pitch-forks, though we're speaking in the spiritual here."

"I can feel his grasp on my chest. My heart I guess."

"That's where he's working at. God's showed it to me in the strong eye of discernment. Spoke it to me just now, as we're sitting here knee to knee in this old *Gospel Tent.*"

"It's like with Judas," muttered Olin.

"Judas? Why'd you say Judas? Why would you say Judas?"

"Because I'm a betrayer. I'm a bold-faced lying betrayer, just like him."

"Nobody's that bad, Mister. Judas was so evil God busted his guts open like a sack of rotten garbage. Spilled them on the ground for the dogs, the cats and the worms. You ain't no Judas. Who you are is a guy Jesus loves and wants to save."

"Hanged himself first."

"That's got nothing to do with the love of Jesus. *Judas* hunged himself. God didn't do that. He hunged himself, and only after he done that did God spill his guts. They say that's the way it reads in the original Greek. He hunged himself which may be the *sin against the Holy Ghost*...though I'm not sure...and it was only after he done that nastiness that God, seeing him dangling and dancing there, finished him off. Showed him mercy really."

"You understand Greek?"

"No. No, but I wish I did. I've got a couple of books from men who do. Back in my truck. I do a lot of studying back there, trying to learn more about God, to make up for my failings in school. I do regret the waste of those days. Thought I was so smart. Anyway, Mister...you're no Judas. That old sucker stabbed Jesus in the back. He was a deceiving Jew. No, you're no Judas, Mister. Nobody's that bad."

Olin leaned forward and covered his face with his big, calloused hands. "O God, I'm even worse, Preacher. You can't get no more worse than me. I betrayed my own child, my daughter. Can you even imagine? You can't get no worse than betraying an innocent baby that never did no wrong and always looked up to you. That's when Jesus says to tie the stone around your own neck and drown yourself in the lake."

"You betrayed your own baby?"

"My daughter."

"What's her name?"

"What difference does that make?"

"None I suppose. Mister Vinson, you're hurting bad."

"I told you my name's not Vinson. That's just another lie."

"Sorry. Is this the truth about your child?"

"She's a gentle little thing. She has a mind of her own, you know, but she'd never hurt anyone or anything. That's why it pains so much to have betrayed her. And now I've done it to her baby too. My own granddaughter. How's God going to forgive this? Again and again the same thing. Didn't even stay for the dedication pictures."

"Your daughter has a baby? Look, Mister I can't claim to know what you're going through. I'm ignorant of the details, and I guess I have no need to know. But I know one thing. I know you need Jesus if you're going to get a grip on this stuff. You're fighting the devil, you're fighting *powers and principalities*…and like I already said the Lord has showed me you're in danger, great danger."

"I've gone to church all my life, Preacher. My folks carried me into the *First Bible Baptist Holiness Church* in my baby blanket. And after my fashion I've always tried to live like a Christian's supposed to live. And I've done it…for the most part. It's just this one thing I can't get straight, I can't stop doing. No matter how hard I try it doesn't work…I keep going back to it again and again."

From the earliest days of her ministry Sister Aimee Semple McPherson was said to have preached that the most dangerous thing for a man's soul was a life-long habit of going to Church every Sunday…and now Evangelist Carrigan could see the truth of that seemingly contradictory teaching. Not that Church was bad…heaven forbid!...but for too many, including this dear man, it got substituted up for facing the reality of sin, for coming to grips with the need all men have for Jesus.

"You can't become a Christian by going to Church, sir. Not even in a baby blanket…and I understand and respect the actions of your dear parents back then. Don't get me wrong. They did the right thing as they saw it. I respect that, but sir, you can't buy your way into salvation by doing good things. I believe that was the mistake of Martin Luther or one of those early preachers. It just doesn't work that way. The *Bible* says, *All have sinned and come short of the glory of God*. And again it says, *The wages of sin is death, but the gift of God is eternal life through Jesus Christ our Lord*. Now you just can't get around that."

"I've heard that. Yeah I've heard that many times. And I believe in the *Bible*, Reverend. It's the *Word of God*, the absolute truth. Every single word of it. But as hard as I've tried to do good things in my life, it's just this one thing I can't seem to get right no matter how hard I try. I just keep going back and doing it again and again. Betraying my baby."

The Evangelist grasped Olin by the upper arm, lowered his head as if to pray, and wondered could it be that the Lord had detained him at the Giantown Dump all these cold and lonely months just to share the Gospel with this one poor soul? Wouldn't that be just like the Lord! Wouldn't that be the sauce on the pie? While he was focused on the *2,000,000 Set Free For Christ* of his vision, God had His eye upon this one who was so tormented. Praise His holy Name! "Fellow, just forget about going to Church since you was a baby. Forget all your good works. Forget all that, and just recognize your own sinfulness. That's why you're having this problem. You refuse to see yourself as a sinner, you refuse to see that you need Jesus right now. You're no worse...but you're no better either. We're all sinners. Everyone last one of us. Blessed be the name of the Lord."

Olin had listened to similar words all his life, and had never been able to make any sense of it. Preachers would take a man who did nothing but good stuff, and then try to claim he was really sinful. It made no sense. You took a man like Wilton Goins, who always had a good word, who always tried to help folks and to keep a cheerful presence, who was a faithful leader in the Church, and then you turned around and called him a sinner. It made no sense. You either did good in this world or you did bad... and sometimes, like himself, you did mostly good, but sometimes really bad stuff got in there any how. You didn't even know where it came from. It just showed up out of the blue, and somehow you had to find a way to deal with it. Or maybe you couldn't find a way. And that was how it was. You didn't need more preaching, what you needed was down-to-earth help to get the bad stuff out. And preachers never offered that.

"What you need to do, sir, is come to grips with the fact that you're helpless in the face of your sin. Only Jesus can save you."

"Preacher, I've never smoked, drank or cussed. I've tried to lead a good life and support my family, and I don't see how God can just turn His back and desert me now. Liquor has never touched these lips. Not once!"

"Now I'm going to tell you this, and I want you to listen carefully. You need to fall on your knees, repent of all your sins... that means be sorry for them and promise to stop doing them... and then invite Jesus into your life as your Savior and your Lord. There's no other way. There's just no other way. The *Bible* says,

All our righteousness is as filthy rags. You can't work your way into heaven. When push comes to shove, fellow, *Ye must be born again.* Period."

"Yeah, I know, I know. Jesus said that, right? To that Joseph of Arimathea."

"Nicodemus. Sorry. That makes no difference. Jesus said it."

"But I've always felt a man sort of works into that born again a piece at a time."

"It's not like that, sir. It's all about Jesus and putting our trust, our faith in Him. There's no short cut, there's no other way. The *Bible* says, For *God so loved the world that He gave His only begotten Son, that whosoever believeth in Him should not perish, but have everlasting life.*"

"That's *John 3:16.* Have I got that one right there?"

"The great word of salvation. Receive it into your heart, spirit and mind. You need a personal relationship with the Lord Jesus Christ. He is the only one who can help you. Mister, you don't need a dumb old preacher like me...you need Jesus."

Olin could see this was going no place. Somehow he and the Preacher would never see it the same way. But the *Bible* had the answer and Jesus was the answer... the Preacher was right about that. He'd listened to those truths all his life, and he didn't doubt them for a moment...but somehow right now it didn't make any difference. That wasn't going to straighten it out with Marva. What he needed was something to help him stop beating on the cattle, to stop killing them, to stop him from humiliating himself in Marva's eyes. He didn't need more Jesus...he had Jesus ... ever since he was a baby. What he needed was some real help. Some way to stop doing what he was doing. What he needed was some peace. He'd gone to Church all his life, he'd followed all the teachings, often double-tithed, triple-tithed one whole year...and when he really needed help none of those things was worth a whit. He loved Jesus, and he supposed it true that Jesus loved him, but what he needed was a word, a word of advice that would make a difference. "You've given me a bunch to think about, Reverend.

A lot to chew on. There's wisdom in the *Good Book*, that's for sure."

"*Thinking's* not the answer. Remember the *Bible* says, *For the wages of sin is death, but the gift of God is eternal life through Jesus Christ our Lord*. There's your answer, sir. Not *thinking*. Not *chewing*. Jesus. Jesus is the answer. Jesus is the only answer."

"Yeah, I can see that. The *Bible's* crystal clear on that. And I know it's true. Every word of it. It's God's *Holy Word*. That much I know for sure. I'll be thinking about everything you've said here. I'll be mulling it over. I promise you that. You can count on it, Reverend."

"This is your moment, sir. You need to kneel down here right now and receive Jesus. You need to put your trust in Him… whether you understand or not. I'll kneel with you …I'll pray with you…I'll be here for you. But it's Jesus who's going to save you, and for that to happen you need to speak directly with Him."

"I'd like to think about it a bit."

"There's nothing to think about. I surely don't mean to push, but you know that. It's a time for simple men like us to take action. Sometimes a man just has to stand up. Jesus is faithful and true, Mister…*the same yesterday, and today and forever*."

Olin looked straight into Carrigan's eyes, feeling in the man as great a sadness as was in himself. "I admire you, Preacher. I truly do. I respect you. You know what you believe, and no matter how it hurts you're going to stick with it. But I'm just not quite where you are. I need to think about all this. Chew on it a bit. Somehow, even though I know you're right, and I know the Bible is true…I'm just not ready. I'm sorry. Really. I'm sorry."

Evangelist John Patrick William Carrigan watched as Olin Ainsley disappeared around a hill of trash. Would he ever see this dear man again? More to the point, would the fellow be one of the elect who turned to the Lord…or one of the many who heard the Word and still turned away from God's mercy, rushing back into the darkness of satan's world? God's infinite capacity for love and forgiveness was the miracle of His grace.

Truly His *Amazing Love* as the old hymn had it. *For I will forgive their iniquity and I will remember their sin no more.*

Unfortunately the tragedy of Man's sinfulness was his seemingly infinite capacity to reject that *Amazing Love.* This fellow was so sad, so very sad. And yet perhaps even this tortured soul would find his way. Evangelist Carrigan certainly hoped so. He liked the cracked skin and the heavy calluses of the man's hands...a farmer's hands. He liked the thickness of his neck and the power of his shoulders and arms. He felt the man's sadness and hurt the same as his own. The *Bible* was written for the workingman, not for college professors. *God's Book* was meant to be grasped in a strong hand, with pages to be turned with difficulty by fingers thickened from hard work and read with eyes worn with care and pain. His own hands, his own eyes were like that, and when he lifted his sweat stained *Bible* he held it with the power of dirt and blood and suffering so it could never be pried from his hands by the effeminacy of the so-called modern world and its false teaching. All praise to the Mighty One, the High King of Heaven. Surely God would not fail him this one time. This poor man would be given one more opportunity to be saved...it was not yet settled for Mister Vinson...he felt the certainty of it in his heart...God's Spirit speaking to his spirit.

Under normal conditions the Evangelist was opposed to *putting out a fleece* as Gideon had done in *Judges*, and so had never indulged in the practice. Though a routine procedure among many of his fellow *Full Gospel* preachers Carrigan felt it smacked of arrogance...a prideful effort to control God. But these were difficult times for him, more troubling than he had ever faced. The cold, the snow, the cutting wind of central Indiana's Winter, the constant wear of tiny meals on his large frame...the loneliness and even futility of night after night spent by himself with no one coming to hear his preaching...these were all things he was used to, indignities he accepted as the Apostle Paul had before him. But the separation from his dear wife and his beautiful babies... so far away in Augusta, Georgia...was wearing him down, and bringing him to a point where he prayed continually for the Lord to ease his burden, to release him...even if but temporarily... from this heavy load.

And so it was, shortly after Olin Ainsley had left, that the Evangelist *put out a fleece*. He would flip open his *Bible* without looking, and he would place his finger blindly on a passage, and reading it he would accept its specific direction to him. *Stay* and he would stay. *Go* and he would go. God would be faithful as Carrigan lifted up what was a cry of anguish and desperation.

Holding his big *Bible* in his left hand, without looking, he let it fall open of itself to the *Book of Ezekiel*...one of his favorites in the *Old Testament*. Then wetting his index finger he touched the page and glanced down at it. Carrigan smiled as he found himself staring at the familiar *Chapter 33, verse 9*. He sighed and began to read aloud.

Nevertheless, if thou warn the wicked of his way to turn from it; if he do not turn from his way, he shall die in his iniquity; but thou has delivered thy soul.

John Patrick William Carrigan knelt in the cold mess of sawdust, straw and dust and gave thanks to his God. The direction was clear...the work the Lord had called him to do at the Giantown Dump was completed. The Gospel had been preached to that special one whom the Lord had drawn to this place, and the eternal decision would soon be made...one way or the other...but he John Carrigan, the servant of God, had been faithful to his calling. His work was completed for this crusade.

He was released. Released not from the call of Evangelist, but released from this place of cold wind and desolation...and called for the present to the warm lands of the American South. The *Gospel Tent* and its prophetic banner would be taken down and stored in his old truck before dusk, and he would enter upon yet another pilgrimage of faith. He would drive straight to eastern Georgia to rejoin his faithful wife and children, that they too might share in the blessings of a gracious God and faithful Savior.

6
Providing A Community Service

In the cold and silent darkness of the early morning hours... under the direction of a heavily disguised Town Marshall Sevier Winslow...four stealthy and well-paid lads from Kokomo methodically scattered bright yellow handbills all along the sidewalks and lawns of Aschburgh as its citizens and dogs slept. A few of the flyers were pasted onto the lamp-posts at the corner of *Goins & Ainsley*...one even on the window of the Bank...and several were attached to the walls of the Post Office, thereby defacing Federal Property. But hundreds were simply scattered along the sidewalks and streets of the downtown area. In the morning a few folks thought it a vicious act of vandalism...but many saw a deeper meaning. And all were relieved to have the information.

PERVERT IN THE PULPIT
Do You Want A
CONVICTED CHILD MOLESTER
In Aschburgh's First Methodist Pulpit?

REVEREND FRANKLIN TUYTER
CONVICTED PERVERT

Reverend Franklin Tuyter, pastor of First Methodist Church of Aschburgh, was convicted of
SEX PERVERSION & UNNATURAL ACTS
in Stonewall County Circuit Court on September 4, 1903.

HOW SAFE IS YOUR WIFE?
HOW SECURE ARE YOUR BABIES?

CHAPTER 11
PREPARATIONS FOR A GOINS
DYNASTY PROCEED APACE

*In which Wilton Goins pursues his program of community
and family enrichment in his own special way. The Methodist
Episcopal Bishop makes a decision. Issues of agriculture and
business are discussed. William Forsyth insists on various
notions relating to smiles and palettes. For her part Marva lays
claim to future greatness. Also, some thoughts are tossed in on
genetics and the size of little Wendy's feet.*

1
Coming To Grips With Problems
Of Both The Urinary Tract & Domesticity

Wilton Goins' lower back had been aching for the past month,
but the best thing Doctor Aiken could come up with was to
proclaim with a big smile…following a humiliating if not sadistic
examination…that some gland or other in his private area was
badly swollen but there was nothing seriously wrong…and
unless something else turned up there'd be no need to *clean it
out*. Who knew what that meant? Who wanted to know?

Drink plenty of water, take an aspirin every few hours, avoid alcohol, caffeine, heavy smoking and spicy foods, take three hot baths a day, don't strain at stool, and face up to the ugly realities of aging. And that was it. Largely irrelevant advice...after all Aiken knew he didn't smoke, drink or eat spicy foods...plus an arrogant aging reference aimed at a fellow who wasn't yet fifty. Stop back in a few weeks if things didn't clear up. Increase the aspirin if the pain continued. Aiken had no more idea what was going on than he did. If Wilton offered financial advice like that to the County's business community they'd take their business to Indianapolis.

He stopped by his office at the Bank and took an aspirin with a large glass of water before continuing on his way to the *Interurban* tracks where he was going to pick up Professor William Forsyth. It was that muddy season of the year when it might snow in the morning, be Springlike in the afternoon, and then freeze up solid at night. He could easily walk to the tracks...which would be good for his back...his new overcoat was certainly warm enough...but if the train was late it would mean standing outside in the Friday evening chill and wind.

Wilton started up the new dark green *Buick* and smiled at the powerful sound of the mint engine. Moving up to this vehicle had been smart and prudent, though of course Marva thought it insufficient. When Wilton considered how much he had given her this past year and a half he had to resist the feeling that his young wife was rather ungrateful.

But of course with a baby at home and another on the way she saw things differently than she had when they were courting. She might only be twenty, but she was no longer the young girl fresh out of *Seminary*. On the other hand, just because a woman had a growing family didn't mean she had to have a *Rolls-Royce*. But try telling that to Marva when she got started about keeping her babies safe and comfortable when they traveled...which was almost never...plus they still had only one child. And then this sudden concern about how their family was viewed in Tecumseh County. He supposed he'd have to deal with the *Rolls Royce* passion eventually, but at the moment the *Buick* was a big step up. And as big a step as he intended to take.

Aschburgh ought to have a proper station like Elwood's. A drop-off, a *stop*... scarcely more than a painted section of road alongside the track...was hardly adequate, but he supposed it too would have to wait until other things fell into place.

That was the prudent way to make progress. It would take some time to restore the Aschburgh he had known back in the *Gas Boom Days*, but there was no reason to doubt a full restoration of the town's pride and power could and would take place. Aschburgh deserved an enclosed *Interurban* station. Not up to the Indianapolis *Traction Terminal* perhaps, but finer than the smelly shacks that sufficed for Indianville and Giantown.

He pulled up alongside the *Interurban* drop-off and waited in the *Buick*, gazing out into the early evening and rubbing his gloved palms together as a light snow began to fall. One thing at a time. Right now everything was about in place for the loan to the Church. Apparently the expansion and paving of the State Road was going to take a lot longer than he anticipated, so the new building would have to be in town rather than outside where their vista would have been larger.

But that had its pluses as well. An in-town location would maximize their local impact, and in the long run would probably be better received in the County. A bit less puffed-up. First Aschburgh, then the County. And once they had Tecumseh County, plus a good base in Stonewall, it would be time to initiate mission churches all over the State. You couldn't have everything you wanted exactly when and where you wanted it. But if you were patient and smart you could take what fell available and maximize your impact.

With Reverend Tuyter pretty much out of the equation many of the Methodists had already come over to *First Community,* and the remainder, the hard-core Wesleyans, would likely follow once they realized a beautiful new downtown church building with professionally designed and installed stained glass windows was in the offing. The *Tuyter Scandal* had shaken the Methodists badly, so the Reverend Doctor Jeremy Poston and *First Community*

Church of Indiana were looking better every day. Especially now that the Methodists...and everyone else for that matter...could see that the money, power and better people of the area were solidly behind the boy.

Jeremy would do fine. Regina would guide him and buck him up whenever that became necessary. The girl kept a clear head, had lots of spunk, and could be counted on to listen to mature advice. And who knew...perhaps the salve Aiken recommended for the boy's face would work and he'd start looking like a man.

Wilton checked his teeth in the mirror, combed his mustache and smoothed his hair. The aspirin seemed to be helping. Recommending Tuyter for the chaplain's position at the *Knightstown Soldiers and Sailors Home* had been another smart move. Tuyter was out, but Wilton and the Church might still need to work with the Methodist Bishop down the road. There was every reason to cultivate the Bishop... who was well connected by family in both the Mishawaka and Fort Wayne communities... and as far as Tuyter went you didn't want to appear vindictive once the fellow was down. There was no percentage in that.

Plus the Bishop, who turned out to be a really fine and practical sort...with good Hoosier sense...was appreciative of the way Wilton helped to resolve what threatened to be a serious embarrassment to the denomination. Of course Frank Tuyter wasn't appreciative, but that was beside the point. A grateful Bishop could be helpful, an elderly angry preacher was irrelevant.

He admired the glisten of the melting drops on the dark green metal of the hood. The Buick was impressive, but not flighty, and Wilton was well pleased. Marva had a point, of course... he couldn't ignore that. It wasn't large enough for the family he envisaged...especially with a son on the way...but perhaps he could pick up a reasonably priced vehicle that would meet her demands. The *Buick* would remain his. She could learn to drive and meet the family's requirements nicely with one of the newer *Fords*.

2
The Bishop Polishes Off A Pervert

"Let's face it, Frank, as far as the Aschburgh Church goes you're finished."

"I've been there for decades, and those folks depend on me, and everyone knows it. When push comes to shove they're not going to accept this. They'll support me all the way."

"You really don't understand, do you? I've had calls from all the police departments in Tecumseh and Stonewall Counties demanding to know what I'm planning to do. I've had three delegations from the Aschburgh, Giantown and Indianville Churches insisting you be defrocked. *Defrocked*, Frank...not just removed from the pulpit. *Defrocked*."

"*Defrocked*?"

"Defrocked, Frank. The shame of defrockment. Given these circumstances I have to say that the local banker, this Mister Goins, who as you know is not a Methodist, has been very helpful to me and very well disposed toward yourself."

"Bishop, believe me, nothing happens in that little town without that man knowing about it and okaying it. Nothing. Not a single thing. The man's a troublemaker...and likely behind the whole thing."

"Unfortunately you're the one behind it, Frank." Bishop Clark Ramsgate was not sorry to see Tuyter out of the Aschburgh pulpit, though he wished it could have been brought about without scandal. Things were changing up there, and if they couldn't put some life into the local Church they were going to end up losing most of their people to this new *Community Church*. But of course Frank Tuyter didn't care about that...his only interest being his own security and comfort. "My advice to you, Frank...and remember there's a reason why I am your Bishop...is to let it go and move forward."

Clark Ramsgate glanced down at his desk and signed a paper, more to have something to do than because it needed signing at that moment. "You've had a good little run over there in Aschburgh, and now that's over. It's come to an end. Like all things in this world. The only one taking your side seems to be that odd little lady who's always sending me notes with pressed flowers. But on the other hand, you've had a secure little position dropped in your lap...a real prize if you ask me...so just enjoy it...over at *Soldiers & Sailors.* Savor your blessings, and then we won't need to pursue this ugly *defrocking* business any further."

"No one's going to defrock me. No one! Not after all these years of service."

"I'm the Bishop, Frank. You're only a local preacher no matter what you may think."

The Bishop settled back in the high backed armchair he used at his desk, and shut his eyes. Many commented on how different it was...not the sort of chair one expected to see behind the desk of a well connected Bishop of the *Methodist Episcopal Church.* But it had come from his mother, in her will, and its cream color and pale blue floral pattern never failed to provide a remembrance of her warmth. His father had it specially made for her by some Amish craftsmen in eastern Ohio, or possibly Pennsylvania. It was never all that clear. Those people were normally reclusive, difficult to establish relationships with, but somehow, for her Dad had managed it. His father's love for his mother had brought the fullness of joy into their home. A beautiful, solid piece of work this armchair. The Bishop liked to feel it brought Mom right into his office.

"I don't deserve this, Bishop. I've given thirty-two years to that town. And now I'm supposed to go off to *Soldiers & Sailors* and be happy to wipe drool from the chins of crazy old men...spend my time listening to their rambling stories about Gettysburg. I deserve better. I really deserve better."

"Two of my mother's uncles were seriously wounded at Gettysburg. These men have served our nation well. Mother's Uncle Thomas lost his leg there. For America, sir. For the United States of America. Frank, I know you are upset, but keep in mind you are a minister, you are not some cheap local politician. Jesus would not have hesitated to wash the wounds of these men, and you, Frank, whether you realize it or not, are the eyes, the ears, the hands and the feet of Jesus."

Without considering it Tuyter leaned forward in his chair, placed his thumb behind the lapel of his wrinkled black suit, and pushed the golden rose pin toward the annoyed gaze of Bishop Clark Ramsgate. "Have you any idea what this means, sir? Have you any idea why I wear this rose? Does it mean anything at all that I was Grand Marshall of the *Giantown Rose Festival Parade* in 1921? Do you have any idea what this means to the people up there, Bishop?"

What the Bishop did know was that he wanted this horrible man out of his office, and off to his new position at *Soldiers & Sailors* where no one of consequence would ever again know of his existence. *Out of sight, out of mind* was a good and a true saying. "Lower your voice, and remember where you are. Those dear people want you defrocked, and frankly if you push me I'll be considering exactly that. Are you aware we keep records? The diocese keeps records. On many things, but also on its clergy. You are aware of that?"

"I've always had good reports."

"Such as they are. But did you know your files have been tampered?"

"Tampered with?"

"Tampered."

"I doubt that, sir. Why would they be?"

"No, it did happen. As near as I can determine sometime around 1904. One of my esteemed predecessors...Bishop Thomas Helms...passed away that year. After a long and apparently most difficult and painful illness. The office was probably in chaos. Anyway...1904...all our records of your conviction and prison sentence...you remember you pled guilty and spent six months in jail back then? Those records...someone destroyed them. Isn't that curious? One doesn't normally see that with Methodist records. We tend toward the meticulous."

"That's all ancient history. Anything might have happened."

"Really? Fortunately the courts and the newspapers keep reliable records so I've been able to verify exactly what occurred. Reverend Franklin Tuyter of the *Methodist Episcopal Church*...the Church of John and Charles Wesley...Reverend Tuyter admitted in open court to being a sex pervert. Remarkable. Disgraced the cloth. And even more remarkable that somehow you could have remained in the ministry, Frank. How was that even possible? Wasn't that when you married the Collins widow? Your dear, dear wife. Young widow of the natural gas fellow. Tycoon they say. She must have inherited quite a bit, and you know what they say, Frank...money does have its way."

"It wasn't like that. Everyone knew I had enemies."

"O sir...O my. I wasn't brought up in a way that I can easily imagine such sordid things. But I will do my duty. They arrested you peeking into a window. And you had been observed by responsible citizens...peeking into others. A pervert in the Church of John and Charles Wesley. A common pervert, sir!"

"I was working for the police, Bishop. At least I thought I was. They led me to believe that and then they entrapped me."

"O, dear sir. Consider yourself fortunate. Between us...just between us now ...those dear people in Aschburgh are right to demand your defrocking. And I would do it in a moment except it would bring even more disgrace on our Church. The real miracle here, Mister Tuyter, is that our friend Wilton Goins...a man you have always disparaged...I have my sources, Frank, and I know what you've said about him...Mister Goins, because of his Christian principles, has rescued you with this fine position in Knightstown. Not many would have reached out to you, but he has. I'm not sure I would have were I in his shoes."

"Bishop, please understand Goins is behind this whole thing. The man wants to control Aschburgh. It's all so obvious."

"Control Aschburgh? Are you out of your mind, sir? Control Aschburgh indeed! You have your last chance. It's been placed in your hands as a grace. Live out the rest of your life in peace. You and your dear wife. Do it for her if for nothing else. Live in peace. And reflect, Frank...reflect."

3
Debarking The Interurban On Friday April 20, 1928

Long past supper-time on that cool and snowy Friday in early Spring 1928 William Forsyth, grip in hand, stepped stiffly from the *Interurban* trolley. Seventy-four years of scratching for a little truth while at the same time grubbing around for a way to live and support a family...all the while fighting to maintain a sense of dignity...it was beginning to catch up with him. Setting his label spackled grip beside the track he lit a cigarette and adjusted the angle of his hat as he watched the shaky lights of the *Interurban* head north through the evening toward Smithville and Power City.

This damn place had less going for it than a gob of spit. He'd be lucky if he had ten productive years left, and the trip up to Aschburgh every other week-end for the last year and a half was wearing...though the money was three times better than excellent...and he had come to treasure the time with Marva and Skoot. It had been way too long since he'd known the company of an attractive young woman who admired him. Other than his own precious daughters of course.

Hopefully that fairy Penn would finally get the Barn Studio painted and insulated by Fall so he and Marva could move ahead with some more interesting and, unfortunately, larger and heavier canvases. Still, they had done good work in the attic space, and the many months of study gave Marva time to get the sense of what painting was all about, even if from the beginning she thought she knew everything. Then again, now that she was expecting once more in the coming Fall their lessons might need to be less intense and less frequent...but he hoped not. He'd grown accustomed to her company and to the good money.

For some reason big...really enormous...canvases were fixed in her brain ... some kind of obsessional thing...ever since he took her to see that *Thomas Cole* in Indianapolis. My God, the thing was 3' x 5'!...and then showing her that second- rate reproduction of Bierstadt's *Emigrants Crossing The Plain* had finished the matter...6' x 9' or some such outlandish size...*big* was in her head, and though he and Steele always preferred an 18" x 24" canvas, *big* it would be for Marva. Once the woman had hold of the notion she wasn't going to budge. No matter how he argued. He would have to live with it, and certainly Mister Goins could afford the canvas and the stretchers.

4
Corn, Vacant Lots, The Dow Jones, Cussing & Muddy Boots

Wilton tossed the Professor's luggage behind the seat, and as they drove out of town, past several prematurely planted corn fields, Forsyth admired the new *Buick*. "It's a beauty. Not much room in this buggy for a growing family though."

"That's why I've lined up a large Ford for Mrs. Goins," countered Wilton. "That'll be plenty sufficient. If she'd ever drive it. I'll bet you miss motoring up here in Greg Penn's *Rolls-Royce*."

"Not a bit. Damned ostentatious. Much like Penn himself. I would've thought he could easily have the renovation of your place completed by now. There's just something effervescent, unsubstantial about the man."

"O now. We're well pleased. It's taken a bunch of time… true…but the contractors he brings on the job do better than a fine job. There's not a single thing that hasn't met with Mrs. Goins' approval. Did you notice the new signs at the *Interurban* stop back there? I'm hoping to see us with an enclosed station within the next year."

"Corn coming up good yet?"

"Still hardly planted. What's in the ground is in too soon. I'd say less than 20% so far. But that much being replanted could result in a big loss. The rain the last two weeks…ever since Easter really…has it too wet for the horses. And now snow. You know, Professor, one of these days this'll all be mechanized and it'll go much faster, much more efficiently. But things change slowly on the farm."

"Too expensive for your average farmer. Tightwads most of them."

Wilton floored the accelerator as they came to a long, flat stretch of paved road. "She'll do seventy and more with no problem."

"Wouldn't have thought you for a speed demon, Goins." Forsyth braced his feet and laughed.

"Lots of surprises in life, Professor. Hopefully, dry as they say it's likely to be the next couple of weeks the rest should go much quicker. But they said dry and warmer for today too. I wouldn't say *tightwad* though. That's a bit harsh for describing good people. *Frugal. Conservative.* Maybe *cautious.* Farming's a tough business, Professor. When you live around here you come to respect these folks and their ways."

Forsyth took a long drag on his cigarette and tossed it. "I meant no disrespect to them." No smoking at *The Old Goins Place.* And he had to watch his language. Had to transform himself every goddamn two weeks for the time up here. "Goins, if you're open to it I'd like to ask your opinion on some business matters. This is a pretty machine though."

"I like it well enough," said Wilton. "Well enough indeed. I'd say I'm well pleased." He pointed toward several black areas alongside the road. "Flooded fields there. All that's going to need replanting which comes out of a fellow's profit margin. See the problem with farming is there's so many things a man can't control. It's not the kind of business I would care to get caught up in. That's why your agricultural community has to be so cautious about the factors they can get a handle on. Like the purchase of machinery and stuff. I grew up a farmer's son …and maybe you did too…and I can tell you it's certainly not an easy life. Not a life for a soft man. Not a life for a man who wants to get ahead either."

"There's a lot of truth in what you say I suppose."

"A man's got to be impressed by their toughness though. *Resilience* I'd call it."

"Interesting. Finance and all. Did you know the *Art Institute* is thinking of investing in some stocks?"

"Now around us here…all of this is going to change in the next ten to twenty years, Professor," Wilton said, sweeping his large hand in an arc toward the darkness. "There'll be machines for everything. And you'll either have them or you won't be able to compete. That's hard, you know, but it's true. There'll be a lot of money made in mechanizing agriculture. A fellow would be well advised to get in on it now, before it takes off. Though with this economy, I don't know. There's too much high living, too little concern about the basics. In a way it's an evil time. So it could turn out to be a while before things develop, and you'd have to figure that in."

"Would you advise the Board to be buying stocks at this point?"

"A lot of these good folks are going under. Which is a doggone shame." He drove in silence for a minute before glancing over at Forsyth. "Stocks? You say the Board of the *Institute* is thinking about stocks? That doesn't surprise me given the kind of flimsy men they are. You just might tell them for me they're probably getting in at the tail end. The worst possible time. They'll end up buying high and selling low."

"Sturdy stuff's what they're thinking. Nothing flamboyant of course. But you think it's a little late? That's interesting. I know nothing of it…not a businessman … but they tell me it's hard to argue with the returns people are raking in."

"Well I sure have *no* problem arguing with it. They're fools and they'll get in over their heads. There's *no free lunch*, Forsyth. Have you ever heard that? I doubt it because I think there's only one fellow says that. Other than myself of course. But when I was a young man, in the middle of that *Natural Gas Boom* business, I heard that very man say exactly that at a meeting in Indianapolis. And when the gas ran dry a few years later I said to myself, *Wilton, it's a humorous saying and it's a simple saying, but it's a true saying nonetheless*. There's *no free lunch*. And let me tell you the fellow that said it that afternoon, down in Indianapolis, was a powerful man, and he could have *demanded* a free lunch, if you know what I mean. One of the first Jewish gentlemen I ever met.

But he didn't demand it because he knew it didn't exist and he'd end up paying double for it in the long run."

"Lots of folks are getting rich though. Surely you can't deny it. I see it all around me."

"Lots of folks are eager to be deceived. It's all paper wealth. Don't believe everything you see in the newspapers, Forsyth. Especially about money. Businessmen are always having a great season. It's always the best year they've ever had. What else do you expect them to say? Don't get suckered."

Wilton pointed out into the darkness toward a grove of trees. "See that? Back of those trees? Brand new brick home. Five bedrooms. Now tell me who needs five bedrooms? Nowadays people are afraid to tell their kids to double up. Well, anyway, that place is empty. I own it now. They got over-extended and I picked it up for little more than a few pennies on the dollar. Me, not the Bank. Nice people, but they put way too much trust in what other people were telling them, if you see my meaning. Beautiful place. It's a doggone shame, but business is business and though a lot of folks, including some of your Board members down there in Indianapolis, don't realize it, business is tough and business is for keeps. I own that place and those nice people are living in a hovel in Giantown.

"By the way, I was supposed to tell you this straight off but I got going on something else. Marva is looking forward to showing you a painting she's been working on this past week or so. She and that little imp Wendy actually. Well, of course, Wendy's not allowed to touch. If you don't start some discipline when they're young it'll catch up with you later on."

"She's a good child. Little Skootums I used to call her."

"Always seemed an odd thing to call a child."

"Marva calls her *Skoot* now."

"Yes. I've heard her call Wendy that. You like children, don't you? I respect that in you, Professor. I'm not really a hugging kind of father, you know, but I love my family. I'm just away a lot. And then the arts are not my cup of tea. Never understood any of that when I was at the University. No substance. No doubt it's a failing in me. Of course I arranged for the development of all the art studios over there. As a favor to Professor Steele, though it was also a business proposition. Anyway I support that kind of thing even if I can't always see what it's all about. There are various returns for supporting the University. But I do like and respect a family man. To me family is the meaning of life. Family and Church and Business. That's the essence of America. And the Church and Business...they exist to help the Family. That's the way I see it.

"By the way, we'll expect you up for Church this Sunday. It's part of our life. We missed you last time, and that just wasn't proper. Even if you weren't feeling all that well. Most of the time anymore I don't feel that well myself. It's just part of life. And Church is part of the bargain we have, as it were. Marva wants it, and that's the end of it as far as I'm concerned. Just like she expects you to be with us for Sunday dinner at her folks. The Ainsleys. By the way, and not meaning to get too personal here, but have you ever had any of what they call *plumbing* problems?"

"Plumbing problems?"

"Some fellows have problems going...that sort of thing. Getting up all through the night. Back aches. Anything like that?"

"No. Never anything like that. I take a regular dose of *Father John's*. Good stuff for a lot of men's problems. Occasionally a little insomnia. Nothing more."

"*Father John's*? Just thought I'd ask. Professor, back to what I was saying ...I like you, and I certainly don't want to be making demands of people, but you're well paid and you're well respected up here, so I shouldn't have to be saying these things about Church and family meals. It may be my house...which it is...but it's her *home*, if you get my meaning. Don't let her youth confuse you. I realize she's only twenty or so, but that's the way it is with Mrs. Goins. She has a strong point of view. And frankly I like it that way. You know how it is. With women. We can't live with them, but we can't live without them either. There's wisdom in that old saying."

Forsyth pursed his lips and stared glumly out at the dark fields. "So you don't trust the Stock Market?"

"Too much risk right now to be trusting a piece of paper, seems to me. You're not thinking of investing are you?"

"Me?" Forsyth smiled. "I'm an artist, Mister Goins. I've no money. No, it's the *Art Institute* that wants to invest. The Board. They'd like to build up a little nest-egg for the school."

"Stocks are all wrong for that. That's my opinion. When you get right down to it the Market's for rich people who can afford the risk. Of course the *Institute's* Board doesn't care because it's not their money they'd be playing with. The Market's not for people like you and me. For my money real estate's always good if a man's not in a hurry. And the Board has no business rushing blind. People who want to get rich quick get broke quick. Real estate's served me well over the years. Of course just small stuff. I've done well…not enough to be rich…but I'm reasonably secure. Don't have to worry.

"The problem is a man needs to be patient with real estate. If you buy right, knowing how things are likely to develop… you can't ever know for sure, of course… but there are ways to improve your chances…it's not pure risk. Buy right and sooner or later it'll probably go up…if you've selected carefully and with some foresight it'll be in demand after a bit and you can name your price. That place back there I pointed out…I'm not so sure about stuff like that…under normal circumstances I wouldn't have that in my pocket…but say you put some money in a rundown neighborhood in Indianapolis…or Indianville or Giantown for that matter…some empty lot or a small building…where the taxes aren't too bad, and where you learn there'll likely be some development down the road…and you wait and just be patient… which your precious Board members have never been good at… bide your time as they say…you'll do o.k. As I say, speaking from my own experience, you won't get rich, but you'll do o.k."

"Buy low, sell high."

"Easier said than done. But that's the general idea. Professor, I want you to let those fellows on the Board know I haven't been generous toward the School only to stand by and watch them go bankrupt over some dumb Stock Market investments. Better yet, I'll let them know myself next time I'm over that way."

"I'd appreciate that. I'm not sure they'd listen to me. You've heard I suppose there's been talk about getting rid of me...getting rid of old Professor Forsyth. Too damn tired and decrepit. Old fashioned. Demands students learn some principles."

"Yes, we've heard that. But it's not likely to happen. Marva won't let it if there's any way. Of course I'm not going to get involved in the operation of the School. Faculty, paper, supplies and so forth. So if it should happen...well, then we'll work something else out that'll be to your benefit. Marva's not going to let you get hurt."

Wilton turned to face Forsyth and grinned. "I married quite a woman. Don't ever get on her bad side, Professor. I sure don't. She knows what she wants, that little lady. On the other hand, she's a good woman. A good wife and an excellent mother to my daughter. Anyway, Forsyth, stay away from fast, easy profits. There's no free lunch."

"Seems damn hard to let all those profits pass you by."

"Hard to find yourself in the poorhouse too. And remember, no swearing or cussing around Mrs. Goins. What you said the last time...between the two of us... was no big deal, but her mother's never heard talk like that. So let's be careful there. The Ainsleys...at least her mother...just won't abide any of that. Or mud on your boots."

"As always I'll watch myself. I always try. Mrs. Goin's has made that clear to me over all this time. I think we appreciate one another, and of course I respect her rules as I do those of my own dear wife."

"We'd really like to have Mrs. Forsyth visit up here for a bit. Do you think she'd like that? Anyway, I don't ever like for Marva to be upset. On this other matter, Professor, you know about paintings, I know money...I know business. Take my word for it. Urban real estate, including the areas right around a growing city like Indianapolis, that's often a sound way to go. If they want to invest that's where the Board should be looking. Just make sure you do your research and know what's likely to develop there. Cautious and sound. The country-side up here is pretty, and it's where I want to live and raise my family...but the city is where you go to make money. Take my word on it. Now no business talk at the house. Mrs. Goins doesn't approve of that in her home. Cash chatter stops at the door. No smoking, no drinking, no cussing, no business talk, no mud on your boots. She just wasn't raised that way."

"Understood. Everything you've said. Understood and appreciated."

5

Saturday Morning: In The Company Of Uncle Billy Discussing Issues Of Child Development & Drawing A Sharp Distinction Between Muted And Muddy

Marva pulled on the cord and rolled the shades back from the new skylights. Bill liked to walk into a bright studio. As usual Greg's contractors had done a beautiful job though Wilton was concerned about heating problems. She fluffed Wendy's curls and straightened up a slumping teddy bear and three dolls who were seated at the child's table in Wendy's corner of the attic studio. At eighteen months Wendy was a pleasant looking, if chubby, little girl with a mass of jet black curls and pale blue eyes like her father's. Everyone fussed about Wendy's beauty and charm, but Marva was not a fool and she could see what was down the road. Wendy would never be a delicate beauty. She would be tall and large-boned like both Wilton and herself, and no matter what anyone said she had already begun to develop the big feet typical of the Ainsleys and Goins.

Marva sat in a rocking chair, stretched out her leg and laughed at the sight of her size 10 shoe. Before her marriage her shoe size was a torment, a constant reminder of all she needed to overcome and probably never would. But following her nuptials she now had a beautiful home, a lovely studio under construction in addition to this one in the attic, a faithful and loving husband, a beautiful baby and another on the way...and though Wilton minimized it, she was certain she had considerable wealth...so her size 10 feet were no longer quite the problem they seemed in adolescence.

"O Wendy, you poor thing. You'll have great big feet like Momma, won't you? Well, Daddy will just buy you beautiful shoes so no one will dare to notice."

"Mamma, Mamma."

"Yes, sweetie. You play with Mister Bear-Bear and the dollies while Momma rests. Uncle Billy will be up soon so I need to gather my strength.

Wendy tossed a doll to the floor. "Ba-Boo, Ba-Boo."

"Uncle Billy-Boom, Skoot."

Screwing up her face and pointing a finger at Marva, Wendy babbled, "Bee-ba, bee-ba."

"Yes, sweetie. Now you can speak clearer than that. I know you can. Bear-bear will be happy to see Uncle Billy too. So will we. Won't we? Bear-bear will go boom-boom, and you'll go in your playpen and play toy-toy."

Why did she and everyone but Wilton speak that way to Wendy? Always with a little squeaky tone. Marva ran her large hands down her sides and sighed. Doctor Aiken insisted she was no more than 3 ½ months, but he had been wrong about Skoot too. And she knew how she felt. Men had crazy ideas sometimes. Thank goodness Momma got Wilton to stop harassing her about moving into a suite in the hospital at the end of the Summer. In Indianapolis! That's all Momma would need …taking care of Wendy along with Daddy. Daddy was more than enough for anyone…the way he was any more. Wilton meant well, but sometimes he had no idea.

She suspected Bill Forsyth would handle a lot of things much better than Wilton. The Professor liked people to see him as a tough guy with a cigarette dangling from the corner of his mouth and his hat at a gangster angle, but when it came to babies he was really involved and competent. She supposed it came from having three girls of his own.

Wendy tossed another doll onto the floor, spilled water from her teapot onto herself, and banged Mister Bear-Bear's head on the table.

"Be gentle, Skoot, be gentle. Bear-bear will have a headache like Momma."

"Mamma, Mamma, Bebe, Bebe."

"Yes, Skooty, Mamma loves her sweet, sweet little girl. Mamma loves her baby so much."

Regina had been amused and teased her when earlier that year she resumed wearing long, floor-length black holiness dresses. But really it was just a matter of comfort. The full dresses were very attractive on her, and if she was going to be pregnant all the time they could be made to fit very loosely. She had grown her dark hair back to shoulder length, and now wore it tied back with a loose black scarf. Pinned up in a bun for Sundays, of course. With a bonnet. In many ways the old styles were more comfortable and practical.

Hearing William Forsyth's heavy step coming up the stairs, she and Wendy looked toward the door. Wendy rushed to her side, tipping over her small chair and knocking a third doll to the floor. "It's Uncle Billy-Boom, sweetie. Here he comes to see you. All the way from Indianapolis to see his Skoot."

"Dada, Ba-boo. Dada, Ba-boo."

"Uncle Billy-Boom, Skoot. Not Daddy. He'll be here in a minny-minny. Uncle Billy is coming to see his Skoot. Don't step on Bear-bear. Be gentle, Wendy, be gentle."

William Forsyth, an unlit cigarette in his mouth, stepped back from the 40 x 60 inch canvas he had set against the wall, studied it for a moment and sat down on a stool facing Marva. "You didn't actually drag this huge wall of a canvas along with you to sketch that, did you?"

"O Bill, of course not. I am capable of making a small sketch and bringing it back here. I may not have as much freedom and strength as you, but I manage to get things done."

He lifted the canvas back on the heavy paint splattered easel, dropped into a peasant's squat, and continued to study it. "Sometimes you puzzle me, Marva. Why would you leave your *Big Blob*...or *Large Mass* as you prefer...so undefined? Surely this is only a starting point, not the end?"

"I'm not at all *sure*. It's not that simple, Bill. It may be a major part of the finished composition. Just as it is. Along with a figure perhaps."

"You're not sure? Along *with* a figure instead of the basis for the figure? The starting point? You're not sure?" He glanced across the room where Skoot was playing quietly in her playpen. "You see what I mean? By allowing Skootums...I probably should start calling her Wendy since she's almost two."

"Two's the cut-off point on cute-names?"

"Somewhere around there. The personality begins to knit and move toward maturity at that point. And she's going to have a strong personality. I've always admired the fact that as an infant she avoided that typical *phony smile*. Your average infant's nothing but a larcenous little poseur. A deceiver. Grinning and snickering and carrying on for attention."

"O Bill, let's not go down that road again. I do not agree with you. Babies are simply happy when they're loved. They are not trying to steal something from us. For goodness sake!"

"I think you're allowing some of these Europeans to influence what you're doing here," he said pointing at the canvas. "There's some odd stuff being done over there. I'm not saying anything against it. I'm usually on the side of the Germans... and innovation has its place. I was criticized in my youth, and I suppose even a wish-washy effeminate madman like that Klimt fellow has something to say. But somehow it's not American. It's definitely not Hoosier. It's a dangerous way to go."

"I can't help but be Hoosier. Don't be silly. And who is Klimt? Someone I should know?"

"Perhaps. But see there's a risk. Even some of the fellows I ran into in Gloucester last Summer. Strong, tanned, heavily muscled fellows...real Americans ...but some of them with their gaze focused on all that Parisian swill. Well, anyway...your average infant is so determined to seek everyone's approval that she's bending over backwards with all that billing and cooing and grinning and sucking. I'm really pleased Skootums never stooped to that level. She's always had her own strong distinctive Hoosier way. And we've done the right thing by encouraging a full range of babbling sounds. I realize it sounds silly sometimes, and you'd hate to be seen making those noises in public...but in the long run her language is going to be much richer. Poetic. Isn't it, Skootums-pootums? A poet-woet. Are you happy to see Uncle Billy-boom? Are you baby-bay?"

"I'm only beginning the painting, Bill. I can change it right now if you think it's so bad. I take what you say very seriously. And I certainly don't want you to think I'm challenging you."

"That's not the point, Marva. Just leave it alone. For now anyway. You have to develop in your own fashion. We'll focus on what's going on there in a bit and see if we can make any sense of it. But before I forget, just so we pace our time properly, will we be eating up here or downstairs?"

"Hildred always serves downstairs. You know that."

"But you're the boss. Surely we could get her to bring some sandwiches up here. You pay her. It would save us so much time. You can't let Hildred set the tone for your home."

"I'm not forcing her to do something that makes her unhappy. The tone she's setting is something we need. You'll want time to go out for a couple of smokes anyway. In any event, Hildred wants the best for this family, and she feels that means meals are always served downstairs, Bill. At the table."

"Fully set. You realize she takes a nip? Your precious Hildred."

"Fully set. So do you. Wilton's aware of it, and he'll deal with it when he feels the time is right. He won't let it slide. And when you smoke outside, please pick up your butts. Anyway, Bill, we'll have more than enough time. Wendy's Aunt Regina will be coming over later this morning to take her for the day. Won't that be fun, Skoot? You and Aunt Nia."

"Nia, nia," agreed Wendy who then burst into tears.

Marva scooped her up and called down to Hildred to bring up a *special bottle* for Skoot. "Poor baby, poor, poor baby. Your *special bottle's* on the way, so stop your crying, stop your crying."

"She's too old for a bottle, Marva. For crying out loud, she's old enough to eat steak. We really need to find a better way to keep her content while we're working.

"It's just sugar water. She enjoys it."

"She's too old, and I'm sure it's got to be bad for her teeth. But you're the mother, you're the boss around here. Still I'll tell you this…when I have servants they're not going to order me about. No cook with a snoot full of bourbon is going to tell me what to do."

"Can we drop it?"

"Fine. Just fine. Let's get about our business then."

Hildred, a thin, wrinkled woman in her late forties slipped into the studio with a *special bottle* in her hand. "I've opened the nipple a bit more, Mrs. Goins. She'll like it better this way."

Marva handed Wendy to the cook and motioned toward a rocking chair in the corner. "Why don't you and Wendy sit over there until Mrs. Doctor Poston arrives?"

"I was hoping to do some cleaning in the kitchen."

"It can wait." Marva walked to the canvas and pointed to the large area of green. "You may well be right, Bill. Perhaps you are. I won't dispute it. But there's a bunch of strength here it seems to me. In this block, or *Blob*, if that's what you want to call it."

Forsyth considered the point…discounted it…and decided to keep his own counsel. "It's amazing to me, Marva, that in little over a year and more of study you've begun to move toward your own style. I'm not saying I agree with everything you do, but then not everyone agrees with me."

"You hate it, don't you?" She looked him square in the eye and smiled.

"Steele would have approached this quite differently. You realize that?"

"You're my teacher, Bill, not Professor Steele."

"Steele's dead. It makes a fellow think."

"You miss him, don't you?"

Forsyth walked over to where Hildred was holding the sleeping Wendy, and took the *special bottle* away from the cook. "He was a good friend and a truly great painter and teacher. Wendy's sound asleep. She doesn't need this."

"Not Skootums?"

"Shall I lay her down in her playpen?" asked Hildred.

"No. Just rock her until her aunt comes if you don't mind."

"When she's approaching two...well, it's time to become Wendy. Our little girl is growing up."

"As far as I'm concerned she'll always be *Skoot*, and as far as she's concerned you'll be *Uncle Billy-Boom*."

"I need to start preparing things for lunch and supper," said Hildred who was not especially fond of Skoot or any other children. She wasn't hired as a nurse maid.

"It can wait, Hildred. Please keep rocking her. Regina will be here shortly." Marva gripped the canvas by the inside of its stretcher and lifted it off the easel, leaning it against a far wall. "I was struck by the *Aschburgh Grain Elevator*. It's really an ugly series of buildings and railroad tracks. Owned by one of Wilton's cousins, I think. I suppose it's a big money maker, but to me it's a great, big blot on the sky over there. I mean, Bill, it's not pretty, it's not scenic or anything like that... it's just a great big thing right there. And it just about blocks out the sun."

"You were trying to sketch it?"

"I couldn't. There were all these farmers around. Even my father. While I was there...I stayed back in my car with Skoot... even Wilton showed up for a few minutes. Later on I tried to sketch it a bit from memory...you can even see where I put Wilton in on the left. But the painting is not about all those little shapes... farmers and cars and whatnot."

"My dear Marva...we've talked of this before. The artist is the prince, the artist is always the king. Stride right in and assume your proper place and role. I always have. You'll find people will step aside...even set things up for you. People inherently recognize the supremacy of the artist. Stride in and they will respond to your power and authority."

"Perhaps. I need to work on that. But don't you think this shape has the sort of permanence...dominance...that's there in the Grain Elevator?"

"The details are good...to the extent you got them. Mister Goins in his black suit. You got him nicely. Notice how all the farmers defer to him. He knows he is in command and doesn't hesitate to show it."

"I'm not sure any of that has a place in this painting. I'm not trying to tell a story or flatter Wilton. Frankly, Bill, I think I may be close to something special here. Something different. But I need to get rid of Wilton. And the others."

"You've been bold, Marva. Very bold indeed."

She glanced down at the weather beaten face of the old *pleine aire* painter and laughed. "I was scared to death. At the Elevator and later up here, when I decided to approach it this way. But then I remembered what you said: *Those who cannot begin do not finish*."

Forsyth, resting his forearms on the sill and raising himself a bit on his toes, looked out the high, small window. "I believe that's probably Mrs. Poston way down the road. The Reverend Doctor must be doing well to afford an automobile."

"Wilton's very pleased with him."

"That's Robert Henri, of course, not me. I lay no claim to originality in my teaching. I freely borrow from the best of the best, the best of the past, the best of the present. Henri is the best of the best. Very ill right now. I doubt he'll be with us much longer. Like Steele. All the great ones are dead or dying."

"Well you're very much alive, Bill. And you're a great one. And you know what? You know what? I'm going to be one of the great ones. I really believe that. I'm going to be a great painter."

"Good girl! Plunge ahead, no doubts, no reservations. Don't wabble about."

"Shouldn't I wake her, Mrs. Goins? So she'll be alert for Mrs. Doctor Poston."

"Let her sleep, Hildred. *Don't wabble about*. I'll remember that."

"Applies to raising children too. Henri says that. About painting. No, no question about it, this is good. Strong. Way beyond what you've done before, though I'm not saying it's perfect. Have you really factored in the force of the *Large Blob*? Do you think?"

"Major mass? *Blob* sounds horrible. Yes, I think I have. The Major Mass, the block of green, is the focus. Don't you think it works?"

Forsyth walked over to Hildred and easily lifted Wendy into his arms. "Hildred, would you make us a pot of coffee? And serve it up here."

"I think it's strong, Bill. I think it's very strong."

"Wouldn't you rather have it downstairs, sir?"

"No. No I wouldn't. Up here. And bring some milk and sugar, would you?"

"Shall I send Mrs. Doctor Poston up when she arrives?"

"I'm not disputing what you say, Marva. But I'd like to see more of a human element. The figure. And at least some emphasis on the slope of the railroad track. I mean that's a major factor in the Elevator. It can't just be ignored. You've got some human shapes over here...probably Wilton and company...but it's all too small, too weak. These are *real people*." He swayed back and forth, soothing Wendy back to sleep. "Would you wipe the corner of her mouth? I don't want her to get a sore."

"People are so intensely drawn to the figure that even when it's small it grabs our attention. Don't you think? Anyway, as I've been trying to get you to see, the *Major Mass* is the subject, the heart of this painting, not people or railroad tracks."

"I can see that's what you're getting at, but I'm not sure you manage it. And I'm not really sure what it might mean if you did. Tell me, what if you were to move to a smaller canvas?"

"Bill!"

"Sorry. Let's not argue. I ought to have told Hildred to bring a third cup. For Regina."

"Regina doesn't drink coffee much anymore."

"Is that a religious thing?"

"She just doesn't like it so much. She drinks tea."

"Well...to each his own. Let's back off this and give some thought to your palette. Because I'm not convinced you've set your palette correctly here. Some of these colors are downright muddy." Skoot began to wake up, and Forsyth placed her against his shoulder, cooing into her ear. "That may be part of the unease I feel about this."

"They need to be muted to get the feel of the scene. A Grain Elevator isn't exactly a festive place."

"I didn't say *muted*, Marva, I said *muddy*. There's a world of difference, my girl. Muted and muddy are not the same at all."

"I set my palette correctly. The colors are *muted*, not *muddy*."

Regina opened the door and stepped in without being noticed by either the teacher or the student. She quietly took a seat and waited.

"And those figures are *right,* Professor. They may be slight, even obscured, but they are right. They pull your gaze in exactly the way I planned for them to do."

"We're having another of our little differences, my dear. Aren't we?" Forsyth glanced at his hand and was surprised to discover he was tightly grasping several brushes. "It's best not to get too heated. Perhaps I should go outside for a smoke. Regina! How did you…?"

Marva rushed over to embrace her cousin. "O Regina. Wendy's been looking forward to spending the whole day with you."

"Has she slept all morning? We're going to do a little shopping."

"No, no. She just dropped off. But she's been so excited about you coming. Bill, would you tell Hildred to send up a pot of tea as well as your coffee? Regina and I need to chat while you have a couple of your cigarettes."

"And pick up my butts."

"O Bill. But yes, please pick up your butts."

CHAPTER 12
YOU WIN SOME, YOU LOSE SOME
& SOME ARE RAINED OUT

A chapter marked by the darkest tragedy, though it starts out playfully enough. The birth of Ribby-Roo and the curious ceremony of waterless baptism. This time Olin hangs around to have his photo taken. Wilton has an inspiration concerning an Autumn Festival, and all enjoy a good home cooked meal. Though there is some tension related to liquor toasts. Joey Birdsall and Marshall Sevier Winslow are summoned late in the afternoon.

1
Dancing In The Clear Sky Of Autumn
With A Pale Yellow Tail

Wilton abruptly pulled off to the side of the road at the sight of a dark blue and yellow object bobbing in the pale blue sky above one of his uncultivated fields. He stood alongside the fence for a moment before recognizing the soaring burst of color...which was at least a hundred feet in the air...as a kite. You saw them in Indianapolis on occasion...children flying them in a park...

282

but he couldn't recall ever having seen one flying in Tecumseh County.

It just wasn't something you saw. Nor something you did. Certainly not on someone else's property...in this case his. Finding a spot in the barbed wire fence where he could get through without tearing his coat, he quickly made his way up the slope of the field to see who was trespassing on his land. You got permission before heading off on someone else's property, even when it was rented out. And no one had asked his permission.

A hundred and fifty yards to the east a small figure in black, his back to Wilton, stood in the wind and sunshine, fingering a slender line attached to the dancing kite. "Hey!" Wilton yelled, but to no avail. Striding through the browning weeds and short growth of the past Summer he quickly closed the distance between himself and the trespasser. But in the minutes it took him to get within hailing distance his topcoat and pants legs were covered with burrs. "Shoot!" he muttered, glancing down and seeing mud on his new shoes.

"Hey, you!"

The Reverend Doctor Jeremy Poston was happier than he had been in months. Married life was wonderful in so far as it completed a man, transforming him from a creature of uncertain prospects into a responsible member of Church and Community. But Jeremy found the institution, and for that matter Regina herself, made demands on him which he was not prepared to meet. Perhaps later, but definitely not now.

He pulled lightly on the string and gasped as the beautiful kite dipped toward the earth and then abruptly soared again, quickly pulling the string through the loose touch of his fingers. As a little boy in Rising Sun he had marveled at his older brother's skill with a kite, and had been filled with pride and delight the day his father declared him old enough to fly his first one.

His mother made the one flying today over these fields, sewing it from nainsook...which couldn't have been easy to get...with a lovely pale yellow silk tail...and presented it to him as a wedding gift. A simple two-sticker, nothing fancy, but fashioned with love.

In a lot of ways a nainsook sail was even better than silk, and certainly was infinitely superior to the patched cotton ones they struggled with back home. Still, until today Jeremy feared to fly his kite, thinking the Aschburgh community would view his passion with the same disparaging amusement Regina showed.

Then this morning, after yet another time of humiliation, the Lord opened to him a way to break free from the unhappiness he was feeling. There were a few unused fields in the area... overgrown places where he could be alone, totally unobserved, free to do as he wished with no repercussions to his ministry. And so on this beautiful Fall morning...thanks be to God... Jeremy tied his rolled up kite to the carrier rack of his bicycle and headed out of town into the countryside to the east of Aschburgh. After pedaling for half an hour he selected a field which looked as though it hadn't been planted in years, and pedaling out into a clear spot, he launched his beautiful blue nainsook kite, with its pale yellow silk tail, into the windy cloud-free sky of the morning.

"Hey, you!"

Jeremy spun around to find himself confronted by the reddened face of Wilton Goins. "Mister Goins! You're covered with burrs, sir."

"What are you doing?"

"Flying a kite, sir."

"Flying a kite?"

"Yes. I hope I'm not causing a problem." He stepped toward Wilton, and with his free hand began to pick burrs off the banker's top-coat.

"Stop it. I'll take care of that later. Don't you realize this is private property, Reverend? What's wrong with you?"

"I didn't think I was doing anything wrong. The field's not being used."

"Well, I suppose it's not. But it is private property, and what you're doing is a bit odd. Around here before you go on someone's private property you get permission."

"I'm sorry, Mister Goins. I had no idea. Down home there's no problem."

"Well, up here there could be, Jeremy. Folks around here are rather particular about property rights. I suppose we're touchy about the government as much as anything. Anyway, this is my land, and of course, you're welcome to use it as long as it's not planted. I don't imagine I've rented this in several years. It's not very good land. My father made a poor swap way back."

"Thank you, sir. For permission. I certainly never intended to show a lack of respect for private property. Have you done any kiting? Maybe you'd like to take the string?"

"Jeremy, there's a lot of socialist thinking around anymore. And you want to be careful up here. We don't take to it." Wilton cautiously fingered the line. "It's got a bit of pull, doesn't it? How high up do you think that thing is?" He stared into the bright sky at the kite dancing now almost straight over them and then darting down and off to the left.

"We've got a hundred yards out, so I imagine it's a hundred and fifty to two hundred feet up, depending on the gusts. Give it a slight tug, sir. We've almost another hundred yards of string."

About an hour later, after the kite had been pulled in, dismantled and rolled up, and securely tied to the carrier of Jeremy's bicycle, they slowly made their way through the field toward Wilton's *Buick*.

"It's an interesting thing, Doctor. I never would have thought a man could get enjoyment from something like that. But you do, don't you? It's really quite a bit of fun. I'm rather well pleased with that hour. Not entirely wasted."

"I've always taken pleasure in it, sir," said Jeremy. "But it's also a time for reflecting on the Scriptures."

"I can see where it could be. But you said this is the first time you've flown your kite since coming to Aschburgh. Why is that?"

"It's simply that I've been afraid it might become a stumbling-block. Really, that's the only thing that's held me back. If it weren't for that, sir...the fear that my example might prevent some from answering the Gospel call…I wouldn't have waited so long."

"Seems like an innocent thing to me, Doctor. If somebody wants to make a fuss about it…claiming some kite's holding him back from salvation…I suspect he didn't want to get saved in the first place. Do you ever find yourself believing in predestination? There's some who just can't be saved, even if they were wanting to?"

"I would find that hard to accept, sir. Given God's mercy."

"That's probably true. His creation calls everyone to knowledge and love of Him, doesn't it?"

"Really, if you think about it, being out here in the midst of God's beautiful world, with a lovely kite flying above you, that should bring a man closer to God. Don't you think?"

"It might very well. I've heard of stranger things."

At the fence Jeremy held the barbed wire apart as Wilton carefully passed through, and then Wilton held the wire as the bicycle, followed by Jeremy, came clear. "Are you using that salve every day? The stuff from Doctor Aiken."

"Yes, sir I am. Every other day actually. I alternate it with an ointment my mother sent me. Something she prepares herself."

"No offence, Reverend, but I'd go with science myself. But whatever you're using, I believe it's making a difference. Does Regina feel it's helping?"

"I believe she does. We haven't really talked about it. Thank you for permission to use your land, Mister Goins. I do appreciate that. By the way, have you heard anything from Reverend Tuyter?"

Wilton unbuttoned his topcoat and folded it inside out and into a bundle so the burrs wouldn't get on the Buick's upholstery. He started to pick burrs from his pants legs but quickly gave it up. It'd give Hildred something to do instead of ducking off to her room to nip at a bottle of bourbon. He wished Marva would just let him fire the woman.

"I understand he's very happy at *Soldiers & Sailors*. Mrs. Tuyter too. They deserve it, God bless them. The Lord always has a place for sinners, doesn't He? Well, Doctor, it's been quite interesting and quite pleasant. I suppose I'll see you back in town. On Sunday if not before."

2

A Few Thoughts While Lying Abed The Day After Delivery

The second child of Wilton and Marva, another girl...Barbara-Jean Winslow Goins, *Ribby-Roo* as she would be known to William Forsyth for her first two years, and *Ribby* to her mother and everyone else for the rest of her long life...was born at home during an early snow on Friday morning November 2nd 1928, a full month after Marva's due date...the which delay Doctor Aiken assured all was not that unusual given recent improvements in modern nutrition.

The baby was healthy, the delivery uncomplicated and everyone but Wilton was well pleased. For his part, Wilton felt Doctor Aiken needed a better computing technique than using his fingers, and he resolved his future sons would be escorted into the pain and joy of this world by competent physicians in a comfortable and properly staffed Indianapolis hospital. And his wife would have a private suite.

Marva was pleased the pregnancy was over, and of course delighted to have another daughter...but she was somewhat unsettled by Wilton's pronouncement that each Fall, beginning the following year, 1929, he would host a *Harvest Festival* for all the citizens of Aschburgh to celebrate the birthdays of his children. Actually he said *sons*, but she knew he loved his daughters and simply and unconsciously expressed his hopes for the Goins Family name. The notion of Wilton placing her daughters on display at some idiotic *Festival* was distasteful to her...but as he grandly proclaimed his intention she held her tongue.

She would bide her time. Three years of marriage, the birth of two children, the management of a large house, with two servants as of last month, and two years under the tutelage of Professor William Forsyth had opened her eyes to what she and her family might become. She was no longer the *child bride* of

Wilton Fox Goins. Though Wilton was of course the head of the household, and though she was scripturally submitted to him… the fact remained increasingly she saw herself the real leader of the Goins Family.

As an only daughter her birthdays had always been major events in the life of the Winslows and Ainsleys, and she intended to see those same magical moments for each of her babies. Skoot's second party, just two weeks earlier, had been delightful. With only Winslows and Ainsleys invited, plus a couple of friends and one of Wilton's cousins, it featured a puppet show starring Wendy's own Bear-Bear, with the stage-set beautifully designed by dear Greg (Bob had rushed it up from Indianapolis at the last minute)…and the entire production executed with remarkable style by Uncle Billy-boom.

Of course nothing ever proceeded exactly the way you planned. In this case Mamaw Belva had done her best to ruin things by insisting on *helping* the new cook with the cake and meal, and naturally there had been tension and tears about that. Marva was not about to have another cook in hysterics. Even Wilton's favorite meal of meat, corn, green beans and potatoes, which Greg said could be prepared by an orangutan, had been ruined for the last couple of weeks as the girl sulked. This coming year, once she had her strength back, Marva resolved to get better control over her mother.

Fortunately Skoot was only two and pretty much oblivious to adult competition and bruised feelings, so in her eyes everything was sparkling. Especially the performance by her grubby Bear-Bear. As soon as Thanksgiving and the Christmas festivities were behind her she would ask Bill Forsyth to begin thinking about next years' birthday pageants. He needed time to discuss it with his theater friends in Indianapolis. And hopefully Greg, with his magic touch, would be able to find time as well. He had said something about Europe and drawings for a theater, but Marva was sure he would make time for her girls and their special days. One of the events, probably Skoot's day, ought to have a hobby horse theme. Greg would adore that.

She respected Wilton, but his silly *Festival* was not going to interfere with her babies' parties...nor would her daughters be put on exhibit to satisfy her *lord's* vanity and ambition. She both loved and respected him. That was not the issue. He was after all her husband and the head of their household...the priest of their family...but the Winslows, and to a lesser extent the Ainsleys, had always had their special celebrations and Wilton was not going to be allowed to change any of that.

He could have his *Harvest Festival*, his State-wide *Community Church*, the restoration of Aschburgh, control of local politics and business, and she supposed, however many millions or billions or trillions of dollars they possessed, and she would support him in all of it if that's what he wanted...but never at the expense of Skoot and baby Ribby. The girls were Winslows, and each was entitled to know the special joys of being a Winslow.

3
Your Average Baby Dedication Is More Or Less Waterless

The baptism of Barbara-Jean Winslow Goins, which for reasons of some obscure foot-note to Reformation theology her parents insisted was a *Dedication*...a baptism without water as near as Greg could make out...marked the first time Penn had been to a Protestant church service since early childhood when his Mamaw Penn, always in conflict with his extraordinarily progressive parents, dragged him along to her local *Brush Arbor*. Since then he had been an observer at many religious events...but European cathedrals and Indianapolis society weddings were hardly the same thing as Midwestern country hoopla.

Despite the baptism of Marva's beautiful baby...remarkably done without even a drop of water...the service had been boring and in poor taste. The congregation's droning was dreadful, and the holy man's lecture...a treatise on the distinction between *righteousness* and *holiness*...totally incomprehensible. Bob wouldn't even come in...claimed he had to protect the *Silver Ghost*...though he covered his bases by presenting Marva with a silver spoon from *Tiffany* prior to the service. Pretending it was no big deal when surely everyone knew Greg had supplied the money for the gift.

Yet also knowing as he did how important the occasion was to Marva and Willie, Greg had been mindful to carefully select the dark green embroidered jacket which had been presented to him in Vienna on the awarding of the contract for the new theater. Now hadn't that been a grand occasion! A new house for avant-garde theater in a city already overflowing with glorious architecture... that was going to be the challenge and the highlight of his career to date. The Germanic peoples, especially the Austrians, knew how to do things with style. The result of a thousand years or so of civilization and refinement. He was so looking forward to spending next Spring and early Summer with friends in Berlin and Vienna, and then continuing on to Budapest for a first-time-ever stay. With at least one day on the beautiful blue Danube.

Bob agreed the traditional Austrian jacket set off his white hair better than anything else in his wardrobe. There was a down-to-earth peasant dignity about the garment. And then, wouldn't you know it...Bob turned around and refused to accompany him to the child's baptism...or whatever it was. Agreed upon the garment and then refused to go inside and attend the ceremony. All because it was simply not possible for Greg to take him to Europe on next Spring's trip. Things had reached a point...a *fine pass* as the saying went...when his chauffer...nothing more than his servant if the truth be told...felt he had the right to set the agenda.

"Who's the little white haired fellow in the funny looking jacket?" Olin said to Belva, breaking a silence of five days. At the conclusion of the service she had elected to block his way and hold him in their pew until the photographer was ready.

"So we're talking again," she whispered. "How very nice!"

"He looks a little...you know."

"It's Mister Gregory Penn. Doctor Penn. You've met him before, Olin. Several times. He's a close friend of Wilton and Marva. The one who's done all the work out there at *The Old Goins*

Place. I can't believe you. I really can't believe you anymore. Are you still living in this world, or are you somewhere off in outer space? The fellow was Wilton's best man. At your daughter's wedding. Marva. You remember her?"All of this was loudly if inaudibly whispered and punctuated with repeated jabs. "Where is your mind anymore? Doctor Penn is a world-famous architect, and for your information...and I've told you this probably three times already...he's coming to dinner this afternoon. Along with Professor Forsyth. Do you at least remember *him*? Believe me the only thing that would get people of their caliber to come to Aschburgh is their devotion to our daughter. Marva and Wilton have some very distinguished friends, and that reflects well on the Winslows as well as on our family. So please be careful."

"Of course I remember Bill Forsyth. Now Bill's a regular fellow, a real man. There's no question about Bill. The man knows dogs and he's not a bad shot. But this little guy...I don't know. He's coming to our house? I don't remember inviting him."

"Doctor Penn. And it really doesn't matter what you know or don't know. Now that you've decided to come back amongst the living, just mind your manners. And you will be in the family photos this time."

"The preacher coming?"

"Of course. The Doctor and Regina. We have them every Sunday, don't we? Regina left right after the Dedication to get things ready. So we would have time to stay for the photos. I just hope Marva can get the photographer to come out to our house for a few more photos so Regina can be in them. I shouldn't have promised her...as much as these fellows charge...but I had to."

"Regina's at our house? Are you claiming I agreed to that too?"

"Just mind your manners, Olin. Try to be civil. At least quiet. It's not fair, but Marva's holding me responsible to see you're in the photos this time. And if you cause any disruption she'll blame me for that too. *You* can't do anything wrong in her eyes. Everything is my fault."

"No one told me a thing about photos. I've never liked having my picture taken, and you know it. You better believe I'll be quiet.

Everyone knows too much already. And I know I haven't been the one to tell them anything, no matter what you say. So yes, I'll be quiet. I might as well. I've very little choice. Very quiet."

"Ssshhh! Let's not have a scene on little Ribby's Dedication Day. We'll make Marva happy and get the photos done, and then we'll head home for a quiet Sunday dinner."

4
Simple Country Fare

The biscuits were set out first. With butter and blackberry jam. Minutes later Belva, still in her apron, hovered about the table as Marva helped Regina carry steaming bowls of mashed potatoes, green beans cooked with bacon, glazed carrots, corn, squash casserole, turnips, stewed tomatoes and yellow gravy from the kitchen. "The chicken will be ready in just a few minutes. Why don't we get settled while it's finishing up? Now be sure to try the biscuits. They're an old Winslow recipe that Regina favors. A real treat. I haven't had them in years, and I know you'll all be delighted."

Olin Ainsley's place at the head of the table remained conspicuously vacant...though unmentioned...as Belva asked Doctor Jeremy Poston to offer some words of blessing. Belva, Regina, Wilton, Marva and their girls, as well as William Forsyth, Bob the chauffeur and Greg Penn shut their eyes...actually Skoot looked around and Ribby...cradled in Marva's arms, cried...and bowed their heads as the Pastor thanked the Lord on their behalf.

As soon as he finished Bob started the biscuits around, followed by plates of butter and blackberry jam. "I do love biscuits and jam," he said, popping a half into his mouth.

"Regina?" Belva dried her dry hands on her apron. "Shall we bring in the chicken to pass?"

Regina continued buttering a biscuit for her husband. "It'll be another couple of minutes, Aunt Belva. I figured it a little wrong. You just relax. It's my mistake. Marva and I will serve. You just sit back and enjoy yourself."

"My brother-in-law said to let you know he's ready any time," said Bob to Wilton. "Norman Overbeek."

"I would think it might be ready by now. We don't want the vegetables to get cold."

"Your brother-in-law?"

"This will give us time to take a little breather and have a nice biscuit," said Regina. "Not that they're anything to write home about. Just sort of a humble country appetizer."

"Norman? The driver/mechanic, sir?"

"O yes. Norman. Norman Overbeek. There's an Overbeek at First Bank of Nappanee. I don't suppose there's a relationship? Let's discuss it later, Bob."

"He knows of a very good buy for you."

"Excellent," said Wilton, savoring a hot biscuit smothered in blackberry jam. "Later on." He broke off a small piece from his biscuit, placed it in Skoot's bowl and motioned to Marva to quiet Barbara Jean. "What's the matter with her?"

"Would you like to hold her, Wilton? Skoot doesn't like blackberry. Give her a piece with butter."

"For goodness sake," said Belva. "She's just a baby, Wilton. Babies fuss a bit, don't they Ribby-Roo? Can I hold her, dear?"

"She's fine," said Marva. "I'll hand her to Wilton if she continues to fuss. Eat your biscuit, Skoot."

"These are superb biscuits, Regina," said Wilton. "You know, Greg, some of the Winslows came down from Wisconsin after the Civil War, and I imagine this recipe came from up there. I believe these biscuits have just a taste of cheddar in them. Cheese. Am I right? Those German folks know how to put a biscuit together.

Plus my Momma Ainsley makes the best mashed potatoes and the best country beans native to Tecumseh or Stonewall Counties. It leaves a man content and well pleased."

"I believe you'll enjoy the beans," said Belva. "Most men are partial to them."

"You just can't beat simple country fare," Wilton continued. "Let's start passing these plates around, but be sure to leave room for the chicken. Take two more of those biscuits, Bob. They're remarkable with the gravy. Anyone know where Olin's at? Pour some of that yellow gravy on the potatoes, Preacher."

While Regina fixed Jeremy's potatoes, Belva buttered another biscuit for him. "We'll have the chicken on the table in a moment, Professor, Doctor Penn. Please check on it, Regina. You've been to Germany, Doctor? My great-aunt Lottie Monona Winslow was of German descent at some point back there. The name was Mann or Mannheim, something along those lines. She married Deloss Winslow, my grandmother's brother. I think I have that right. I believe mother always said it was Monona and Deloss. Marva? Though I have no idea where the Monona came from."

"I'm busy with the babies, Momma. Regina will check after she finishes fixing Pastor's plate."

"She loved sauerkraut. Aunt Monona. Which is what we always called her. I suppose she was really Aunt Lottie but we always called her Aunt Monona. That's a very unusual jacket, Doctor."

"Please call me Greg. It's Austrian. I admire a good kraut."

"Monona always resented that as an insult."

"I was referring to cabbage."

"In any event it's an attractive jacket. Wilton, you know how Olin is. He's probably fussing at something in the barn. I'm sure he'll be here in a second. He never misses his Sunday dinner."

Greg Penn, his hair fluffed for this special moment, stood up from the table with Belva's finest glassware in hand as Bob moved around the table filling everyone's glass from a tall bottle of imported grape juice...the rich purple of the grape juice sharp against the dark green of Greg's peasant jacket. "Ladies and gentlemen, I would like to propose a toast."

Wilton smiled and tapped a spoon on Skoot's high chair, signaling her to be quiet and pay attention. Doctor Jeremy Poston sighed, placed both hands flat on the table and lowered his head. All conversation stopped and a certain tightness filled the air of the farmhouse dining room. Was the chauffeur actually pouring alcohol?

Greg tilted his glass in a gay salute to Wilton and Marva. "To my dear friend and college chum, Willie Goins. I can only say, old boy, I stand in awe of your powers. At the advanced age of…well, let's just say advanced…you have done it again! Bravo! And to the lovely and gracious Marva, gifted painter, devoted mother, and long-suffering mate to this old coot, I congratulate you on the birth of yet another gorgeous daughter. And finally, to you, Barbara-Jean, beautiful baby, greatly blessed in your wise selection of parents, we welcome you to this world, darling, we welcome you to the joy, to the festivity of life. And of course, we can't forget Wendy, better know as…."

"*Skootums*," whispered Forsyth.

"Better known as Skootums. Congratulations on your new baby sister." He lifted his glass high and smiled at all. "Everyone. To our wonderful friends. *Prosit!*"

Professor Forsyth and Wilton sipped from their glasses, but Belva stared at Greg, seemingly dumbfounded.

"Down the hatch, Grandma. To your health."

Regina backed in from the kitchen with a large platter of chicken, placed it in the center of the table and sat down next to her husband. "That white meat on the side is for Skoot. I set it off to cool a bit, Marva."

"Good work," said Wilton. "Greg is always the tease. Well, old buddy, you've had your joke at my expense. Now it's time to dig in."

Doctor Poston, his head still bowed, could not believe what had just occurred. A liquor toast! Did the elderly midget have no sense of where he was…or was it a deliberate attempt to show contempt for the clergy…as well as for the Lord Jesus?

Belva cleared her throat. "Well, that certainly was very different and very nice, Doctor Penn. Doesn't that chicken look good? Better late than never. You are blessed to have a wife who is such a fine cook, Reverend. Very nice, Regina. Very nice."

His glass in hand, William Forsyth rose. "Perhaps one more toast."

"Girls, I believe we've forgotten to put out the tea. Excuse me, Professor. We've both sweetened and unsweetened. We'll have it in just a second." Belva excused herself and motioned to Regina and Marva to join her in the kitchen.

Forsyth sat down resolved to propose his toast to Marva later, perhaps before dessert. Bob, seated next to him, borrowed a pencil and scribbled a note which he passed along to Wilton.

Rolls Phantom in Greenfield. Excellent. Lady died.
Hardly driven. Son wants to sell VERY cheap.
Norman says need to act quickly. Extra parts free.
Son thinking of selling to someone else. $8,000.

Wilton glanced at the note and shoved it into his pocket. Left with Barbara-Jean in his arms and Wendy leaning perilously from her high-chair, he called after the ladies. "Marva, Regina, Belva…take a moment. The tea can wait for goodness sake. Our dear friend, Greg Penn has brought us a wonderful gift. Several bottles of imported grape juice from the Mediterranean. Brought all the way from Indianapolis. I think we need to acknowledge this exquisite gift."

Greg and Bob darted about the table pouring more grape juice for all. "It's a gift of love," said Greg. "I believe it's the *ambrosia* of ancient times."

"A delicious *non-alcoholic* grape juice," said Wilton.

"Non-alcoholic, Mister Goins? Yet it was served in an alcoholic manner."

"But non-alcoholic, Pastor," said Wilton. "Served with great affection. By my closest friend. Shall we join Professor Forsyth who was about to propose a toast? Remember now, it's non-alcoholic grape juice, and this is a joyous, light-hearted occasion. It's my Barbara-Jean's Dedication Day. Why don't we all give it a shot?"

Professor Forsyth, Bob the chauffeur and Greg Penn stood, glasses of grape juice in hand. Wilton handed the baby back to Marva, patted Skoot on the head, and stood. "Please everyone, stand with our friends, lift your glasses and share in the Professor's toast. Professor?"

Forsyth rubbed the back of his hand across his mouth, lifted his glass and said, "To Marva Winslow Goins, an excellent student who has become a fine painter, and may well become an excellent painter if she is allowed to develop her gift."

"Down the hatch!" said Greg. "Bottoms up!" said Bob the chauffeur. "Prosit!"

The grape juice was sipped in silence by the ladies, and with sulky suspicion by Reverend Poston, and then everyone sat down to finally get to enjoy their Sunday meal.

"Well now, that was very distinctive, Professor. Very distinctive and very nice," said Belva. "Not something you would want to do every day...but quite nice. Now, girls, I'll need your help to bring the tea from the kitchen."

"I'll get it, Momma," said Marva, handing the baby back to Wilton. "And you just stay where you are, Regina. But keep an eye on Skoot."

"Are liquor toasts typical at your dinners in Indianapolis, Mister Penn?" asked Jeremy. "Somehow the tradition doesn't seem very Hoosier."

"Indianapolis dinners are fine after their fashion," said Wilton, fingering the note in his pocket. He wondered how *cheap* and $8,000 could be used in the same sentence. "But as far as I'm concerned they can't compare with your good solid farm fare. Put some more of that yellow gravy on your potatoes, and be sure to sample Mamaw Ainsley's turnips. Simple American country cooking is still the best. Break open a couple of biscuits, Professor. Just ladle that gravy all over them."

"There's no beating it," agreed Forsyth.

Setting down two metal pitchers...one labeled *Sweet* and the other *Tea*... Marva sat next to Wilton who had handed Ribby over to Regina when she came over to pat Skoot on the back. "Did you feed Skoot some chicken?" Marva whispered to Wilton.

"We were waiting for you. You know she won't eat for me. She swallowed too much biscuit. Had to whack her on the back."

"Momma, where did you say Daddy was? Wilton and I were well pleased to have him in Barbara-Jean's photos. He is going to join us I hope. You know he loves chicken with yellow gravy."

"Toasts are just a normal part of civilized society, Reverend."

"They're not usual up here. Liquor toasts. It's against the law for one thing. As far as I know. And it's inappropriate in a Christian setting."

"He may have gone up to the cattle shed over by the woods," said Wilton. "Or even over at the new barn. Or the kennels. He loves those dogs."

"Laws are made to be broken, Reverend," said Greg, savoring the grape juice. "Anyway, this is grape juice, not whiskey. I believe it's what they say Jesus drank at his Final Meal before His execution."

"He might very well be doing something with those new hunting dogs of his. There's a bit of chipped ice in that covered bowl," said Belva. "And plenty more in the kitchen. I have no idea what he's up to. Your father keeps his own counsel any more. Serve the tea while it's still cool, Marva. Isn't she the best baby, Regina?"

"Last Supper, sir. And it was the crucifixion. Even grape juice can set a bad example when it's treated like an intoxicant."

"We'll talk about that *cheap deal* of yours later, Bob."

5

One Of Those Truly Dreadful Accidents, Incidents Or Things

Not being at the table when the ladies served chicken and biscuits with yellow gravy, plus not being there when you had guests... especially the Preacher...that was not something a proper man did...definitely not something Olin Ainsley would do. No matter how upset he'd been this past year. And he had been. No question about it. You could tell from things he'd repeatedly done and said. The man had problems…within him…not with the farming operation.

Wilton knew the business and the property were sound. Olin paid his bills on time and never over-extended himself. He wasn't a man to be careless about money. He'd never maintained more horses than he could actually use, and was cautious about buying a lot of this new machinery. On the other hand, he and Belva had always had rough edges that grated against each other. She wasn't an easy woman to live with. But then how many women were?

$8,000 for an automobile wasn't cheap no matter how you figured it. Plus the cost of this brother-in-law Norman. But prices were going up, and you had to add in the cost of shipping a *Rolls-Royce* from England. The dead woman had had to pay that. Still, it was a lot of money. Eight times what he paid for the *Ford*. Just so Marva could cruise around Aschburgh in English luxury.

Not knowing what to expect, Wilton told the women he'd check for Olin over by the cattle shed and the kennels before checking the new cattle barn and the horses. But his sense was Olin would most likely go to the old barn, which was kind of a second home for him. So that was where he headed. The big sliding door was padlocked, but several boards had been loosened on the far side, and careful not to rip his new topcoat and suit, Wilton pried back a large plank and eased himself inside.

A strong smell of decay, perhaps blood…it had been years, but he recalled his childhood revulsion on finding his father slaughtering…made him shake out his linen handkerchief and place it over his nose and mouth. Light filtered through the gaps between the planks on the side of the barn so that he could see piles of straw scattered about.

Something in here was dead and rotting. All the stalls were empty and dry, which was as he expected. For the past several months Olin had slowly and reluctantly moved livestock out of here and over to his new barn across the creek. Far away from the house, in response to Belva's complaints about flies and the smell of manure.

"Olin? You in here, buddy? Olin?"

As he turned from the empty stalls he could make out a large, dark shape stretched on the dirt floor in the back of the barn. O Lord, he thought. Olin. But it couldn't be. Not with this stench. Olin had been at church, dressed up, suit, shirt and tie. Even stayed for the photos this time. Which pleased Marva. What the dickens was it?

"Well, I'll be! Son-of-a-gun!"

Wilton glanced down at the rotting, bloated calf and brushed away several flies which having struggled to stay alive into late Fall were now rewarded with so rich a feast. Bluish white maggots throbbed about the entrails, for a half-hearted effort had been made to gut the animal, and intestines and organs had been pulled part way out of the slit belly. He expected to see the throat cut, but it was intact. Something else had killed the calf.

"Shoot!"

Swatting aimlessly at the languid flies he stepped back and scrapped the soles of his shoes against the ground. What a stinking mess. Olin had been hiding this. Why else padlock an empty barn? Unable to complete the butchering, or more likely *unwilling* since he had slaughtered all his life...hadn't even bothered to hoist the animal...he left the botched job and locked up the barn. This was not the man he had known all his life.

"Olin! Hey, Olin!"

As he climbed the stairs...hardly more than a home-made ladder placed at a steep angle...leading from the dirt floor to the hayloft ten feet above him, he glimpsed Olin's scuffed black Sunday shoes dangling several feet above the dusty floor of the loft... slowly twirling across the slits of sunshine breaking through the old walls. A drop of liquid fell from the heel of one shoe. Olin had gone and done it.

"Aw shoot, man! How am I supposed to explain this to Marva? You doggone coward. You son-of-a-gun! Now isn't this a pretty sight. You miserable...."

The smell of the calf filled the hayloft. Doggone! When he was about ten he and his father found Uncle Howard Goins the same way. Back then, only a boy, he'd handled it poorly, shaking and crying and even puking…unable to accept that someone he knew, from his own family, who had joked and worked with his father, had gone and done a crime so horrible that God would send him straight to hell for it.

But over the course of a lifetime he supposed he'd become hardened to it. Seemed like every couple of years a Tecumseh County farmer killed himself. Usually gunshot, but sometimes like this. He'd known of more than a few. Though no one wanted to admit it, it was becoming a normal part of the stress of farming. These fellows didn't spend all their time sucking on a piece of straw. Of course it rarely got reported that way. You had to protect a man's family and reputation … plus it wasn't anyone's business anyway.

Leaning against bales of hay piled eight feet high all around the loft, Wilton rested his hand against the rough wood of the makeshift ladder Olin used to climb to the beams up by the roof, and studied his friend's silent body, still spinning slowly on a rope tied to the highest beam. He probably sat hunched up there for a bit, his head touching the underside of the tin roof while he fixed the rope about himself. His neck looked to be broken, so he probably didn't flip about while suffocating. Likely wouldn't have suffered much once he made the decision to push off.

There was often a blessing if a fellow looked hard enough. Much as we messed things up, God was still loving. It just wasn't like human love. Still, *all things work together.* "Well, you've gone and done it now, you son-of-a-gun. No turning back. And no point in me getting bent out of joint about you, is there? You've left me with bigger problems. I'm the one's got to tell Marva and Belva. Not you. You just skipped out on the whole mess. Aw shoot, Olin! I always thought you were a Christian…thought you were more of a man."

Surely this was going to tarnish the memory of Barbara-Jean's Dedication Day. No getting around that, no getting around the loss for little Wendy and the pain for Marva…but for certain there was no reason for it to be more than an unexpected sudden death. No reason at all for it to torment and torture needlessly. You'd think Olin would've seen that and had some respect and concern for Marva and his grandchildren. A man was supposed to protect his family. That came before his own needs. It just did, plain and simple. Family came before everything. Before business, even before God, truth be told. This was a doggone selfish thing. A *damned* selfish thing. Son-of-a-gun. Shoot!

Wilton removed his top coat, jacket, vest, trousers, white shirt and tie, and folding the garments into a neat pile, laid them on a relatively clean bench. He felt foolish...it was way too cold to be running around in his underwear...but a man had to do what a man had to do.

He climbed up the ladder, careful to avoid splinters, aware Olin had made this same trip less than an hour earlier, and grasping the rope he pulled Olin's corpse close. Firmly gripping his dead friend's arm he steadied him and searched his pants pockets for his old jack-knife. Once this was over he resolved to take a hot bath and wash his hair real good. Olin probably used this very knife last week to slit that calf. Doggone! He grasped the corpse by the shirt collar, sliced the rope and let his childhood friend and father-in-law flop onto the hay covered floor, setting up a cloud of dust.

Best to continue the climb to the roof and cut the rope off the beam before fussing with Olin. One thing at a time. Belva would wait...patiently...maybe sensing what he had found out here. They'd all be eating cake and sipping coffee or tea. Each detail he covered here would make it easier for Joey Birdsall, the coroner and undertaker, to cooperate by looking the other way.

He needed to get it cleaned up and smoothed out properly. That was the thing. Then Joey would have less struggle doing what needed to be done for the family. Actually, within reasonable limits, the longer it took the better. Marva and Belva would give him a solid hour to check out the new barn and then go way on up to the horses and all.

Wilton struggled to get the heavy hayloft ladder off the high beam, and let it fall crashing to the floor. He stored it the best he could behind bales of hay in the shadows against the far wall, and tossed some loose hay over it. A proper ladder would be much lighter and easier to handle, but you could never get Olin to spend the money.

Cutting the noose off Olin's loose neck was distasteful for sure, but dragging his heavy body over to the edge of the steep loft ladder was just plain hard and left Wilton breathless and gagging. He'd always been strong and taken pride in his physical condition, but right now he had to admit his age and his years behind a desk at the Bank had taken a toll.

Lining the corpse's shoulders up with the loft ladder...Olin's head hanging loosely over the edge of the hayloft...and grasping his friend's ankles, he flipped him heels over head, tumbling, rolling and sliding down the plank ladder stairs and sprawling on his back on the hard ground below. He just hoped Olin's head wouldn't come loose. Marva would not understand that...she would not be well pleased. Though he supposed Joey knew how to cover up stuff like that.

Pausing in the chill air to consider what would make things easier for Joey Birdsall, and Marshall Sevier for that matter, he took a broom and smoothed out the drag path on the floor of the loft, he covered up the tiny pool of urine, and tossed some more hay over the ladder. Although he was very cold, before getting dressed he went back downstairs to check the position of the corpse. Having pulled his friend's shirt collar up to cover the rope marks as best he could, he stepped back to give the scene a final check.

Ultimately there was nothing he could do about the rope marks which were still clearly visible, but he knew he could count on Joey Birdsall and Sevier Winslow. They were good fellows who understood how things were done. The real problem would be to keep those marks hidden from Marva and Belva. He stooped by the body and rubbed a light coating of dust around Olin's neck and face, pulled the smudged shirt collar up a little higher and held it in place by pulling Olin's neck-tie tight. That would've made him mad. Olin always hated a tie. Son-of-a-gun!

Wilton checked one last time. Not too bad...not too bad at all. Nothing that couldn't be overlooked if a fellow was willing to overlook. After dressing himself carefully and brushing dust from his trousers and shoes, he slipped back through the loose boards on the side of the old barn, took several deep breaths of fresh air, pulled up the collar of his topcoat and headed back toward the house.

Belva stood near the window watching as he approached the house. "Did you find him, Wilton? Did you tell him his dinner is cold?"

"Yes, Belva I found him. But--"

"Where? Where is he?"

"Belva, I think you ought to--"

"Something's wrong, isn't it? Tell me, Wilton. He's been hurt! O Lord, where is he?"

"Sit down, dear. He's taken a bad fall, I'm afraid. A really bad fall. I'm afraid there's nothing to be done. He's gone, Belva. He's just plain gone. I'm so sorry. Let me get everyone here into the parlor. We need to be together. And I've got to make a call."

6
BELVA'S SUNDAY CHICKEN

Take good sized old hen
Put pieces in Mamaw Winslow's black pot and cover with enough water
Good pinch of salt and bring to rapid boil and reduce
Vegetables and seasoning
Continue until hen is tender but not too so
Strain broth. Leave fat. Add some yellow but not too much
Flour and water until just right
Place hen in gravy and serve with Tempie Phipps biscuits

7
The Family Struggles With Death &
Some Issues Of Humanity

Greg Penn curled up in a cozy armchair in a corner of the over-heated parlor ...a tartan comforter draped about his shoulders...

watching the others struggle with the impact of the tragedy as he puzzled over the homey imprecision of the splatter stained recipe. Much as he wanted to help and to comfort, he felt he was more effective as a steadying influence. At least until the police arrived. Willie would be in charge then.

"Bob, would you get nice cold glasses of water for everyone? Not the children of course. I suspect they're too young. This is a lovely room, Belva. So warm and cozy. You've done a beautiful job with it. I find, at a time like this, an old-fashioned parlor is very reassuring, very comforting. Did we have Tempie Phipp's biscuits?"

"Thank you, Doctor Penn. Those were Regina's. Tempie's were never that fluffy. Are you sure you're warm enough?" Belva whispered, choking back her tears. "O Marva, he's gone, he's gone. We'll never see him again. Why won't Wilton let us go to him?"

"He doesn't think we should right now, Momma. Wilton knows what's best."

The Reverend Doctor Poston and Regina sat by the window. Regina, her eyes reddened, reached for her husband's hand...but without thinking Jeremy brushed her fingers away. "Perhaps we could have a word of prayer."

"Wouldn't one of Ted Steele's *Brown County* landscapes look appropriate over the sofa, William?" Greg asked Professor Forsyth. "A prayer? Do you think that helps those who have passed?"

Forsyth, who desperately wanted to get outside for a cigarette, stared open mouthed at the architect. "No one ever called him *Ted*. Not even Mrs. Steele. *Professor Steele*. Are you serious, man? There's been a death here."

"Perhaps your own *Portrait of Alice?*"

Jeremy Poston cleared his throat. "When folks are ready we can form a circle of prayer and lift up the family."

"It would be nice there, wouldn't it, Greg?" Marva murmured, wiping away tears with her hand. "I adore that painting of Mrs. Forsyth. From the moment I first saw it. Dear Alice in her blue gown. It's a work of genius, Professor. Greg, you're very sweet.

I'm so grateful to have you with us right now. Would you like to hold Skoot? She's a little upset by all the sadness."

Regina left Jeremy standing in the center of the room, and walked toward the kitchen. "I think I'll give Bob some help."

Belva blew her nose and took Greg's hand. "You are a comfort to me, Doctor Penn. Thank you for staying with us. I just don't see how he could have fallen, Wilton," she said, really speaking to herself. "He's run up and down those hayloft ladder stairs for years."

"They're very steep and a bit damp. He seems to have slipped," said Wilton. "I'll know more after Joey Birdsall and Marshall Sevier get here. Right now the best thing is for all of us to stay together. I'll let you know everything I find out."

Greg stared at Skoot who was crying and had a greenish substance flowing from both nostrils. "Hold her, Marva? Hold the child?"

Professor Forsyth glared at the tiny architect. Comfort indeed! The things people would say! "In your arms, Penn. In your arms. Marva's asking for your help. She needs to comfort Mrs. Ainsley. Her mother, man. You comfort Skootums for God's sake."

Returning from the kitchen with Regina, Bob the chauffer set down a tray of water glasses, and grinning broadly lifted Wendy into Greg Penn's lap. "There, there little girl. Now that's a comfy lap, wouldn't you say?"

Regina leaned across Penn and wiped Wendy's nose. "There, Skootie, that's much better. Let's not get Mister Penn's nice clothes snotty."

"Thank you, Regina and Bob for being human," muttered Forsyth. "It's a miracle some people even know how to breathe on their own." He gestured toward Jeremy who was still standing in the center of the room. "I believe the Reverend is planning to pray. With us or without us."

Wendy pulled Greg's comforter from his shoulders and squiggled out of his lap. "Well, this is quite something. I don't think I've ever held a child before...have I Bob?"

"Perhaps we should wait for things to settle down a bit before praying," said Belva.

"Not so far as I know," said Bob. "Your work tends to be rather more adult orientated, sir. But you do quite well with grown-ups."

"My God, Penn," said Forsyth, scooping up Skoot. "You're supposed to cuddle her, man. Cuddle her. Comfort the baby." The old artist sat next to Marva and began tickling Wendy. Wilton smiled at them. The man was really a good fellow. Outspoken and a bit vulgar, but he had a good heart, and he'd been very good for Marva these past two years.

"That old barn was like a second home to him, Marva. Maybe if I hadn't insisted on the new barn. But I just don't understand how he could get hurt in there. I want to see him. Wilton, I want to see him. Please take me over to him."

"I'm sorry, Belva. We're going to have to wait on Joey and the Marshall. I'm afraid the law is very strict in a situation like this."

"O Momma, it'll be all right. Wilton knows what to do. We'll come through this all right, won't we Professor? Won't we, Wilton? Wilton will tell us what to do as soon as it's o.k. He'll know exactly what to do. O God, why? Daddy!"

"Try not to get the babies upset, dear," said Belva.

"It's all so terribly sad," whispered Greg Penn. "Bob, why don't you pass the glasses of water? I love those glasses. You can't find cut-ware like that in Indianapolis any longer, Forsyth. You know, this is just one of those truly dreadful accidents…incidents or things…things that happen, that go wrong. You'll have the same situation, the same kind of accidents on a construction site no matter how well you've designed things. We had a foreman…I mean an experienced man…topple from the roof of my new synagogue in Cincinnati. Sixty feet. Landed on his head. Awful, just awful they said. The rabbi was touring the site when it happened, and I imagine that was very comforting. I find Hebrew people have more compassion. I've yet to meet a really mean-spirited Hebrew. But these incidents will just seem to happen. For no reason whatsoever. I don't suppose there's any satisfactory explanation."

"God remains in control," said Jeremy. "The Lord has compassion. Even for the Jew. But His ways are not our ways."

Greg Penn raised his hand to silence the minister. "Take no offense, Reverend Poston. But having studied the horrors of the Albigensian Crusade I find I can no longer believe in a merciful God. I hope we're not distressing you, Mrs. Poston?"

"No, no not at all," said Regina who hadn't heard his remarks, and wouldn't have been concerned if she had. "Skoot just adores you, Professor Forsyth."

Jeremy didn't know what State Albigensy was in...nor who had preached the crusade there...but if hearts had been warmed and souls won at the altar he couldn't see what this little man was so upset about. "There's no horror or shame in a crusade, sir. God uses that anointed preaching to achieve His ends."

"I suppose," said Greg dismissively. "What is your doctorate in? I assume it's from *Indiana* or *Purdue*? Willie and I went there. *IU*. Though my doctorate is from *Massachusetts Institute of Technology*. You've heard of it I suppose? Be careful of the baby, Forsyth. They can be very fragile."

"There's got to be a reason. There's got to be," Belva whispered to Marva. "Is Barbara-Jean all right?"

Wilton crossed the room and patted Belva's hand. "I'll wait outside for Joey and Sevier. We'll get through this, Marva. We'll all miss him terribly, but we'll be all right. We're a family."

"Should we call the church?" she asked.

"Doctor Poston's here, Momma," said Marva.

"Of course."

William Forsyth tickled Wendy. "Little Ribby-Roo and little Skootums-pootums. That's what you are. A little Skootums-pootums. Even when everything else goes wrong, Mrs. Ainsley, we still have the babies. I don't know what I'd do without my girls. They've seen me through some very dark days. Skootums and Ribby-Roo will always be a comfort to you."

Greg Penn listened intently. "Would you like me to take the child, Professor?"

"No, I most certainly would not."

"Suit yourself. These old-fashioned armchairs are so comfortable. You can say what you want, Reverend, the old craftsmen knew how to make a chair."

"You are such a comfort to me, Doctor Penn," said Belva. "Would you like a warmer blanket?"

"I am a Doctor of the Word of God," Jeremy said to Penn.

"There's been a death," said Forsyth. "Both of you stop your blathering."

"Don't you think it helps to have normalcy in our conversation? I'm more than willing to spell you for a bit," Greg added, gesturing toward Wendy with his index finger. "Do folks around here still have the wake in the home, Reverend? Doctorate of the Word of God? That's a new one to me. You know, they laid my grandfather out like that, and they still do it that way in much of Europe. Ghastly. No embalming over there. When it's my time I'm going to be cremated."

"Be quiet! My God!"

"Perhaps we could have a word of prayer now that we're all settled."

CHAPTER 13
ONCE IN A LIFETIME
ARRANGEMENTS

Some things kind of get worked out in this long chapter. But new issues are raised. We meet Josephuston Birdsall in the context of his vocation and as he struggles with new ideas. Made privy to Wilton's offer, we also share in his visionary insight into the future import of colored funerals. In the determination of Belva and the Supper Committee to control events we see disturbing reminders of humanity's insistence on trying to dictate destiny. Many other things occur within the drama of Olin's funeral, and there is even an unseemly effort to undermine Professor Forsyth's virtue.

1
Nothing More Than A Simple & Tragic Slip And A Fall

Joey Birdsall, rail thin and 5'10" tall, had since childhood cultivated a stoop shouldered look and a voice rarely raised above a comforting whisper, and as a consequence tended to be thought much smaller than he actually was. Now in his mid forties, Josephuston Birdsall had taken over the *Birdsall Funeral Home* twenty years earlier upon the death of his father Verritton Birdsall.

Soon afterward and to no one's surprise he was appointed to replace his father as Tecumseh County Coroner, had remained in that office since, and was likely to hold onto it until he died. Thought highly effective in dealing with both the quick and the dead, Joey had a well deserved reputation for being discreet and mindful of local concerns and community values.

At about three o'clock that afternoon he smoothed out a small and tidy canvas tarpaulin alongside Olin's body which lay sprawled on its back with the right eye open and the left eye half shut. Carefully running his hands over his short black hair which had been mussed up a bit as he squeezed between the boards on the side of the barn, he knelt carefully to examine the head and neck of the corpse, taking special care to avoid getting barn filth on his new black suit.

"Isn't this just the most tragic thing, Willie? The Ainsleys, as you well know better than anyone, have always been a sound family. Just real fine people. Well regarded and well respected."

Wilton noted the *Willie* and took it to be a very good sign. Joey would have called him *Wilton* or even *Mister Goins* had he been in one of his officious moods. Olin's death was to be treated as a family matter...and so he was *Willie*.

"These tragedies happen even in the best of families, Joey. It's the nature of life, and I've always thought it to be one of the redeeming qualities of our blessed town that we deal well with these kinds of things. Olin's gone, and that hurts of course, but he's in God's hands now. Truth is he's been gone for some time. He hasn't been the Olin we grew up with...he's been someplace else. Our concern has to be for Belva. And Marva and the babies, of course. And the family's reputation."

"Yes, yes," Joey Birdsall whispered, lightly patting Olin on the head. "Now I hope that even in your grief and shock you haven't touched him. The coroner has to deal with the body, Wilton. Untouched. Difficult though that may be."

"Haven't put a hand on him. It may have caused some hurt, but I even stopped Belva from coming out to fuss on him. I know the law, Joey, and I don't take liberties."

"Of course. It's all just so sad. We see altogether too much of this sort of thing."

"Pardon?"

"Early and unexpected passing. Especially in agriculture. You and Olin and myself...we were all in school together. It makes one think."

"Hmmm. Makes a fellow think is right."

Joey slowly moved Olin's loose head from side to side, and ran his finger around the rope burns on his throat. "From hitting his neck on the edges of the steps, I imagine. Do you think Belva will want him shown here at the house or up at the *Birdsall Home*? It's whatever she wants, of course. The family's needs and wishes come first. That's always been the *Birdsall* motto. The main thing is that Belva and Marva be comfortable."

"That's important, of course, but there are other concerns than what she wants. Belva will probably tell you she wants him here at *The Old Ainsley Place,* but that's not a good idea, Joey. That's not a good idea at all, and it's not about to happen."

"You see her needs being met more fully at our *Home?* That would of course be my preference."

"As you say, it's her choice. No one's denying that, but I would prefer the viewing...visitation as it were...to be at your place, with the service at our Church. I'd like to avoid nibbing and prying and so forth. You know how these people can get."

Joey held Olin's head between his hands, and then shut the corpse's eyes. "We see this so much anymore. The eyes bugged out like that. Very unpleasant for the family, but we know how to handle it. So I understand your preference, Willie, but if Belva disagrees how shall we focus on meeting her needs?"

"You see a lot of protruding eyeballs? The result of falls I imagine."

"Most likely. Willie, if there's any rope around I'd stash it away if I were you. Someone might trip on it."

"Right. Excellent point, Joey. The bottom line is it's going to be at the *Birdsall Home* and *First Community Church*. No matter what," said Wilton. "That's not open to debate."

"So it would appear. What kind of accommodations do you imagine Belva would prefer? More and more we're finding families prefer our *Full Home Service*. It makes everything so much easier on the family."

"The most expensive casket and so forth."

"I don't like to focus on cost...but the highest quality, of course. Olin was a fine man. We'd lost contact a bit recently... but a fine fellow."

"He deserves the best. And, Joey, we'll work all this out so everyone's well pleased. These things can always be worked out. A lot of people don't realize that, but if there's one thing I've learned through the years it's that things can always be worked out. Give a little to get a little. We do need to have the casket open though. And his head looking good. That's a must. That's an absolute must. Otherwise... well, you know how people can get. You know how people around here can talk. Turn a perfectly honorable thing into a scandal if you know what I mean."

Joey Birdsall, still kneeling on the tarpaulin, tugged on Olin's pants so his ankles were fully covered. "More and more we find people appreciate all that we're able to do at the *Home* for their loved one. We have all the latest facilities and mechanisms so things move along nicely. But whatever the family wants, of course. That's paramount." Olin's left eye slowly began to reopen. "Isn't that something? I'll take care of it later. He'll be resting easy and look just fine." He wet his thumb and worked on a smudged bruise on Olin's forehead. "An open casket will be no problem at all. We handle tragic falls like this more often than you might think."

"Frankly I have no idea what Olin wanted, but he was a Deacon of our Church, so the service ought to be there, led by Doctor Poston. He and Regina... Mrs. Poston...Winslow of course...are up at the house right now. Comforting Belva. This service will be a very important event in the history of *First Community Church of Indiana*."

"Doctor Poston has done some fine services at our *Home*. He seems very comfortable in our setting."

"Not this one though. I realize it makes a problem for you, and you've already got quite a job. The last thing I want to do is imposition you, and I don't like to insist on something I know is going to be an imposition, but...."

"O we'll make him very comfortable, very presentable. Olin's no problem. There, that's better," Birdsall whispered as he smoothed down Olin's few wisps of hair. "Bald fellows have it tough, don't they?"

"He's dead, Joey. Already starting to turn gray, and pretty badly banged up if you ask me. We can't even get that eye to stay shut."

"Yes, he is, poor fellow. But we can smooth all that out. Mortuary Science has made remarkable strides. Remarkable. You can't imagine the difficulties we faced in my father's time."

"Verritton Birdsall was a fine man."

"This is, in its way, so tragic. Don't you think? Olin was still a young man."

"Our age. I'd hardly call that young...more like his prime. But regardless, we need to keep our focus on helping Belva and the family. Sparing them unnecessary pain. That's got to be our bottom line. Now those are his best shoes. You'd of thought he might have changed them. Pretty scuffed and beat up from all this. Tragic fall and whatnot. Will you be able to use them?"

"A little spit and polish. They'll be covered with his blanket anyway. But I do appreciate your concern, Willie. A lot of people will send us dingy old things, so the poor fellow's toes are hanging out. We'll have Olin looking nice and spiffy. Very proper. Very comfortable. Does he have any high collared shirts? We're all so fond of Olin and Belva."

"You hardly see couples like them anymore. "'til death us do part. Totally inseparable. Would one of my shirts do? Given the difference in chest and so forth? But we're both 18 in the neck."

"18? You're really an 18? That's deceptive. Because of your height and build I imagine."

"Thick neck and thick head."

"Couldn't be better. The shirt that is. One of your shirts. It has to be cut down the back anyway so I can tuck things in or splay things out a bit. But your absolute *highest* collar...that'd fit the bill. One of those old-fashioned ones. Now we will need a clean suit. These trousers can't be used, if you see what I'm saying. And I'm not going to be able to clean this tie up adequate. So a good suit, clean underwear is always nice...you'd be surprised the number of families that forget that...socks and a simple tie."

"Olin did hate a necktie."

"I'm afraid anymore it's a must for a proper viewing. Plus it'll tighten up the collar...and...well...if you see what I'm saying. By the way, Louise and I were there for baby Wendy's Dedication, you know. Must be over a year now. The Church was so crowded and somehow I never got around to mentioning how nice it was to you. Sorry we had to miss today though. For the new baby. We sure would have liked to have been there.

"O...and I need a recent photograph. Definitely a recent picture. That just helps so much. Our church, *First Methodist...* we're still going there even after all this Tuyter mess...we're hanging in don't you know...well, we're preparing for our *Late Winter Tenderloin Supper.* The few of us that's left. Biggest fund raiser we have. That was one thing Reverend Tuyter was good at...not that I'm excusing him of course."

Wilton stepped around Olin's body checking for any obvious mistakes that might still make it tough on Joey to go along. Though Birdsall hadn't seemed to have any problems so far. "His leg must've got twisted like that in the fall, don't you think? So many things can get whacked up in a fall like that."

"I'd imagine. It'll be easy to straighten out. We know how to do that." He stood up, and very lightly tapped Olin's leg with his shoe to get things lined up a bit. "That looks better already, don't you think? Willie, what's your sense of all this, just between friends, don't you know?"

"A simple and tragic slip and a fall. Nothing more."

"A simple and tragic slip and a fall. That's exactly what I'm going to put down. *A simple and tragic slip and a fall.* That'll do fine."

"Joey, not to push and not to get nibby, but have you and Louise thought about coming over to *First Community?* I can guarantee you'd be very, very well received, and have pretty much any committee assignments you want. Or none if that's your preference. You're the kind of people we're seeking after. I can tell you for a fact business people are well appreciated at *First Community*, and unlike a lot of churches a business man's views are taken pretty much for Gospel. We treat our Pastor good, we take care of our property, but first and foremost we balance our budget. Our guiding Scriptural principle is, *You can't spend what you don't have.*"

Josephuston leaned over and rubbed his knees. "They get so sore anymore. Arthritis I imagine. I appreciate what you're saying, Willie. Louise and I both appreciate your principle. A lot of churches need to learn that. But what with Tuyter gone… and I really doubt he was a child molester…not that he wasn't a pervert, a peeping tom, and that's bad enough…anyway, we've been trying to hang in a bit and see how things go.

"But I will tell Louise what you say, and see about her thoughts. She's a bit tired of all this, and personally I'm leaning your way. You've got a sturdy little Pastor there…not a pretty fellow…but for my part I think that's often a good thing."

"A pretty preacher is always trouble. That's right up there with a load of debt. We'd all be well pleased if you were to come our way, Joey. There'd be a seat on the Board for you. I guarantee that. And Louise would have whatever she wanted. And I'm not meaning to make light of your *Tenderloin Supper.* That might well be something that could be carried over to *First Community.* I doubt we could do three a year like you folks have done. But we could certainly have one big one. You know up until recently Olin here loved those *Tenderloin Suppers* of yours. Never missed them until last year. Can anything be done about that eye? It's not going to look good for the ladies."

"I'll have it shut and get rid of all that puffiness for the visitation."

"I mean now. O.K. if I put my handkerchief over his face?"

"Suit yourself. I'm finished. But I wouldn't bring the ladies in to see him at this point. Let me get him to the *Home* and settle him down a bit."

"Marva says after her first year at the *Women's Seminary* she and her folks were motoring down in Brown County...and Olin drove his old *Ford* straight through the night to get back for that *Start Of School Tenderloin Supper* you used to have in early September. Flat tires and over-heating and whatnot. Now that's commitment. Knocked down eight tenderloins at that meal she says. Quite a guy! On this other thing...this Tuyter business...the way I see it, Joey, I don't want a preacher who's peeking in my bedroom window. At my wife. And I don't want him peeking in yours either. I don't want him peeking at my Marva, and I know for sure you don't want him peeking at your Louise. But, on the other hand we are Christians, and as I told your Bishop, I'm glad I was able to get Tuyter a good position over to Knightstown. The *Bible* says to hate the sin but love the sinner and help one another out whenever it's practical and feasible."

"Eight tenderloins would about be the world's record. So I think there's maybe a bit of exaggeration going on there. But the man did love his tenderloins."

"He did that, he surely did."

"Personally I agree we're better off without Tuyter. The fellow is a pervert...but more than that he'd just been around too long. He probably went back...what...twenty-five, maybe thirty years. Way too long. When a minister's in town more than three or four years he starts to think he's part of the community, and in the long run that makes for trouble no matter what anyone says."

"You can work it out...provided you keep the reins on your man. The problem with Tuyter was over the years they just let him run loose, do whatever he wanted. Anyway, the fellow's gone now, and I'm sure he's happier where he is. So it looks to you like a simple and tragic slip and a fall?"

"Farming's a dangerous business. Am I right? Banking's a much better way to spend your productive years, in my humble opinion."

"Has its advantages. Good hours, like they say. Right? Now will his head be a big problem? Keeping it steady and in place for the viewing? Can that be braced so you can't see the steadiers? Plus it's swelled up a bit. I don't want it tilting funny."

"Not a problem at all. Despite the break everything's reasonably tight. Sometimes you actually see them fall off. Sorry. I oughtn't to have said that. But my men will be very careful. We'll want that lock opened or cut off so we can take him out the barn door. And get some of that stink out of here."

"That's from a dead calf."

"O. Well, it'd be good to get it out. By the way, Willie, we're thinking of expanding our facility. We're badly needing another space for viewing, and a nice little cozy room for the families to gather in private and chat. Maybe even a little more expansion than that. With all the progress in our field you need to be constantly updating your equipment and work-space. That's our current vision for *Birdsall Home*. We've been dreaming about it for some time now, and maybe this is as good a moment as any for me to speak to you about it."

"My door is always wide open to you and your facility, Joey. Wide open. Through the *Birdsall Home* your family offers a great service to our blessed little town. Just like your Daddy did. Watching him and listening to him…that's what taught me what it meant to be a Christian man. He was a genuinely good no nonsense businessman and a good Christian, and you don't see that combination enough anymore. Nowadays your average Christian thinks *business* is a dirty word."

"And my Grandfather was quite a man too."

"And your Grand-daddy too. Talk about family. Let me put it this way, Joey…expansion of the *Birdsall Home* would definitely be something the Bank would look upon with favor. Many things, even some good and deserving things, why we have to be cautious about…frankly we have to say no to lots of good things …we hate that, but given the state of the economy right now…. You know, Joey, a lot of your Washington bureaucrats, who've never run a business, why they think things in the economy are going to continue to expand indefinitely, but we don't see it that way.

We're simple people…folks who've got their hands dirty…and we know better. You can't spend what you don't have. Common sense tells you it's got to stop soon. Still, expansion of the Birdsall family business…it's a certainty…we wouldn't give it a second thought. Joey, *Aschburgh Savings & Trust* will stand behind you all the way. 110%."

Wilton and Josephuston made their way through the loose planking, and came around the corner of the barn to inspect the padlock. Since it looked very rusted, and he didn't want to go back to the house to search for the key, Wilton picked up a good sized rock and gave it several whacks until it popped. Two Birdsall assistants…actually high school age Birdsalls…quickly disappeared into the barn with a large wicker basket. Joey ducked inside after them. "Be very careful of his head. Make sure to give it full support. Keep it on. I don't want a mess. And look out for the right leg. It's busted up bad. If you screw anything up I'll hold you both responsible."

Rejoining Wilton outside Joey looked up to savor the early evening sky. "Except for the really bitter cold I do love the Winter. God's creation is wonderful, Willie. He really has done a fantastic job, you know? He's a gentle and a gracious Lord. And I want you to know I appreciate your support. You've always been the man to make things happen in this town. How are the rates? It's been a while since we worked something out with you."

"We would view you with favor. I can say with certainty you would be seen as one of our very best customers. Very favored. Very best."

"That's decent of you. Very decent. We'll be able to fix up those nasty cuts on his neck so you'd never even know they were there. Poor fellow. It's just such a tragic thing. But we have a special putty and extraordinarily precise make-up nowadays. And lighting is getting much better. It's not like in my father's day. But I will need that high collared shirt. The absolute highest you have. One of those old-fashioned ones if possible. And a recent photo."

"I've made a mental note. I imagine he hit his neck several times as he crashed down those stairs. Ladder really. The edges of those rough boards will slice right in."

"Severed his spine."

"Broke his neck clean. Joey, why don't you stop by my office in a few days? Naturally I'm going to be tied up with all this. Getting the women settled down and whatnot. Not to mention the holidays. I would have thought the Marshall would have been here by now, this being family. But Sevier Winslow always has been a bit of a rascal. A good man, but still a rascal. Even before he became a widower."

"Now that was a funeral. I'll bet every police department in the County was present for Mrs. Winslow. Well respected people. And Stonewall County too. But anyway, we don't need the police for this. Coroner is fine. I'll let him know my findings. And Doctor Aiken too. He doesn't like being called out of a Sunday."

"One other thing, Joey. Maybe as a special favor. There's no need for an autopsy, is there? Marva wouldn't like for her Daddy to be messed with. Sliced up and all."

"Heavens no! There's no need for that. We're friends, Willie, and this is Aschburgh. Tecumseh County for goodness sake. We know how to take care of our own people. And you can be sure the boys will make Olin very comfortable. They'll support his head nicely. A simple and a tragic slip and a fall. An unfortunate and a sad thing. Young as he was. I'll see if Marshall Sevier can get some of his police friends as an honor guard. Maybe those State Troopers. They really look sharp. I imagine Marva would like that."

"Joey, on second thought, instead of you coming to the Bank why don't I just stop over by your place with the loan papers? Save you the trouble and get this thing expedited. Maybe as part of Olin's arrangements. Which I'm sure you realize are going to be substantial."

"Whatever the family decides...but I'm sure that you will want to give Olin his due honor."

"But, Joey...I'm sorry, but I have to emphasize this again...an open casket is a must. We cannot abide a closed casket. And his head has to be fine. Agreed? I can't negotiate on that. Whatever it takes that casket needs to be wide open and he needs to look good. And steady. No wobbling. I don't know if it's possible, but maybe a metal rod in there. Because you know some of those women are going to push at him. Then as far as our business, why we can just work things out one, two, three. Any sense of what size loan you're going to need?"

"He'll look better than he has in years. We'll even clean his ears and his nails, which is something Olin pretty much stopped doing. Of course many of your farmers don't. Now I don't mean to sound critical. Anyway, an open casket is no problem for us. We handle situations like this all the time. Willie, the funeral business is not what it once was. Those horse and buggy days are a thing of the past."

"So we might be talking more than just a lounge for families?"

"I think that's fair to say. We're looking at a substantial addition to our physical plant. By the way, when you come over my Louise just got her Notary Stamp so any papers we work on will be fully squared and legal. To put this to you fair and straight...we're looking to be the largest *Home* in Tecumseh County. Which I'm sure you of all people realize will mean a major expansion for the *Aschburgh Florists,* plus up to ten jobs for local folks helping out around the *Home*, not to mention all the other money we'll pour back into the Aschburgh economy. And the construction itself. We're easily talking tens of thousands at first, and much more as we find ourselves able to accommodate multiple services."

"Are your boys waiting on you? With Olin?"

"No. I'm sure they've taken him back to the *Home* by now. They'll make him real comfortable. I've got my own vehicle. Now you take the *Winters Home* in South Bend...Marvin Winters who got us the tickets for that Army game? Wasn't that something?... he's processing ten and more many weeks. Almost four hundred last year. Now that's close to unbelievable. Of course it's a big town and he's got two older facilities plus his new one. Marvin's got families coming in from all over the area. Believe it or not, he recently had two from the Niles area. Up in Michigan. Basically because of his new facility. He can provide everything…even cremation… though of course he doesn't publicize that. He's got everything from the very lowest cost service…which I feel is kind of embarrassing actually…unless you're talking derelicts with no family…on up to the most complete service you could ever imagine …the sort of thing you folks would want for Olin. Marvin's *Home* even gets some Amish people…which is incredible given the way those people are."

"Sounds a little grandiose for Aschburgh."

"Granted we're not South Bend…but do the math, just do the math, Willie. I believe we can be of service to people in Indianville, in Giantown, and everything in between. Most folks are hurting for a sympathetic, down-home approach, and that's exactly what we offer. I'll know the full extent of the expansion by late tonight, and when you stop by tomorrow for the arrangements I'll have all the numbers we need. We can just type everything up in my office and have Louise notarize the whole shebang. Ultimately I intend putting Marvin out of business."

"As far as South Bend! I like that. That's vision, Joey. I imagine I'll want to take the papers back to my office for a final look see."

"Suit yourself. This is just so tragic for the family. So tragic. We especially want to save the ladies as much pain as possible. The whole town's going to be at the visitation. And more. Way beyond the town. Over the years Olin has just been a big part of this total community."

"These things always are sad, Joey. But we get through tough times because we care about one another. And we know how to work things out. That's the strength of Aschburgh. By the way, Joey, sorry I missed the last couple of *Lions* meetings."

"Attendance hasn't been what we'd like recently. A lot of folks take the *Lions* for granted. But your preacher always makes it. We really appreciate him. Though we surely have missed you, Willie."

"It's always good to be missed. How's the family?"

"Well you may have heard Louise has been having some problems. Women's things. But otherwise we certainly can't complain. Having that door open really airs out this place. Though the stink is going to take more than fresh air."

"I'll have one of my fellows come over and shovel up that mess. The calf I mean."

"That'll do the job. Most of your stink is from that. These situations can be so unpleasant. Especially for the ladies. All these flies....I've always disliked flies. I think I'll stop by the house before I leave. Pay my respects and wash up a bit."

"That'd be well appreciated. And I'll plan to have everyone at your place tomorrow...say around 10. That be o.k?"

"Just fine. Make it 10:30 though. I'll have a special arrangement set up for you in the selection room. Only our finest mahoganies. Plus a gorgeous walnut. Unfortunately the walnut's extremely heavy, but I know Olin would love the craftsmanship. Nothing but top quality. Given the standing of both your families that's proper. This only happens once."

"We'll select a good one. That's not an issue. Just be sure his casket is open and his head looks good. I want that head sturdy, his eye shut, and press down all that swelling. Whatever you have to do you do to get the swelling out of him. I don't want any talk...I don't want any talk at all. I simply won't abide any talk about this."

"Open, Willie. Open casket. Wide open, looking good, and no talk whatsoever."

"I'm fortunate to have a friend like you, Joey. I'm truly looking forward to assisting you in the expansion of your facility. And profits of course."

"We're both fortunate, Willie. I'll be honest with you now... no matter how things are starting to look everywhere else...it's a good time in my business. Service to be provided."

"And money to be made."

"And money to be made."

2

Green Bean Casseroles, Tickets For Olin's Funeral & The Cincinnati Synagogue

As they arrived back at the house Joey suggested to Wilton that it might prove wise were the ladies allowed to grieve in their special feminine fashion...at least for a bit...while he and Wilton sat down with Doctor Poston to advise him of the family's plans.

"At this point, Jeremy," said Wilton, "I agree it's best we just let the ladies settle down a bit."

"They'll need to purge some of the sadness from their systems before we can really discuss things sensibly with them," said Joey.

"I believe my Regina will be a great comfort to Belva and Marva," Jeremy offered. "Regina, dear, there's someone at the back door," he called to his wife. "Would you get that?"

Regina, who had been hugging her aunt and cousin, left to answer the knock with Barbara-Jean in her arms, and returned a few minutes later with Mary and Marty Kimes, a frail elderly couple who brought a green bean casserole. Joey and Wilton quickly moved to greet them and usher the Kimes to Belva and Mara, while Regina, first tucking the baby back in her bassinette, carried the bean dish into to the dining room.

"I'm always struck how quickly word gets around," Joey whispered to Wilton. "And you know, it was the same in my father's day, before we had hardly any telephones in the County. Farming people have an amazing sensitivity. Somehow they just know."

"And they always come. Even frail old ones like Mary and Marty. It's almost like these folks will keep beans or macaroni and cheese in the oven just *in case*." Wilton grinned as they rejoined the minister.

"I understand you'd like Brother Olin's service at the Church, sir," said Jeremy, brushing crumbs from his suit.

"Will that be a problem, Reverend?" asked Joey.

"Not at all. Provided it's scheduled properly."

324

"Jeremy, I'd sort of like for us to stop using the *Brother* and *Sister* business, if that's o.k. with you,"said Wilton. He pulled up a chair, and gestured to Joey to join them. "To put it frankly it's a new day for *First Community*. The Church has moved across the tracks into the better section of town so to speak, and over here we don't say *Brother* and *Sister*. Now I know *First Bible Baptist Holiness* used to, but on the other hand they never had any Bishops, whereas for *First Community*, why a Bishop seems to be not so far off. A couple of years at most. Maybe a lot sooner."

"A Bishop?"

"That's a big move, Wilton," said Joey. "Around here nobody but Methodists have a Bishop. Well, the Catholics I suppose. They go right on up to Pope. And that's bishops all the way. One atop another so to speak."

"*First Community* and its mission churches will have a Bishop. Maybe with full robes. We'll have to see. And Jeremy, take my word for it, Bishops do not say *Brother* and *Sister*, at least not when they're being serious. Enough said."

"A big, big move." Joey waved toward the dining room as Regina ushered in another elderly couple, Elton and Mary Passwater, who were carrying a pot of green beans flavored with bacon.

"Good to see you, Joey. You doing good?" Elton called out as Regina, with little Wendy in tow, led them across the parlor toward the intimate group gathered around Belva and Marva.

"Now, you make sure he behaves himself, Mary," joked Joey. "And keep him away from those pies."

"Thanks for stopping in, folks."

"I'm sure Mister Goins has a good sense of the community and the Church, Reverend. You'd be wise to listen to his experience. Wilton," Joey whispered, "Not to stick my nose where it has no business being, but shouldn't they be leaving the casseroles, pots and stuff in the kitchen?"

"Let's just let the ladies handle that. They know what they're doing."

"You're probably right. Now on this matter of Olin's service, I know you all want the service up at the Church, but I think it's fair to ask if you'll be able to seat all his guests? The whole County will come to share those moments with him. You know that. Just look at all these folks showing up with casseroles and goodness knows what all. All the farming people will be there. And we'll see them coming in from Stonewall County, and very likely Jefferson and Buchanan. Who knows?... even Grant and Madison."

"I think it will be more manageable than that,"said Jeremy. "I didn't know him that well, but I never saw that he was close to too many people."

"That's because you're new here, Reverend. We're not just talking about people's friendship with Olin, nor even respect to the Ainsley family," Joey whispered. "You'll have at least as many bringing respects to the Goins. So you're talking about the two most respected and influential families in Tecumseh County."

Wilton stood up and grasped Joey's shoulder affectionately. "I think that's laying it on a bit thick, buddy."

"Willie...Wilton, I'm not, and you know it. Now please don't walk away."

"I'm not going anywhere. Just need to stretch out my knees a bit."

"If there's any other family that's as respected...though I suppose no longer quite so influential...it's the Winslows. And Belva and Marva and Regina, they're all Winslows...and they'll let you know it too."

"That's the truth," said Wilton, laughing. "I thought I married an Ainsley but I actually married a Winslow. You agree, Jeremy?"

"Yes, sir. Mrs. Poston's very particular about the Winslows."

"And your Marva...Mrs. Goins...and your Missus... Regina...they've always been favorites there...of the Winslows, I mean. Those folks have favored on those girls since they were babies...everyone knows that...you never speak against them to a Winslow...not that anyone would of course...so you can count on every one of them, the Winslows, being at the service. They'll have problems with the old lady, Jennie Garnett Winslow, if they're not at it. For Marva and Regina if not for Olin and Belva. And for Belva too. That's a fact...and that's a big family. See it's not a question of Olin being somebody's best friend. Though many were close to him over the years. Difficult as he could be. No offense now. You'd be surprised."

"Goodness," said Doctor Poston, beginning to realize the immensity of the task before him. "It's kind of like Rising Sun and Switzerland County in a way. I had no idea there were so many family connections up here."

"O we got them," said Joey. "And there's Nestleroads in there too, though I'm not clear just what that connection is."

"Olin's step-brother...by his third wife...the step-brother's third that is...he lost the first two...one in an accident and the second some other way...married a Nestleroad...the third wife... and his kids by her all carry the *Nestleroad* as a sort of family name. Twilla Jean Pefley is that branch. Twilla Jean Nestleroad Pefley actually. Never cared much for the woman, but she always sends a little something for Marva's birthday. And then we may very well see a bunch of Foxes. I haven't kept in close contact, but I wouldn't be at all surprised to see my uncle Emmett George Fox, plus his family...which is large...very large...from over to Weller County."

"You see what I'm saying, Reverend? So you've not only got the Nestleroads, you've got the Pefleys as well. And now we learn of the Foxes...who I've never even met. I didn't know that, Will... Wilton. About the Foxes in Weller County. I'll need to make a note of that. Emmett George Fox. The Pefleys are a smaller family, but they carry a lot of weight in Democrat circles, of all things. So you can expect a bunch of Democrats from Stonewall County. For sure. That whole crowd is very clannish. How do the Foxes usually go, Wilton?"

"Not sure anymore, but they used to be dependable. Back in my father's time they were strong for business. We were at the *Nestleroad-Pefley Christmas* last year," Wilton added. "Mostly nice people, but now they seem to have gone some Democrat. Some of them...the younger ones anyway." He stepped away for a moment to check on Belva and Marva, but both seemed to be thriving under the influence of neighborly condolence and gossip. Regina, back from storing more casseroles, was holding Barbara-Jean again while Wendy had fallen sound asleep in Professor Forsyth's arms.

"Joey's got it all figured out, Reverend," said Wilton. "You watch out for undertakers now. Always keep your eye on them."

"My family has provided faithful service to Tecumseh County families for almost a hundred years. And you know we're trying to get out from under that *undertaker* label. I prefer Funeral Director."

"Sorry. I spoke out of turn. Your family has cared for this County for generations now. And done a wonderful job...as do you, Josephuston. I meant no disrespect. But I do apologize. I spoke out of turn. Way out of turn. No disrespect was intended to you or to any of your Birdsalls."

"We've been friends for a long time, Wilton. But I want you and the Reverend to understand we're going to have four or five hundred for this Church service. Maybe more. And you don't seat more than two hundred in your present sanctuary. O I know you've got plans, but I'm talking about now. And when you think about the Grange and the Lions and the Masonic Lodge...and if we're lucky the Giantown and Indianville Rotaries...Olin had contacts with both, though he wasn't a member so far as I know. Don't you know they'll be wanting to have a separate Masonic service? You could easily see a couple of thousand for the viewing. Especially if the weather's good. Of course that'll be at the *Home* and we can handle those numbers."

"You can handle them with lines up and down *Goins Boulevard*...and a four hour wait."

"A couple of thousand!" gasped Jeremy Poston. "Am I expected to be there for that? For the entire visitation?"

"Reverend, for Aabert Winslow...he was the great-grandfather...or one thing and another...of all these Winslows and Ainsleys and Goins and Pefleys and I suppose some Nestleroads and probably a few other families that momentarily escape me... though I very much doubt the Foxes...the viewing line was a seven hour wait. Seven hours. We had folks passing out on that line.

Now you might not think it, but a lot of the older people really enjoy these events. You can't get them to go home. I've had to flash the lights more than once. Many of their friends, especially from other communities...they meet them only on these occasions. It got so on Aabert's line...they said he was over one hundred...but we never could document that...we had to provide chairs and ice water...we even kept a hearse ready...only as an ambulance, you know. And...and I believe Wilton will back me up on this... Aabert was not that well thought of...not by some anyway."

"The man was mean and lecherous. Ancient as he was you had to watch your women around him. Now that's said in confidence, Pastor. He broke his wife's heart more than once. But that's the kind of thing you sort of keep to yourself. Joey, you're sure Olin will look fine for this visitation?"

"Just fine. We're talking about large and greatly respected families here, plus Olin was generally a well liked man."

"As long as you didn't get in his way."

"That's true. You had to be careful what you said. Had to leave him alone sometimes. Even back in school. He could get a bit explosive if you pressed at the wrong time."

"Do you gentlemen remember about the loaves and the fishes?" Jeremy smiled and folded his hands over his swelling paunch. "I think it's revelent here."

"In Luke. Five loaves and two or three salted fish," said Joey. "A beautiful instance of God's love and provision. The word's *relevant*. The other is kind of *boisterous* I think. *Revels* and all. What you said."

"For sure."

"Seven loaves and a sack of catfish," said Wilton. "Depends on which Gospel you read. Sort of like those apostles couldn't make up their minds." Wilton slapped Jeremy lightly on the shoulder to let him know the last was a joke. Regina was doing a good job of fattening the boy up, but he wasn't getting any smarter or prettier. He'd make a good Bishop. "What's your point, Doctor? The Lord will provide? Of course He will...He always has... but we've got to do our part too. God can't do it alone. There's such a thing as initiative, get-up-and-go. America's built on that.

That's why you'll find the majority of responsible members of the Church are Republican."

"We need to put our trust in Him."

"Everyone knows that," said Joey. "What's your sense, Wilton?"

"Well, there's only one place in the County that'll seat that big a crowd. But frankly I'm not sure it's acceptable. In fact I'm about certain it's not. In the final analysis Olin was a Church man, a Deacon of the Lord Jesus Christ."

"Blessed be His name."

"I was thinking the same place," said Joey. "But unlike you I think it'll work fine. The Church is the people of God, not a building. And it seems to me the high school gymnasium is the logical spot...really the only place. Plus Olin was always a big supporter of the basketball team. I believe he kept season tickets. And went whenever he could see his way clear."

"He played when we were in school. Remember that, Joey? Of course that was kid's stuff compared to what we've got today. And Olin wasn't much good."

"The high school gymnasium is not God's place," said Doctor Poston. "I've heard there's been instances of swearing in the bleacher seats. And cigarettes."

"How can you say that, Reverend?" said Joey. "How can you say God's not in the midst of that game? Those boys pray. It's like Wilton says, they depend on God but they also put out a lot of sweat. God can't sweat for a fellow. I mean they're our kids. You've got *Bible* readings by the teachers twice a week over there. They honor our country every morning. Plus the team prays before and after every game. Win or lose. And they sure don't lose much...let me tell you. Coach Noffsinger never allows anyone to stay on the squad if he misses those team prayers. They're good Christian kids. And so are the coaches. Most of them anyway."

"Joey, I'm thinking of what you're saying, and I can't take issue with any of it. You're right on target. 100% as usual. It's all well thought out," said Wilton, waving to Orvin and Kendra Nestleroad who had just dropped off a casserole. "Now those are real good people, Reverend. Orvin and Kendra. Nestleroads.

Tithers. And more. You have an electric bill that you can't pay, Orvin's your man. It's worth a little calling on your part. We ought to get them over our way. Get them out of that dead *Friends Church*. Let them know we'd treat them good. Why don't you pay them a little visit?"

"Nestleroad?"

"*First Community Church* has got to be the place for the service. I realize that makes a problem for you, Joey…and I hate to see that, I really do…but that's how it's got to be."

"You're sure?"

"Yeah, it just has to be. Why don't you let me and Doctor Poston come up with a plan, and I'll let you know tomorrow when I stop by the *Home* for things. I'm leaning toward that walnut rather than the conventional mahogany. You agree?"

"It's a superior rest. It really is. Personally it's pretty much my preference. Though there may be another…higher up the line…we never get a call for it around here…too refined I suspect. Let me think about that."

"And let's not forget to ask Marshall Sevier to have that special State Police Honor Guard for Olin. In full dress uniform. Do you think we can get them with rifles? Mention to Sev that Marva and Regina would be well pleased if he would arrange that. There'd be a nice honorarium for each man, of course. That group is sharp, and they have truly outstanding uniforms, Reverend. Every one of them a Christian. Baptized…for the most part by immersion as far as I know. They've got this extra braid and doodads. I believe the ladies would really be touched by that flamboyance. And Joey…and this is important…please tell the Marshall I personally would be truly obliged to him if he could grant me this special favor of the rifles. And while I hesitate to mention this…and I know it'll mean nothing to Sevier…let him know I will be lunching with the State Superintendent in the near future. Not that that means a thing of course."

"I'll chat him up a bit this evening," said Joey. "But I don't see how we can do this, Wilton. All these folks are not going to fit into the Church. You're going to create unhappiness for people coming to pay respect. Anyhow, that's how I see it. That's not a way to begin Olin's rest. But as I've told you before, the family's wishes come first. That's always been the Birdsall motto."

"I appreciate that, Joey."

"And...don't hold this against me now...I don't know how I let this slip my mind earlier...like I say, I've got another thought on the casket. We may be able to secure a best, top-of-the-line, water-proof and air-sealed mahogany...triple polished ...which is superior to anything available anywhere in this entire country. I don't usually stock it...that's why I forgot. Now I'll have to order it from down to Batesville...provided they have it, of course... and it'll take up to two days, but it'll be worth the wait of an extra day, and maybe I can speed them up. They'll ship it by way of Richmond. Generally speaking, the walnut is my favorite... *except* for this superior, triple-polished mahogany. We don't use it often because...well, frankly it's out of the range for most of our clientele. But you'll probably want to give it some thought. I'll put in the order so you can see it, and then if you say the walnut, why it's the walnut, and I'll send this superior triple-polished air-tight mahogany right back to Batesville. Marva and Regina and Belva will adore it though. They'll get great comfort from it. From knowing this superior quality is Olin's rest. And that's a significant factor in the days and months that follow."

"What with Spring rains I imagine. I appreciate it, buddy. Appreciate your looking out for my ladies."

"Down home a lot of the old folks still use a simple pine box."

"But now as for the special Honor Guard, I'll note it down, but I can't promise you the Marshall will be able to pull that off. Those fellows came up for the Klan rally in Elwood last year... of course with the indictments that's all cooled off a bit...but normally they don't travel that much out of the Indianapolis area. I'll check, but don't get your hopes up. Is that little fellow... the one over there talking to Marva...is that your friend from Indianapolis?"

"I can do it myself if I have to, Joey. If you can't pull it off. The State Police Honor Guard. I've got other things to do...as you're well aware...but I'll get it done if you can't. I want them at both services. *Both*. But they don't need to be there for the visitation. And lest I forget, be sure to have that Masonic service at the *Birdsall Home*. Maybe before the visitation begins. We don't want that in our Church. Nothing against them...they're fine people after their fashion...but services in our Church are done by the Doctor here. Only by the Doctor."

"No Willie, please let me take care of the Honor Guard. I'll get it done. I'll have them here. Without fail. *Two services*? You said *Both* if I understood."

"We can easily do two services. Heck, we can do three if we need to. It's our Church. Who's going to tell us different? I'll bet neither one of you thought of that, did you? One service after the other. With some immediate family members assigned to each one. And I'll be at both. Now visitation...that can be at the *Birdsall Home* or at the High School...whatever works for you, Joey. Though there'd be no need for folks to wait outside in the weather if we use the High School."

"On reflection I prefer the *Birdsall Home*. It's just more respectful. For Olin people won't mind waiting in the weather. We're talking the Ainsleys...Winslows... Pefleys, for goodness sake. And the Goins, of course. Nestleroads. People will be happy to wait. The weather won't trouble them."

"Two services!" exclaimed Jeremy. "I can't do two services, Mister Goins. It's too draining."

"Yes you can," said Wilton. "Three if necessary. I'm thinking tickets, Joey. I'm thinking tickets for each service. We'll have some order that way. And the *Home* it is for the visitation, but you'll be responsible for those folks on the line. Get them blankets, hot drinks...whatever they need. You just make sure the old ones don't catch a chill. I don't want a bunch of funerals blamed on our family."

"No one does *two* services, Mister Goins. And I don't understand about tickets."

"Reverend, each one of those mourners will leave their individual service thinking of *First Community* as a packed out, on-the-move Church that knows how to do things right. They'll experience a full Church, with a remarkable State Police Honor

Guard, with rifles and full colors...American, State and County...
if there even is such a thing...a Tecumseh County flag...do you
know, Joey?...plus a top-of-the-line coffin...am I right about
that, Birdsall?...or is it *casket*?...plus a distinguished minister in
full robes, with a doctorate and handsome stripes on his sleeves
to prove it. A funeral ought to be an evangelistic opportunity,
Reverend. We'll show the whole area just who we are. And when
you're appointed Bishop... and I'm sure it's going to happen a
lot sooner than you think...people will know precisely why, and
they'll know how proper and well deserved that appointment
is."

"But tickets, sir?"

"Joey, I surely don't mean to push, but I'm asking you
and Louise to think seriously about joining us. Switching your
membership to *First Community*. I can assure you, you will both
be well received with full respect, and I know you will find our
Church and our services more than adequate in distinction."

"Like I said, we've been considering it. We really have. And
we both appreciate your invitation. But as for this two or three
services plan of yours...I don't know. And tickets? Are you
serious, Wilton? People are not used to anything like that, and
I'm not sure how it will be received. Some folks may see it as a
little puffed up."

"Pray about it, buddy. Pray about it. You'd have the pick of
whatever you want. Louise too. And listen, don't fret on the funeral
services. There's nothing puffed up about *First Community*. We're
plain common folks. I'll have tickets printed up and distributed
through the various local banks, post offices and stores. All over.
I've got a few contacts...and that way we'll be sure to get more
or less an even number at each service. The tickets'll be labeled
1 or 2...3 if we need it...and we'll just assign folks. Most of the
close family...which you're right is a bunch and a half...will be at
the second service so they can head out to the cemetery and get
back to the house in time for the meal. And not be just hanging
around. Marva and I, and maybe Belva if we feel she's up to it,
will be at both services. And I know Marva will get some help
with the kids from Regina. Mrs. Doctor Poston."

"Tickets for a funeral, Mister Goins? I just don't know what to say. We're going to charge people to come to a funeral?"

"The tickets will be free. To guarantee seating. Why not? Jeremy, my middle name is *Lets Work It Out*. I've no patience with people who can't adapt. You've got to learn to deal with the situations you're given. Take problems and turn them into opportunities. I'd take an offering at my mother's funeral if I thought we needed the money. Who's going to tell me different? And Olin would be one to support me all the way. Tomorrow morning, Joey. At the *Birdsall Home*. I'll have all the papers. We'll settle everything...though of course I'll have to review it all later on. So Louise won't need to notarize anything tomorrow. Joey, Pastor...with all due respect to Olin...this is going to be big."

"Fine. Willie, who is that odd fellow? I'm asking you again. Maybe you'll answer me this time. With the white frizzy hair? Talking to Marva."

"He calls it *fluffy*, buddy. That's Doctor Gregory Penn. We were at school together at *IU*."

"The architect? Then that's his *Rolls-Royce* out front. My Lord, that's a car. Did you know Penn did the initial drawings on the *Winters Home* in South Bend? I believe he did them personally. Well, maybe not...but he reviewed them. He gave them a work area that's simply beyond belief. Of course this was back before he was really established. I just saw in the papers where he's designing a Jewish church... what they call a Temple...in Cincinnati. Plus an opera house someplace in Europe next year. You wouldn't think a little fellow like that...sort of peculiar looking really... could handle all of it. And the older gentleman with Mister Penn? Holding your little girl."

"I don't believe Mister Penn or the other gentleman are Christians," said Jeremy.

"Professor William Forsyth, the well known artist from Indianapolis. One of the leaders at the *Heron Art Institute*. Known and respected all over the world. I believe he's a Methodist, Jeremy, but seeing how much he smokes I doubt he's a regular. Marva's private teacher and a good friend of our family. He's working out very well. We're well pleased with him. The other man, sitting next to them is Bob, Greg Penn's chauffeur. Now Bob's a good fellow. Very knowledgeable about automobiles and getting practical things done. Very helpful to me. I'm considering employing his brother-in-law. Also a very handy fellow to have around. Instead of those oafs I've got now."

"I hope he doesn't smoke in your home," said Doctor Poston.

"Isn't that something? A world famous artist and Mister Gregory Penn right here in the same parlor in Aschburgh. I must pay my respects. Do you think he might be interested in our upcoming construction in Giantown? Maybe the Professor would consider some of the decorating."

Belva and Marva were surrounded by four elderly farming couples, so Joey could hardly be faulted for not spending time with them. He headed across the big room toward the three men, the oldest of whom, the elderly painter, was singing or humming to the sleeping Wendy.

"Sleep a-bye, sleep a-bye, sleep a-bye, little Skootums,
Sleep a-bye, sleep a-bye, sleep a-bye, little one."

Best not to take note of something so embarrassing. Some people couldn't help but behave foolishly around small children. "I believe you're Doctor Gregory Penn. What a pleasant surprise to find you here. I'm Josephuston Birdsall, the family's funeral counselor. Were you close to Mister Ainsley?"

Greg glanced up at Joey and spread his tartan comforter over his legs, taking care to pull his feet onto the sofa and tuck the blanket carefully around them. "The room may be warm...but my feet get so cold out here in the country. My God, Bob, look out the window. It's snowing again. I dread the ride back home."

"I'll start the engine up ten or fifteen minutes early so the heater is toasty."

"It's not toasty in the back seat, and you know it."

"Perhaps, just this once, you could ride up front with me."

"No. I absolutely hate snow. That's why I avoided the trip to Vienna this Winter. Those Austrians think it's all so pretty. Do you think we'll be all right? We need to get home this evening no matter what. And *someone* decided we have to drop off the Professor first. Whose idea was that?"

"Yours."

"I'm sure it wasn't."

"It was. But we'll be all right. The *Ghost* handles well. And the heater is working fine. Especially up front. Anyway it's just light snow showers. And it'll keep those Klan morons in-doors when we pass through their silly town."

"So that's your *Rolls-Royce* out front? *The Silver Ghost*. I couldn't help but notice. It's a magnificent machine." Joey rubbed his palm against his trouser leg in anticipation of a handshake.

"You asked am I close to Ainsley? The farmer who got killed? No, no, not at all. I never met the man before this morning. At the baby's baptism. And then only to nod. Well, I suppose I must have met him at Willie's wedding. I had some sort of role there, didn't I, Bob? I'm a friend of Willie and Marva. Mister and Mrs. Goins. Wilton Goins and I were at school together. And you? Josephus is a Jewish name, isn't it?"

"My friends call me *Joey*."

"But your name is actually Josephus?"

"Josephuston."

"But you're Jewish?"

"Methodist. It's a Biblical name."

"People often think my name is Gregory. But it's not. Did you know that about me, Forsyth?"

"I'd never given it a moment's thought. Lower your voices, the baby is sleeping."

"My name is actually *Alexander*. But after my father gave me that name he had second thoughts. Felt it was effeminate. So he always called me *Greg*, and it stuck. Isn't that interesting? Truth be told I like *Greg* well enough. But *Alexander* has a little more panache to it I think. Did you know that about me, Bob?"

"Of course. But you don't like it when I call you Alexander."

"It just feels a little odd. Plus the last time you actually called me *Al*. That I definitely don't like. And I believe you knew that at the time."

"Suit yourself, sir."

"Mrs. Birdsall...my wife...Louise...my better half as they say...and I were admiring your design of the *Winters Funeral Home* in South Bend. We were up that way a few weeks ago."

"Funeral Home? O yes. That was so long ago. Who did the drawings on that job, Bob?"

"Tommy. I'm surprised you don't remember."

"Tommy, of course. He's a fine boy. I'm afraid I wasn't personally involved, other than to check the final drawings. Tommy is extraordinarily competent for someone so young. At the time of those drawings. Gifted is one thing, but it's not much without competence. I try to instill that in my young men. Bob, please make sure the *Ghost* is properly prepared. Don't you find that *better-half* business overdone, Mister Josephus?"

"The automobile is fine. I'll warm it up now if you like."

"We absolutely have to get back this evening. I have appointments in the morning. And I don't want one of those flat tires in this blizzard."

"We've *never* had a flat tire. I *never* have flat tires. I really resent your saying that, sir. And it's not a big storm. It's only snow showers."

"You won't be staying for the funeral, Mister Penn?"

"Perhaps we can get back for it, but I doubt it. Forsyth, how about you? I'm sorry about the flat tire business."

"O I'll be back for the service. If nothing else I owe that much to Marva and Wilton. Plus that way I get to see my Skootums and my Ribby-Roo. Frankly I prefer the *Interurban* to your *Showboat* anyway. I imagine I'll catch the late train tonight."

"You will? Skipping Irvington will get us back a little earlier, Bob. If we don't slide off into a ditch."

"We've *never* slid off into a ditch. I have *never* slid off into a ditch. Are you deliberately trying to upset me? Why do you say these things? Do you even listen to yourself? Sir."

"But you are personally designing that Jewish church, aren't you?" asked Joey. "No, it's not called that is it? Temple...Jewish Temple."

"In Cincinnati. Yes. *Synagogue* actually. Hebrews make a distinction of sorts. Some Hebrews anyway. Our firm is also supervising the actual construction. You've admired it, have you?"

"Well, I haven't actually had time to get down there. But I've read about it."

"O. That stupid article in the *Star*. You know the one, Bob? That critic just abhors me. You have to realize newspaper reporters and critics are all frustrated artists. So they hate creative people. We remind them of their failure. You need to take the time to go down and see the work for yourself, Mister Bird. Make your own assessment...never depend on vindictive critics. They'll betray and mislead you every time. It's their very nature. Like reptiles. The building's due to open in the Spring. Spring, Bob?"

"Late Summer or maybe the Fall, sir. The investigation of that accident delayed everything."

"How stupid. Well, Bird, you need to see it for yourself. You too, Forsyth. In fact, Professor...and here's a deal for you! Try to resist this one. If you make the trip down there to see my work I'll redesign those horrible studio windows of yours. At a reasonable cost. Because we're associates of a sort. We'll get rid of all that fragmentation of the light that torments you so."

"At a reasonable cost!"

"Hebrews are outstanding people. Through the centuries they've always appreciated art and the finer things in life. And they never quibble about costs when it comes to art. Were you aware of that, Professor?"

"That's a sweeping generalization. Some Jews are fine, some are morons."

"What a terrible thing to say. Hebrew people have always been kind to me."

"Those were probably the morons."

"You're working yourself up into one of your cranky moods, aren't you? I take back my offer on the windows."

"There's been a death, man! A tragic, violent death. These babies are left without a grandfather."

"So very tragic." Joey tried to seize the chance to get back into the exchange. "I was admiring your exquisite automobile as I came over to the house. Have you had it long?"

"I didn't even know the man. How tragic can it be? How long have I had it, Bob?"

"We've had it over four years, sir."

"Are you sure? That long? O what do I care! Are we about ready to leave? I asked you to clean off the windshield half an hour ago. And you said you'd warm it up. Please listen to me, Bob. When I say something it's meant to be taken seriously. Forsyth, what about you?"

"I prefer to take the *Interurban*."

"The public trolley?"

"The public trolley."

"As you please."

3
OLIN F. AINSLEY

Olin F. Ainsley, 49, a lifelong resident of Aschburgh died at 3:27 p.m. yesterday, the result of a tragic farming accident. Mr. Ainsley was born in Tecumseh County to Molton Ainsley and Cilla Foggon. His entire life was spent within a few miles of the house in which he was born. He married his beloved wife Belva Winslow, who survives him, on Saturday June 9, 1906 at the parsonage of the First Bible Baptist Holiness Church of Aschburgh with the Reverend Harmon Hoheimer officiating. Mr. Ainsley was a prominent Tecumseh County farmer. He was a founding Deacon of First Community Church Of Indiana where he also served as Assistant Chairman of The Board, and as Assistant Chairman of the Pastoral Advisory Committee. For many years he served on the Board of the Winslow Memorial Cemetery.

A member of the Stonewall County Beef Breeders Association, he was also a life-long member of the Tecumseh County Grange, a twenty-five year member of the Masonic Lodge 427, and a faithful member and former Vice-District Governor of the Lions Club International. Until the last few years Mr. Ainsley regularly attended meetings of both the Giantown (downtown) and Indianville (Country Club) Rotary Clubs. He also enjoyed for many years an association with the Benevolent & Protective Order of the Elks.

Mr. Ainsley greatly enjoyed fishing, admiring his livestock, and spending time with his family and grandchildren. In his youth he loved to play basketball, and was a distinguished member of many outstanding varsity teams at Aschburgh High School.

In addition to his beloved wife Belva he is survived by his daughter Marva (Mrs. Wilton) Winslow Goins, numerous nieces and nephews including Regina (Mrs. Rev. Dr. Jeremy) Winslow Poston, and two grandchildren. Mister Ainsley was preceded in death by his parents, his older brothers Ansman, Virgil, Max and Marvin, as well as two sisters Maxine and Vergie. Visitation for the community will be on Sunday from 6 p.m. until 9 p.m., on Monday from 1 p.m. until 4 p.m. and from 6 p.m. until 9 p.m. at the Birdsall Funeral Home, on Goins Boulevard, Aschburgh. Masonic services will be held at 5:30 p.m. on Monday at the Birdsall Home.

Two services to accommodate all family, friends and members of the community will be held on Tuesday at 9:30 a.m. and again at 11 a.m. at the First Community Church of Indiana, Ainsley Street, Aschburgh, with The Reverend Doctor Jeremy Polson presiding. Funeral Director Josephuston Birdsall advises that in order to insure the comfort of all who wish to attend, seating passes are required for attendance at either of the services. These passes are free and readily available at any of the following locations: Birdsall Funeral Home, Aschburgh Savings & Trust, and all local Post Offices and Banks, as well as most reputable merchants throughout Tecumseh and Stonewall Counties.

Burial will be in the Ainsley-Foggon Family Section at the Winslow Memorial Cemetery outside Aschburgh. Arrangements are handled by the Birdsall Funeral Home, Josephuston Birdsall, Director.

4
A Resonant Deepening, An Organic Enriching & A Certain Filling Out

The complexity of the arrangements for Olin's three visitations and twin funeral services, along with delays in getting delivery of the super-deluxe, triple-polished casket from Batesville...not to mention some confusion about the printing and distribution of the tickets...resulted in an awkward delay of some eight days. But as Joey Birdsall pointed out to Wilton the natural processes of death and decay, coupled with certain unforeseen and unavoidable circumstances during the embalming process... while distressing in many ways and especially painful for the *Birdsall* reputation...did present certain long-term blessings for the family in so far as there was a significant thickening and a firming in the neck area. *All things work together for good to them that love God.*

Although Belva, Marva, Wilton and Regina were granted an early and to some extent satisfactory viewing of Olin on Tuesday morning, less than two days after his *tragic slip and a fall*...the rest of the community, which certainly had its share of gossips, nibbers and malcontents who could be counted on to scrutinize and even poke the corpse, had to wait a full week for the scheduled visitations. By that time Olin's remains had undergone what a chagrined Joey Birdsall referred to as a resonant deepening, an organic enriching, and a certain filling out, so that it became next to impossible to recognize the old familiar visage, let alone conjecture on the reasons for his tragic and abrupt demise. Everything sort of filled out and filled in as it were.

At each of the three visitations, held at the Birdsall Home on Sunday evening, Monday afternoon and again on Monday evening, long lines of mostly elderly rural Hoosiers, bundled in coats and hats, snaked along the cold and windy sidewalks of Goins Boulevard, and then slowly passed through the many inter-connected rooms of the *Birdsall Home*, jerkily processing, staggering and eventually stumbling past the magnificent open casket which was barely able to contain the *deepened, enriched and filled out* body of Olin Ainsley. Though many were inclined to gasp, they quickly regained their composure, hugged Belva and Marva, blew kisses to Regina who, seated next to William Forsyth, held Barbara-Jean and played with Wendy, assuring all the family that Olin looked peacefully asleep, at rest in the arms of his precious Lord.

*Right now he's in that new and glorified body and he's wearing
his crown and rejoicing in the Lord's throne room, Belva. I'll
bet Olin's happier than he's ever been. Won't it just be wonderful
when we can all be with him up there, singing and praising in the
presence of Jesus? O how I long for it.*

*He's a' looking down and a' saying, "Stop all your crying and
a' fussing. I'm having a wonderful time in my glorified body.
Loving my Jesus." Bless his heart.*

*I do believe Jesus looked about Him and surely said, "Heaven's
not complete without Olin. Without him there's something
wonderful missing up here. I just got to have him. He's the apple
of My eye." So Olin's with his sweet Jesus now. He's got that new
body, and he's rejoicing and tossing his crown in praise of his
Lord. Bless God. Ain't He the best!*

Open criticism of the work of the *Birdsall Home* was unheard
of in Aschburgh. The family had been providing a special service
to the community for four generations, and had been a major
economic force for as long as anyone could recall. Criticizing
people like the Birdsalls just wasn't something a person did. Still,
Joey was aware of whispers, looks and hints.

*Somehow he just don't look the same, Joey. It's kind of like
Olin's up and gone. I'm sure you did all you could, all that
anyone could do. But it's kind of sad. For the family and all. He's
just kind of got all that big bloat.*

*Might be time to kind of close her up. We had to do that with
Uncle Jeff.*

*I'm sort of sensing Belva might appreciate a little help there,
Joey. You know. Making the hard decision. Shutting it on down.*

The whole rigmarole of all this double service, printed tickets
and casket delays left Joey Birdsall more dejected than he had
been since Louise moved them to separate bedrooms. Normally
being of service to a local family in grief left him with a warm
sense of fulfillment, but these bloated and distorted remains
reflected poorly on his skills. And it was even more distressing
in that it was all so pointless. The walnut casket would have been
fine. And had they used the High School gym none of this would
have happened. Visitation would have been Monday and Tuesday

past, the service and burial Wednesday late morning, and there would have been none of this *deepening and filling out* business.

Willie Goins had his reasons, and Joey understood that and appreciated Wilton's assistance in expanding the *Birdsall Home* for the benefit of the community, but distributing tickets for two services at the Church…still to be endured…was unheard of around here or any place else for that matter, and all this puffed up pridefulness about the necessity for holding the services at *First Community* had delayed everything needlessly and led to an aggravation of the initial fluid retention error. Sometimes a man just had to wonder why God would allow these kinds of things to happen.

Joey and Wilton sat opposite each other in huge dark leather armchairs in Birdsall's private office on the top floor of the *Home*, an imposing three storey Victorian mansion in the center of the decaying town. The finest bit of surviving architecture in Tecumseh County.

"I'm well pleased, Joey. So far I'm more than well pleased. The services will have a long way to go to top these visitation times."

"I have no idea how you can say something like that, Willie. I appreciate all you've done for the *Home*…I know the size of the loan and the relatively low interest rate was all your doing…and I know you mean to be polite and friendly at a difficult time for me…but I just don't see how you can sit there and tell me you're satisfied. The simple fact is…and this is strictly between the two of us and not to go beyond this room…Olin looks ghastly. And everybody knows it."

"I'm glad you're pleased with the loan and all that. The interest rate just couldn't be any lower. Look, Joey, he is dead after all. I mean there's no way we can pretend Olin's not rotting away right in front of us. That's just the way it is. Don't get yourself in a fix about it. Anyway, I've been meaning to ask you, are you still considering consulting with Greg Penn about your plans for the new *Giantown Home*?"

"You can't be serious. Did you see how he brushed me off at the Ainsleys?"

"On occasion Greg's a little self-focused."

"And there's no way we can afford his fees. The *Birdsall Home* is not paying for that dwarf's *Rolls-Royce*."

"Now that's beneath you, Joey. That's just nasty, saying something like that about one of my closest friends. I know he's a little different, but he's also...just maybe...a genius. Well...I don't know enough about that to say for sure. He may just be odd. And smart. But I do know this...there's nothing wrong with a man having a *Rolls-Royce*...a man is entitled to a little luxury if he's earned it and can afford it...who's going to say he's not?...and if you can get yourself under control, and figure out a respectful way to approach him...and were you to actually engage him... that would be received well by men of vision throughout this whole area. And not just Tecumseh County either. I talk to a lot of people."

"I'm sorry, Willie. I don't know where that *dwarf* business came from. Things had been going so well, and suddenly with this botched job on Olin...and that's exactly what it is...I'm not going to tell you otherwise...it's got me very worried, very concerned. *Birdsall* is sound...don't get me wrong...but we've got some stiff competition coming right next door...into Beauville."

"*World Famous Architect Turns His Attention To Historic Aschburgh and Giantown, Indiana.* I'll bet Greg would have a headline something like that in the *New York Times*. Beauville's nothing. Forget Beauville. Greg hasn't even finished with my house, and he's already had a couple of nice write-ups in the *Indianapolis Star*. And he's planning to have a reporter come up this way for a big spread on Marva's *Barn Studio*...as soon as it's finished. The man knows how to toot his own horn. I respect that. Having *Penn & Associates* draw up the plans and supervise the work on your new place...that'd be something for Giantown, this County and ultimately for Aschburgh as well. He wouldn't even have to come up here...just have his associates do it and approve the designs. Who's ever going to remember Beauville and their two-bit shovel-toting undertakers?"

"His fees alone would eat up all our available funds and then some. I just can't afford to carry that much debt no matter how famous he is. We'll go with Tom Chappell. Ol' Tom does pretty good work. And he's cheap."

"The man can't even read. To work on a magnificent new *Birdsall Home*?"

"I'm the one who writes the checks, Willie. You can't spend what you don't have."

"Of course. I recognize that. But here's what I'd like for you to consider. This is not just a matter of business. It is that, of course...ultimately everything comes down to a matter of business...but it's even more a matter of *vision*. Greg Penn is a man of vision. Tom Chappell is still struggling with the alphabet. And I'm not saying anything against ol' Tom."

"And you call me cruel. You certainly are saying something against him. Plain mean. It's beneath a man of your standing. Tom does quality work for a fair price. And he's a good fellow. We've known him and his people for years. We buried his parents as well as his grandparents."

"I believe we can sort this out, Joey. It's workable. I'm not one to toss money out the window...surely you know that...but there is wisdom in spending some to make lots. Prudent spending, of course."

Wilton stood by the window and looked down *Goins Boulevard* toward his non-descript Bank building. "A lot of these buildings from the *Gas Boom* days need to be torn down. Less than twenty-five, thirty years old, and they're falling apart. Because the builders had no vision, no sense of possibilities. *Where there is no vision the people perish*. David said that in the *Psalms*. For a few dollars we could knock down a lot of these wrecks and put in a nice downtown park. *Birdsall Memorial*. Honoring Verritton. With a picnic area for families...and for visitors who come to share in our vision. They'll want to see the improvements, including the work on this building. And later, after they've left and reflected on what we're doing in Aschburgh, they'll be drawn to your new *Birdsall Home* in Giantown. Plant trees all along Goins Boulevard, spruce up Ainsley Street by the churches, renovate the Bank...or tear it down and start all over again. Joey, I believe you and I working together can transform Aschburgh into a showcase of rural Hoosier civilization."

"*Letter to the Hebrews* I believe. And you're thinking of Greg Penn for all this?"

"I am. Or perhaps *Proverbs*...definitely not *Hebrews*. We need his name, his vision, his stamp of approval, his ability to publicize, to catch the eye of the national and international press. One of his up-and-coming associates could do the actual work... which would lower the costs a bit...I'll bet we could negotiate an agreeable fee."

"With all due respect to you and to your family, Willie, I think you're out of your mind. This man is putting up some kind of opera house in Austria, and you think he's going to come to Aschburgh?"

"Wake up, Josephuston. Wake up! He's already here, isn't he? He's already involved in the life of Aschburgh."

"That's just for you and Marva."

"He'll listen to me. Because he'll see the long-term advantages to himself." Wilton picked up a photo from Joey's desk. "Verritton Birdsall. Your father dreamed big. Now that's a fact. Your father had more vision than anyone in his day. And that's why you've got this thriving business, and why you're moving on to expansion in Giantown, and why you're the County Coroner...do I have to go on? Verritton Birdsall brought in the top people of his time, and that's why your Daddy's renovation of this building is still an architectural wonder. Am I right?"

"No, you're on target there. He was a man of vision."

"Of course he was. When folks look at the *Birdsall Funeral Home* they think of Verritton, your Daddy...and they think well of him. Now that's a fact. Your Daddy will always be a well respected man."

"Thank you, Willie." Joey took Verritton's photo from Wilton and carefully replaced it on his desk, first pausing to dust the frame with his handkerchief.

"Stand up to your Daddy's standards. He would be so pleased to see Aschburgh on the verge of a renaissance."

"Renaissance. That's a strange one. Wasn't that back in Europe?"

"The original. But this is a new move, and it's going to start here in Aschburgh. In Tecumseh County. And it won't just stay here either. It'll be in other rural counties across the Midwest where the authentic values of real America have been preserved. People are yearning for something genuine, something American, something Christian."

"You've really been thinking about this."

"Joey, we are going to be the heart of a great social and religious movement, the *Community Church of America*. That's where *First Community Church of Indiana* is headed. Folks are looking for genuine revival, and I have dreams of financial blessing flowing from that revival and from our conservative and progressive vision."

"You're tying together a big Church and profits?"

"The Lord has shown me His blessing for America is unending wealth predicated on the conservative Christian principles of compound interest and devotion to His Son. God hates socialism. Just look in the *Bible*. This so-called boom economy that these politicians and bureaucrats are giggling about is going to *implode*, Joey. That's the opposite of *explode*. I mean it's going to collapse like a cheap pin-popped balloon. And soon. God has shown me exactly that, and you just see if it's not so. Booms always do. Boom! It's going to blow sky high and ruin millions of greedy people, but you and I and Aschburgh will thrive because of fiscally sound planning based on Biblical principles. Properly discerned Biblical principles. Compound interest and solid investment is God's way. A man's got to know where to put his money. God expects that of His people."

"He sure doesn't do the investing for you though. That's up to you. You've always thought big. And Christian."

"What counts is God's plan. I believe Verritton Birdsall...your Daddy... understood that. We want to discern God's plan, and we want to walk in it. I see a new Christian Renaissance rising here in north central Indiana, not far from the Mississinewa, a river the Indian people recognized would bring a full and rich life to this land. Naturally it didn't happen for them because they didn't follow Christ, but it will happen for us because we are faithful to His vision. And God's call is capitalism, Joey. American capitalism."

"I've never even thought about these things, Willie. Sometimes you amaze me."

"Buddy, I'm not an idle dreamer. I went to university, but I didn't stay there. You've known me all your life, and you know I'm nothing if not a practical man. *If it ain't broke don't fix it.* But, Joey, Aschburgh and Tecumseh County are broke. So we've got to fix them because God says so. We can make this town and this County thrive once again. Because that's what God wants."

"It's big. It's a big vision you're talking about."

"If you think about it…it was your Daddy's vision. But we'll never realize it with a man like Tom Chappell. Don't get me wrong…I like Ol' Tom. He's a good fellow. But Tom's not the man for this. I'd hire him in a heartbeat to fix my roof. No, not Ol' Tom. Not for this job. You consider Greg Penn, Joey. He's worth every penny. Aschburgh deserves the best. When this American Renaissance comes…rises up out of small town America…the *Aschburgh Birdsall Home* and the new *Giantown Birdsall Home* will be centerpieces of a revived civilization. Well, that may be a bit strong. But they'll be the basis for a good, sound return."

"It's big…very big." Joey sat behind his desk, and opened a small folder with the plans for Olin's funeral. "But I have to think about it. Maybe talk with you some more. More down to earth stuff. For the moment though, could we review some of the arrangements for Olin? I really need to turn this situation around. I've got to do something with this mess. Sorry…that was again a bad choice of words. I'm a little unsettled. But it's so troubling to have your work doubted and questioned by everyone this way. The situation with the tickets…is it going o.k?"

"Everything's in place, everything's good. Marva and I will be at both services. We're kind of hoping Regina can help a bit with the kids. Most of the rest of the family, including Belva, will be at the second service. Doctor Poston has the Church all set up…family sections reserved…and he's fired up to go. This is a big step for him. Took a little doing, but like I say, he's fired to go. Folding chairs are set for overflow."

"It still sounds strange to talk about tickets for a funeral. We've never done anything remotely like this. O yes...Sevier will have the Honor Guard for both services. Full dress uniforms and rifles."

"Vision, Joey, vision. I'll take good care of those Honor Guard boys. I won't take them for granted. Olin was a well respected man...after his fashion. This is a major event for *First Community*. I believe these services will be a turning point. God's going to see to that. By the way...Olin needs closed up. Everybody's checked him out, the point has been made, so it's time to shut the lid tight. Not just me thinks that...but the ladies too...time to close him up for good."

"Consider it done."

Standing with his back to Birdsall, Wilton looked back down *Goins Boulevard*. It was hard to believe that God began all this a little over three years ago, with the vision of the crossed *Goins Boulevard* and *Ainsley Street* signs. Who could tell where He would lead next? "Joey...Greg Penn. Keep your focus. He's the key. Greg Penn's the cornerstone. Forgetting the Bank loan for a moment, how much more do you think you'd need to get *Penn & Associates* and do the job right?"

"I can't borrow anymore money, Willie. I simply can't."

"Wouldn't have to be a loan as such. That's not the only way to get things done. It could be something like a quiet purchase of a half share in *Birdsall Homes*. A silent and very quiet partner... someone you could trust...who wouldn't stick his nose in the day to day operation...someone who loves the Lord and believes in *Birdsall*. I would imagine you could negotiate something like that so you'd have enough for Penn plus all the work here and in Giantown, plus enough left over to set you firm for quite a while. Just a thought."

"*Birdsall* has been strictly a family business for four generations."

"Near as anyone could tell it still would be. Plus the notion of family is a big one. Bigger than most people think. Biology isn't all it's cracked up to be. We've got to be a little more progressive in our thought processes. Just something to consider. A little bug in your ear, so to speak. Funerals are an interesting sort of proposition when you reflect on the nature of the need. A couple of years down the line I could see a big *Indianville Birdsall Home.* The reason I say *down the line* is we would want to avoid too much expansion too fast. That can get a fellow into a lot of hot water. But manageable growth would come soon enough. Probably an *Elwood Birdsall.* And how far off would *Fort Wayne Birdsall* be? I mean, what would it take to project an *Indianapolis Birdsall?* Maybe out by that reservoir Clarence Geist is digging. Not that I trust that scoundrel…don't ever trust Geist, Joey…he's always got an angle…but as the City grows and starts to push out in ten years or so there's a lot of new development going to take place around all that water Geist's creating. Plus most of these places… excluding Elwood of course…have got a lot of coloreds, and those folks need to be served too. By their own naturally…but that doesn't say who owns the *Homes.* Just use another name…Weaver or Barber or Pettiford. So there could be facilities for that need too. But all this would depend on Greg Penn being brought in of course. With lots of publicity. Plus a very quiet silent partner."

"Indianville? Fort Wayne? Clarence Geist? I don't know, Willie. You're moving too fast for me right now."

"Just an idea, buddy. Putting that little bug in your ear."

5
World's Best Husband, Daddy & Papaw

Wet snow whipped across the *Winslow Memorial Cemetery.* Belva and the immediate family were seated under a double-sized dark green *Birdsall Home* tent, the side flaps pulled down to protect them from the wind and weather. With the State Police Honor Guard packed into the tent alongside the grave, Reverend Doctor Jeremy Poston saw no easy way to squeeze himself in at the head of the flower covered casket, which was suspended over the wet grave. He was fortunate to get inside the tent at all what with all these guests. You would think the Honor Guard could have waited outside. Jeremy stood uneasily at Olin's feet, his Funeral Manual carefully marked and in hand. With his collar pulled up against the biting chill, Jeremy…wishing he had worn the long underwear Regina laid out…shifted his weight from foot to foot in a futile effort to drive off the cold as he waited for the hundred or so folks who had taken this wet and dreary journey with Olin to gather in the face of the wind for the final words and benediction.

Wilton, comfortable in his Russian fur coat and sable hat… sat between Marva and Belva…both of whom were sobbing. He winked at the sergeant in charge of the Honor Guard. The boys had been well pleased with their honorariums. A small favor that might come in handy down the pike. Regina…seated in the row behind them…passed her tiny embroidered handkerchief to Belva and signaled to a bored Marshall Sevier Winslow that she needed his clean handkerchief for Marva.

Wilton gestured to the Pastor to approach the family…which Jeremy did with great caution…angling in from the other side of the grave…mindful of the stories of preachers slipping on wet clay and sliding under the casket and into the ghastly hole. "Mrs. Ainsley would like to ask you something, Doctor," Wilton whispered across the casket.

"Thank you for everything, Jeremy," Belva gasped, wiping at her cheeks. Everyone told her it would soon get easier, but instead it was becoming harder. She missed Olin so much. She missed his special ways so very much.

Jeremy motioned to the Honor Guard to make room…leaned carefully against the side of the casket, reached out his arm, tried not to knock any flowers off…and made some motions as though to pat Belva's hand. "He's with Jesus now. Mister Ainsley knows the fullness of the joy of Jesus. He's so much better off than we are."

"Thank you. That's a blessed assurance." She was surprised and a bit chagrined how little she thought about Jesus during this whole ordeal. She missed Olin, missed his smell, his silences, his stubbornness. But honestly she felt nothing about Jesus. Or Olin being with Jesus. In fact, she was shocked to discover she didn't really believe Olin was with Jesus. Or anywhere for that matter. Except in that enormous casket. Olin was gone and she was empty. Maybe the spiritual vision would come later. "Thank you, Reverend. You've been so helpful through all of this. Did you want to say something to Jeremy, Marva?"

Marva, her nose and mouth covered by the Marshall's huge handkerchief, shook her head no.

Jeremy nodded. "He's resting in the everlasting arms."

"Yes. Yes he is." Belva wiped her nose as discreetly as possible. "That's so comforting. With Jesus. Thank you for those words. For everything you've done. We'll never forget." She stood and moved forward...the officers quickly stepping back for her and Jeremy...and she placed her palms on the smooth casket. "In your final remarks, Reverend...."

"Yes."

"I really should have said something to you before the services at the Church."

"It's a difficult time for you."

"Do you think you could mention, just briefly, just in passing, that Mister Ainsley was the world's best husband, Daddy and Papaw? Could you do that?"

"Of course I'll do that."

"All three. In that order. You won't forget?"

"I'll make a little note in my book right now."

"Husband, Daddy and Papaw."

"The world's best."

"The world's best husband, Daddy and Papaw."

6
Not Too Much, But Not Too Little

Regina hoped Jeremy hadn't caught cold at the cemetery, but if he had it would be his own fault for refusing to wear the long underwear and galoshes she had set out for him. Serving a proper meal for their family was turning out to be a bigger problem than she had imagined. When you added all the Winslows, Ainsleys and Pefleys there were just so many of them...plus Nestleroads...

and Belva was accustomed to setting a nice table. There were even a few Goins that no one but Wilton knew. Unfortunately the ladies of the *Supper Committee* tended to treat these *After Cemetery Meals* as just another covered dish. Belva and Marva would be expecting much more.

Since little Mister Penn and his chauffeur hadn't been able to make it because of the snow she planned for only eight immediate family, including Professor Forsyth, Jeremy and herself and the babies. And then she quintupled that for the other family members who chose to stay...and then a few more chairs for deacons who felt entitled to hang around to eat. Hardly a small number, but by borrowing good tables and chairs from the Winslows, the Pefleys and one of Wilton's cousins she felt she was prepared to see everyone served as though at a quality restaurant. Something elegant and relaxing...the sort of thing Wilton and Marva were accustomed to...at least when they went to the *Indianville Country Club* without the children. She was disappointed with the Ainsleys though. You'd think they would have helped out in some way.

Wilton's remarks at both services had been touching and uplifting. Though it was a funeral and a sad time, the entire service had been enriching, almost glorious in a way. Jeremy was so dignified in his Doctoral robes...and his skin was greatly improved...and Mister Goins so poised and appropriate as usual. Unknown to many...but now shared by his closest friend...Olin Ainsley had been revealed as a man who had prayed for many years for a new and revived Aschburgh, and for a Church that would literally evangelize the entire State and nation. As Wilton shared the full scope of his old friend's dream, Olin Ainsley was revealed for the visionary he had always been.

But Regina was learning life didn't remain on those high peaks of inspiration. Now, as the Pastor's wife, as well as a member of the immediate family, she would have to do her best to supervise this meal. She had been compelled to consent to a typical buffet-style serving table...though it would only be used for seconds... and perhaps desserts would have to be presented that way.

But she had been firm that the family would be served at their places...with good linen...and Belva's best china and glassware.

The glasses filled, and everything waiting to comfort them when they returned from the snowy cemetery. But of course it hadn't worked out quite like that. This was still the old Aschburgh.

The shock had been wrenching, but Wilton, realizing what had happened, took her hand and whispered, "The *Supper Committee* has to do it their way…they always have. They're wrong, but we need to be bigger and to love them. Belva and Marva and I…we all know how hard you tried to do this right. And we love you."

The beautiful tables and chairs were removed to who knew where, and had been replaced by long ugly church tables which were covered with stained oilcloth. Shoved against the far wall of the large room the *Supper Committee* had placed two uncovered serving tables jam packed with salads, casseroles, plates of meat and vegetables, pies, cakes, cornbread and biscuits. Nearby, a smaller table, covered with old discolored paper, was piled high with cracked plates, glasses, cups, cheap silverware and a ragged assortment of napkins, all carted in from the Church kitchen. On this already over-burdened table a spot had been left empty for a coffee pot and two jugs of tea…sweetened and unsweetened… which were to be brought out just before the meal began.

Aunt Greta Nestleroad and Ethelynde Redding, the president and vice-president of the *Supper Committee,* struggled to spread an extra large oilcloth over two tables, and paid no attention to Regina. Finally the matrons managed to maneuver the tables so the covering would almost fit. Both ladies, life-long members, annoyed Jeremy and amused Wilton by insisting on continuing to refer to the Church as *First Bible Baptist Holiness*.

Stepping back to admire their work they stiffly acknowledged Regina who remained standing in the doorway with Wilton, struggling to hold back her tears. Greta waved perfunctorily while Ethelynde gave a slight smile. "The others are all out in the kitchen. Millie and Gwen have been here for hours. We could've used a little help."

"I thought we were going to set the dining room tables…with Belva's good china. Didn't we agree to that?"

"Did we?" said Aunt Greta. "There's no room for this whole family at those nice tables. Anyway, they'd only get the tables scratched up. The Pefleys don't have much anymore, and they can't afford to have their only table damaged. And why break Belva's good china?"

"And leave the mess for her to clean up. She's got enough on her mind, poor thing," added Ethelynde Redding.

"We would have washed the dishes," Regina protested. "And you know this family's not going to break any dishes or scratch any tables. Those old Church tables won't give us any more room. This isn't what we agreed to."

"Do it anyway you want." Aunt Greta started to remove her apron. "I'm getting too old for all this. I've done more than my share over the years. It's about time for the young women to do some of the work."

Wilton placed his arm around Regina, and smiled at the matrons. "This is very nice, ladies, very nice. We really appreciate all your hard work. Over the years you've made the Church what it is."

"We've done it this way for a good many years without any problems. I sure don't mean to fuss, but some of the younger ones have no idea all that needs done," said Ethelynde as she swiped at a few indelible stains on the table covering.

"Us young'uns still have a lot to learn," said Wilton.

"O Wilton! You are such a joker."

"I'm sorry," said Regina. "I didn't mean to give offense. I'm really sorry."

Ethelynde and Greta surveyed the room with satisfaction. "You've been raised here all your life, Regina. You ought to know better. We're just simple folks, and Belva Winslow has always been just as common as the rest of us. She's never thought she was any better. She's wasn't raised up to think of herself as fancy. That's never been the way Winslows are. The Winslows have always been common...and proud of it. As have the Ainsleys."

"I didn't mean she wasn't. Common that is. I just thought...."

Ethelynde ignored Regina and went on with her musings. "You know, I went to school with Belva. I think there were more

Winslows in the school than any other family. Before she ever looked at Olin Ainsley. You remember, don't you Wilton?"

"I was much younger."

"O Wilton!"

"Belva's got deep roots here. And so do you, Regina. I respect all your education at the *Seminary*, but just remember your people are from Aschburgh. You're a Winslow and you'll always be a Winslow. You'd do well to get an apron and be of some actual help. A critical attitude doesn't do anything but hurt. Wilton, would you mind to straighten up that silverware? Make yourself useful."

Jeremy Poston was totally focused on spooning onto his plate the traditional Hoosier church dish of chicken and egg noodles ladled atop mashed potatoes as Wilton leaned over his shoulder to offer congratulations. "Your remarks at the grave were just right, Doctor. Not too much, yet not too little. Just perfect. *The world's best Papaw* was excellent. It just rang true. And I know it touched Mrs. Goins."

"I'll have to admit, sir, it was Mrs. Ainsley who asked me to say that."

"She did? Of course. She'd mentioned it. At the grave. Well it was all very fine. Just the right touch. It's those small things that make all the difference."

"He'll be missed."

"Yes, I suppose he will. But Olin's vision remains with us. For the community and especially for the Church."

"Unfortunately I never got to speak with him about those things. He always seemed a little distant, but I suppose that was because I'm new to the area. I certainly didn't know he felt that strongly. I suppose I always thought of him as caring for his family, his farm and his cattle."

"Well, you aren't far off the mark there. Olin loved this farm, and he surely loved those cattle. Plus he was always one to keep his own counsel. But I know he would have been deeply appreciative for your remarks, and the way you conducted both services with warmth and dignity. They say there were over three thousand at the visitations. Sounds like a stretch...but that's Joey Birdsall's count and we'll let him have it. I figure about six hundred total at the two services. Major overflow. Major. The Deacons did a remarkable job of serving those dear folks. I don't think there was a one that had to stand more than a few minutes."

"You could see he was deeply loved."

"A good family man and a faithful Christian. The world's best Papaw. Greatly appreciated, Doctor. Greatly. As they say, *You done good*."

With Regina off in the kitchen Marva found herself much too busy with Skoot and Ribby to pay attention to her weeping mother. She wondered if she would ever get back to her studio and her painting. Belva's grief...constant, public and seemingly inconsolable...surprised her, and though she didn't like to admit it, shocked and offended her as well. Marva was still slightly numb and stunned by the sudden loss of her father, his dreadful appearance in the casket, and the disruption his death brought to her own life...but responsibility for her children, her husband and their guests required that she maintain control. That Belva didn't seem to care was hard to excuse.

"Momma, you're making Skoot and Ribby very unhappy," she whispered. "This is not the time to forget all you taught me. You need to wipe your eyes and thank the ladies for all they've done. They've worked very hard to put this dinner on. Especially Aunt Greta and Ethelynde. It's simple respect and courtesy."

Belva wiped at her tears and kissed Wendy's sticky hand. "O sweetie Skoot, Papaw loved you so very much."

"Momma. That's not helping."

"We should have buried him ourselves."

"What?"

"Not let strangers shovel dirt on him. We should have buried him ourselves."

"It's not done that way anymore. No one does that. We would have looked like fools. Especially not in the middle of a snowstorm."

"We owed it to him."

"Momma, pull yourself together. *That's* what you owe to Daddy's memory. A little self control."

"I'll try, Marva. I'll try. Why don't you go and thank the ladies for me? I'll watch my babies. I miss him so much."

"We all miss Daddy. Of course. But we still have the family, and we still have our friends. Others are hurting too, you know. Not just us. We need to think of others a little bit too."

As all this was transpiring Greta Nestleroad waited until it was clear William Forsyth was heading for the desserts before making her move. "The walnut cake and the chocolate cream pie are both mine. Are you partial to sweets?" He was certainly a very distinguished looking man…though he absolutely reeked of cigarettes.

"I try to limit my intake, dear lady. Perhaps a small bowl of fruit salad."

"I've never seen your paintings, but I'm told they're very pretty. Doctor Poston, our young minister, tells us you're quite world famous. And yet you've remain devoted to Indiana."

"Ohio born but Hoosier in my blood and bones."

"I admire that you haven't forgotten where you come from despite your renown. Are your pictures shown at the State Fair each year?"

Forsyth eyed Greta carefully. Was the damned old bat trying to be obnoxious? More likely she thought she was amusing.

"I go only to see the livestock. I'm partial to the pig barn."

"I've always wanted to *pick up the brush* as they say. I think pictures tell a story so much better than words. A thousand words. Don't you? Exactly what are your paintings about?"

CHAPTER 14
HARD TIMES BUT GOOD FISHING

The Great Depression descends upon America, Lora Winslow Goins is born, Norman is compelled to help out, Greg Penn receives recognition, while Wilton Goins, showing signs of aging begins to eat more chocolate and expresses great disappointment, Ziporah Winslow Goings enters this world, Marva makes a sad journey home, an unscheduled exhibit is cancelled, and the fishing remains good.

1
The Day Of The Lord

The *Black Days* of October 1929 were hardly noticed in Aschburgh since few folks took a paper. But Wilton Goins observed what was happening, and saw in it the hand of God.

Then as the season turned toward Christmas and folks took note that ten good workmen had recently been laid-off at the *Tecumseh County Brickworks* there was just the inkling of a sense that these might no longer be such good times. *First Community Church of Indiana*, under the leadership of The Reverend Doctor Bishop Jeremy Poston...but actually sparked by the maternal concern of Regina Winslow Poston who made a point of browsing the Goins' paper when she visited her cousin ...prepared

Christmas packages for each of the ten families, guaranteeing a happy holiday for the children as the town passed through what experts in Indianapolis were now calling a *Normal Temporary Down Turn & Correction.*

Despite this growing unease...during the early years of the decade, as soup lines appeared in Chicago and the Salvation Army initiated a small operation in Giantown...girl babies arrived with regularity at *The Old Goins Place.* And though Wilton continued to look for a proper heir, each daughter was received with great joy by both her parents. And even more so by *Aunt* Regina who had taken to spending a good part of each day with her cousin and nieces, while back in town her own husband toiled over his episcopal responsibilities. The old farmhouse... brilliantly restored under the demanding eye of Greg Penn, and equipped with an adjoining *Barn Studio* beyond anything even Professor William Forsyth had ever imagined...was a place of joy, comfort and creativity.

Pleased to see his young wife and children, as well as dear Regina, cozy and well protected, Wilton turned his attention to what he knew was going to be a long and protracted period of suffering for the community, brought on by a national frivolity encouraged by government functionaries and cheap politicians who cared not a whit for the pain and confusion they caused. Without true repentance, without a cleansing of the national heart and a return to the way of holiness, America and his beloved Aschburgh and Tecumseh County, were headed for an economic and social cataclysm brought about by moral corruption.

Sitting in his simple office at the Bank, and staring out the window upon a wet and deserted *Ainsley Street* he flipped open his *Bible*, fumbling around the *Samuels, Chronicles* and *Kings* until he found the passage he was seeking. He leaned back in his chair and considered the nature of the times, pleased he had not given in to the pressures to renovate the *Bank*. The new Church was up...though it had to be built on *Ainsley Street* rather than outside town as he would have preferred...the *Aschburgh Birdsall Home* renovation was completed and the *Giantown Birdsall Home* a reality...though neither as grand as Joey or Greg's young associate would have liked…the Lord had been gracious to give them the years of plenty to achieve so much…but clearly they had now entered upon the lean years, and there would be no further building, no further expansion, until the Lord gave the sign.

As he had repeatedly told the Bishop, the days of Amos were upon them to preach and to practice a life-style of repentance. For the sign of good days from the Lord would not come again until the American people…including the people of Tecumseh and Stonewall Counties…fell upon their faces and repented of their sinfulness. Surely how could that prosperity come again if the heartland, the one place where Biblical values were still treasured, did not itself lead the way in penitence? Indiana, and especially the blessed north-eastern portion of the State, was now God-called to be the location and the people that would model faithfulness for a nation which in its pride and arrogance had lost its way like unto Israel of old.

2 Chronicles 7:14 was from this day forward his watchword. *If my people, which are called by my name, shall humble themselves, and pray, and seek my face, and turn from their wicked ways; then will I hear from heaven, and will forgive their sin, and will heal their land.* The Father's command to Jeremy was clear: *Preach this Word. Preach it again and again, and as My Bishop, lead My people and My nation into a spiritual purification that all may see the American nation strong once again, the economic and moral dynamo driving God's glorious plan toward the fulness of His time.*

Unfortunately Jeremy remained Jeremy despite his new robes and title, despite the clear call of God. Every Wednesday morning, given clear weather and wind, he flew his kites. The boy meant well and after his fashion worked hard…the kite business was harmless enough, even fun at times…but he lacked the potency of say a Savonarola or a Calvin or a Luther…or for that matter even a Billy Sunday. *First Community Church* was content and happy and growing…if more slowly than Wilton would have liked…but the boy's primary concern remained local Church functions, his new robes, and setting up his office at the Church. Especially the arranging and rearranging of that doggone office.

Shoot! An office on which he had already dithered away a full year. And if his mother didn't stop sending up new furnishings and clutter from Rising Sun the contemplating and navel gazing over the room was likely to continue forever.

2
Celebrating The Birth Of Lora Winslow Goins

It was while in this frame of mind and devout reflection, in November of 1930…at what was actually the 2nd annual *Harvest Festival* hosted by Wilton Goins to celebrate the births of his children…that he initiated the practice of distributing free turkeys to the unemployed of Aschburgh…excluding only those occasional undeserving men who were known to have never seriously sought work. In that first year of the new decade, to mark the birth on October 15th of Lora Winslow Goins, *Lorry-Lo* to Professor Forsyth…who had only recently returned from an extended *plein-aire* trip to California…Professor Forsyth that is, not *Lorry-Lo…Lo* to her parents…a small sack of Florida oranges was distributed along with each of the fifty free birds presented to the worthy unemployed.

3

Mrs. Willetta Barnes and her girls spent the week-end with her son Delmar and his family in Newcastle where he is employed as a chief mechanic.

4
Wilton Maintains A Positive Attitude In The Face Of Hard Times

Two years later, in the Fall of 1932…during the heat of a presidential campaign which Wilton clearly saw was leading the United States to fully embrace Socialism if not Bolshevism…and despite some early signs of moral cleansing over in Europe…of all places…in blessed America there was certainly no move toward national repentance. Only a lot of self-pity and whining.

The Bishop…who had recently pleased his older relation and Chairman of the Board by calling for prayer and fasting at least once a month…had thus far still not fully realized the urgency of God's call upon him…and so as a direct consequence of the Bishop's failure to fall on his knees, as well as the moral failure of all too many others, life had turned even bleaker for the people of Aschburgh… though Wilton continued to be favored, finding himself able to pick up numerous choice bits of real estate for little or nothing…to be salted away for a better time… and as a silent partner he was discovering that the funeral home business was every bit as reliable as he had supposed.

5

To All The Good People Of Our Town:

I respectfully ask and draw attention to the matter of who are these men loitering on the edge of Aschburgh? Near where the tracks cross Old Uptegraft Road they are often burning wood and probably trash items in a big barrel. I would think folks might see the danger of fire in that section of town where there is much kindling lying about. Also there are mostly older wooden buildings. Couldn't they find someplace else? And another thing I want to say is this Light Saving Business the One United World bunch are pushing for. Just like they jabbered away about the League of Nations and so forth. The way I read my Bible God made the day to have 24 hours, not a whole bunch more which would only be used for mischief. Those of us on the farm found out a long time ago that God knew what He was doing and the animals know what time it is. Let's pray for President Hoover, for if these other foreign fellows gets in our nation is doomed.

Mrs. Deloss (Gwenda) Cheek
Aschburgh Taxpayer

6

Celebrating The Birth Of Stephanie Winslow Goins & Remembering Mamaw Ainsley

Concerned by the number of local men who no longer evidenced any desire to pick themselves up by their own bootstraps, Wilton hesitated and deliberated over the *Harvest Festival of 1932*. Still, urged on by his children's Aunt Regina…and realizing that if local businessmen didn't do something the way would be left clear for Roosevelt and his Socialist agitators…at the Thanksgivings season and in celebration of the birth on September 15th of Stephanie Winslow Goins, *Steppy-Step* or *Step,* a free holiday dinner for the newest unemployed and their families, with all the fixings and more, was hosted by the *Bishop's Faithful Men* and the *Women's Supper Committee of First Community Church of Indiana.*

Following the Charity Dinner, the doors of the Church were opened to most of the remaining unemployed in town who were invited down to the cellar to share in the left-overs and the distribution of relief. Wilton took note of the sensitivity of the ladies as they made sure the best left-overs got to families with younger children. Later that evening, under Wilton's personal supervision, twenty-two bags of *American Freedom Apples* were given away along with the *Poor Birds,* as the turkeys had come to be styled around town.

Then, in a gesture which very nearly caused Wilton to choke-up, the *Ladies Society* of the Church enclosed Mamaw Belva Ainsley's recipe for *Apple & Walnut Stuffing* on a small card bordered in black to commemorate her unexpected passing earlier that year.

7

PeeDee LaReneau, class of '33 and basketball star for two seasons, is winning laurels for himself in Kansas. A clipping, kindly provided by his grandparents, Mr. & Mrs. Clyde LaReneau, from the Waterside Daily Press, Waterside, Kansas,

> *stated: LaReneau, the whirlwind forward on the Waterside
> YMCA teams, seems to be speedier every game he plays. Last
> night he was in only a portion of the game and still netted 12
> points for the team. It is safely predicted he will play more
> minutes in the immediate future.*

8
*Professor Forsyth Casts Gloom Over The Birth Of Ziporah Winslow Goins
& A Return To Bible Baptist Black*

Despite the heat the birth of Ziporah Winslow Goins on July 22nd 1933, marking the end of a difficult pregnancy, was greatly welcomed, a pick-me-up for a depressed Marva. Sadly the beauty of the late Hoosier Spring and early Summer had been ruined by the abrupt and vicious dismissal of Professor Forsyth from his long-time position at the *Herron Art Institute* in Indianapolis, leaving Marva bitter and devastated for several weeks as she struggled to understand how someone named Donald Magnus Mattison, an outsider no one had ever heard of, could come into their State from *Yale University* and abruptly and heartlessly destroy so much beauty and greatness.

As usual Wilton was wonderful and supportive, offering to intervene with business associates of his and get things back the way they ought to be...but for some reason Bill Forsyth would have none of it, insisting he was capable of taking care of things himself. Dear Professor Forsyth was manly and had a healthy self-respect and pride that set him apart in her mind...but the decision to refuse Wilton's offer had not been wise. Oftentimes it was best to listen to Wilton.

Bill was aging, and although he was as vital a painter and teacher as ever, she knew he didn't have the energy for the battle. It was a serious...a very serious mistake. Instead of finding himself with a comfortable position in his mature years Bill had been tossed out onto the street, and had actually been forced to accept hand-outs from Mister Roosevelt and his Indianapolis cronies...begging for some kind of made-up work down at the new *State Library*. The greatest painter and teacher of his time reduced to the red dole.

And then in the late Winter of the following February, under horrible stress as he watched his beloved wife and daughters forced to take little jobs to pay the bills, her wonderful teacher and companion suffered a devastating heart attack. And for month upon month Marva lived with the fear of losing her closest friend and artistic advisor. Neither Regina's loving care nor Wilton's purchase of a new automobile for her and the babies had been able to lift her spirits.

Unable to see Bill because of his grave condition she spent many days grieving even as she painted, her burden eased only by the memories and the skills he had shared with her. Often she would reflect on their days together in the *Barn Studio* when as equals they had first begun exploring the possibilities of the new building and enjoying one another's company.

It was during this period of grief, lasting several months, that she was encouraged by the memory of her mother to recommit herself totally to the wearing of black Bible Baptist Holiness dress. Following new fashions as a young bride was understandable and even forgivable, but she was right to gradually move back toward the old way...and now, still bearing some remorse for her mother's sudden death and even more hurt because of Bill's constant struggles, she fully committed herself.

The dresses...which she ordered from England...could be modified so they weren't dowdy...as a young girl she hadn't appreciated the extent of her control and authority over the style. Floor length instead of ankle length...and black certainly didn't have to mean dull. Not merely for comfort during her pregnancies ...but all the time. A distinctive statement of who she was and who her people were. Regina, who had continued to wear the *old dress* after *Seminary*, encouraged her, noting how well she looked in it, and even accepting for herself some of Marva's modifications and improvements. And, Marva joked to herself, the long dresses covered up her and Regina's big feet.

9

The Strongly Disapproved Excursion To Irvington

Then in June encouraging word arrived from the town of Irvington. Professor Forsyth, confined to bed ever since his February heart attack, was now getting up to paint for short spells. On two occasions Marva had even been able to speak briefly with him on the telephone, and they had begun exchanging notes. Able to sit in his yard and chat with friends and neighbors when strong enough, he described himself as *ready to get on with it*. He wrote how he intended to make another trip to California the following year, and he even thought some of his recent sketches might be developing his work in entirely new directions.

In mid-August, anxious to show Bill some of her new work, she and Regina packed up Skoot, Ribby, Lo, Step, and baby Ziporah...whom she longed to hear her old friend christen *Zippy-Zoo*...into her brand-new black *Rolls-Royce Phantom*... and driven by Norman Overbeek, her young and highly skilled but frequently irritable chauffeur...with two of her smaller canvases jammed alongside him in the front seat...took off for the Forsyth home in Irvington, on the northeast edge of Indianapolis.

Pointing out that Zip was too young to make such a long trip, her husband had strongly disapproved of the excursion...which in any event had proven a disappointment when Forsyth suddenly took a turn for the worse and was unable to see her for more than a moment and a wave. Wilton sulked a bit on that occasion, demanding on her return that she take Zip for a thorough check-up by Doctor Aiken.

But as Wilton later shared with Regina, he recognized what a great burden Marva bore in caring for five little girls. Her relationship with Professor William Forsyth, he patiently explained to their young cousin, helped to take his wife's mind off the tedium of housework and motherhood, and in that respect it was a positive and innocent matter. In any event, Doctor Aiken assured them Zip was fine...plus it was obvious the old painter was going to die soon anyway.

10
Celebrating The Festival of 1934

That November the *Harvest Festival of 1934* proceeded as scheduled, celebrating the lives of all of the Goins children. On the other hand, the year 1934 had been very hard for the business community throughout Tecumseh and Stonewall Counties. In addition to a continuing series of lay-offs, bankruptcies and closings in Giantown and Indianville, the *Tecumseh County Brickworks*...located just outside Aschburgh, and the town's largest employer...indeed the only surviving example of the glory days of the *Gas Boom*...finally gave up the ghost, and without any notice to Wilton or to the workers abruptly padlocked the doors.

It seemed to Wilton that by the evening of the *Festival* fully half the men in town were just standing around with their hands in their pockets. And sometimes pathetically extended for a hand-out. Always a proponent of local control of government... deeply suspicious of what went on in places like Indianapolis... and increasingly outspoken in his disdain for the anti-Christian and anti-Business atmosphere of the preposterous *New Deal* in Washington...Wilton watched with interest the development of strong leaders in Europe. As he drove around town in his *Buick,* observing occasional clusters of men who ought to have been at work...in particular the bunch who gathered daily at the *Old Uptegraft Road* near the *Goins Elevator,* not far from where the *Goins Branch Road* led out to his home...he mused about the practicality of democracy for weak people like these men.

The supposed *New Deal* of the Roosevelts and this Harry Hopkins...a communist buddy of Eleanor's...seemed to him a sickly and contaminated contrast to the strong, healthy leadership that was leading the German and Italian economies into days of vigorous prosperity. Fortunately most of the local business people who were still productive...including himself and Joey Birdsall... strongly opposed the efforts of these Washington collectivists to provide makeshift jobs, intruding themselves into the fabric of Hoosier life through the insidious and demoralizing dole. *Close enough for government work* was the standing joke at the *Rotary* meetings.

The source of aid to a man down on his luck ought to be the Church. That was God's way, pure and simple. Just last night he had checked it, wanting to make sure he was staying on track with God's will. *It is not reasonable that we should leave the Word of God, and serve tables. Wherefore, brethren, look ye out among you seven men of honest report, full of the Holy Ghost and wisdom, whom we may appoint over this business.* Short and sweet. *If any would not work, neither should he eat.* Local and effective. And the Church could and would do a better job than a bunch of reds.

But if that weren't enough…and why it wouldn't be he couldn't imagine… then the local business community ought to step in as he himself frequently did… and if for some reason even they couldn't straighten the situation out, then the local township Trustee ought to be more than up to handing the problem. But… and much to his surprise…Wilton was coming to see that right now even these old stand-bys didn't quite do the job. If able bodied men simply refused to work, then the best efforts of Church, Business and Local Government would be pointless.

Under these circumstances…which were obviously a by-product of the moral corruption of American society and the creeping Socialism that had been entering the country ever since the European War…then a strong, well-focused leader might very well be what was called for…a vigorous, self-confident fellow able to impose discipline upon an anarchic people filled with self-pity and defeatism. Put a stop to all this *New Deal* talk about changing the clock around and introducing confusion and instability into an already bad situation.

He looked for someone with a vision…a man who, when the unions and the social workers demanded a hand-out, wasn't afraid to say a firm *No*. He could well live with a man like that. He would be well pleased with the leadership of a man like that. His own efforts were constantly being abused, and it was reaching the point where the cost of turkeys was draining his resources to such an extent he wondered how much longer he could go on helping people who refused to help themselves. At the *1934 Harvest Festival* three hundred and fifty small hens were distributed along with seven walnuts per needy family. Wilton noted that with each passing year fewer and fewer families stopped by the Bank to thank him.

11

The Loyal Women's class meeting, planned for Tuesday at the home of Mrs. Orie Hull, was postponed a week on account of the sickness that has been going around.

12
Reflections On Decline

Over the years Marva had consistently refused to attend any of the *Harvest Festivals* sponsored by her husband. The decline of the community, the lethargy she saw even in some of her own relations…especially the two youngest Pefley boys…got her down. The Aschburgh she had known as a girl, the town she had returned to as a young bride, was disappearing, replaced by an ugly and false reflection of what it had once been. Fortunately she could be grateful to the Lord for five healthy and happy girls, for the joy the children had given Mamaw Ainsley during her final years, for the friendship and love of Regina, and especially for the inspiration of Bill Forsyth and the world he had opened to her.

But then she worried that Wilton had aged so much since their marriage nine years earlier. He simply was not the man he used to be. While in spite of all her pregnancies…and the constant hubbub of the girls as Regina fussed over them…she felt more vigorous than she had when mooning about schoolgirl dreams back at the *Seminary*. With years of steadily accumulating knowledge and skill to build on, Marva seemed to grow more confident each day.

Wilton, on the other hand…and despite the fact that he rarely spent time or energy on his girls…no longer had the endurance and enthusiasm he and his cronies had taken for granted for years. He had begun walking with a noticeable limp, and for several years now his sturdy posture had been giving way to an ever increasing stoop. More and more he was looking like that simpering Joey Birdsall. Doctor Aiken cautioned that his heart, while still up to the job, was missing the occasional beat and certainly wasn't growing any younger.

There were days, realizing his strength was ebbing, that Marva actually felt sorry for him. The men around town still tipped their hats, but the simple fact was that all his hopes for a rebirth of Aschburgh were falling apart. Wilton continued to spout the same old message of a Midwestern renaissance, but the reality was stagnation at best. The daily sight of able-bodied men standing around doing nothing was intolerable to him and sapped his own vitality.

Fortunately his mind was as sharp as ever, though even there as he entered into his mid-fifties and had to come to grips with old age...she noticed he was becoming increasingly preoccupied with some of his odder notions about God and His plans. The latest was this obsession about President Roosevelt changing the clock. And yet in spite of all of these signs of decline, Marva was deeply grateful for his sound financial judgment and his care in providing for her and the girls. Despite terrible times which had crippled quite a few of their relatives, Wilton's wisdom left them...while not actually rich...he was very clear about that... Rockefeller and Ford were rich...more comfortable than she had ever thought possible.

13
Waiting For Norman To Stop Playing

Glancing up at the 13' ceiling Greg Penn insisted upon for the *Barn Studio* Marva had to admit he had been right and she had been wrong when she demanded no barrier between the floor and the roof. Heating would have been impossible, lighting would not have been improved, and the vast storage and nursery space of the upper storey lost for no purpose whatsoever. She tied a large smock over her dress and admired the new set of *Winsor & Newton* Kolinsky sables Wilton had presented her at Christmas. Who ever had told him about Kolinsky sables?

Light from the eight windows Greg placed along the northern wall of the barn poured into the large clean space of the main studio. Northern light was a *must* both Greg and Bill insisted on. Painters required northern light. Absolutely. And she didn't particularly disagree, but the fact remained that for the most part light was light, and she liked to have the full flood from both studio exposures, north and west.

If it became too bright, or the sun was setting, curtains could always be pulled. But this morning much of the light she treasured was missing because Wilton's boys...who he had promised to get rid of as soon as Norman started...those immature incompetents he kept around for odds and ends...which Norman ended up doing anyway...hadn't bothered to remove the heavy shutters from the west windows. In their laziness figuring the windows on the north were enough. Well they weren't enough. She wanted all the light.

Wrapping her coat around her she stepped outside and began to fiddling with the latches which held the wooden shutters tightly over each window. Without a ladder she'd not be able to reach the top latches...but possibly by standing on a nearby bench she might be able to do it. Marva dragged the bench closer to the wall, and standing atop it, began pulling the latches free. But the shutter...which had been constructed to resist the wind, snow and ice of Indiana Winters...weighed more than she expected, and lifting it free of the window casing she found herself staggering back and forth on the bench.

Regina rushed up behind her and grabbed hold of the shutter, steadying things enough that Marva could regain her balance. "Thank you. My goodness. That was pretty shaky. I'd like to get the rest of them."

"What are you doing, Marva? You said you'd watch the babies while I looked for Norman. Have you left them alone?"

"O they're fine. Help me while I get the rest of these. Is Norman coming or not?"

"Sometimes I can't believe how you've become." Regina left her standing on the bench and rushed into the Studio and up the stairs to the nursery where she found the girls quietly playing. She loved the bright and cozy nursery Mister Penn created for her babies, and he had been right to put it on the second floor away from Marva's painting areas. Away from all the poisons, the turpentine and who knew what else.

Having the nursery closer would have made no difference. Marva always promised to keep those dangerous things under lock and key, but she never did. Too much trouble was her excuse. Which, of course, was no excuse. When she was involved in painting Marva paid no attention to the babies even if they were right next to her. Upstairs...away from the clutter and all the tools and turpentine and danger of the studio...where there was quiet and peace...the way girls ought to be raised...playing quietly with their dolls...upstairs was best. Upstairs was safest. Regina loved her cousin, but there were times when she had to admit Marva was not the conscientious mother everyone thought she was. Not that she didn't love her girls of course, but painting always came first.

Skoot and Ribby, 8 and 6, were off at *Aschburgh Elementary*... the same building she and Marva had attended once *James Whitcomb Riley* had been shut down...but Lo, Step and baby Zip were still young enough to need her every morning and afternoon while their mother scratched away at her canvases. What Marva sometimes seemed to lack as a mother Regina supposed she made up for in her dedication to her art. And there were signs that her paintings were coming to be appreciated beyond Aschburgh. Some businessman in Fort Wayne recently bought several. So who could say?...it might amount to something yet.

Regina yearned to bear Jeremy's children, but since that did not appear likely to happen she was grateful for the way things were working out. Marva was gifted far beyond what either of them had imagined when they were schoolgirls, and as much as she loved her children...and Regina never doubted her love...she simply didn't have the time and the energy they required. The

Lord knew what He was doing, and the gifts he denied one were provided to another.

She made herself comfortable on the floor and began helping Step and Lo who were busy cleaning a bedroom in the sprawling dollhouse Professor Forsyth had sent them at Christmas...while little Zip crawled around the floor, exploring anything and everything she could reach...every now and then pulling herself upright in preparation for starting to walk. Regina crouched down close to the floor in order to see into the recesses of the dollhouse, and when she turned around found herself staring at the hem of Marva's dress.

"I got most of them off," said Marva. "But two are still stuck or jammed or something. You would have thought Greg could come up with something a little easier. The amount of money I paid. Don't you think Lo ought to be talking clearer? You don't think she's slow do you?"

"She will. When she's ready. She speaks fine. Doesn't shut up when she feels like it. Clarity will come. Won't it, you pretty girl? Mister Penn said he needed the sturdiest shutters he could get. Because of the weather, and you planning to use the studio all year round. He wanted to be sure you were warm. And the babies."

"The girls are fine. Do you have what you need?"

"I'd like to bring them downstairs later, if that's all right. If you would clear off a safe area for us. Or we could stay in the sitting room, and they'd be able to see your paintings...and even to see you a bit while you're working."

"Why?"

"So they begin to have some idea of what you do."

"The sitting room is for people who want to look at my work. Completed work. It's not designed for children. They'll be too noisy."

"But it would be nice for them. Just once in a while."

"They wouldn't understand. Maybe when they're older. You're so wonderful with them. So Greg Penn thought it odd I would be painting here all year long?"

"No. He never said *odd*. Only he thought you might paint in the house…the attic…during the Winter."

"Of course I'm going to paint out here all year long. There's no space in the house. Did Norman say he was coming? I really need his help. Did you happen to check on what Hildred's making for lunch? I think Wilton was wrong to give her this second chance. Since she's been back I never know what to expect. When she might next turn out to be intoxicated."

"Please wait on the shutters. It's too dangerous. You need Norman's help. Come see how Step and Lo have cleaned up the dolly's bedroom. Here, have a look what a good scrub they've given that room. Hildred's doing a good job, Marva. Don't be so critical. Her father was a drinker, and naturally she struggles with it. We all know that. But she's trying very hard. She really loves this family."

Step grinned and moved back so Marva could look inside the dollhouse. Marva bent down and kissed her on the forehead. "That's beautiful, Steppy. You and Aunt Regina are doing a beautiful cleaning job. And Lo too."

"They're such wonderful girls, Marva. Lo misses Ribby a lot. They're so close. I'm hoping maybe this coming Fall the school will take her a year early. They did that for the youngest Wasson boy. I'll bet Wilton could arrange it if you would ask him. And look at baby Zip. Look how happy Zippy is. You great big girl, you great big girl."

"Shouldn't she be walking by now? Is that man coming or not?"

"Norman? He's working on the motor. The poor fellow was all covered with grease. Anyway, he said he had it *ripped up* or something, and he couldn't just leave it, but he'd be over as soon as possible."

"As soon as possible? Since when does a *Rolls-Royce* need all that work? He's just amusing himself. And I'm just supposed to wait while he plays with the car?"

"That's what he said. And it didn't look to me like *playing*. He'll be here as soon as he can. The poor man can't do three things at once. Why don't you go back to your work? You've plenty of light. Lo has some new paper dolls…from her Daddy…and we're all going to play with them. You've enough light, Marva. Nothing's ever perfect in this world."

14

Miss Mary Stiney who lives near Backcreek Methodist Church spent Saturday night with Miss Lovelle Planck.

15
Doing Whatever She Feels Like Doing

The attic studio had not only confined her to the house…so that Wilton and the cook Hildred and Regina and the children and anyone else who happened to show up could interrupt her whenever they chose…but the worst thing about working in that studio was it had restricted her to miserable little canvases. Tiny things. 18" x 24"…that sort of itsy-bitsy shape that Bill and Professor Steele favored. It made sense for a *plein-air* man. And had been…in a way…all right as long as she and Bill were still in a pure teacher / student relationship…puttering around with landscapes and little dippy portraits…but that had changed years and years ago…and to remain with canvases that size would have suffocated her.

The first time she stepped into Greg Penn's creation…not a building, he said, but a *creation*…the first time she actually had a sense of its space…Marva stood silently beside the tiny architect, afraid to say anything, to do anything that might make the studio go away, explode like a dream abruptly shattered…turn out to have been nothing more than a hope. But it had been real…it did not go away…and slowly, and very quietly and privately, she incorporated its space and its simple design into her idea of who she was and what she was to do. So that today her studio and her art were no longer just something she possessed…they were who she was… they did not exist without each other.

O not that she wasn't also a wife…not that she wasn't also a mother…and a good friend to Regina…but her studio, all it

377

meant, all it allowed her to accomplish, was really who she was. She slid a taboret with a glass palette atop it closer to the easel on which she was working. Greg was a funny little man, but he had known exactly what she would need.

His contractors totally gutted the old barn, leaving in place only the essential structural beams, all of which turned out to still be sound. And then he began from scratch, creating a two storey space, with enormous ceilings and a studio area completely surrounded by large windows. Storage, which had been such a problem in the attic, was moved to the rear of the building... and if that ever became full... which seemed unlikely...the entire upstairs...except for the nursery, of course...was free for expansion.

She would never have thought of including the sitting room off to the side of the studio. A place for reflection...for Bill to relax and to share his thoughts on painting and on her work. Of course now that he was no longer able to make the trip she had turned it into a little gallery, a pleasant place to show her latest canvases. Certainly not an area for children. Where had Regina come up with that notion?

Resting on one of the two enormous easels in the studio was a 5' x 8' canvas with the outline of a cadaverous man in black topcoat and derby, his hands jammed into his pockets, glaring out into the room...the grill of an automobile off to his left. He was unpleasant but dominating. Suppose she gave him red shoes? Or maybe a red derby. She grinned and ran her hand over the edge of the canvas. She could do anything she wanted. *FORD*. A block of red in the upper right corner, possibly running into his left shoulder. Or a splash. Something less defined, more dynamic. Bill would hate that. He'd demand to know what it was. It *was* red. Period. A red *splash*. Not a *blob*...a *splash*!

16

Cleaning Up With A Dirty Rag

"You wanted my help?" asked Norman Overbeek. He leaned against the far wall, a smudge of grease on his forehead, scratching at his short blond hair as Marva blocked in the red splash. "That's odd, isn't it?" said Norman.

"What?"

"That mess of red. I never saw that before. It's an interesting idea though."

"Mess of red? There's a lot of things you never saw before. You've got grease on your face."

He was an attractive man, she thought. But very young. "I need your help to get the shutters off a couple of windows. And while you're here would you help me move some of those canvases to the back?"

"I probably ought to wash my hands first. O.K. if I use the sink back there?"

"That's only for brushes and things. Use this," she said, handing him a rag.

"You've made a point many times I'm not to touch your paintings," he said as he picked one up and moved it toward the racks in the storage area. "Plus Mister Goins' boys are supposed to take those shutters down. Not me."

"I'm asking you. Mister Goins so-called boys are lazy idiots. Did you wipe your hands?" She rushed after him. "Be careful with that. I don't want it just shoved in the rack. I'll help you to put it away."

"I know how to handle it and I'm not going to scratch anything. If you'd let me do my job things would go much better. And yes I wiped my hands. With the dirty rag you gave me."

"Is there something wrong with my car? Regina said you've got it all broken up. I may be needing to make a trip to Indianapolis at very short notice."

"The car is fine. I've got the engine apart."

"Apart? Suppose I need to use it."

"I'll fit it back together." Norman carefully slid the painting into the rack, and with Marva tagging along beside him headed back for another painting. "For servicing. Lubrication and to check for wear...any problems...that sort of thing. You've got to be continually maintaining a fine car like that. But it's in good shape, and as soon as I'm given time and allowed to do my job I'll reassemble it."

"As soon as you're given time."

"And allowed to do my job."

"Well, maybe I'll give you the time."

"That would be appreciated."

"But I need those shutters off first. After you put this painting away."

"The shutters are off as soon as I'm out the door, Mam."

17
The Reich Honors One Already
A Sagamore Of The Wabash

To The German People & All Aryan Peoples Scattered Beyond The Reich:

Already we are seeing the results of our new policy of encouragement of German arts and thought in the Fatherland and other civilized areas of the world. Throughout the advanced peoples proud voices are raised in celebration of the new German architectural vision of Power, Strength and Blood. *The corruption of so-called modern architecture is being swept aside like so much rotting trash.*

Even as we ourselves already proclaim the glorious achievements of Paul Ludwig Troost, and we point with heartfelt pride to his Haus der Deutschen Kunst *in our dear Munich, and of Albert Speer and his magnificent* Zeppelintribune *in Nuremberg, so we ourselves also must pause already to note with fatherly pride the work of those architects struggling valiantly outside the protective arms of the Reich to uphold clean, healthy and vigorous standards in their monumental work.*

Each of these honored today has created structures not only declaring Aryan values for our age, but further embracing our standard of Ruin Value *for the ages to come. The architecture of the new Germany is not only for today, but we see clearly thousands of years into the future and we build today so that the very foundation stones of our creation will be viewed as sacred ruins by those Germans of a distant age.*

*In the face of the corrupt and decadent architectural influences
of barbaric semites and primitive africans, these three strong
voices honored today already are standing firm and are declaring
their conviction that from this time forward our German values
shall in the future be the final standard. Therefore, we ourselves,
speaking in the name of the German Reich and of all German
peoples both within the Reich and temporarily separated from it,
proclaim already these three to receive the Reichschancellor's
Supreme Citation For Architectural Excellence:*

*Markus Annenberg Kalsius of the United Kingdom
Wendell Berendorf of the Union of South Africa
Gregory Alexander Penn of the United States of America*

Adolf Hitler

Reichschancellor

18
*The Impact Of The Louisville Library
Frieze Upon Adolf Hitler*

The awarding of the *Reichschancellor's Supreme Citation For
Architectural Excellence*...presented in advance before the world
press with considerable fanfare on a snowy Munich morning in
late February 1935...had taken Greg Penn and everyone else in
American architectural circles completely by surprise. While he
didn't know the work of the other two fellows...and he wished
the German authorities had checked with him about his name...
this award stood as the apotheosis of his career to date and the
total vindication of his dogged loyalty to the monumental neo-
classical style so favored by Mister Hitler. A style routinely
mocked by Greg's lilliputian critics as *BIG HEAVY STUFF*.
Well, let them mock now. *BIG HEAVY STUFF* was the stuff of
the future.

Greg was painfully aware that last year's award by the
Governor of Indiana ...declaring him a *Sagamore of the Wabash*...
had been greeted with hilarity in New York and Cambridge.
But the *Indiana Limestone Quarry Association* hadn't laughed.
Men who appreciated stone more than sitting around cafeterias

sipping bad coffee and looking for *WPA* hand-outs hadn't laughed. The stone-cutters and masons hadn't snickered. Daniel Chester French's dear family had wired congratulations. Which meant a lot more than the bitter witticisms of the rag-tag *East Coast Bauhaus Survivors Social Club*. Gropius, Mies Van der Rohe…all squelched! Deservedly so. The entire Bauhaus rabble decimated. Someone needed to stop them, and now, by this proclamation and award, they were halted. Dead in their tracks. Stomped. Smashed. Squashed.

Not that he agreed with every single one of Adolf Hitler's policies…or even knew what they were for that matter…or had an inkling what all this *Ruin Theory* business was about. But the fellow's totally unexpected yet delightfully insightful decision to award him *The Reichschancellor's Supreme Citation For Architectural Excellence*…or something like that…left him breathless and speechless and overwhelmed. Naturally he would have preferred not to be included with the other two men…but that was politics…and with any luck his medal would be presented in a separate ceremony.

He supposed the *Louisville Library* had been the work to catch the eye of the authorities in Berlin. The Germans and he shared an enthusiasm for Daniel Chester French's rugged sculpture, and he'd heard that several of them adored the similar pieces he had worked into the Kentucky frieze. A la the *Brooklyn Museum*, though he doubted they knew that obscure work of French. In any event, the similarities, such as they were, weren't really that close. French's work was only one of many influences, but when it came to the *Louisville Library*…that was 100% pure Penn. Hopefully they wouldn't pay any attention to the *Cincinnati Synagogue*. That unfortunate association could end up ruining the whole thing.

The presentation ceremony in late March…at which the *Reichschancellor* himself was expected to bestow the medal… followed by a triumphal tour of Germany and Austria…would set the tone for his career from that point forth. And would silence all the nonsensical criticism about the leaking roof of his *Theatre of the Creative Consciousness* in Vienna. Did they think he was a roofer?

He would share the triumphant tour with Bob, savoring Germany, Austria and central Europe...and concluding with England which in many respects was an integral part of the Germanic world. Bob was insisting on lots of time for the *McNear Body Works* and the *Rolls-Royce* people. Apparently he had some ideas for improving the heating...and then there remained the whole matter of getting some properly fitted curtains for the *Silver Ghost*. All of that business had dragged on for years now, and absolutely had to be settled once and for all.

There was even the possibility...now that Chancellor Hitler had placed the mantle upon his shoulders...that Greg would be asked to design a new *Rolls-Royce* limousine. Which would represent a handsome fee...plus a new vehicle for sure. But of course nothing was certain. He wasn't even certain he'd want to do something like that. It all seemed a bit *Bauhaus*.

19

Because of redecorating of the interior of First Friends Church there will be no services of any kind for two weeks. Friends are encouraged to pray with their families at home.

20
Why Not Bring In Father Coughlin?

Wilton slowly unbuttoned his vest and took several deep breaths. Marva said he wasn't putting on weight...or if he was it didn't show...and he supposed she was right, but everything felt tight, making it difficult to get a good breath. As Bishop Poston entered his office Wilton pushed back from his desk and gestured toward an empty chair.

"Thank you for coming, Jeremy. I've been meaning to stop by the Church office, but somehow I keep putting it off. There's always something."

Jeremy tugged at his trousers and adjusted his jacket as he sat down. He was pleased with the new suit Regina picked out. Recently he had begun wearing a clerical shirt and collar...a new experience for Aschburgh...and this rather expensive black suit set the collar off quite nicely.

"Pleased to oblige you, sir. I know you're very busy."

"Yes, I suppose I am. Well, let me get right to the point, Jeremy. Mrs. Goins and I have been quite well pleased with your recent sermons. She was saying last night how you're hitting all the essential points...and hitting them strong too."

"Thank you, sir. I think when the preacher lets the Lord speak...through him, you know...then God's message comes forth loud and clear."

"Yes, I imagine it does. That's what's supposed to happen, isn't it? But we've also been noticing quite a few empty seats recently. Have you observed that?"

"Actually attendance is up a bit. Since January we've been averaging 221 of a Sunday morning, and that's including two Sundays with heavy snow. If it hadn't been for the weather we'd of been up around 230."

Wilton reached into a desk drawer and pulled out a large bar of milk chocolate. He broke off a small piece, popped it into his mouth and offered the bar to Jeremy. "Marva suggested I eat some of this to give me a bit more oomph. Try a bite."

"No thank you. It'll ruin my lunch. No church in this area has ever shown attendance figures like ours."

Breaking off a second bite of chocolate, Wilton paused, and staring at Jeremy, held the candy bar in his hand like a pointer. "Do you realize we built the sanctuary to seat 500? And it was constructed so we could easily expand to 1000? You remember that? That was the vision."

"Of course. But given the economy and the local situation numbers like that are unrealistic. If we set our goals too high we're going to end up disappointed. I prefer to aim at a realistic target."

"I don't ever set unrealistic goals. I set goals to make us stretch. Anyway, son, God has set the goals for us. Jeremy, Jeremy…what are we going to do with you?"

"Sir?"

"You've been here how long, son? Ten years?"

"Just about. Ten years in December. One of my first duties was to officiate at your wedding."

"Yes. We were well pleased, Marva and I. Well pleased. Jeremy, do you have any idea how successful I was by the time I'd worked ten years? Two years really. Two years was all I needed to establish the base of my fortune. Two short years."

Jeremy ran a finger inside his clerical collar. "I'm still getting used to this thing."

"It looks quite good on you. Clothes are important, no matter what anyone says. Two years was all it took me, Jeremy. Two brief years. Everything that's come since then was built upon the foundation of those two."

"I think I hear what you're saying, sir. But the Church is not a business, so it's really not the same. The Church is the bride of Jesus Christ. Even though we have a budget, it's not a matter of a balance sheet. Fundamentally that is."

"The Church is a business. Period. Everything is a business, Bishop. Everything has a balance sheet, son. Everything has a bottom line. Let me be frank…." Wilton wiped his forehead with his handkerchief, and slipped the chocolate bar back in his desk. He thought he might get sick. "I've given you a brand new building. I've given you seating for 500 with easy expansion to 1,000. I've given you an academic degree, I've given you distinguished credentials. A very decent salary…plus I've made you a Bishop--."

"Sir--"

"No, hear me out. Where are the mission churches? Where is the evangelism? Where are the 250 missing people every Sunday? 500 ought to be our minimum. Do you see what I mean? Jeremy, do I have to do it all myself? Son, you are a Bishop!"

"Please don't get yourself upset, Mister Goins."

"I'm not upset. But I am concerned. More for you than for myself. My success is established."

"With all due respect, sir, it is Jesus who has given us a new building…and it is Jesus who has provided every single one of those seats. And I believe, sir, in His perfect timing every single one of them and more will be filled. If that is His will."

"*If*? How can it *not* be His will? Let's not blame Jesus for our own deficiencies."

"And He will fill them with the right people. And sir, I don't mean to boast, but my title is no more and no less than a confirmation of my anointing."

"I don't need sermons, Bishop. I'm tired…things are going on within me…I don't even know what…anyway, the last thing I need is another sermon. What I need is to see this Church grow according to God's vision. Which is the same as my vision. And that growth is not happening. *That's* the bottom line. The business is not growing the way it is supposed to."

"My goodness, sir! Aschburgh has less than a thousand residents. One of four already attends our Church. Others are considering it. We need to appreciate that. And be thankful. You're asking too much. Too much of me, too much of the Church, too much of yourself. That's my honest opinion."

"Don't lecture me, son. I'll be the judge of what's too much for Wilton Goins. You think too small. I want all of those thousand people. And more. Outreach is not limited by the size of the local community. Outreach is limited only by a lack of vision, faith and courage."

"With all respect, sir, I think that's pretty strong. I work very hard."

"Perhaps. I don't mean to push you too much. I'm going to try another piece of this chocolate. Marva says it has a raspberry tinge. Change your mind?"

"No, thank you. I don't really like chocolate."

"Neither do I. Regina bought your suit?"

"She selected it. Actually she and your Marva. Sister Goins. In Indianapolis. Then I had to go down there to have it fitted."

"It's quite nice. *Mrs.* Goins. Skip the *sister* stuff. It sets the wrong tone."

"*Brooks Brothers.*"

"*Brooks Brothers.* As far as I know they don't have a store in Indianapolis. All my suits were fitted in New York City."

"It's not *from* Indianapolis. But you can pick it up there...at *Winslow & Sons*...they're some kind of relative...they work with *Brooks Brothers* in New York. Things are changing, sir."

"Things are not changing *that* much. Anyone can sew a *Brooks Brothers* label into a suit. *Winslow & Sons*? I'd double check that if I were you. But back to what we were saying. Do you realize you have no competition for the market? Absolutely none. The *Methodists* have basically shut their doors. The *Christian Church* is getting ready to go into permanent siesta, the *Friends* have 15 on Sunday, there's no *Baptists* anymore. So where's the competition, where's the obstacle? There's no *Baptists*, there's no doggone *Presbyterians*!"

"We're *Baptists*, Mister Goins. You and I. I'm a *Baptist*. I'll always be a *Baptist* no matter what we happen to call the Church."

"Now *there's* your problem, right there. You're stuck in the past. You've got a denominational mentality. We've had the same people for years. We don't go up, we don't go down. The same 250 in a half empty Church."

"Perhaps we built too big."

"You just said Jesus built it! Anyway, there's 1000 and more folks right outside the door."

"Maybe we missed the Lord's perfect will. Mister Goins, with all due respect, 250 is a good sized Church for this community."

"There! Now you've gone and said it. It's out of the bag. That's exactly where the problem lies." Wilton reached into the desk and popped another piece of chocolate into his mouth. "250 is not a good sized Church for me!"

"Too much of that chocolate is not good for you. I'm sure Mrs. Goins didn't mean for you to eat it all the time. Have you tried *Father John's Medicine* that I showed you? My mother recommended it, and Sister Poston has me take that morning and evening. I think it's made quite a difference in my vigor."

"For *this* community, you say. 250 for *this* community. And what you really mean is *Aschburgh*. When I say *community* I mean Tecumseh and Stonewall Counties, I mean Indiana, I mean the Midwest, I mean the whole blessed United States of America! And beyond! Now there's a vision. All the way into Mexico and Canada. I'm sorry to be raising my voice…but you have no idea… no idea what our potential is…no idea how large my dream is."

"I believe I've done my part, and I don't think there's any place for blame. No one's at fault here. I mean, what would you suggest, Mister Goins?"

"What would I suggest? What would I suggest? Bishop I would suggest we need someone with big ideas. Someone with ideas as big as mine. Let's have some massive meetings. Thousands of seats. Put up a tent. Hold it at the High School. With major figures coming in to speak and sing. Why haven't we invited Father Coughlin to speak? Because he's a Catholic? Who cares? People listen to that man, and he'd fill our Church. Have you heard him speaking about *Franklin Double-Crossing Roosevelt*? Now that's strong stuff. And right to the point. Doggone it, Bishop, we could get Billy Sunday. He'd come once he learned of our vision. Let's bring in these fellows with national reputations. Let's start an *Aschburgh Bible College*. You've got a Doctorate. Use the thing! You could be the president. Are you with me, son? This is the way to proceed. What would I suggest? Let's start a mission church in Irvington. Another one in Terre Haute. Evangelize Indianapolis. This is the way I think. Big. Big and on the move. Let's make our mark in Kentucky. Get started in Illinois. Let's bring in Father Coughlin and get something moving to counter Roosevelt and his commie red supporters. Let's elect one of our own as governor. The Klan did it, so why not Christians? You see what I'm saying? Do you have the vision, son, do you have dreams like this? Do you have any ideas, Jeremy? Do you have any ideas at all?"

"Is it that you're disappointed with my performance, Mister Goins?"

"Yes. Yes, I'm very disappointed. That's a good way to put it. Bishop, you're a big disappointment to me. Aschburgh is a disappointment. The Church is a disappointment. I thought everyone would see what we could achieve. But I'm afraid I'm surrounded by people who lack vision...and at the same time God is sapping my strength. And it's not acceptable, Jeremy. It's not acceptable. Everyone, including you, is totally lacking vision, lacking good old American get-up-and-go. You've got no Christian entrepreneurial spirit, son."

"I think you're being very unfair, sir. You're not proposing to break my contract are you?"

"Perhaps, perhaps. Contracts are made to be...o I don't know! Son, I need for you to show some initiative, some get up and go. I can't be doing all these things myself. I need for you to take some action, to grow this Church into a powerhouse. I need for you to take control of this community and beyond. Jeremy, you do understand I'm not feeling so well recently?"

"Yes sir, I do. And I'm very sorry."

"I'm sorry too, but that makes no difference. Doctor Aiken says my heart is not what it used to be. In my body, I mean. My heart for the vision is as great as it ever was. You're aware sometimes I have dizzy spells? That I've fallen? You're aware of that?"

"Yes, sir. I'm so sorry."

"Don't be sorry, Jeremy. My dizzy spells and falls mean you need to be the man I need you to be. I can't do it on my own anymore. I need a strong man at the helm of *First Community*. And you can be that man. But you have to step forward and assume full authority. I've never been one to ask for help, but I need your help. Jeremy, I need for you to be strong."

"Sir?"

21

To the Editor and All Taxpayers of Sherman County:

Dear Sirs it has come to the attention of this writer that our SHERIFF, if that is what he is, has seen fit to PAY certain teachers-pet INMATES otherwise known as CROOKS for doing favors. I hear the going rate is 10 cents per day. Once in the CROOKS hands this PAY is going for TOBACCO. Taxpayers ought not be paying for SIN.

A Concerned Taxpayer

22
A Promise To Bring Home Some Father John's Medicine

She saw he was unable to eat the beef stew Hildred made because of the trembling of his hands. He tried once, but put the spoon down when he realized he was going to make a mess. This was something altogether new, and though she tried to look away so as not to embarrass him, Marva was very concerned. She sent Hildred off with the girls to get them ready for bed, and telling Wilton she was exhausted, she urged him to come to bed even though it was only seven-thirty.

"The boy has no idea what I'm talking about, Marva," said Wilton as he pulled off his socks and rubbed his big toe. "Absolutely no idea. I'm not sure I can fall asleep this early."

"And? That's still sore, isn't it? I know it's early, but it'll help me to rest."

"What do you mean *and*?"

"Is your foot better? I think you need to show it to Doctor Aiken before it gets infected. They say things like that could be diabetes. And that spot on your leg. Have your hands been bothering you?"

"Don't be silly. It's just a bad toe-nail. Marva, the boy's got to go. That's your *and*."

"I'm more concerned about you. Did you eat some of the chocolate I sent?"

"Yes. Maybe too much. It's hard to limit yourself to a little piece. Jeremy recommended...really his mother recommended... something called *Father John's Medicine*."

"It's a very effective tonic. Regina's taking it, and I've thought about it for you. It certainly can't do any harm. But let's don't get yourself worked up about Jeremy. Jeremy is Jeremy. Nothing has changed and nothing will." She sat beside him on the edge of the bed and put her arm around his shoulders. "You used to be able to stay calm about these things. Did the chocolate give you more energy?"

"I need a strong person in that pulpit. I've plenty of energy. I know you're going to disagree, but I can't allow personal feelings to influence my decision. The boy has got to go."

Marva fluffed up two pillows...and urging him to lean back in the bed and rest while she got ready, she rubbed his leg. "At least that spot's not any bigger. A strong man would only cause you problems, Wilton. And until you're feeling better that's not something you need. Anyway, Regina is my cousin and my best friend. Since Daddy and Momma died Regina has been the one person in town I can depend on. Except for you, of course. You know, I thought Regina and I might take my car tomorrow and have Norman drive us to Indianville...to the *Country Club* for lunch. Do you think it's all right for us to be seen there? Because of the liquor. They do serve the best luncheon."

"We were married there. Had our reception is what I mean. You and I have eaten there. Of course it's all right." He fumbled with the Giantown newspaper as he watched her undress. "Regina is a good person. I know that. I've always said that. But that's not the point. Jeremy is the problem. Perhaps you can change your plans. I have something for Norman to do...and I'll be using the *Rolls* tomorrow."

"I depend on Regina. Anyway, you have your *Buick*. We agreed the *Rolls* is my car, and Norman is my chauffeur. We agreed to that, and I was very pleased you cared that much for me. I need it for the girls. But as far as Jeremy and Regina are concerned...let's remember that Regina is a Winslow."

"Every time I bring up the miserable job Jeremy does you throw Regina being a Winslow in my face. What am I supposed to do, Marva? I know you depend on her, I know she's your best friend, and I certainly know she's a Winslow. But what am I supposed to do? Should I just ignore her husband's incompetence because she's a Winslow?"

"You're going to make yourself sick again. Do you like this pink gown?"

"Marva, let's not discuss this any more. Yes, yes I like it very much. It's very becoming. You've always looked well in pink. Let's just go to bed...early as it is."

"It would be a good idea for you to simply ignore Jeremy's failings. I noticed your hands shaking a tiny bit at supper. Have you had that before? Maybe you should see a specialist. In Indianapolis." She sat across from him and began brushing her hair. "You still like to watch me, don't you?"

"You know I do."

"Wilton, Jeremy's probably doing the best he's capable of. It's not necessary for everything in life to be perfect."

"I haven't heard the girls at all since we came to bed. Isn't that unusual?"

"They're being very good. Hildred's with them. They're trying hard not to disturb us. Your hands?"

"You know, I never agreed the *Rolls* was your car. I bought it to help you out, that's true...but I never said it was your car. You just said that and I didn't challenge you. And it's the same thing with Norman. You don't need Norman. What possible use do you have for a full-time chauffeur?"

"I'm not going to see my cousin's life upset just because her husband is incompetent. Let him be incompetent for goodness sake. Really, Wilton. You're a successful and respected man, with many friends, a devoted wife and five loving daughters. It's enough. Or at least it ought to be. You push yourself too hard. I'll finish with my hair and we'll go to bed."

"It's unusual to have the girls so quiet."

"Hildred's with them, and I told her how their noise upsets you. She's putting them to sleep...reading stories...that sort of thing. She's not Regina, but she does a fairly good job with the girls. No one is as good with them as Regina. I'll check on them later. After I see you've fallen asleep. I want to be sure you get a good night's rest. Wilton, Norman is a big help to me around the studio. Lifting and fixing things. It's not just his being a chauffeur. I would think that would matter to you. That I don't have to struggle with things. You know I can't trust those *boys* you keep around. I've given you five babies, and I simply can't lift the way I used to."

"You know I love you, Marva. But the fellow has to go."

"Norman?"

"Don't be silly. Do you realize I have to do everything at the Church? The man has absolutely no ideas. No spunk. No spark. Don't you usually kiss the girls good-night?"

"I will not lose Regina. Even if you're not concerned about me and my feelings, doesn't it matter that your daughters adore her? I would think the happiness of the babies counted for something. And I am taking her to lunch tomorrow. In the *Rolls*. With Norman driving. How long have you had that tremor in your hands?"

"I'll hire a girl for the nursery. What they call a *nanny*. A local girl. Someone you know. I want you to have whatever you need."

"No you won't. I don't want any *nanny*. Regina is my friend and my cousin. And a Winslow who shares blood with our children. I will not give her up."

"Well, Jeremy has to go. Blood or no blood."

"Don't make yourself sick. This is why you're getting those tremors. On my way back from lunch I'll stop and get some of the *Father John's Medicine* tomorrow. A large bottle. It'll be good for both of us. To settle us. And something for your toe." She put out the lights and slipped into bed beside him. "I'll check on the girls in just a bit. Right now I need to make sure you're all right. I will not lose Regina."

"Shoot!"

"Don't swear. You never used to swear."

"*Shoot!* is not swearing, Marva."

"It's not what I want my girls to hear. I don't ever want my little girls to hear their father swear like that."

23
My Savior Smells Of Turpentine

April was close enough to touch as Marva tightened the ribbon of her bonnet, pulled a comforter across her lap, and shut the glass partition between herself and Norman the chauffeur. In a cold March rain the limousine headed south toward Irvington, toward the home of the Forsyths.

Earlier...unable to control her emotion as she realized the meaning of this journey...she had sobbed as she hugged each girl. She was furious with herself... even as her tears flowed...for upsetting the children who until then had been delighted at the prospect of staying home with their Aunt Regina.

Dragging along the unfinished portrait of Professor Steele was probably silly, as Alice...Mrs. Forsyth...had said...but if through some miracle Bill was able to look at it, to respond to the likeness of his old friend, it might make the end easier for him. Perhaps for all of them. Of course the painting was not the sort of thing she wanted to do anymore...not the sort of work she wanted associated with her name. But Bill didn't need to know any of that.

The Bishop had been concerned that she try to get Bill saved... but that seemed absurd to Marva. Men like William Forsyth were not the same as other people. They lived under different rules...and their relationship to God wasn't the same either. Who was the Bishop to say Bill wasn't saved? Saved by his art. Saved by his embrace of the Holy Spirit, the force which drove all creativity. Professor Forsyth was a great artist, a man with a profound creative insight and a capacity for love and friendship that someone like Bishop Poston would never grasp. God would welcome her friend and teacher as she knew God had embraced

Professor Steele. It was the Jeremy Postons of the world…leaders of the Church…who might find the door barred.

A lot had changed in the last ten years. More than anyone else it had been William Forsyth who brought so much freshness into her life. It was amazing how the application of color to canvas had transformed everything. Wilton had almost no understanding of all that had changed within her this past decade. But Bill knew.

Norman rapped on the window to get her attention, and picked up the speaking tube. "Will you want to continue to Indianapolis after stopping at the Forsyth's?"

"No. Just the Forsyth's. I'll be there a while."

"Not on to Mister Penn's?"

"He's in Europe. In Berlin as we speak. No, just the Forsyth's."

"Mister Goins said he might be needing me later in the day."

"Mister Goins is quite capable of doing without you, Norman. I may decide to stay overnight. I'll have to see."

She replaced the tube, and shutting her eyes recalled that first meeting with Bill Forsyth in Professor Steele's old fashioned studio atop the University Library. She supposed she loved him from that very first meeting. Gruff and often rude… though never to her…older than her father, his clothes stained with paint, stinking of cigarettes and turpentine. Not as she loved Wilton, and not as she had loved her parents. Perhaps she loved the creativity in him…loved that passion…but she couldn't really separate any of that from the man.

Sometimes it seemed the girl of 1925 and the woman she was today had little connection. But Bill said she was wrong, that the woman had been in the girl and the girl was still within the woman. Perhaps that was true, but even if it were it didn't mean very much. The simple truth was she had changed. Marriage, children, and especially Bill had altered her, and today things were different, very different. And would never be as they had been. She had struggled with the deaths of her parents, and with the change in her relationship with Wilton…and as she accepted those changes she discovered she liked the person she had become.

She was pleased with who she was and who she was in the process of becoming. Bill, and no one else, had given her that.

Alice and two of the Forsyth daughters, Dottie and Connie, were in the bedroom with him when Marva, painting under her arm, arrived at the old house in Irvington, shook hands with Evie the youngest of the girls, and then feeling that was not enough, hugged her. The grounds around the house were drab but she knew how beautiful it would be in another six weeks as the shrubs and flowers began to bloom. Last Summer and during the early Fall, recovering from the heart attack and still weak, Bill had enjoyed sitting outdoors on the warm days, surrounded by the smells and colors and by his many friends.

"How is he, Evie?"

"Not well. He's in and he's out. Let me take your coat and your bonnet."

Evie's face was reddened and swollen with tears. That's how I must have looked when Momma died, thought Marva, displeased. She leaned the painting of Professor Steele against the wall.

Alice Forsyth...much older but still striking and dignified, much as her husband had painted her in their youth...quietly shut the door of the bedroom behind her, and joined them in the kitchen.

"Marva, thank you for coming. Bill asked about you earlier. He knows it might be close, and he wanted to see you just in case."

"Is he awake?"

"He just drifted off again. Would you like to see him? Dottie and Connie are there. Evie, would you make some tea? I'm afraid he won't be able to look at the painting. He's really not up to that, dear."

"I understand. I just thought...." She sucked in her breath. No silly blubbering.

The Professor lay on his back, mouth open, staring blankly at the ceiling. Marva was shocked by his loss of weight, by the yellowing of his skin. Three weeks earlier he had looked pretty well, seeming to recover much of his strength. Why had they shaved his mustache?

Connie patted his hand, and whispered to Marva. "Did you bring the painting? He asked for it, and we told him you would."

"It's in the kitchen. Alice thought…. Well, I'll get it."

"Daddy, Mrs. Goins is here to see you. Marva! Mrs. Goins! She brought her painting."

As she stepped back into the room carrying the canvas Marva was surprised by the loudness of Connie's voice.

"Daddy will need for you to speak up, Marva."

"Professor?"

"You'll have to speak louder than that," Dottie whispered.

"Daddy! It's Mrs. Goins. She's come to see you!"

"How…painted…?" the old man mumbled.

"I don't understand!" Marva tried to speak loudly.

"Steele." Forsyth strained to lift his head. "How?"

"Don't wear yourself out, Daddy."

"How have I painted him? Is that what you're asking?"

"How?"

"The way he was the first time I saw him. With you. At the easel…outdoors. Working on one of his paintings of the *Observatory*."

"Me?"

Connie held the painting up for him to see, tilting it back and forth in the dim light. "I don't think he can see it," she whispered.

"Me?"

"Yes, you're in it. By Professor Steele's side," Marva lied.

Connie smiled and leaned the canvas against the wall. "Daddy!"

"He's back asleep," Dottie whispered.

For the next half hour the three women sat by the bedside, ignoring the Professor and chatting. Alice and Evie, carrying a tray with cups and tea, joined them.

"His breathing is so heavy," said Alice. "I wonder if the smell from the painting is troubling him."

"It's barely noticeable, mother," said Connie. "Actually his breathing is better than it was. Fix his pillow, Evie."

"Skoo..."

"Daddy! What? What did you say, Daddy?"

"No, Professor. Skootums had to stay home!" Marva shouted.

"Good."

Alice Forsyth fussed with the pillows Evie had just rearranged. "We'll get that turpentine smell out of here, Bill."

"Smell...leave it. Damn...."

"Mrs. Forsyth is afraid the smell will bother your breathing, Professor."

"No." He struggled to sit up, but quickly gave up and settled back onto the pillows. "Up. Up."

Connie picked up the canvas, and certain he couldn't see it, held it up over him. "How's that, Daddy?"

"Paint is...."

"What?"

"Paint."

"I don't understand, Daddy!"

"Paint...smell...save...."

"Daddy? Daddy!"

"He's off again. What was he trying to say?" Alice muttered. "I think the painting wore him out."

Alice imagined he was just rambling, but like Connie...Connie who was a painter herself...Marva thought she understood. Had he tried to speak of the savior? She didn't want to put words in Bill's mouth...he wouldn't like that. But she wondered what he was thinking, what he was seeing. The familiar smell of turpentine? His words hardly made sense and she supposed she was going to have to accept them for what they were.

For most of the three hour trip back to Aschburgh Marva kept her eyes shut. She had no intention of crying in front of Norman. What she was feeling was her own business. Alice asked her to leave the painting, and she surprised herself by refusing.

But it needed to be revised. Or destroyed. And then, after time had passed …and if it survived…and if they were still certain they wanted it…she might loan it to Connie. If it survived. If the changes worked. If it was any good. Which she doubted.

The savior smells of turpentine. Maybe Bill meant that and maybe he didn't. But why not? Her savior did. Marva looked out at the wet, empty fields and sighed. The Professor had it right as usual. *My savior smells of turpentine.* She would decide about this painting before continuing with the Ford canvas. Forsyth and Steele at the Observatory. Or maybe just Steele. She wasn't sure she could bear to paint Bill. But she could smell the turpentine.

24

Concerning An Exhibition Cancelled Before Scheduled

ASCHBURGH ARTIST, MARVA WINSLOW GOINS, LOSES TEACHER TO DEATH

Aschburgh July 6, 1935

Exclusive to The Giantown Tribune

By E. Marvin Tugwell, Staff Reporter

Word has but recently reached this reporter of the passing some months ago of artist William Forsyth in Indianapolis. Respected throughout the State for his various art works, Mister Forsyth is certainly best remembered as the teacher of prominent local artist Mrs. Marva Winslow Goins. Mrs. Goins is the wife of the well known Tecumseh County banker, businessman and Christian philanthropist Mister Wilton Fox Goins. Mr. Goins, a life-long resident of this community, recently described his wife's paintings as "remarkable". Speaking of an upcoming exhibition of her paintings in our capitol city he was outspoken in praise. "We are all well pleased with this much deserved recognition of Mrs. Goins' talent and hard work." Mrs. Goins, who was unfortunately not available for an interview by this reporter, was for several years the foremost student of Professor Forsyth.

However, her husband points to the fact that her style is completely unrelated to Forsyth's whose painting he described as

399

rather old fashioned.

Funeral services for William Forsyth were held earlier in Indianapolis. Burial was in that city.

Further information about the upcoming exhibit of the paintings of Marva Winslow Goins will be reported in this newspaper as available.

"I'm appalled."

"Appalled?"

"Horrified. *You* did this. *You* actually did this. *Old fashioned*! You're quoted!"

"I was interviewed. You know they make up half the stuff they print."

"They made it up! Don't think I don't know how you do things."

"How I do things?"

"I thought you would have more respect for Bill. This is humiliating."

"You're over-reacting. It's only a local paper. My goodness. He misunderstood. The man did his best."

"I not upset with the *reporter*, Wilton. And what exhibition?"

"In the Fall. This Fall. At the *Heron Institute*. It's being arranged."

"By you."

"And others who admire your art."

"No you're not."

"Not what?"

"Arranging anything."

"I'm not?"

"No, you're not."

25

Two local fishermen, known to one and all around here since their skill with rod and line is unquestioned, spent Thursday at their favorite spot, and for their valiant efforts produced a fine string of crappies, as well as other varieties from the depths. Mrs. Gula Dickens, who we hear is related to one of these fellows, reports a fine meal resulted.

CHAPTER 15
ENOUGH IS ENOUGH

Wilton Goins subjects the modern world to incisive analysis. Poor
Birds are distributed, but Norman withholds twenty-five or maybe
twenty-six. All efforts at economy are fiercely rejected, and the
Spirit Of Ecstasy is rubbed in Wilton's face.

1
The Giver Of The Final Feast

One hundred and fifty men, most in rough, torn canvas jackets,
with cloth caps pulled down over their ears, mingled in the cold
drizzle of a late November evening in 1938, hands jammed deep in
their pockets, packing the sidewalk and overflowing onto Goins
Boulevard. The majority were native to Aschburgh, though
more than a few walked in from surrounding communities in
the hope of getting one of the *Poor Birds*. This year their wait
would be wet and lacking any semblance of festivity since the
rain and cold forced the 9th *ANNUAL ASCHBURGH HARVEST
FESTIVAL* indoors at the storefront *Masonic Temple* right next
door to the *Aschburgh Bank & Trust*.

The large Masonic meeting room, its plate glass windows
looking out upon the cold and wet crowd, was packed with

Aschburgh and Tecumseh County notables seated at five long tables, with Wilton Goins, Joey Birdsall and The Reverend Doctor Bishop Poston on the dais. Half a dozen ladies from *First Community Church* shuttled back and forth serving dinners of steak, mashed potatoes, corn and green beans to the assembled gentlemen.

Damp cartons of chickens and small sacks of potatoes lined the rear wall. Wilton doubted there would be enough chickens to go around this year, but he had done what he could. Times were hard for everyone. *Poor peoples can't be choosy* was an old and a wise saying. Folks had to be content and gratefully take what they were given. Because they weren't going to get much more.

Norman the chauffeur stepped out into the drizzle, his collar pulled up against the damp chill, and with a long steel pole began to lower the *Masonic Temple's* awning. Mid-way he stopped, and leaning the pole against the wall, studied the *Rolls-Royce Phantom* across the street. Strolling over to the car he carefully surveyed the length of the limousine, and finally, satisfied none of the men had touched the vehicle, he stepped back and finished rolling down the awning.

"Stay away from that automobile or I'll see to it there's no dole handed out tonight. There's probably not going to be enough stuff anyway. So prepare yourselves. But hey, *poor peoples can't be choosy*. Am I right?" Still grasping the pole in his fist he stood under the awning, and eyed the crowd of men standing around him.

"Bishop Poston ordered the awning down to keep some of you out of the rain. Why he's so worried about you I have no idea. Some of you aren't even from around here. And as far as I'm concerned you ought to go get a job. Just like me. And I mean all of you. But evidently the Bishop is troubled about you catching cold. So enjoy it while you can, fellows. The dole rations will be handed out in a bit. After Mister Goins says his speech to the gentlemen inside."

Once the chauffeur stepped back into the warmth, twenty men jammed themselves under the awning. Those in the front row pressed their faces against the steamed glass to watch Bishop

Poston offer a word of thanksgiving and grace, and as they gazed at the notables slicing their steaks and buttering their rolls, Joey Birdsall rose to introduce Wilton Fox Goins, the *Giver of the Feast.*

After ten minutes of general remarks and joke filled introductions of various town and County officials, followed by a series of Masonic announcements, Joey turned toward Wilton who, his face buried in his notes, ignored him. "Gentlemen, it's sure not necessary for anyone to introduce Mister Goins in this town. Some have said Wilton Fox Goins is Aschburgh, and I certainly would not be one to quarrel with that assessment. Most of us around here have *growed up* with him, as they say, and through the years we've known him to do many really good and generous things for our community. Often anonymously... because that's just the way he is. Now of course the smartest thing he ever done was to get Miss Marva Ainsley, one of the Winslow girls, to marry him. I'm still not sure...homely as he is...how he ever managed to pull that one off."

Joey smiled at the grins and laughter of the men...missing the annoyed look Wilton cast in his direction. "Seriously though fellows, Wilton's done a lot of good, and one of those things is something we'll all get a chance to take part in a little later on this evening. Which is the handing out of what's come to be called *Poor Birds* and some other stuff to the hungry at this festive time of the year. Though personally I've never seen why anyone willing to work--"

"Joey," Wilton whispered loudly. "Enough."

Several men seated near the dais grinned and elbowed each other. "Time to let the boss have his say, Joey."

"Well, shoot...I was just getting warmed up. But I suppose I ought to shut up and sit down."

"You said it, not me."

"So, without anymore ado, let's hear from the president of the *Aschburgh Bank & Trust*, Mister Wilton Fox Goins, the Giver of this *Annual Harvest Feast... Festival.*"

Wilton placed his notes on the rostrum and waved off the applause of the Community Leaders. Now just shy of sixty, he remained an imposing figure in black...though his hair and mustache were gray and his shoulders slumped. After deliberately rearranging a few of his papers, he looked up and smiled.

"Enjoying your steak dinners, gentlemen? You know I think before we do anything else we need to take a moment to show our appreciation to the ladies who have come out on this cold and rainy evening to see to it that we have a delicious hot meal. Let's give a warm round of applause to the *Ladies Society of The First Community Church of Indiana.*"

As they applauded the six white haired ladies in aprons, Wilton motioned for the men to rise to their feet. "Remain standing in appreciation and respect if you please, fellows. Ladies, I speak for all the men here tonight when I say you are the heart and the soul of Aschburgh...indeed of Tecumseh County. Without you we would be nothing. Thank you...thank you so very much."

Wilton smiled and led the men in a final burst of applause for the blushing women. "God bless you, ladies. You may be seated, men. Thank you for your enthusiastic and respectful courtesy to our dear ladies. By the way, and I hope this isn't out of place...if you're looking for a Church home where the ladies really know how to put on a covered dish, you want to be sure to check out *First Community.* I may get in trouble for this...but I truly believe we have the best cooks in Tecumseh County."

"Stonewall County too."

"There you've said it. Stonewall County too." As the men shuffled their chairs and resumed eating, Wilton pulled his watch from his vest pocket and made a point of noting the time and carefully placing the watch on the podium. "Gentlemen, with your kind permission, I'm going to move right along as you continue to enjoy your delicious meal. And although Joey's already made some introductions, I want to call special attention to the presence this evening of my good friend the Honorable Chester Armour, mayor of Giantown, all of our very diligent Tecumseh County Commissioners, members of our esteemed School Board, and all the Aschburgh and Beauville Town Board Members. Welcome Mister Mayor...good to see all you fellows...and lest I forget... honored reverend clergy...Bishop Poston and others.

"I have also received regrets earlier today from the Honorable Tom Studder, mayor of Indianville, whose wife is critically ill. Mayor Studder asked me to say that he covets our prayers for Madonna. I'm afraid it doesn't look too good. So remember the Studders...especially those two little girls...as you spend time in your prayer closet. We serve a mighty and a gracious God. Now fellows, I want you to know we certainly appreciate your making space in your busy schedules to fellowship with us this wet and chilly evening. And I trust that you are enjoying yourselves and getting plenty to eat. The ladies tell me there's seconds and more, and they're setting that out on the tables by the door to the kitchen. So you just help yourselves...we're not going to make a fuss about it...we're all just plain common folks.

"Now I'll do my best to be brief, but I have given a great deal of thought to what I am going to share with you tonight, so I would appreciate your bearing with me. And don't worry about disrupting me if you get up to get some seconds...or thirds... that won't bother me at all. This *Annual Harvest Festival* which I initiated almost ten years ago to thank God for each of my precious and beloved children... these *Feasts* as some have taken to calling them...have become very dear to my heart. Nevertheless, even as I thank the Lord for the health and happiness of my five girls, as I thank Him constantly for a wonderful family, and... as Joey has so humorously pointed out...for a loving, beautiful wife who puts up with me and does her best to keep me on the straight and narrow...."

Wilton paused as the men laughed and elbowed each other. "Marva knows how to handle you, Wilton."

"She surely does. Bless her heart." Wilton grinned. "Everything I have achieved I owe to my precious Marva and to the Lord. I thank God every day for my wonderful wife. And I hope you fellows do the same with respect to your dear ladies."

"Amen," intoned The Reverend Doctor Bishop Poston from the dais.

"Fellows, this leads me into my point this evening. God has blessed me and God has blessed you. Yet despite that blessing... and maybe there's a message here ...each year at this event, each year since 1929, we have witnessed that mob of idle men out there on the street to be getting bigger and bigger. Now maybe I'm wrong. Tell me I'm wrong if that's how you see it...tell me I'm exaggerating."

"No. Sad to say, you've got it right, Wilton."

"So I asked myself...I said, Wilton, you live in the most richly blessed part of this great blessed land of America, and what are you doing to improve things? That's what I asked myself. Am I improving anything by handing out bountiful Thanksgiving dinners each year? Now mind you I enjoy doing this, and while it's a significant personal expense...Mrs. Goins and I have felt it was a justified expense... something above and beyond our tithe and even double tithe. So that's not an issue.

"But then the answer came back...perhaps from the Lord... I'm not sure...*No, you're not improving anything, Wilton. You're probably making things worse.* Not that I mean to aggravate the problem, of course...but each and every year there's more and more hungry, more and more who are no longer working, and often I'm afraid not even willing to work anymore because... it really pains me to say this...not willing to work because it's become too easy to get free food by begging."

"Wilton, there's some out there that's not even from Aschburgh...or Beauville...or Giantown or Indianville for that matter."

"Exactly. Now I don't want to get political here. Just like at the supper table we try to keep politics and religion out of our business and lodge discussions."

"Amen to that."

"I respect both parties...Democrats and Republicans...and I know we have at least one Democrat with us this evening...and very happy and honored to have him here too I might add. So it's not that. But I have to say it sure wasn't like it is now when Mister Hoover...who is a Christian man...was in office.

"Say what you will, those were good days, blessed days. Now here again... we've got to tell the truth on this...it has nothing to do with politics...today we've got socialists and even communists in Washington telling us what to do, how to live, how to run our businesses…claiming things are getting better under them. When we can just look out these windows and see things are getting worse, not better."

"No one can deny that."

"That's for sure."

"I've got it on good authority…a man who knows what's going on…that they're even talking again about changing our clocks. Changing the time of day so as to give us more hours to work… when the fact is they're taking jobs away…and we don't need our clocks changed.

"Fellows, as the *Bible* says, I've got eyes to see and ears to hear…and I can see and I can hear those shiftless men out there on the street. A street named after my family…named by our town to honor my family…who were common farming people who never took a day off except the Lord's Sabbath. Yet now we've got men standing around in the rain. I have called them a mob and maybe that's a bit strong, a bit lacking in grace and charity…I don't know…but that's what they're becoming. You just give it another year."

"You're right about that, Wilton. Time is running out."

"I know I am and I know it is. Begging for a handout. Able-bodied, healthy men begging for a handout. Since when do Hoosiers beg? Since when do Christian men beg? My Daddy would have died before he sunk that low. He didn't have the education most of us have, but he knew how to think straight and how to speak his mind. Daddy would tell us kids, *Even a one-armed man can chop wood*. He'd say that. Just think about it. There's a lot of common wisdom in that saying. Now just like you, I know my *Bible*, and the *Bible* says for us to care for widows and orphans, and I say if we don't do that we aren't Christians."

"Amen," said the Bishop as he left the dais to go get seconds.

"But those fellows out there are strong, once capable men, and the *Bible* says of them if they won't work, they don't eat. Now that's hard…I realize that…and I wish I didn't have to say it…but I didn't say it…I just quoted it. God said it. Fellows, streets packed with able-bodied men looking for a handout is not the Aschburgh I've known all my life. And it's sure not the

Aschburgh I want my girls to know. Am I making this up, or am I making some kind of plain common sense to you?"

The Bishop, who was pouring gravy on his mashed potatoes, called out, "You're right on target, sir."

"That's for sure."

"Well, there you have it. Thank you, Bishop. I sure didn't come here tonight to talk politics or religion. I'm just a local businessman trying to make an honest dollar…like most of you. But if our businesses and our freedoms are to survive sometimes we need to get serious like this. Mister Roosevelt is strutting around in his fancy car, chomping on his fancy hundred dollar cigarette holder, and he's telling us everything's getting better. *Happy days are here again*. That's what he's singing. Well, the happy days we had under Mister Hoover are not here again. Men, it's not getting better, it's only getting worse.

"Now here it is. Bottom line. I have decided, gentlemen, that I am no longer going to play pretend about this situation. I'm not allowing some Washington bureaucrats to be changing my clock, and I'm not helping Roosevelt and the communists by hosting these handouts. After tonight the free meals stop. This is the last one. The last *Harvest Festival*.

"There's better ways I can praise the Lord for my girls. I never meant for it to get out of hand like this. With your help I'll distribute some Thanksgiving dinners tonight…the last of the *Poor Birds*…but then that's it…we've done our piece. And we've got to get serious about changing things in our town, and in fact in our nation."

"You're speaking my mind."

"You're not afraid to tell the truth, sir."

"No, I'm not. By the way, just to set the record straight. Those are quality birds back there against the wall. They're sure not *Poor Birds*. So if anyone would like one to take home, you just tell my driver, Norman, and he'll set it aside for you. There's no sense letting them go to waste on men who won't work. Norman, would you lift your hand so the gentlemen know who you are.

"You know, I want to see men like you fellows in the Statehouse, and I want to see men like you in Washington. We need some

Christian men in those places. Men who've run a business, who've had to go hungry so they could put their profits back into the shop, who've known the pain of being forced to let some good people go in order to make ends meet...who know how things are done in the real world. Now what I'm about to say next may seem a little radical to some of you, but please hear me out."

"You've got my attention, Wilton."

"Right this very minute a very dear friend of mine...some of you may know him...Greg Penn...."

"The little fellow?"

"Yes, that's him. A tiny body but a big mind and an even bigger heart. My friend Greg is making his fourth trip to Europe in the last three years. Normally I'm not one to pay much attention to what's going on in Europe, but this time I have studied it. Greg's in Germany right now, then he's going to Austria, and then I believe to Czechoslovakia...that one's a mouthful...places that are joining themselves together because of the good things that are happening over there."

"You mean Hitler?"

"Some of us don't care for this Hitler fellow very much. I know I sure don't agree with all he says. Though I certainly am happy to see that he despises communists and is getting rid of them. Quickly. We could use some of that here. But for the most part I prefer someone who speaks good, plain American. Still, here's what I want you to consider carefully.

"What Greg Penn has told me is causing me to pause and take a careful second look. Fellows, business is booming in Germany. Now that's a fact. Greg Penn tells me you can go anywhere over there and you won't find a single workingman standing around with his hands in his pockets. No one's leaning on his shovel the way these *CCC* boys are. There's none of this *WPA*, and none of these other government boondoggles over there.

"The simple fact is there's no unemployment in Germany. And no crime in the streets. You steal...they shoot you. How about that? Problem solved. Not everyone deserves to go through a full courtroom process. No relief, no handouts, no begging, no government meddling in business. No communists telling you what to do. And you don't need to lock your door at night.

"Over there there's none of this stuff we're seeing outside these windows. How long before these men are trying to break into my bank or into your store? How long before your wives are afraid to leave the door unlocked? They probably already are. Whatever anyone wants to say against Hitler and the Germans, and I suppose there's a lot that can be said, they will not put up with able-bodied men standing around in the rain with their hands in their pockets waiting for a hand-out.

"You know what really breaks my heart, men? My friend Greg Penn...a native Hoosier, a man who's had a successful career here in Indiana...hey, I know he's tiny and he's different...but he's a rock solid business man who's built up a thriving architectural business. When a man like Greg tells me he can no longer afford to do business in America because of the unions and the laziness and the waste they promote...and so he has to look across the ocean to Germany and Austria....

"Gentlemen, that just about breaks my heart. I went to *Indiana University* with that man, and now he feels he has to leave America if he's going to make a fair profit on his investment. Because Americans don't want to work anymore. That tells me we've got to do something. We've got to get a Christian man in Washington who will take action about these follows loitering outside these doors. Somebody who'll stop tossing our tax money around like it's confetti."

"Amen to that. You're on target, Goins. You're making a lot of sense."

"There's too many of these communists in the schools too."

"Fellows, politics is not my cup of tea...frankly it's a dirty business for people who'll do things behind your back. But something needs to be done, and I for one can't just sit back and shut my eyes any longer. I'm tired of seeing everything we've worked so hard for go up in smoke. Frankly...and I never thought I'd be saying this...I'm tired of seeing the men of Aschburgh become nothing more than bums on relief. They used to take pride in honest sweat, but today they're nothing but bums on relief. Now that's exactly what Roosevelt and his thugs have done to the people of this town. That's what Roosevelt's done to America, men. Bums on relief.

"Before we do this for the final time...how many would like a bird to take home? Hold up your hands, fellows. I count fifteen. Norman? Sixteen? O.K. sixteen it is. Norman, make sure there's sixteen set aside, and maybe four more just in case. So a total of twenty. We'll hand out the rest of these *Poor Birds* because otherwise they'll just rot...and I know none of us believes in waste. That's not our way. We weren't raised to waste. But then that's it. There's two more hands, Norman. Twenty-two. From now on we take care of orphans and widows...but no more than that. We either stand on our own two feet, like they're doing in Germany, or we'll end up begging for scraps from Roosevelt's commie table.

"Well, that's about all I've got to say. I apologize for speaking at such length this evening. And I apologize for speaking a little bit politically. But somebody has to tell the truth...somebody has to be willing to take the consequences. It might as well start with me."

"You done good, Wilton."

One after another the leaders of Tecumseh County...and a few from Stonewall...rose to their feet to applaud the *Giver Of The Feast. The Giver Of The Final Feast.* Ignoring them, Wilton stared down at the rostrum as he gathered his notes into a neat stack. When he glanced up at the applauding crowd he raised his hand to silence them and then motioned with both hands for them to sit back down.

"Gentlemen, I see the dear ladies are serving cake and ice cream even as I speak. And coffee. How could I have forgotten their preparations for our delight? Coffee's on the way, and I'm sure there's tea. Thank you, ladies. Thank you so very much. Let's just take our time and enjoy our dessert and coffee, and then we'll get rid of those birds and call it a night. After we're ready...had a little time to digest this wonderful meal...share some good fellowship...thank you again, ladies...Bishop Poston will show us how he wants this *Poor Bird* hand-out done. I wouldn't imagine it'll take us all that long. And don't forget to pick up a bird before you leave. Better set aside twenty-five birds, Norman. Make it twenty-five...twenty-six."

2
The Morning Of January 2, 1939

"In peace is the way I would like to eat my breakfast, Marva. I have a busy day ahead of me...what with taking the girls to the circus and all...and you're making me to dawdle."

"And when this great plan of yours unfolds are my girls supposed to walk? In the rain, in the snow? From all the way out here in the country? My little girls walking these isolated, muddy roads all by themselves? Is that also part of your great plan, Wilton? Sometimes you don't seem to care about them...or about me... not at all."

"You're a good wife and mother, and I love you very much, so I'm not going to say anything."

"That's so nice of you."

"Surely you can see you're being melodramatic...plain ridiculous. I'm not planning to sell the *Rolls* before Summer anyway. We've got at least six months to work things out. Six full months. For goodness sakes, Marva. This is no time to be getting yourself worked up with the baby due."

"Due right around the time you sell my car. I want the *Rolls* and I want my chauffeur for my babies. Since when do we have to worry about money?"

"Now there! Now right there! You've gone and said it. I knew that's what you've been thinking. And that's precisely the attitude that leads to bankruptcy. Marva, if I don't worry about money then you and the girls won't have any."

"So now we're going bankrupt? Let me quote you. *The Goins know how to get along in this world. We're not people who need anyone's help. The Goins make their own way.* Now that's exactly what you said when you stopped...stopped abruptly...giving even a tiny bit of food to those poor families."

"I never said any such thing. Those people were as good as stealing from us."

"You most certainly did say it. Let me tell you something, Wilton Goins. I cannot drive with an infant in my arms. I need my *Rolls-Royce* and I need Norman to drive and to help me in the studio."

"O shoot! Now this is all to make a point, isn't it? This is all to make a point! This is all about that women's rights speaker you had at that Women's Group, isn't it? Admit it."

"I've asked you not to swear in my home, around my girls. I don't even attend *Psi Iota Xi* meetings. That's Regina's group... and for your information they do wonderful work. I may just start to attend if you're going to make such a fuss."

"Now I didn't mean anything against the ladies or their sorority. For goodness sakes, Marva. But you know the girls are my daughters too. I'd never do anything to hurt them."

"Maybe it's time for you to act that way and protect them."

"That's just plain unfair. You're still furious with me about the Fall *Harvest Festival*. When is it going to stop? That was almost two months ago. You know that was a decision I just had to make. If a man is really a man he has to be able to say, *No*. For the future of the town I cannot let all our young men be turned into beggars. You know I did the right thing. We've talked it over, and you said you understood. I mean I've explained it all to you several times. My goodness, let's be reasonable."

"I want the *Rolls* for my babies. I want the *Rolls* properly maintained. Even improved. I want a new heater installed. Their new heaters are much better than what I have to put up with. And I want Norman. I want my chauffeur. You're not getting rid of Norman."

"Marva, this is a business decision. Pure and simple."

"No."

"Aw shoot!"

3

First Community Church of Indiana
125 Ainsley Street
Aschburgh, Indiana

January 2, 1939

The Very Venerable Father Charles Coughlin
The Radio Priest & The Fighting Priest
The Shrine of the Little Flower
Little Flower Church
Royal Oak, Michigan

Dear Very Venerable Father Coughlin:

I have the honor of writing to you on behalf of one of our members who desires to sponsor you as our guest speaker during our late Spring revival. I am sure I do not need to tell you that this is a great honor to you personally as well as to your esteemed church and denomination.

The cornerstone of our SEARCH FOR SOULS EVANGLISM PROGRAM will be a full week of Spirit drenched meetings. Suggested dates for our revival are Sunday April 23rd for both morning and evening services, followed by evening services from Monday through Friday the 28th. And of course should you have great success in your preaching we are prepared to continue the meetings for as long as souls are being saved and the Lord Jesus tarries.

If those dates are not ones which agree with your schedule we can choose Sunday May 28th for both morning and evening services, followed by evening services from Monday through Friday June the 2nd. Please let me know which days will be best for you and I will do the rest.

Suitable accommodations will be provided for you at no cost, and you may be assured there will be a generous honorarium for your labors. The member who will sponsor you wishes to remain anonymous, but I can assure you that you will be well cared for as he is a most accommodating individual and an outstanding Christian.

We are all most interested to hear you speak on the Last Days, the Supremacy of Scripture, the necessity of Baptism in the name of the Trinity, and the evils of Pentecostalism. Your sponsor would especially like to hear you speak about how current events, particularly in Germany, Spain and Europe relate to the above. He is also interested in your views on the Communist conspiracy in this country. Of course, within the doctrinal boundaries of the Bible Baptist Holiness Church you will have complete freedom as the Spirit directs.

We are greatly looking forward to meeting you this Spring, and are confident we will be well pleased with your ministry. Please advise us as to when you will arrive and if you have any special dietary requirements.

Very truly yours in Christ Jesus,
The Very Right Reverend Jeremy Poston
Doctor of the Word of God
Bishop of the Church in America

4
Later That Same Morning At The Bishop's Residence

Since it was easier on Marva, and Regina always drove out in her little *Ford* to be with the girls anyway, the cousins normally met for their early morning coffee and chats in the Goins' kitchen. But this morning, since Wilton had taken the girls in the *Rolls* to the circus matinee in Peru, Marva decided to drive his little *Buick* into town to join Regina for a cup of tea in the warm but drafty kitchen of the *Bishop's Residence*.

"I would have preferred to come out to the farm," said Regina, pouring a cup of tea. "It's too chilly for you with all these drafts. Anyway I don't like to think of you driving all that way by yourself. Suppose your tire exploded? Would you have preferred coffee?"

"I really needed to get away from the house, Regina. Tea's fine. Everything about the house suggests Mister Goins' presence. Even when he's not present, he is present. Isn't that silly? I used to get so lonely when he was away...but not anymore. I never thought I'd come to feel this way...I'm sure you don't feel like this about Jeremy...and my Momma certainly never felt this way about Daddy...but Wilton weighs on me...Wilton weighs on me all the time."

"Don't say these things. It's just the weariness of your condition."

"I wish it were that simple, but the fact is Wilton has become a hard-hearted old man. Do you remember how he was when he was courting me? When we were first married he was so young and full of happiness. He took me to New Orleans, to Memphis, all over the South...but he'd never do that today. Suddenly he's become a mean tight-fisted old man. I'm really afraid for my babies. He doesn't care about them at all."

"Marva, please don't talk that way. You're upsetting me. He's taking them to the circus. Have one of my shortbread cookies."

"The girls love them. I put a dab of strawberry preserve on them, and I can't get the girls...especially Skoot...to stop eating them."

"Wilton is a good man, Marva. You have to realize he and Jeremy both bear weighty responsibilities. It's not as though they're workingmen or farmers. When they make decisions they have major effects on the town and the County. Sometimes even the entire State. They can't always do what you or I think would be nice."

"If you really knew Wilton you wouldn't take his side." Marva nibbled on the cookie and sipped at the tea. Over the years Regina had turned herself into a remarkable cook. What else could she do, living with the Bishop? "Don't misunderstand. Canceling the *Harvest Festival* doesn't bother me that much. It's even a relief. Some years he would even take one or two of my girls down there around those people. But taking food away from hungry families, that's what bothers me so. Wilton has no charity in his heart any longer. If he ever did."

"You're not thinking clearly, dear. You're not being fair. Mister Goins has gone out of his way to take the girls to the circus. All the way to Peru. How many fathers would do that?"

"It's the hardness and mean-spiritedness that's come into him. It wasn't there when we first were married."

"Marva, my goodness. Jesus says we're under the covering of our husbands. Even when we may have private reservations."

"That's Paul, not Jesus."

"Not to dispute with you, but it's all the same. You can't just pick and choose with the *Bible. All Scripture is given by inspiration of God, and is profitable for doctrine, for reproof, for correction, for instruction in righteousness*."

"I'm well aware of that. Do you realize there are families who depended on Wilton's *Poor Birds*? Have you ever gone by the Funkhouser place? I think it's on *Wesley Circle*. Near the old Methodist parsonage."

"That old place has fallen down. The parsonage."

"Maybe so, but I'm told those children had no coats and no shoes all this Winter. And just a dirt floor in the house. Can you imagine? If she were still alive my Momma would have had the *Ladies Society* out there caring for those little things."

Regina knew Belva Ainsley would have done no such thing. She wouldn't have even noticed the Funkhousers. Anymore than Marva would. But this wasn't the time to argue the point. "The Funkhousers have been slow for generations. I can't remember that they've ever worn shoes. They don't like shoes...none of them. And remember we are planning to distribute Easter baskets. I'll make sure the Funkhousers are at the top of the list."

"You're showing too much compassion for him, Regina. He takes my vehicle and my chauffeur whenever he feels like it...but he keeps his sporty *Buick* for his own pleasure. And the way he treats these poor people just fills me with shame."

"Would you like another cookie? Some more tea? Why don't you put a dab of my preserve on your shortbread? Just like Skoot."

"I'm famished, and at this point a couple of cookies won't matter very much. I believe you're the best cook in the Church. No one can light a candle to you."

"I've worked hard to learn. Uncle Sevier was hardly one to teach me. But Jeremy just loves to eat, so I had to learn."

"Maybe you could teach Hildred a thing or two. All she cooks is Wilton's favorite meal: beef, corn, beans and potato."

"Hildred does just fine. She keeps a clean kitchen."

"So you say. When a woman has to do something she just goes ahead and does it. My mother was like that after Daddy's accident. She learned everything about that farming operation, and she surprised everyone by doing a better job than Daddy ever did. But that was Momma."

Regina spread raspberry preserve on a cookie and handed it to Marva. The truth was the *Old Ainsley Place* fell apart after Olin's death. It had been Wilton who took charge of renting things out and managing to save the house and grounds for Marva and the girls. "We don't take the paper, but Jeremy says there's been some articles about times getting better real soon. And then you and I will be more than busy with the new baby…and then there's going to be no time for all this stuff and nonsense."

"The fact is he's not treating me well anymore. After I've borne him five healthy babies, and soon a sixth. I think he's grown tired of me. His arrogance is going to cause God to curse our family."

"God doesn't curse babies because of what their father does. Heavens!"

"Who's picking and choosing Scripture now? This is good on the shortbread …but the preserve I really like is the one you served at the last covered dish."

"The blackberry. Quite a few complimented me on that. I'll bring some out for you and our babies."

5

Truly Remarkable News
Lucky Lindy & Michigan Preacher
To Be Feted At Aschburgh Event

Aschburgh January 14, 1939

Exclusive to The Giantown Tribune

By E. Marvin Tugwell, Senior Staff Reporter

Word has only just reached this reporter of a remarkable Spring visit to our own Aschburgh by American aviation legend Charles

Lindbergh, better known as Lucky Lindy.

Bishop Jeremy Poston, ecclesiastical leader of both The First Community Church of Indiana and the Community Church of America denomination advises that Mister Lindbergh, eternally famous for his solo flight across the desolate Atlantic Ocean as well as for his courageous stance for American freedom, will be the lead speaker at the SEARCH FOR SOULS meetings to be held at Aschburgh's First Community Church of Indiana. There will be special music and delicious refreshments every evening.

The Very Right Reverend Bishop Poston is a native Hoosier with his roots in historic Switzerland County. Married to Regina Winslow of the highly respected Winslow family of Tecumseh County, he holds an advanced degree in Theology from the Switzerland Bible Institute of Holiness and is also the recipient of a Doctorate of The Word of God. Well respected in Church circles for dynamic and probing preaching, Bishop Poston also handles an enormous administrative burden as the head of a growing denomination, but this reporter found him to do so with considerable aplomb.

Assisting Lucky Lindy in this upcoming gala event will be Charles Coughlin, a Catholic minister from Michigan who is highly regarded in that State and is known to his followers as the "Communicating Pastor".

Seated behind his massive desk in his executive office, a sculpture of praying hands poignantly before him, Bishop Poston confided to this reporter that while details of Lindbergh's appearance still are being worked out, the event is a certainty. The exact date and time of Lucky Lindy's arrival in Tecumseh County will be announced shortly, and all members of the community will be invited to meet him and to hear him preach.

All in the community interested in further information about Bishop Poston's ministry are invited to feel free to telephone him at the Church office in Aschburgh. Or better yet visit the new Church building on Ainsley Street for one of their many enriching worship services.

6
GREAT BAFFLEMENT

Wilton sat quietly in the bright sanctuary and fought the urge to
vomit. Breathing slowly and deliberately, he gulped air and tried
to focus his mind on the Church but found that too upsetting.
He loosened his vest and tie and wiped sweat from his face. His
father died of some sort of heart problem...died relatively young
too...but this wasn't his heart, it was more of a problem in his
stomach. Perhaps because he left the house so upset, refusing to
finish breakfast and slamming the door.

The simple fact of the matter was he found himself under
enormous pressure because of the failures of the people around
him. And now there was this ridiculous newspaper article, and
he knew he would be the one expected to defuse it. Jeremy was
certainly at the top of the list of failures in his life. All his efforts
over the past fourteen years...and yet the Church was still
moving in the wrong direction...all because of Jeremy's apathy
and incompetence.

Still stuck in Aschburgh...even the tiny mission effort in
Kokomo stifled because Jeremy couldn't bring himself to move
it along. Nothing was working out the way Wilton had hoped.
Aschburgh had become a poorhouse. All the old Hoosier values of
thrift, hard work and honesty were mocked. *Aschburgh Savings
& Trust...* always the bedrock of the Tecumseh County economy...
was now sustained only by investments made outside the State...
too often with less than desirable associations. He would have to
find the energy to negotiate a sale if he was going to protect the
girls' future. Nothing was as it should be. Everything at loose
ends. Except for the Funeral Homes of course. The steadiness of
those businesses and the potential of his real estate holdings were
all that sustained him in these times of darkness and turmoil.

"Mister Goins, it's good to see you," said Jeremy as the
Bishop strolled down the center aisle. "Isn't this new carpeting
wonderful? I've been waiting over fifteen minutes for you. In my
office."

"I just sat here for a few moments of quiet reflection, Doctor."

"Are you all right?"

"Just fine. A little warm perhaps. That's why I loosened my tie. Aren't we heating the Church a little too warmly? And do we need so many lights on?"

"I have those corrected attendance figures for you...someone multiplied when they should have divided...and I've developed some thoughts...plans really... that I want to share with you. Shall we go back to my office?"

"I'm concerned about the newspaper article."

"O yes. That's just dreadful."

"Have we actually invited Mister Lindbergh? And he said, Yes? To come to Aschburgh? I find that hard to believe. That he would come, and that you would be so stupid as to invite him after what he's done."

"I think we really need to sort that all out. Shall we go back to my office?"

"You go ahead. I'll be with you in a couple of minutes. I have a few prayer concerns I need to lift up."

A large print of Jesus in the Garden of Gethsemane hung behind Jeremy Poston's clean and highly polished desk. Just as reported in the *Tribune* the only thing on his desk was a cheap bronzed statuary of Durer's drawing *Praying Hands*. A small display case against one wall held five copies of the *King James Bible* and a mint *Matthew Henry*.

Wilton glanced at the print of Jesus as he settled himself into a chair. All of these items were from Rising Sun he was sure. His stomach was quieted some, but he continued to sweat, and he mopped his face with a handkerchief.

"Would you like a glass of water, sir?"

"Please."

"Perhaps you'd like for me to call Doctor Aiken?"

"No need. Just the water." Wilton sipped and stared at the blood sweating Jesus. A righteous man paid a price.

"The Lord is good and compassionate, overflowing with love and mercy. Don't you agree, sir?"

"Can you explain the newspaper article? It's ludicrous, and it's going to make us look like fools. Have you actually written to Lindbergh? I sure don't fault him for accepting that *German Eagle* medal...what else could he do, and what's wrong with it anyway?...but for the moment the fellow's *persona non grata*. We sure don't want him in the Church. That's why I asked you to get Father Coughlin... someone with a little more balanced reputation. Did you actually write to Lindbergh?"

"I wanted to, but I couldn't. I don't have his address. But I do have those corrected attendance figures for you. Someone just made a little slip-up."

"O Jeremy, Jeremy. What are we going to do?" The urge to vomit was returning, and Wilton rubbed his stomach and began taking deep breaths.

"My mother sent this paper-weight," said Jeremy. He held up the *Praying Hands* for Wilton to see. "Mrs. Goins, being an artist, would really appreciate it. Perhaps I'll get her one. But please don't mention it to her. This is only a copy, of course. The original, which is by an Italian and is done in marble or granite, is in the big museum in England."

"May I have another glass of water?"

"Though she never studied it my mother has a good sense for art. Are the corrected figures what you need? I've been evaluating our seating problem."

"Seating problem?" Wilton was sure if he could hold on a few more minutes this would pass.

"It wouldn't cost that much to put up a very nice fabric screen. We could easily block off the back half of the sanctuary. It would be portable, of course, but it would close off those portions we don't want to use."

"Don't *want* to use?"

"You have to admit we built too big. Our eyes were bigger than our stomachs. Those empty pews make people feel we're not growing."

"Well, *we're not growing.* We're not growing here, and we've had to shut down the Kokomo mission. We need to get back some of the vision we had when we first started the Church. How could you have even thought of inviting Mister Lindbergh? No one wants to hear from him right now."

"I think a screen...tasteful of course...would lift morale enormously. And ultimately that might stimulate some growth. But with all due respect, sir, I've done about all that I can. I don't see where I have any more room on my plate."

For a moment Wilton's vision blurred, and he feared he was about to faint. But now the spinning was easing, he was beginning to feel better, though he was still sweating. "Isn't it hot in here, Jeremy?"

"Despite what people say, I have more sheep to care for than most pastors."

"You're a Bishop, my boy. Anyway, what about this newspaper article? How does Lindbergh get in the picture?" Wilton tossed the Saturday Giantown *Tribune* on the Bishop's desk. "I skipped my breakfast and came here immediately to find out what's going on. Lucky Lindy? Who said anything about inviting Mister Lindbergh? How could you do something so stupid? Not that I don't respect everything he's done...but this is the wrong time."

Slowly moving his finger from line to line Jeremy scanned the article. "Well, I don't know, sir. But it seems to me the reporter just got everything all wrong. I have no idea why. Or how. I doubt I ever even mentioned Mister Lindbergh. Or not this way. For one thing he's not ordained. And for another thing...as I said...I don't have his address."

"He's not ordained? What's that got to do with anything?"

"No, he's not, sir. I'm sure of that. He's strictly an airplane pilot. I may have mentioned his name, or made some reference to him...but I never said what it says I said. You know how reporters are. Can I get you another glass of water?"

"Please. Do we at least know if Father Coughlin is coming? Did you send him a letter? Did you remember to invite him? And may I have that glass of water?"

Jeremy filled the glass in his private bathroom, and glancing in the mirror realized he was sweating as heavily as Mister Goins. Perhaps the heat was turned up too high.

"Actually sir, I have a copy of the letter I recently posted to Mister Coughlin. And I had a response from him yesterday, though I don't think he's fully committed himself just yet." The Bishop fumbled with a batch of papers on his desk, eventually locating the Coughlin letters. "Here it is, sir. The one I sent to him. We can't allow a non-ordained person like Lindbergh in our pulpit. *Bible Baptist Holiness* by-laws stipulate that. I never said anything about him, and I don't know where that reporter got all that stuff."

"How many times do I have to tell you we are not *Bible Baptist Holiness*? We are *Community In America*. Let me see that letter you sent."

Holding it in one hand and wiping his face with the other, Wilton scanned it and tossed it back on the desk. "If I'm not mistaken *Venerable* means the fellow's dead and gone to heaven."

"I very much doubt that. He's a Catholic. A Roman Catholic."

"And?"

"You can't be saved if you believe in the Pope. The *Bible* makes that quite clear."

"Jeremy, Jeremy. Let's me see the letter Father Coughlin sent you."

Very Right Reverend Jeremy Poston
Bishop of America and Doctor of the Word of God
First Community Church of Indiana
Aschburgh, Indiana

Your Eminence:

In the name of Our Blessed Mother and her devoted Little Flower I greet you and give thanks for your recent letter of inquiry and for your generous offer of prayer and support.

As you know our radio broadcasts are heard all over America and even in large parts of Canada, the land of my birth and a nation desperately in need of our prayers and the ministry of Holy Mother the Church. The cry of our heart is for all Americans to devote themselves to Mary the mother of our Lord and to the precious Little Flower. Our heart is lifted with joy when we think of you and all who take a stand for the Church against the wickedness of the Jews, Franklin Double-Crossing Roosevelt, and the communist hordes who would destroy our great land. I want to assure you that despite things you may have read in the press our ministry continues to be blessed by his Holiness Pope Pius XII.

Would you, Bishop of America and Doctor of the Word of God, Very Right Reverend Jeremy Poston prayerfully consider generous contributions to both our radio ministry and to our special concern for The Shrine of the Little Flower here in Royal Oak? Pledges of regular monthly support are most appreciated as they guarantee the consistency of our efforts to share the devotion to the Little Flower with a needy world. Your contributions will be gratefully received and appreciated, and will receive a special blessing from His Holiness.

In closing allow me to ask for your prayers for our brethren in Spain, Germany and Italy who are faithfully taking a stand against godless communism. Remember that they are putting their very lives in jeopardy that America may remain free.

In the faithful service of Our Lord, of His Blessed Mother and of the Little Flower,

Father Charles Coughlin
The Radio Priest

"This is his response? This is the whole thing?"

"It is quite a nice letter, but it's a little hard to see how his letter responds to mine. But on the other hand they say he receives more correspondence than anyone in America, including King Roosevelt."

"Perhaps you need to write again. Or telephone him. That would probably be best. I'll try to get the newspaper mess straightened out."

"I really don't have the time to take on even more responsibilities."

"O Jeremy."

7

A Gold-Plated Spirit Of Ecstasy

Many months had passed since the scandal of the Lindbergh/Coughlin meetings at which neither great man made an appearance. It was now late June as Joey Birdsall, suit jacket folded neatly over one arm, stepped out of the heat and into the cool of the *Aschburgh Bank & Trust* and wiped droplets of sweat from his face and neck. He nodded to the tellers as he headed back to Wilton Goins' office.

"Hot enough for you?"

Wilton sat behind his clean, glass topped desk fingering a carefully wrapped brown package. "It just came in the morning mail, and I'm wondering if I shouldn't toss it out the window."

"Something nasty?"

"No. Nothing much really. Just yet another annoyance. It's one thing after another."

"How's Marva doing?"

"About as well as can be expected. When a woman's in that way, you know. She's about as big as she's going to get, so it's more or less a difficult time. A continuation of difficult times. Another week at most, I imagine." Wilton rotated the package on the desk top. "From England. Can you believe it?"

Realizing he wasn't going to be asked to take a seat, Joey helped himself to one of the leather chairs across from Wilton's desk. "When are you planning to take her down to Indianapolis? To get her settled in, you know."

"It's not going to happen. No matter what I think. I've given up trying to get her to do the smart thing. Doctor Aiken'll have to be it. Indianapolis is too much of an excursion and too much expense…according to her. Can you believe it? So what am I supposed to do? I'm only the husband and the father."

"A fellow can only do what he can do. But Aiken's getting pretty out of date. Louise says he doesn't keep up. He doesn't even listen to her half the time, so we've started doctoring in Giantown. With Bragg."

"You only hear good things about Bragg, but Aiken'll just have to do for me. There's tons of bright, up-to-date young doctors around...but we have to settle for a middle-aged guy with shaky hands and no idea what's happened since he left medical school. And no concern. But he's the one Marva wants, and I'm finishing fussing with her about it. After five children you'd think she'd learn. The woman gets more stubborn with every one. What's on your mind, Joey?"

"Just social. Wanted to say, hi."

"How's our *Giantown Home* doing? That was a nasty accident up there. Both of those young kids dead. Sad."

"Doggone shame. Just kids. I've known both families for years. We served their grandparents and probably their great-grandparents. From over to Galveston. Originally from Ijamsville. But like I say we've known them for years and years. Even when they were up there. Long ways from us back then. Sad. Same old stuff. Love, speeding, guzzling beer. They're both with us, but it looks like the families are going to want separate services, which...since there was no official engagement and the girl's folks didn't fully agree on the boy...well, I think it's only right. Anyway things up are fine. The services will be separate, but we'll get both of them. Couldn't be better. From England you said? Something for your *Rolls*?"

Wilton pushed the package to the edge of the desk. "I'm well pleased with the way the *Home* is working out for me. It's a service to the community and it's a sound return. And for you as well."

"We're averaging two, sometimes three services a week up there. In Giantown. People are looking for old-fashioned care for their loved ones. Which is precisely what *Birdsall* provides. Plus I'm starting to explore what you suggested. Over in the colored section. What would you think about maybe starting that up in the next year? With a colored director, of course. Different name and so forth. No clear tie to us. They need the same quality service as we do, but it'd have to be handled with some tact. Discretion, of course. If anything comes of it, you'll be pleased with the kind of return we can get on that. How's that sound to you?"

"Colored money's green, same as White. I've always believed that in my heart. I've never understood all the animosity. But you do want to move with some caution. We could tarnish our reputation with some folks around here. If it got out. Handling colored bodies. Folks wouldn't want the same person who worked on them."

"Exactly. By the way, Willie, I noticed you're still driving the *Buick*. You thinking of selling the big one? You're aware I'm in the market?"

"The *Rolls-Royce*? That's something I've learned not to discuss. Marva'd have my head. See, that's what this is all about," he said, pointing to the package. "No, I've decided we're keeping the *Rolls*. Well, maybe we're keeping it. It's Marva's car. I'm still not sure just when the transfer took place, but it did. It all of a sudden became *her* car. Can you imagine, Joey? I mean you and me and Olin we grew up together around here. All of us dirt poor. Didn't even have shoes. Well, not you I suppose. But anyway, why do people like us need a car like that?"

Wilton stood and stepped into his private bathroom. "Excuse me while I take a handful of pills. I've got to do this three times a day now. There's no end to what Aiken's got me taking. It's just plain ridiculous. I may just follow you guys and go see your man Bragg."

"All those pills are another thing we didn't like about doctoring with Aiken."

Back in his chair Wilton resumed fiddling with the package. "Let alone a uniformed chauffeur. A chauffeur is bad enough, but she went and ordered two uniforms for him. Can you imagine? Two! You have no idea what it costs me to keep Norman lounging around looking pretty. Given the economy it's not something we can afford anymore. If we ever could. Still, if I was to sell that car locally...well, that'd rub it in her face, you know. And I really can't afford to do that. I'm still thinking I'm going to sell it... but not locally. Making decisions for the *Bank* is a lot easier than living with that woman."

"Any woman. That's for sure. Can't live with 'em, but you can't live without 'em either. Well anyway, I'd been thinking of picking up something like your *Phantom.* You're right about the economy right now...but the way I see it Roosevelt will take us to war no matter what he says. He's going to want to jump in over there to help his Russian commie friends out if nothing else. And like it or not that's going to give our economy a healthy boost."

"Franklin Double-Crossing Roosevelt is what Father Coughlin calls him."

"He's got a lot of good things to say...Coughlin...though Louise doesn't trust the collar. Isn't that the way it goes? Of course I can see your point too. I'd just want the *Rolls* for special events and things. It's not that I'd be rubbing it in Marva's face. So then that package is for the car?"

"Something she ordered. To make a point. Put me in my place."

"Like you always say, Wilton, things can be worked out. So I thought if your vehicle was on the market--"

"It's not, and as far as I can see it's not going to be either. No matter what I want. I wish it were. I truly do. Joey, you can actually see the needle on the gas gauge dropping as you drive! There's no reason for folks like us to have a vehicle like that. We're country people when you get right down to it. And glad to be. Common. I mean what's wrong with the *Buick*? Goodness sakes, we could have four *Buicks* for what that thing costs me. But when and if I do sell...which I doubt I ever will...ever *can,* really...I'm afraid I'll have to do it outside the area. Outside the State probably. If she ever saw someone else driving that car... well, you can just imagine."

"Think Mister Penn might be interested in selling his?"

"Wish I knew. It's like he's disappeared over there in Europe. Nobody's heard a thing in months. I understand his family checked with the embassy, but they don't know either.Vaporized or something. He's probably gone off to Czechoslovakia or some such place. Joey, you simply don't have to put up with what I do, so I don't think you can appreciate the constant pressure. Louise is a good wife to you."

"I've got no complaints on that score. That's for sure."

"You know why there's all these fancy British insurance stamps on this thing?" He held the package up in front of him, balancing it on his thumbs. "Once I learned she ordered it... needless to say she didn't check with me first...I looked into it and found out what the thing was going to cost. Well over five hundred dollars! This little package right here. That's why all the insurance stamps. My goodness! Marva's a country girl...she's a *Bible Baptist Holiness* girl...where does she get these ideas?"

"Five hundred dollars?"

"More. O it'll be a lot more before it's finished. Can you imagine? My father never saw five hundred dollars at one time in his whole life. Never."

"Remember she's been a good wife to you, Willie. And a loving mother to your girls."

"I'm not saying otherwise. I'm not talking against Marva. But that's hardly the point. We don't even know anyone who drives a car like hers. Let along anyone who keeps his own chauffeur. Uniformed. *Two* uniforms! Frankly it's kind of embarrassing."

"Well, there's Mister Penn. The chauffeur. But of course he is different. To be fair, Willie, you're the one who bought her the car. And Norman was hired by you."

"I never bought it for her. She just claimed I did. But I suppose maybe I did those things when you look at it that way. But that's not really the point, Joey."

Wilton set the package down on the desk and slowly revolved it between his hands. "A gold-plated *Spirit of Ecstasy* hood ornament. That's what's in here. Gold-plated, if you can imagine. Not fake...real gold-plated. I'm just hoping she didn't change the order to solid gold. Of course I know where she gets all these ideas from. It's all this artist stuff. Between Greg Penn and all those lessons with Professor Forsyth she's picked up all these artistic notions. Joey, that's plain and simple the biggest mistake I ever made. The studio, the lessons...all of it. So now it's *her* Rolls-Royce and it's *her* chauffeur...*uniformed* chauffeur....hers, hers, hers. There's no end to it. And it's all a part of this world-famous artist notion she's got."

"Maybe it would be better to stand up to her right now...
before things get worse...and just go ahead and sell the *Rolls* no
matter what. Even sell it locally. Maybe you need to rub it in her
face. Put a stop to this attitude once and for all."

"I'm not denying her talent. I'm not saying that. I think she's
more gifted than Forsyth and Greg rolled together. And when
you get right down to it I'm not wanting to deny her anything she
wants...but there's got to be limits. I don't know but I may just
turn around and send this thing back to England unopened. A
five hundred dollar hood ornament! The woman is just pushing
me too hard."

"I wonder, Willie, I just wonder," mused Joey. "If Penn's
staying in Europe maybe his *Rolls* is up for sale. Perhaps I'll
check with his office."

"Afraid not, buddy. The Indianapolis office is shut up tighter
than a drum. That's part of the whole mystery and the shock of
it all. Apparently everything went over there. Berlin or Vienna...
he talked a lot about both, and had business in both places. And
then there was the Hitler award. Did you know Lindbergh got
one last year too? Anyway, he took the *Rolls-Royce* with him. On
the ship. You want to talk about extravagance! No one's heard
from either of them...Greg or Bob...the last eight months or so.
So who knows what's going on? Biggest doggone mistake I ever
made, that's for sure."

"Mister Penn going to Germany?"

"Encouraging the whole painting thing. I have no control
over Penn. No one does. But who knows, Joey, it may turn out
I'm completely wrong. There's some smart people down at the
Herron who feel she's got what it takes for a big career. So who
knows? I don't understand it myself...sticking red all over Henry
Ford's shoulder. Why would anyone want a painting of Henry
Ford anyway? There's plenty of photographs of the man. But I'll
be the first to admit I know next to nothing about art."

"Art's a strange business. I always felt that Forsyth was a bit
of a blowhard."

"And she takes good care of my girls and my home. I've got
no complaints there...but then neither does she...she's got all

sorts of help. Who else around here has a chauffeur, a cook, a cleaning-lady…a maid really…not to mention all the help she gets from her cousin Regina? It's just put all kinds of ideas in her head. Inappropriate to where we live, to the kind of common people we are."

"Not that it's my business, Willie…but if it was me, and I was having these kinds of problems with Louise, I think I'd put my foot down and regain some control. I'd sell the car and I'd sell it locally. Whether she liked it or not. But suit yourself. You know your situation best."

"That's where this whole *Spirit of Ecstasy* business comes from. Doggone, what's so bad about a *Buick*? Her cousin Regina would give her eye teeth for a *Buick*. A lot of women would be well pleased with a *Ford*, let alone a *Buick*."

"That's for sure. Willie, it occurs to me, given your good sense, you may be selling real soon. No matter how things look right this minute. I'm sure we could handle it all tactfully, so there'd be no offense to Marva."

"I'll sell you a gold-plated hood ornament. *Spirit of Ecstasy*. Cheap at seven-fifty."

"Throw the car in and it's a deal."

"I'd really like to sell the car to you, but it's not going to happen. I can't afford the aggravation. Not with my heart. Shoot, Joey, I'm still young…I've got a lot of good years yet…I'm not going around looking for trouble. She'll say I'm rubbing it in her face if I sell that car. I know she will. She'll say I hate my children. And I just cannot afford all that aggravation. She'll never let it go."

"Because of your heart? I hope you're taking your medicine."

"My heart's a factor. You saw all the pills. But it's more just the plain upset. I used to be able to deal with the upset, but anymore it's too much. When Marva gets a fuss up you have no idea. Never yells, never even raises her voice, and everyone thinks because she's wearing those old-fashioned *Bible Baptist Holiness* dresses…and of course the bonnets…especially the bonnets…. Well, they're all wrong about that stuff. Marva wears those clothes because she looks good in them and because she likes to stand out. Simple as that. It has nothing to do with holiness. Not to say she isn't a holiness woman. I mean a good woman. But Joey, when she gets a fuss up I can't eat, I can't sleep…I'm too tired for this stuff. I'm still a young man, but anymore I'm too old for constant upset."

"But you're regular on the heart medicine?"

"I'll bet I take six pills." Wilton rotated the box holding the hood ornament. "You have no idea, no idea at all. It's reached the point where the woman does whatever she wants. A thousand dollars for a hood ornament…it's nothing to her."

"A thousand dollars! You haven't even opened it yet. They told you five hundred, didn't they?"

"Who can say? And you know what I'm going to do with this thing? And it'll probably turn out to be solid gold for all I can guess."

"I hope you not going to do anything foolish at that kind of money. I didn't think you could just go and modify a *Rolls*. Isn't there some kind of regulation and restrictions in the contract?"

"Can you believe it? That's exactly the sort of thing she's tied me to. You can't even do what you want with your own property. I own it, but I can't change it unless some Englishman says so. Now isn't that a pretty picture!"

"It's approved then? This ornament?"

"O it's approved. You better believe it's approved. I'm sure she and her chauffeur have taken care of all that. They'll sell you one made out of jade if you'll pay their price. You know what I'm going to do with this, Joey? And I'm ashamed to say it. It's just pathetic. I'm going to bring it home, give it to her arrogant chauffeur…and I'm going to smile while he installs it."

"Just stand up to her, Wilton. That'll settle it."

"I can't. She'll get angry…you might not realize it…her anger…but I will. I can't stand for her to be angry with me. Can you imagine? This is precisely what a woman can bring you to. To avoid the aggravation, to avoid her not speaking to me, this is the state she's brought me to. The woman's brought me to my knees. She's turned me into a beggar. Turned me into a pathetic beggar."

"Now, now don't get yourself so worked up. It's just not worth it. Well, look, Willie…I just wanted to drop by. Kind of put a bug in your ear as they say. About the *Rolls*."

"I appreciate it. That's what friends are for." Wilton walked over to the window and looked out on the hot street. "*Spirit of Ecstasy.*"

"Pardon?"

"The hood ornament. *Spirit of Ecstasy.* Can you imagine? *The Spirit of Ecstasy.*"

"Isn't that something? That's what they call it? *Spirit of Ecstasy.* Well, Willie, I am in the market. You keep me in mind. Just in case."

"Nothing's going to turn up, Joey. Everything's going to go her way. She's killing me. I believe she's deliberately killing me."

"Now, Willie."

CHAPTER 16
SEPARATED BY CENTURIES

A chapter in which the birth of Wilton's sixth and last child is viewed in relation to Adolf Hitler's invasion of Poland. Also some consideration of Modern Art, the cost of parts from England and further thoughts on the relationship of race to the protection of beloved corpses. Wilton and Joey discuss certain gaps, failures and suspicions.

1
New War, New Birth, New Ideas

On Friday September 1, 1939 Adolf Hitler invaded Poland... Britain and France declared a state of war with Germany two days later on Sunday the 3rd ...while that same Lord's Day King George VI, courageous if reluctant and frequently tongue-tied, rallied the English people to *stand calm, firm and united in this time of trial* ...yet in spite of all this European activity there had still been no word from Greg Penn or Bob, nor had their *Rolls-Royce Silver Ghost* resurfaced.

In America, earlier that Summer, on Monday morning July the 3rd, Lamar Ainsley Goins, the first and only male child of Wilton and Marva Goins, was born... and was declared by his father before the congregation of *First Community Church Of Indiana* to be a *Blessed Child,* dedicated unto the service of the Lord. Asked years later...long after her fame was firmly established...about the use of Ainsley rather than Winslow... Marva responded quite honestly that she could not remember why she and Wilton had named Lamar that way.

Lamar Ainsley, safe in Indiana from the strife of the Old World, was a fairly normal child, neither remarkable nor especially deficient, greatly loved by his sisters and his Aunt Regina Poston, tolerated by his mother...who after ten years of preparation and disciplined work was only then just beginning to be accepted as a serious painter in Midwestern circles...and largely ignored by his father who continued to do battle with assorted physical problems as well as financial, Church and community matters during what turned out to be the final years of his life.

Marva had to prod Wilton to pull some strings and employ some pull, but eventually the youngest girl, Zip, was given special permission to stay the full day at school...attending both morning and afternoon Kindergarten classes. And now with all five girls safely at Aschburgh's *Elementary School* Marva was free...for the first time in ten years...to indulge herself with hours of exploration and experiment in the studio.

Shortly before his death Bill Forsyth told her her studies were over and, "Now it's time to paint. Paint and paint and paint." Which was all well and fine, but of course Bill had meant paint as he painted, plus he had no idea what it meant to try to paint with five or six children scurrying around all the time. After their fashion, she supposed they were fairly good and quiet children... nonetheless, Marva was pleased she had never given in to the motherhood urge. She took satisfaction she had never substituted changing diapers for painting. It would have been easy to do, just as it would have been easy to paint the way Bill painted...but neither of those options was acceptable.

Fortunately, with some new ideas from a young man she ran into from time to time at the *Art Institute's* Life Sketch Class, she began to move in a new direction which seemed to hold promise. She was even receiving a small amount of recognition in Indianapolis and Louisville. Not that she fully grasped Larry Sackroth's ideas on color and shape, but she was certain he was on to something and...with help from Regina and the local school system...it was going to be possible to explore these new directions. And this new baby was not going to stand in the way.

With a little time and freedom to work she believed she could take these ideas beyond anything Larry Sackroth had done with them. For one thing Larry wasn't that bright, and for another he lacked the basic skills Bill Forsyth had drummed into her. And who could tell the future of all that *push and pull* stuff he rambled on about? Though...left alone and given the opportunity...she just might figure it out.

Regina, resigned to never having a baby of her own, arrived in her battered *Ford* Monday through Saturday shortly before nine...having fed the Reverend Doctor Bishop and seen him off to his study where he did whatever it was that he did...and telephoned the school to be sure the five girls arrived safely and had their lunches. If the weather was good she and Lamar Ainsley might even go across to the studio to visit with Marva for a few minutes.

But more often than not they left Marva to herself and kept to the big house where Regina lavished years of pent-up affection upon the baby. While across the way...in the *Barn Studio*... Marva, with notes on all of Larry Sackroth's ramblings, and an excitement about her hard earned freedom, focused her energies on a new conception of painting.

One late September morning Aunt Regina and Lamar Ainsley, the baby bundled in a plaid comforter and cradled in her arms, sat in a rocking chair in the *Barn Studio* and waited patiently for Marva to acknowledge them. "Pretty baby, my beautiful baby,"

Regina whispered in Lamar's ear. "My precious big, beautiful baby."

Marva, big-framed and strong, her hair just beginning to gray at thirty-two, wore a large, heavy white smock over her dress. During her years studying with William Forsyth the garment remained pristine...for Bill insisted on a neat and clean studio. Recently though, as she explored more of Sackroth's ideas on primary colors and strove for greater freedom in her work, she was amused to find the smock frequently splattered with bright colors.

Ignoring her cousin and her baby she sat on a stool and nibbled on the handle of her palette knife. Bill Forsyth would have hated this painting...but Bill was dead and good as his basic ideas were she knew she needed to leave them behind and move forward. The painting wasn't right...it wasn't even moving in the right direction...but it would be silly to panic and throw its future away. The right direction would become clear if she gave herself enough time...and she was determined she was not returning to the landscapes and portraits she and Bill Forsyth labored over for nine years. If nothing else the *Ford* painting with its red splash... which no one but Larry Sackroth appreciated...showed she had long been on the verge of a breakthrough. This new one would go beyond the *Ford*.

"Is it finished?" asked Regina, less to learn about the painting than to call attention to her presence.

"Of course not."

"Well I'm glad to hear that. Wilton has no legs. Why is it such a thick jumbled mishmash where his legs should be?"

"What makes you think it's Wilton? I never said that. It could be anyone. Or no one."

"It looks a bit like him. Maybe not. Were Skoot and Ribby feeling better this morning? I stopped by the school and dropped off some extra sandwiches for the girls' lunches. Step forgot her sweater so I left one for her."

"You carry extra sweaters with you? Plus sandwiches?"

"I made a quick trip back home to get a sweater I had. Either you or Hildred forgot to send enough sandwiches."

"You fuss too much, Regina. Always stopping by the school. Hildred makes sure they have their lunch. I'm sure they had enough. And sweaters or whatever they need. And don't you think Wilton can get them there on time? He's quite capable."

"I'm glad they're in school, but I do miss them."

"They're better off in school. Skoot had us running all over the place this morning trying to find her glasses. It's something new I'm trying."

"What?"

"This canvas. It's a different approach."

"Because of that fellow you met at the Sketch Class? The one from Milwaukee?"

"Larry. Larry Sackroth. He's represented by a gallery up there."

"Aren't there women in the class you could associate with? Not that there's anything wrong...."

"I appreciate your help with Lamar Ainsley."

"He's my little angel. Aren't you Aunt Regina's precious angel boy?"

"Hildred rinsed out a clean bottle for him. Evidently Lo threw up at breakfast, but she seemed better so I sent her off to school. Her temperature was more or less normal."

"You could have let her stay home, Marva."

"It's important for them to be at school every day. You and I never missed school."

"We could have had some fun and not been in your way. This little one'll be ready for some cereal soon. Don't you think?"

"Try if you want to. Aiken says it's too soon...but if it is he'll just puke it up. It won't hurt him."

"Don't you think there should be some legs in there? Whether it's Wilton or not."

"It's not."

"Is the green splotch supposed to be grass?"

"I don't want to talk about it, Regina. The painting's just developing. I need to think about it...to concentrate. Not gossip."

"O! Well, little Lamar Ainsley and Aunt Regina will just get out of your way."

"Sorry. I need a little time to myself. To think things through. Hildred's gone shopping to Indianville with her sister. But she put a sandwich for Wilton's lunch in the icebox. I doubt he'll come home though. He'll pick up the girls after school. Or Norman will if he forgets. One way or the other they'll get home."

"Well, we'll just putter around the house. Just a little putter, putter, putter... won't we, pretty boy?"

"Don't fuss over him so much. You'll end up making him effeminate."

"I will not! What a thing to say."

2

The Drive Home From School

It was shortly after four-thirty that afternoon when Wilton, chauffeured by Norman, left the school for home. New carburetor parts ordered from England had taken a little longer to install than the chauffeur anticipated...but the girls had been allowed to sit outside the principal's office until their father arrived, so no great harm was done.

"Runs like a top, Mister Goins. Don't you think? It took a little extra time and effort, but a job worth doing is worth doing well. That's what I think."

"Daddy, Mrs. Hiatt said my drawing was the best in the school," said Skoot. Tall and dark, like her parents, but showing signs of the extra weight she would carry for the rest of her life, Skoot hated the thick glasses she was forced to wear.

"Next time you order a part from England I'd appreciate your letting me know in advance. I'm sure we could have found American parts at half the price."

"Perhaps. But not the same quality."

"No perhaps about it. Do you think we could install extra seats here in the back? There's plenty of room."

"Seats?"

"With me and the girls back here it's way too tight. Step, please sit on the floor. You'll be fine."

"Why can't we stop for ice cream?" asked Step. "Aunt Regina always takes us for pop and ice cream when she picks us up."

"I know I told you the carburetor wasn't working right. I spelled it out for you, and I told you I had to order new parts. From England. The problem is you paid no attention to me. But new seats? On top of what's already there? That'd be quite a job. Expensive to say the least. But I suppose it could be done. We'd need some help from England, of course."

"I don't care what your Aunt Regina does. Ice cream will ruin your appetite. You did mention the carburetor, Norman. You did. But I never thought you'd just go off on your own and order the parts. We need to get together on these things. You think it would be costly? I don't see why we have to contact England all the time."

"Mrs. Hazelbaker said my drawing was the best," said Ribby, holding up a piece of manila paper with crayon scrawls all over it. "It's better than Skoot's."

Wilton stared blankly at her. Where had her blue eyes come from? Maybe Olin's people? A few of the more distant ones were redheads. "She did? Best in the class? Well, that's very nice."

"Mine was best in the school."

"Maybe in the future you should just order the parts yourself, Mister Goins. *Rolls-Royce* doesn't make cheap stuff. But if you want cheap parts…well, that's up to you. The engine won't run as well, but I imagine it'll still run. Now if we start messing around with the seating, and tying into the frame…well, you're going to ruin the structural integrity of the vehicle. But that's your decision, sir."

"That's not what I'm saying, and you know it. Just let me know before you go and order something. I want to be consulted. I was totally puzzled when this package arrived out of nowhere. What kind of integrity? At a substantial cost too. The package."

"All you had to do was open it up. Or send it back. On another matter, are you going to be doing one of those *Harvest Festivals* this year? Because if you are I'd like us to use a different vehicle for that night. I don't want those people crowding around this automobile again."

"Lo's throwing up, Daddy!" Step shouted as Skoot punched Lo and pushed her away and on top of Zip, the youngest, who began to cry.

"Definitely not. Never again. Lo, stop it. Stop throwing up in the car. Just stop it, girls. You're making a mess for Norman to clean up."

"Daddy! Skoot pushed Lo," said Ribby, always protective of her younger sister. "I'll rub your back, Lo. Try not to throw up. Zip, don't cry. We'll be home soon. Norman and Aunt Regina will clean it all up."

"We've seen the last of the *Harvest Festivals*," said Wilton, glancing out the window as they left the town behind and headed into the country. "Can you get me some ideas on more seating back here? I wouldn't think it's that big a deal."

"Step's so mean," said Skoot.

"I am not!" shouted Step. "I didn't want to get Lo's puke on my dress."

"I thought maybe you'd start the *Festival* up again, what with the new baby. But you're completely right, sir. Those people don't appreciate it. They're a lower element."

"Can you get me some information?"

"I can do that, sir. No ordering though. I won't do that. Just your information. But no matter what they say, if you ask me it's a very bad idea."

Zip, who suddenly realized Lo's vomit was smeared in her hair, sobbed all the harder.

"There'll be no more *Harvest Festivals*."

"You're right on that and everything else, Mister Goins. From now on I'll let you do all the ordering for maintenance...plus all the planning for destroying the structure of the vehicle. And in case you're not aware, with all this war stuff going on it's no picnic getting parts from England. You need the right contacts... with all due respect, sir."

"Dear God,"muttered Wilton as he wiped vomit from his trousers. "There's no need to get into a huff, Norman. I don't appreciate your sarcasm. And I do acknowledge your expertise. And I understand the supply problems right now. Just get me the information I need to make a proper decision."

3
German Notions Floating Around The Barn Studio

She gathered that a lot of these ideas circulating in the Milwaukee area…and apparently Chicago too…had come out of Germany years before. But it was all new to her and she had to start somewhere. They were almost certainly clichés in Germany by now because even Bill had mentioned seeing early examples of these things years and years before when he studied over there. He'd deplored all of it of course…but then he'd never been easy with anything that deviated too far from Professor Steele.

But how you could consider yourself a painter and just pretty much ignore the whole issue of perspective was beyond her. Without depth…no real front, no back…things simply wouldn't look right. Real life involved perspective. Not *push and pull*. Push and pull wasn't how the human eye worked. There was depth, there was a front, a middle, a background.

When you boiled down all of Larry Sackroth's verbiage she supposed he was simply insisting the canvas had a reality in and of itself. Not a copy of reality, but its own reality. The three dimensional world, the world of perspective, that was something else…a whole other reality. And the two needed to be kept separate or you found yourself lying about the way things really were on the canvas.

Which perhaps had some truth to it, but then Larry showed up for the *Life Sketch Class* and drew the model in three dimensions. Or the appearance of three dimensions. When she pointed out that discrepancy he merely laughed and said perspective was a *cheap trick*. All of which might point to Larry's confusion…but there was always the possibility his notions might just hold out the promise of a fresh direction for her. Everything was in a state of flux and she needed time and space to figure things out. Which was yet another reason to be thankful for Regina's obsession with the kids.

Confused or not, Sackroth was on target when he said the old painting was going to be shoved aside by the camera. Especially now that they were apparently working on a really good process for color photography. Still…for the moment she wasn't prepared to go so far as Larry. The figure would remain at the heart of her painting. Wilton, or whoever the man was, would stay in this new one. Perspective would stay. At least in the figure. But what Regina called the *mishmash* would stay too. Blocks of pure color and texture. Wouldn't that shock Bill? Using his *Big Blobs* that way!

4
Confronting Sackroth & The Age Gap

Wilton Goins and Joey Birdsall sat in their newly renovated offices on the second storey of the *Giantown Birdsall Home*. While Joey opened two bottles of *Coke,* Wilton…his baggy black suit needing alteration because of a recent weight loss…leaned back and studied the room. He had placed a desk and chair for himself in an adjoining space, but it was merely to stake out the territory since he rarely got up to Giantown any longer. And even when he did show up he had no energy to give to the funeral business.

"This is very nice, Joey. Very nice. *Plush* as they say. Who's that? In the picture. With his arm around Grand-daddy Aberton?" He pointed with his black walking stick to one of several photos on the wall behind Joey's desk.

"That's one of my favorite family photos. From the early days of the business in Aschburgh. Quenterton Birdsall is the other man with Grand-daddy. He was a distant cousin. Didn't stick with the business long though. Went into medicine and did quite well for himself in Louisville. He's the one married into the Lexington Todds…the Todds that's descended from Abraham Lincoln's wife Mary's side. That's where that small branch of Kentucky Birdsalls all come from. Doctor Quenterton Birdsall.

In a way a direct descendent of President Lincoln. At least part of that line anyway. By marriage as it were...if not quite immediately direct."

"Moving the office up here to Giantown, Joey, that surprised me at first. Not letting me know, you see. This being my business too...well, you ought to have let me have a say."

"It was strictly a personal thing, Willie...not related to the business at all...so I didn't see it involving or troubling you. Is having the main office up here an inconvenience?"

"Probably not. As long as your being way up here doesn't impact on your Aschburgh commitment. I wouldn't want to see that happen. The *Aschburgh Bank's* supported *Birdsall* all the way. There's no Giantown money in our business. To put it another way I went out on a limb for you. And naturally I like to be reasonably close to my business interests."

"I can see that, but the fact is Louise wanted to live in Giantown. Primarily for the cultural opportunities up here. Band concerts and so forth. That's the sum and the substance. I don't think we ought to make too much of this. It's just a matter of having my office closer to my residence."

"I'm sort of wondering if the time hasn't come to include Goins in our name. *Birdsall-Goins*. Something like that."

"Let's not push too hard, Willie. *Birdsall* is a long established name. We've agreed to that from the get-go. Once you start monkeying with that name you're going to lose a bunch of good will built up over generations. Anyway, like I said Louise just wants to be closer to all the cultural activities up here. That's the whole thing. My heart's still in Aschburgh. And quite frankly, Giantown's not the end of the world."

"That's debatable. And your money? Still in Aschburgh?"

"And my money. Such as there is. Willie, I'm a bit surprised you'd even be asking about all this. Louise and me are keeping our basketball tickets for *Stonewall-Tecumseh*. We have the same seats reserved for next season. Center court. Nothing's changed. We're not out there supporting the *Giantown High* kids. I suppose I should have let you know about our move sooner, but my goodness, we still have our Aschburgh offices. This is the twentieth century. There's such a thing as telephones. And it's not debatable...it's a fact...Giantown is not the end of the world. You can get here from Aschburgh in half an hour."

Wilton took several pills from his pocket and washed them down with a swig of Coke. "More blood pressure and heart stuff and improvement of digestion. Or so Aiken says. Plus they've got me swallowing a tonic every morning and night. You ever take this *Father John's Medicine*? Marva's got me on it."

"You've been taking off some weight."

"Marva went and fired the cook. Of course she's done that before, so I don't know how long it's going to last. You remember Hildred? Marva said she was *arrogant*. The woman'd been with us for years, and knew exactly how I liked things. Got the kids ready for school every morning. Now I've got to put up with Regina to make my breakfast and get them all out the door. She let Hildred go on a whim. No thought about my meals. Anymore I'm lucky to get a sandwich for supper."

"Hildred?"

"Hildred Philippe. I'm sorry if I pushed you a bit, Joey. Charlie Philippe was her husband. But I worry about our old town. It's got so much potential...but no matter how hard I try I can't seem to get it to turn around. It's like the old Aschburgh we knew is gone. Gone forever. And the Church. I've even had to put up with all that push to change the name back to *Methodist* or *Baptist*. Which would be moving in the wrong direction entirely. But I've been forced to put up with it. I listen and I smile. Which never would have happened before. No one would have dared. So it's all going backwards. It's really not the business...it's the Church and Aschburgh itself. That's all that's got me so off my balance."

"Well Louise and I are not leaving the Church, Willie. I suppose what with the distance and all, the snow'll keep us away a bit more...plus we're spending a bit more time down South... but our tithe will stay with *First Community*...or whatever you decide to call it. Even when we're away. Personally we'd prefer *Methodist Community*...though I imagine that's distant to you. Given your background and all."

"I think I better have a glass of water. My head is spinning a bit. They give you all these pills to improve your digestion and then the things make you dizzy. I think maybe this pop has me a bit out of focus."

"Just try to relax a bit. You have to stop worrying so much. Have you considered taking a little time off? Maybe get yourself a new cook, and eat a little more? Or put your foot down and get Hildred back. So she was married to Charlie Philippe? I don't think I remember her, but we took care of Charlie. You know, Willie, it wouldn't be the worst thing if you stood up to Marva every now and then. Sorry...that's none of my business. But I mean you're worked up about Aschburgh and Hitler and Roosevelt and the Church...not to even mention losing this Hildred ...it's too much on a fellow, Willie. Too much. I hope you don't take offense, but you're not looking that well."

"I don't have the energy I used to. That's for sure. Could I have that water? I seem to be lacking enthusiasm."

"How's that? Water? Of course. Your voice is dipping some too. It seems to me this Church business is at the heart of all the stress you're under. Not to minimize this red President of ours. But you carrying the whole burden of a new denomination is way too much on a fellow. Too much for anyone. Did you know there's been a feeler from the *Methodist* Bishop? He'd be willing to help ease the weight of all this. Louise is still quite close to his wife. And of course, as you know, the *American Baptists* see enormous possibilities. And Jeremy would fit perfectly into either one. *Baptist* or *Methodist*. Of course he couldn't call himself a Bishop anymore, but I'm sure he can live without that title. At least I hope he can. So you see, you don't have to live under all this horrendous pressure."

"It's almost beginning to sound attractive. Much as I dislike any and all denominations. Especially *Methodist*."

"Those things can be worked out, Willie. *Methodism* is an easy-going faith. It's adjustable. Don't let these things be a burden to you. Now I know you don't want to hear this, but it may even be time to consider retiring. At least partially. Just taking it easy. Going down South for the cold months. I mean it's not that you can't afford it. We're thinking about building a Winter place around Augusta, Georgia. You can play golf right through the year...though you don't want to be there in the Summer...and they're developing some of the best private clubs in the nation."

"We're not becoming *Methodists*. Period."

"Well...so what's wrong with *Baptists*? Having the denomination...makes no difference which one...behind you would remove a lot of the headaches. Give them to someone else."

"First of all, I don't like golf. It's a waste of time. Secondly, all denominations are rotten. All they want is control over our Church and our money. And we're the ones that built it up. We left the *Baptists* for good reason. A long time ago."

"But *American Baptists* aren't like *Bible Baptist Holiness*. These are stable people...good people. It's a much superior group. I prefer *Methodist,* but I'm willing to compromise on *American Baptist*. I believe we could grow under them. And have some peace. They're not a contentious bunch."

"A *Baptist* is a *Baptist*."

"Well...anyway. Feeling any better? More water? Are the negotiations for the *Bank* still on track?"

"Moving along. As you well know. But you can't just *sell* a Bank. Every government bureaucrat in Indianapolis and Washington is trying to get his finger in the pie. Every one of those scoundrels is looking for a little slice. This is what Roosevelt and his cronies have brought us to. Father Coughlin has been right all along. A bunch of grafters and bamboozlers. And now they're trying to crucify the man."

"Roosevelt?"

"He's the crucifier not the crucified! Coughlin."

"Still, from what I hear it'll be settled soon. Things are moving along. That'll give Marva and the kids the security they need. Coughlin's too controversial for my taste. Plus you don't want to encourage the Catholics."

"At least Catholics are respectful. Joey, Marva already has all the security anyone could want. I don't know what you're talking about. The woman is completely provided for. And more. Lots more. Security!"

"Shouldn't have stuck my nose in. Sorry."

Wilton rested his hands on the head of his walking stick and stared at the floor. "Because of fear of the Pope, you know. He keeps them in line. Catholics. That's how things should be run. They don't get worked up like some crazy old Baptist who thinks he owns the Church. And don't believe everything you hear about the *Bank*." Wilton pulled himself to his feet, and leaning heavily on his walking stick moved stiffly to the window overlooking the Tecumseh County Courthouse. "Joey, just between you and me. Old friends. And not to go outside. I wouldn't normally bring this sort of thing up. But just between us. And it stays in this room. Can you agree to that?"

"Pardon? What are we talking about here? Is this about the Catholics?"

"Personal stuff. Not to leave this room. I'm having some concerns. Have you ever had trouble with Louise?"

"Wilton? What has my Louise got to do with anything? What is this about?"

"You know. With another man. Louise? You ever dealt with anything like that?"

"I can't believe you're asking me this! You're way out of line here, fellow. Of course not. Louise is a good wife."

Wilton turned to face his old friend and business partner. "I'm pleased to hear that. And I'm sorry to have asked that so inappropriately. So clumsily. Seemingly. But then, Joey, you and Louise are the same age. We were all in school together. You know in some ways you've always been smarter than me."

"That'll be the day."

"I've not always been very smart, Joey. I went and married a girl twenty-seven years younger than me. That's hard to believe when you put it that way…that starkly…but it's true. Twenty-seven years. It seemed a good move at the time, but now I wonder."

"Are you losing your mind? Marva's borne you six beautiful children."

"Five…no, no…six…you're right. Six counting this boy. That's pretty stupid of me, isn't it? Skipping the boy."

"Your first son."

"I suppose he is. Anyway, my last. I don't have that kind of energy any longer. I'm not even sure about this last boy."

"Willie! God forgive you for saying such a thing. I don't want to hear any more about this."

"You're right, Joey. You're right. Let's talk about something else. I apologize. Let's just change the subject. I'm just beside myself a bit with all these tonics."

Joey took a file from the center drawer of his desk, opened it and set three photographs on his desk. "Sit down and take a look at these. They just came in the mail."

"Pictures?"

"These are the latest *Stratoseal Eternally Protective Caskets* from *American Casket*. I think it'll sell very, very well. Especially in our *Colored Home*."

"*The Weaver Home*? You think they can afford something like that? A lot of those folks don't even have a job. And most of the rest are picking up trash or digging ditches."

"*The Weaver Home*. We'll open in a couple of weeks. A simple set-up and very low-keyed. Nothing like this place. But money's not the issue with them. They'll come up with it. Colored people want to protect their loved ones the same as anyone else. There's no difference in people. Especially when you get them to thinking about rain and the way our clay up here holds onto water."

"*Stratoseal*? Sounds like something in these *Buck Rogers* comics. *Stratoseal*. Names are strange sometimes. What kind of name is Sackroth? You ever hear of a name like that? Sackroth?"

"Almost sounds made-up. Jewish, I suppose. What about it? Someone from the East coast?"

"Milwaukee. I think Marva may have an interest in a young fellow named Larry Sackroth. Maybe beyond an *interest*. When it gets to a certain point you look at your children differently. You wonder."

"Willie, this is outrageous! You said we would drop the subject. If it was anyone but you I'd tell you to get out. I'm really shocked. Marva's a good wife to you. A religious woman from an outstanding family. An honorable woman. Shame on you, Willie. Shame on you. I'm really disappointed."

"Don't get too high and mighty until you've thought about it. I certainly never would have imagined anything like this. Not in a million years. Especially with a Jewish fellow. But I never would have thought I'd be unable to be the husband she wants either. That's just a fact. I try but I just can't do what I used to do. And Aiken says there's nothing he can do about it. I should just get used to it. Can you imagine that? Get used to it!"

"You're being ridiculous. I don't want to hear this. It's embarrassing. You need to talk to some specialist about these things. But it's definitely long past time for you to retire and get some rest. That would probably straighten the whole thing out."

"I really think it's all these fancy intellectual, artistic ideas Professor Forsyth brought into our home. It's destroyed the moral tone."

"Are you losing your mind?"

"Easy for you to be critical, Joey. With you and Louise being the same age. So if you lose some type of physical things it's a thing you do together. Lose it that is. Plus sharing the same interests and hobbies. You have no idea what it's like to have to deal with this age gap. To be married to a woman thirty years younger than you who thinks she's some genius or something. Who makes these crazy demands on you. Just realize...I was born a century before her. A hundred years, Joey!"

"Twenty-seven years. A woman who's kept your home, and who's given you six lovely children...who's lifted your name in respect."

"No man should have to put up with a thirty year gap. I'm from the 19th century...Marva's all 20th."

451

CHAPTER 17
A CLEAN SLATE

Joey cleans mashed potatoes and gravy from the eyebrows of Wilton Fox Goins as Tecumseh County braces for the storm. We learn of a line so long its beginning merges with its end. Marva remains calm, makes clear her commitment to critical Christian values, and asserts the natural authority of the Goins. And through it all the grass still grows in the Spring and the snows still fall in the Winter.

1

Dr. J. D. Planck, Secretary of the Indiana Anti-Saloon League will be the chief speaker this Sunday evening at the Union Service to be held at First American Baptist Church of Aschburgh, according to the Reverend Jeremy Poston, long time Pastor of the church. The congregations of Methodist, Friends, Baptist and Wesleyan churches throughout Tecumseh County will join in the service. As part of the program a play will be given by local talent. In light of recently raised concerns, Reverend Poston points out that the various churches will bear the full cost of this service and no taxpayer money whatsoever will be employed.

2
A Notable Passing

Having lived a full and rich 61 years Aschburgh's noblest son, Wilton Fox Goins, was declared dead...some said officially, some said unofficially...at 12:22 p.m. Friday, December 5, 1941, by his school-mate, life-long friend and reluctant business partner, Josephuston Birdsall, Tecumseh County Coroner.

Though he had been ill and failing for several years, needing the aid of a highly polished cherry walking stick with a silver head, and having grown cranky and forgetful...often irritated with people whose names he could not recall...the tax-payers of Aschburgh...even business acquaintances who saw him and spoke with him every day...tended to view the retired banker as a granite monument who would forever be on display in downtown Aschburgh.

Even so, as the saying goes, *God forbid, if something should happen*....well... *something* did happen...as it inevitably does... and so it was that on that Friday December the 5th 1941 while attending the monthly *Lions* luncheon at the Masonic Hall, and as he...that is Wilton Fox Goins, a full year retired...was explaining to Joey Birdsall exactly why America needed to remain neutral in the raging European and Asian conflicts...and as he was savoring one of his favorite meals...meat loaf, mashed potatoes soaked in brown gravy, creamed corn and green beans cooked with bacon...without so much as a whisper or a whimper or a moan... with his eyes wide open...he jerked forward and departed this earthly life before his head slumped onto his plate.

For the moment stunned by this abrupt end to their conversation, Joey Birdsall pushed back from the table and patted his lips with a napkin before calling for help. Instantly he and Wilton were surrounded by a small group of concerned men eager to help and to deny the obvious but unacceptable event which had just played out before their eyes.

"Mister Goins has fainted."

"What happened?"

"Somebody get him a glass of water."

"Is he o.k.?"

"A sip will bring him around."

"Loosen his tie."

"Lay him gently on the floor, fellows," ordered Joey. With his soiled napkin he wiped mashed potato and brown gravy from his old friend's forehead and eyebrows, adjusted his nose which had been jammed to the side by the abrupt crash into the plate, and loosened his food-splattered neck-tie. He wondered how best to handle the matter of Wilton's share of the business. Unfortunately Wilton always made certain everything was documented just so, with every loophole closed. Still there'd be no need to proceed with some of the odd ideas his friend had been prone to these past few months. "Anyone know where Doctor Aiken is? He was supposed to be here today. Somebody see if you can find him." He leaned over his friend's body and discreetly shut his lids.

Joey looked up into the bloodshot eyes of Lillard Joyner...the sergeant-at-arms of the *Aschburgh Lions*...and shook his head from side to side. In turn Lillard faced the crowd of men gathered around, pursed his lips and announced, "He's gone. Nothing we can do. Someone get the doctor so we can handle this according to the full rules and regulations."

As it turned out Doctor Aiken...who had never been strong on rules and regulations...was speaking on *The Advance Of Hoosier Medicine: The Saga Of A Tecumseh & Stonewall County General Practice* at the *Indianville Rotary Club* luncheon meeting that very afternoon...and so was unable to attend to his old patient in these moments following Wilton's *actual* demise but before his *official* demise. All of which caused some confusion and dismay among those unfamiliar with the distinction between the way things had to be done according to Indiana law and the way things were actually done in Tecumseh County.

Among those naives, those innocents, the question was immediately raised, *Was Wilton Fox Goins officially dead without a doctor's approval?*

"What're we going to do, Joey? Is Wilton actually dead? Are we allowed to move him without the Doc's o.k.?"

"Can we move him? You think I'm going to leave my old buddy on the floor all day? We don't need any doctor. I'm the Coroner. He's dead when I say he's dead."

And so it was that Joey Birdsall, acting in his official capacity as County Coroner, made the final and the official call on his own...settling on 12:22 p.m. as the official moment of death... more or less. As to whether Wilton was truly *officially* dead, the dispute between Dr. Aiken and Josephuston Birdsall raged throughout World War 2.

In the midst of the pain, shock and turmoil of that memorable afternoon, under the leadership of the funeral director and Coroner himself, Wilton...who had never accepted the change from *First Community Church Of Indiana* to *First American Baptist Church Of Aschburgh*...though he had been too enfeebled to put up much resistance...was draped in one of the *First American Baptist Women's Society's* best cotton tablecloths and carried out the front door of the *Lions Den* and onto *Goins Boulevard* by three of the more robust of Aschburgh's *Lions*.

Outside, warmed by a bright Winter sun, and under the close supervision of Norman the chauffeur...who though not overwrought at seeing the remains of his cranky employer...was very much concerned about his own future...Wilton Goins, his knees tucked up to his chest to make room, was carefully laid on the back seat of Marva's *Rolls-Royce Phantom* for the short trip up *Goins Boulevard* to the receiving door of the *Birdsall Home*.

Word of the disaster spread up and down *Goins Boulevard* and *Ainsley Street* during the early afternoon. But such was the confusion and the dread of the community...and such was the gulf which existed between the ordinary citizens of Aschburgh and Marva Winslow Goins...that had it not been for one of the ladies... the unnamed *gal* whose meat loaf recipe was favored by Wilton...thinking to call Regina at *The Old Goins Place*... Marva would have been one of the last to learn of her husband's departure from this world. And indeed might not have sensed that all was less than well until Wilton failed to turn up at the supper table.

It was a full two hours after Regina, with Lamar Ainsley on her hip, rushed out to the *Barn Studio* to share the news with Marva… who was as one would expect so shaken that she put down her brushes and determined to do no more work that day…that Joey Birdsall drove his freshly simonized black *Packard* up the curved driveway and parked right behind the splattered black *Dodge* pick-up of Herschall Hoddupp, the school superintendent, who had protectively gathered up the Goins girls as soon as he learned of the tragedy.

Slowly but steadily the stunned town was pulling together. Just as it always had done before in times of lesser calamities Aschburgh now marshaled all its resources to aid the stricken family of its greatest citizen. Green bean casseroles were prepared on stoves all over town and out into the surrounding countryside and beyond.

Regina, still carrying two year old Lamar Ainsley, answered the front door, and immediately took her girls from the flustered school superintendent and sheltered them with hugs and kisses. "Mister Hoddupp says Daddy has gotten dead," Skoot whispered to her. "Ribby and Lo heard, and Step too. Zip doesn't know. But she knows something is bad."

Ignoring the superintendent and Joey Birdsall, Regina, Lamar Ainsley still in place on her hip, knelt in the vestibule and hugged the girls with her free arm. The older sisters, who had been holding themselves under control for the sake of the younger ones, now began to sob. "O my big girls. My big, brave girls. My precious Lamar Ainsley. Aunt Regina will take care of all of you. I won't let anything bad happen. Everything is going to be all right. Daddy is with Jesus now. Daddy is happy with Jesus. But Aunt Regina will always be here for you. Let's each of us be brave for our baby brother, for our precious, pretty Lamar Ainsley."

All six children were ushered into the parlor by Regina who rearranged the pillows scattered on the sofa so they could sit near their mother. "Give Momma a hug," she urged. Marva held Lamar Ainsley on her lap and stared at her weeping and frightened daughters, vaguely amazed there were so many of them. How Regina managed to care for that many children was beyond her.

"Let me take Lamar Ainsley, Marva," Regina whispered. "The girls need you."

Marva handed the baby back to Regina and turned her attention to the funeral director.

"It was all so very peaceful, Marva," said Joey. "It was natural and gentle. As though he just fell asleep. He was with his closest friends…doing the things he loved to do…and with the brush of a holy breeze the Father took him home, quickly, painlessly and gently."

"Did he say anything, Joey?"

"Love and peace were all about him."

"We're all so very sorry, Mrs. Goins," said the school superintendent. "If there's anything we can do…."

"Anything at all. Nothing is too large, nothing too small. You need but speak it," said Joey whose thoughts were already given over to questions of casket selection, visitation, services and interment. Fortunately Wilton had suffered no injury other than the broken nose, so it wouldn't take that much to get him ready. Joey would be able to focus attention on the arrangements.

"Thank you both. I appreciate your bringing the girls home, Mister Hoddupp. That was very kind and thoughtful on your part. I know how busy you must be. Thank you. Regina, come sit by us. The girls…all of us…need to hug for a little bit."

The School Superintendent let himself out as the five girls, Lamar Ainsley and Marva sat together on the sofa. Aunt Regina moved around them, hugging, kissing, wiping and comforting. Joey Birdsall, fingers and palms pressed together before his lips, sat in a comfortable armchair in the corner of the large parlor and considered the best way to proceed. "Perhaps we ought to notify the Bishop…that is to say, Reverend Poston."

"Wilton still liked to call him Doctor Bishop. He didn't much care for the change back to Baptist. Just his little quirk,

I suppose." Marva squeezed Regina's hand. "Would you check that I closed everything up in the studio, dear? Be sure my new canvas is all right. I left in such a rush. And please make certain I sealed the turpentine. I may have left some rags around too. The last thing I need is a fire. And my brushes...I'm afraid I didn't have time to clean them properly."

"I really should stay with the girls," Regina protested. "The paints can wait."

"Please, Regina. I won't have any peace. The girls will be fine. They can go with you."

"It's so sad," said Joey as Regina, Lamar Ainsley back on her hip, quietly left the room followed by the five girls. "He had so many plans to do good. No one loved Aschburgh and our people the way Wilton did."

Marva sighed and considered her situation. Wilton's death was, of course, a surprise. The way it happened. But he had been sick and getting weaker and more erratic all the time. So it wasn't really a *big* surprise. Maybe more a shock than a surprise. The problem, she supposed, lay in her being so busy she hadn't really had time to prepare for what everyone else could see was coming. And so now all the arrangements, the contact with local people, the decisions...all of that, which could have been done in advance, had to be taken care of in the next day or two.

"Where did the girls get to?"

"They're with Regina," said Joey. "Lamar Ainsley too."

"Well...of course." She needed to get through these next few days...which were going to be difficult...so many strange people coming to her house...not to mention the time surrounding the funeral and all that would entail. But things would settle down. She needed to keep that in mind...before her...to help get through this ordeal. It would only be a few days. A week of disruption at most. Then she could get back to work. For now she needed to securely lock the Studio so none of these visitors could get in there.

"I appreciate all your help, Joey. I think we'll be fine. Regina's such a boon to me."

"A boon?"

"A help."

"She truly is," whispered Joey. "It's so important to have a close friend at a time like this. I am so pleased you have her. A boon. And your faith, of course."

"He's in a better place."

"Yes."

"Joey, why don't I stop by in the morning to complete all the arrangements? I'll have Norman bring me in. Regina can watch the kids. But in the meantime please make sure the initial obituary is in the morning papers. I want Giantown, Indianville and Indianapolis. And of course we shouldn't forget Beauville even though they're only a weekly. You might see about Bloomington too. New York, Memphis, New Orleans...those can wait."

"That won't be a problem. Well, maybe Indianapolis. They're sometimes difficult to deal with on short notice."

"Isn't it often short notice?"

"Of course. Well, we'll see. Wilton sketched it all out for me some time back."

"He did? Did he foresee his own passing?"

"No. Nothing like that. As you know, he was in good health. Right up to the end. I just think he didn't want you to be bothered with it when the time came. Will it be all right to proceed with what he gave me? It's fairly complete."

"I suppose. It's nice he thought of me. But one thing he might not have included. I do want our joint-ownership of *Birdsall* spelled out in the obituary. It was important to him. And it's very important to me. All his plans for the business. Also make sure Lamar Ainsley is included. I want all the children listed by full name. Including their middle names. And I want our family ties to the Winslows, Ainsleys, Nestleroads and Pefleys spelled out. Everyone always forgets the Nestleroads. I'll leave it up to you how best to word that."

"Well...Marva, that's something we were always very discreet about."

"What? My family?"

"No, no. Of course not. The joint-ownership of the *Birdsall Homes*. Wilton handled it as a matter of some discretion. I'm not sure he would want it made public at this time."

"Well, Wilton's gone. Hard as it is I'm already coming to grips with that...I have to for my children's sake if for no other reason...so there's nothing to be discreet about. After that last transaction you and Wilton entered into the Goins family owns 60% of *Birdsall* and I want it reflected in the obituary. Wilton's business ties were important to him...and they're important to me....and they will be important to our children. *Senior partner* of the *Goins-Birdsall Funeral Homes*."

"It's only 57%. I can show you the documentation if you'd like. Why don't we sleep on it? We can always insert a sentence later."

"I'll be calling the paper myself to make sure it's included, Joey. I don't mean to push you, but I will have things done the way Wilton would have wanted. We're only running the obituary two days. Things must be done the way Wilton would have wanted. Right from the first."

"Marva. After all these years I think we can trust one another."

"Just be sure it's in there, Joey. Please. Do that for me. For Wilton. Be sure it's in there. Along with the *Bank*. And that he was active in real estate...and his early ownership of many of the natural gas wells. We still own a lot of that land around *Power City*. And of course all that around the reservoir. In Indianapolis."

"It's considerable."

"Yes, it is. There's a lot involved here. And I don't intend that any of it should be overlooked."

3

To whomsoever this may or may not concern:

This current Jap and German war, if that is what it is, won't last long because there's nothing to them. But the problems some of us who pay taxes face day in and day out and have done so for years are not going to be changing unless someone steps up and takes a swing. So here's my best shot.

The suggestion at the recent School Board meeting that those of us who work hard and pay our taxes should socialize the system by paying for text books for people who refuse to buy their own is another one of those steps toward bankrupting this County and this State if not the this whole Country. I for one don't suggest to stand for it.

Parents are responsible for their own kids. I am not responsible for yours and you are not for mine. Take care of your own. I take care of mine. Buy the books yourself.

Twilla Jean Gaw

Aschburgh

A hard-working parent

4

Respect On A Scale Hitherto Unknown

All the local churches agreed to cancel the *Union Worship Service* planned for the evening of Sunday, December 7th...because of Wilton's passing. Then at noon on Monday December the 8th, as the rest of the stunned nation rallied under the leadership of Franklin Delano Roosevelt, a long line of mourners stretched to the west from the steps of the *Goins - Birdsall Home*, far down *Goins Boulevard*, then around the corner of the old *Aschburgh Savings & Trust* (since Wilton's retirement renamed *First People's Savings*), and then north along *Ainsley Street* to the *First American Baptist Church of Aschburgh* at which point it doubled back east all the way down *Winslow Lane* to the overflow parking lot of the *Funeral Home* where the end of the line merged into its beginning.

In the long experience of Joey Birdsall this was unparalleled. For the end of the line to touch the beginning. Respect shown on this scale...a line stretching throughout the entire town...and doubling back again!....had never before been known in Tecumseh or Stonewall Counties.

Despite the damp and cutting cold northwest wind of early December this line was three times the length of Olin Ainsley's, and that one had been over a six hour wait. Two deaths had been directly attributed to the Ainsley line...who could tell what today's toll might be? Which of course Joey wanted to avoid if possible.

But the problem for Joey was if you showed compassion too early you would only encourage them. They actually enjoyed standing on these lines. It was the only amusement a lot of these older folks had. Comparing one line to another. But so many of these dear people were ailing and up in years. Perhaps after some of the really shaky ones had been forced to give up and had been taken home...which was where they clearly belonged in the first place...he'd send a few chairs out to the line. Deaths during visitation were not a good thing for the *Birdsall* reputation.

Around three that afternoon, four hours after the visitation began, having conferred with Marva, and choosing to interpret her cryptic remarks as a begrudging blessing of his plan, Joey dismissed the back half of the line, directing them to do everything in their power not to hurt or offend the family, but rather to return the following day at eleven in the morning to show their due respect and affection. Pointedly he reminded them no one would be permitted to sign the book until after they paid their respects at the casket. In fact the book would be placed alongside the family at Wilton's head and would not be accessible to folks who tried to flit in and flit out again.

The longer he reflected on this tremendous outpouring of respect the more Joey felt he ought to follow the remarkable example of devotion set by Wilton himself at Olin Ainsley's funeral. If tickets were appropriate for Olin's services they certainly were called for at Wilton's. They would schedule not just two, but they would have three *admission-by-ticket-only* services at the Church. The precedent had been set by Wilton himself... and there was still plenty of time to distribute the tickets.

Sadly Marva would have none of it. She thought two days of afternoon visitation were *outrageous if not actually puffed up*, to use her words…though eventually, pressured by the good sense of Regina Poston and realizing she would be able to get back to work soon enough, she consented to at least that much. But no further prideful displays. She would tolerate only one service and absolutely no tickets.

"I never agreed to that for my father, and I certainly won't have it for Wilton. Mister Goins was above that sort of cheap huckster trick. There'll be no tickets. First come, first served. The rest can wait in the street. Be sure to reserve two pews for the Mayors, the School Board, Commissioners and so forth. You'd better make it three."

To Joey *first come, first served* seemed coarse and insensitive, if not plain vulgar…though reserved seating for the dignitaries eased his mind a bit. When he considered at least four mayors, upwards of thirty school board members when you took all the schools in the two counties into account, probably twenty or more commissioners and who knew how many members of their official staffs. And the business community. You couldn't forget the business community. Wilton's peers. You couldn't very well seat some in the reserved section and then turn around and not seat them all. Plus you had reverend clergy…you always had the reverend clergy at something like this. Marva hadn't even considered the clergy. He was going to need at least twelve pews… figuring eight people in each one…and that was tight. Probably too tight for dignitaries. They usually sat six across. So with four pews across the whole church he would need two…no, three or four full rows up front. Maybe more. Stores and businesses in both counties would be encouraged to close for the service. With first come, first served who could tell who might show up?

And the ushers would have to be alerted to recognize all these dignitaries. To distinguish them from the regular people. And they'd have to be taught how to escort them to their seats. Just like at a wedding. The best way to handle it would be to hold everyone else outside the church until all the dignitaries had been seated. He would need Marshall Winslow's help for that. But since Sevier was a member of the family…and a dignitary to boot…it was going to be necessary to call on the State Police for crowd control on the streets. Very few people realized all that a funeral director had to take into account.

But whatever happened the family's desires came first. That had always been the *Birdsall* motto. No matter how harsh and inconsiderate Marva's terms were. Such as her insistence on a closed casket at the Church, depriving the community of one last good-bye. There was no need for a closed casket. It wasn't like with Olin. Wilton looked good.

"The family's needs and wishes come first, Marva. That's always been the *Birdsall* way, and I believe in it with all my heart. But an open casket would be a great testimony to the love of the Aschburgh community for him. He was very well respected. Wilton was never thought of as an ordinary man. People would be well pleased to behold him one last time."

"They were terrified of him, Joey. Many of them hated him. Let's not be silly."

"O no. Don't say such a thing. No one feared Wilton. He was a beloved man."

"Wilton wasn't like these people...and they didn't know or understand him ...let alone love him. I think our *Funeral Home* needs to pay more attention to what the Goins want. It is the *Goins-Birdsall Home* afterall."

"I don't think that's fair, Marva. I'm doing my best to be helpful. To meet your needs."

"Regina and our children are not being put through the ordeal of multiple services. Not by my own *Funeral Home*, not by my own Church...whatever it's called at the moment. One service. One short service. With a closed casket. And the children are leaving early today, and they will not be at tomorrow's visitation. They'll be at the service...but I haven't decided yet if they'll be at the cemetery. But I doubt it."

"Folks are going to be hurt, Marva. Folks are genuinely going to be hurting. They'll want to see his little ones at tomorrow's visitation. People will be waiting in line for hours and they will be expecting to see Wilton's children. I think you owe them that much. Don't you think?"

"I don't owe anyone anything. I've earned everything I have. Our children will not be there. On public exhibit. They'll be safe with their Aunt Regina."

"I'm sure Wilton would have--"

"I don't think he would. But frankly I don't care. This is getting tiresome, and I have things to do."

"Well...anyway. I think he looks very nice. Don't you? He's always been so distinguished. Even when we were boys. Perhaps I can set several loud-speakers outside the Church so everyone on the street can hear the Reverend's remarks... especially the eulogy. I know for a fact he plans to speak of Wilton's devotion to Aschburgh and to our dear people."

"Joey, are you out of your mind? Have you heard anything I've said? I don't want this turned into a circus the way you and Wilton did with my Daddy's funeral. That's not going to happen. If you set up loud-speakers I will walk out of the church and there will be consequences. You may be the undertaker, but *Goins-Birdsall* is my business. I am the controlling partner."

"He's at peace with his Lord now. Praising the Lord Jesus. That's the main thing. But surely Wilton wouldn't have wanted me to leave all these poor elderly folks out in the weather. He wouldn't have wanted them alone on the street to catch their death of a chill. The Wilton I have always known was a man with a heart filled with compassion. Especially for the poor and for the old folks."

"Wilton is gone, Joey. I know that's hard to accept...I'm having my own struggle with it...but that's the fact. My concern now is for my family and my business interests. There's no Wilton anymore, so we'll proceed the way I think best."

5

Fire completely destroyed the barn and contents, including cows and sheep, on the Molton Welschel farm Friday night. Mr. and Mrs. Welschel were in Giantown at the time attending the Christmas basketball tournament where Giantown easily triumphed over La Fontaine.

6
The Christmas Wreath

On Wednesday December 10th, as HMS *Prince of Wales* and *Repulse* went to the bottom of the Strait of Malacca and the American garrison on Guam was captured, Jeremy Poston conducted a brief funeral...with closed casket...for Wilton Fox Goins who would probably have preferred three lengthy services...with tickets ...and a wide open casket.

Immediately after the service Aunt Regina Poston... chauffeured by Norman who was relieved his position was in no jeopardy...took the six children home while Marva rode to the *Winslow Memorial Cemetery* in the *Goins-Birdsall* limousine.

A light dusting of snow blew across the Christmas wreath on Wilton's highly polished walnut casket as it was borne to the grave-site and placed beneath the *Funeral Home* canopy. Hundreds of ordinary Tecumseh County folks, plus most of the local dignitaries and members of the better families...including the Mayors of Giantown and Indianville...huddled closely together in the small cemetery in a democratic but futile effort to stay warm.

Jeremy Poston...still disappointed that the *American Baptists* had been adamant he surrender both his titles of *Doctor* and *Bishop*...but nonetheless feeling liberated now that he and *First American Baptist of Aschburgh* were finally free of the oppressive presence of Wilton Goins...breezed through the brief service of interment expressing the grieving community's sympathy for Sister Goins and the dear, dear children...whose absence, as well as that of his beloved wife, he failed to notice.

"Bless them and give unto each the consolation of Thy loving grace in this the Winter season of their bereavement. And dear Father, we givest thanks unto Thee as Thou hast embraced Thy servant Wilton Fox Goins in so far as he has entered unto his rest in Thee who art the resurrection and the life. Amen."

Jeremy gave the nod to Joey Birdsall who then stepped forward. "This concludes the services for Wilton Fox Goins. The family wishes to thank each of you for your presence today, and you are all invited to a brief luncheon to be held at the Fellowship Hall of the *First American Baptist Church*."

The Reverend shook a few hands and offered final condolences to Marva before walking briskly to his new *Buick* which was parked near the entrance to the cemetery. As a young and naive clergyman he often rode with the bereaved family, but over the years he found that not only depressing but also inconvenient since it left him trapped at the cemetery as people chatted and dawdled. Nowadays, with the authority and wisdom of experience he always brought his own vehicle and parked at a safe distance from the cortege so he could depart quickly.

Marva took the Christmas wreath from the casket and setting it on her chair stood to the side of the grave to receive condolences. She was pleased to find herself dry-eyed and relieved that all this was almost at an end. Wilton would be missed of course... he had been a faithful if often distracted husband and a well meaning if often out-of-touch father...but now, five long days after his death, she was anxious to get on with things and she was confident of her abilities. All that remained was to see him properly buried in a manner befitting their family.

"We can leave whenever you'd like, Marva," whispered Joey. "We're at your disposal. The limousine is all warmed up for you."

"I'll stay until the casket is lowered and the grave filled in."

"We try not to do it that way anymore, dear. We didn't do that for your Daddy or your Momma. Even the Nestleroads no longer do it that way."

"We probably should have. For Daddy and Mommy. I'll wait."

"You'll catch your death of cold. Please let me take care of this. I know how to handle these things."

"I'll shovel at least some of the earth into his grave."

"We really don't do it that way. Times have changed. Marva, believe me it's very difficult and messy with the heavy clay we have around here. That's why I hire men to do it. You'll hurt yourself and get your clothing all dirty."

"Get some men from the Church, and get us enough shovels. I'm not having hired help bury my husband. I'll wait."

"I hear what you're saying, but your guests will be arriving for the Church luncheon. They'll be expecting you there. For condolence and comfort. You owe it to them."

"Would some of you men help me?" Marva called to the Church deacons who were standing nearby, waiting for her to leave. "I need some strong men to help me fill in the grave after Mister Birdsall lowers Wilton's casket."

"Sure. Certainly, Mrs. Goins. We'd be greatly pleased to do that service for you and for Mister Goins."

"Charles," she said to the oldest and feeblest of the deacons. "Perhaps you would stand by my side while the others do the shoveling. I would appreciate the wisdom of your counsel."

"Suit yourself, Marva. *Birdsall* believes in doing things the way the family wants." Joey angrily yanked up the collar of his overcoat and walked off in a huff to get his grave-diggers to lower the casket. The woman was as difficult and bull-headed as Willie had always said.

"Remember, fellows…with some sense of dignity. Button your coats. Fix your hair, Smithburn…it's sticking up in back. Try to look appropriate. No talking, and definitely no laughing or joking. I hope no one's been drinking. Just lower it slowly, with dignity, and then get out of the way. But you better hang around. I'll need you after she finally leaves. How many shovels do we have in the truck?"

Joey stood off to the side and brooded. He would probably have to pull all that clay out and start over again after she saw fit to leave. And have to pay the men for just hanging around. It would all need to be redone the right way or the grave would turn into a sink hole by late Spring, and he'd never hear the end of it from the Cemetery Trustees. When push came to shove, because she was insisting on doing everything her own way, it was going to cost him twice as much as it ought. And who was supposed to pay for that? Who was going to have to dig into his pocket to pay for that?

Once the casket was lowered, more or less appropriately, Joey distributed six shovels to the deacons. The men lay their top coats on the grave-site chairs, and prepared to toss cold clumps of clay onto the casket. Marva, in her long black coat and bonnet...the hem of her dress and coat already stained with soil...asked one of the deacons for his shovel. "Please come and help me, Charles," she said to the old deacon. "I would like to do the first shovelful or two myself. And the final few."

It took the better part of two hours...and two of the deacons had to be excused because of breathing problems...but she did it the way she wanted it done. She had wanted to make a point and she had made it. "Mister Goins will be well pleased. I want this left as it is, Joey. Don't have your men change a thing. Just send them home."

"The Trustees won't be satisfied, Mrs. Goins. We'll have to tidy up some."

"The Trustees are my family. Everyone of them. I'll take care of the Trustees. When the clay settles we'll fill it in in the Spring. It's a Goins grave and the Goins will fill it in."

She thanked each of the deacons for this service to the Goins family, and as Joey...his shoulders slumping more than usual... walked off to dismiss the grave-diggers Marva placed the Christmas wreath atop the mound of damp clay. Escorted by Charles the deacon she slowly made her way to the waiting *Goins-Birdsall* limousine.

"You've got mud on your coat and dress," said the old man.

"Yes."

"Well, it'll come off I suppose. There's worse things than a little mud."

"The loss of a loved one certainly. But family and faith sustain me, Charles."

"Very true, Mrs. Goins. The Lord created the family before He created the Church. Bishop Poston showed me that in the Scripture. There's wisdom in that for those wise enough to see it."

"**Mister Goins was always a man of wisdom.**"
"**Christian wisdom. And Christian compassion.**"
"**Christian wisdom and compassion.**"
"**I'll say Amen to that.**"

7

Hail & Farewell
A GREAT CITIZEN
A COMPASSIONATE BENEFACTOR
NEVER TO BE FORGOTTEN

Giantown Tribune

Sunday, January 18, 1942

By E. Marvin Tugwell, Special Assistant Editor

Though the tears of sorrow have scarcely begun to dry following the death last month of Wilton Fox Goins, this reporter feels compelled in these moments of national tragedy to speak out for the values that make America and Americans the greatest nation and people the world has ever known and very likely ever will know.

The cruel double blow of losing the beloved Mister Goins and then two days later having to face the treachery of the Japs attacking American boys at Pearl Harbor has been hard for many of us to deal with. But were we only to look to the personage of Wilton Goins we would see in his resilience, in his faith in God and in democracy, and in his basic human kindness the very resources that have always made America great and have made our Hoosier home to be the very backbone of our great Nation.

Tecumseh County was a far different looking place when Wilton Goins was born here in 1880. Farmland stretched as far as the eye could see, and scarcely a large city was to be encountered. But the Hoosier values of hard work and honesty, of faith in God and loyalty to the Nation were strong, and young Wilton imbibed them at his parents' knees. It was these very values which sustained him throughout his long life, and it is these values which will sustain America during the conflict ahead.

A hard-working and scrupulously honest businessman, Mister Goins never hesitated to reach out to his fellow man, perhaps no more so than during the recent hard-times when on his own, and with no government assistance whatsoever, he sustained the hungry and unemployed of his native Aschburgh.

It was typical of the man that both his primary business ventures, the Aschburgh Savings & Trust and the two Goins Funeral Homes, were always employed for the betterment of his fellow man. This was an individual who when the churches of his town were struggling to survive looked to the future and founded a new church, his beloved First American Baptist Church of Aschburgh, a Church which will continue to honor his name even as it lifts up the Cross of Christ.

This was a man who never forgot from whence he came, a family man who cherished his six beautiful children, and who was devoted to his faithful wife and help-mate.

We citizens of Tecumseh County would do well to study and emulate his example. We must never forsake the values of integrity, faith, love of family, and devotion to America which were at the core of his life. Let us draw strength from the example of this great Hoosier, this great American, Wilton Fox Goins.

We shall not soon see his like again. And so in the memorable words of the Latin poet Catullus we unite in declaiming, Wilton Fox Goins,

HAIL AND FAREWELL!

LaVergne, TN USA
27 July 2010
191054LV00005B/5/P